Airs & Graces

ERICA JAMES

An Orion paperback

First published in Great Britain in 1997
by Orion
This paperback edition published in 1998
by Orion Books Ltd
Orion House, 5 Upper St Martin's Lane,
London WC2H 9EA

An Hachette UK company

Reissued 2008

A CIP catalogue record for this book is available
from the British Library.

Typeset by Deltatype Ltd, Birkenhead, Merseyside

Printed and bound in Great Britain by Clays Ltd, St Ives plc

The Orion Publishing Group's policy is to use papers that
are natural, renewable and recyclable products and
made from wood grown in sustainable forests. The logging
and manufacturing processes are expected to conform to
the environmental regulations of the country of origin.

www.orionbooks.co.uk

Erica James grew up in Hampshire and has since lived in Oxford, Yorkshire and Belgium. She now lives in Cheshire. She is the author of twelve novels, including *Gardens of Delight*, which won the 2006 Romantic Novel of the Year Award.

By Erica James

A Breath of Fresh Air
Time for a Change
Airs & Graces
A Sense of Belonging
Act of Faith
The Holiday
Precious Time
Hidden Talents
Paradise House
Love and Devotion
Gardens of Delight
Tell it to the Skies

To Edward and Samuel
for their love and sense of fun

ACKNOWLEDGEMENTS

Thanks to Big G for the belief, and to all those who answered my questions, no matter how personal.

Grateful thanks to Jonathan at Curtis Brown for being there for that crucial 'man to man' session.

Thank you, Jane, at Orion for the gentle words of encouragement and for almost convincing me I could do it.

And as ever, enormous thanks to Helena and Maureen for the never-ending supply of friendship and good times.

But my special gratitude must go to Alwyn for his supreme act of bravery on the M25 and A3, and for having a carrier bag to hand. Thank you.

PART ONE

April

The Song of the Lords-and-Ladies Fairy

Here's the song of Lords-and-Ladies
(in the damp and shade he grows):
I have neither bells nor petals,
like the foxglove or the rose.
Through the length and breadth of England,
many flowers you may see –
Petals, bells, and cups in plenty –
but there's no one else like me.

In the hot-house dwells my kinsman,
Arum-lily, white and fine;
I am not so tall and stately,
but the quaintest hood is mine;
And my glossy leaves are handsome;
I've a spike to make you stare;
And my berries are a glory in September.
(BUT BEWARE!)
Cicely Mary Barker

Chapter One

Crantsford was the last place in which Ellen expected to
see a young teenage girl begging for money.

The prosperous small market town didn't lend itself
easily to being a backdrop for the tired figure hovering
outside the Patisserie. Its narrow, winding roads, some
cobbled and lined either side with pretty Georgian bay
windows displaying old-fashioned jars of humbugs,
Jacques Vert separates and Lladro china, gave off an air
of Easy Street; the young girl, on the other hand, smacked
of Queer Street.

Ellen sensed that the girl hadn't much experience in
what she was doing, and turned away at the uncomfortable sight of passers-by offering little more than stony
disapproval at the sight of an outstretched hand in their
midst. She cupped her own hands around her eyes and
peered through the window of the travel agent's where
Hermione was cruising the shelves for the holiday of a
lifetime. She could see one of the assistants approaching
her, ready no doubt to humour the old lady once more.
They were quite used to her regular flights of fancy. Last
month it had been talk of a trip on the Orient Express.

A few moments later Hermione came out onto the
street with a bundle of glossy brochures. 'Egypt,' she said
briskly, 'I rather fancy the look of the Nile.'

'And I rather fancy a cup of tea. Shall we?'

Ellen linked arms with her elderly friend, not because

Hermione was in any way fragile and unable to cross a road alone, but out of love and gratitude – there had been times during the two years since Roger had left her when Ellen herself had been more than a little fragile and it had been Hermione who had been there for her, sure footed and rock solid.

They crossed the road and came upon the young girl. With nobody else on the pavement outside the Patisserie there was no avoiding what Ellen had tried earlier to ignore.

'Twenty pence?' the girl said, her voice unsure as if she knew she was pushing her luck.

Ellen reached into her bag. Excluding the money she had set aside for that morning's treat with Hermione, she knew she had only twelve pounds with her and that was to last until after the Easter Bank Holiday. She opened her wallet and pulled out a pound coin, but then hesitated. It suddenly felt too much. The girl would think her ostentatious, would probably thank her lucky stars to have stumbled across someone so gullible. Visions of the girl, later that day, high on some mind-altering drug flitted through Ellen's head. You read such stories, of children doped up to the eyeballs to simulate hunger and deprivation, when in reality . . .

Oh, to hell with reality!

She dropped the coin into the proffered hand and tried to smile in a sympathetic and understanding kind of way.

'Thank you,' the girl said, but there was no smile. Ellen felt annoyed, not with the girl for failing to show gratitude, but with herself for confirming the hypocrisy of charity. Sure, I'll give you money, but here's the deal – in return you have to make me feel good about it.

'Very commendable of you,' Hermione said as they pushed open the door to the Patisserie and waited for a waitress to come and show them to a table. 'Though it might have been of more use to the girl to have invited her in with us. She looked unspeakably hungry to me.'

'I've a table free now in the window,' a waitress greeted them importantly in a larger than necessary frilly pinny, the size of which Hermione and Ellen had long since decided denoted that this particular waitress was superior to the rest of the staff, who all wore tiny plain aprons. 'How many are you?' she asked Ellen.

Ellen hesitated. For most of her life she had rationalised and analysed to the point of what she thought was absolute certainty in any decision-making process and then more often than not had regretted the outcome. And since she had been on her own she had grown worse, analysing everything she and everyone else did and said; questioning motives, seeking out hidden agendas and exploring all possible means of justification. Hermione called it her 'rationalising to the point of inertia'. But just recently she had tried hard to act with more spontaneity. She thought of the pound coin she'd just given away and seized her moment.

'Three,' she answered quickly, and without risking a look at Hermione she turned and went back outside onto the street.

Hermione took her seat in the window and decided not to be put out at being deprived of Ellen's undivided attention. She watched Ellen approach the girl. She read the young girl's body language – surprise first, followed quite rightly by suspicion and then shoulder-shrugging submission as Ellen led the way. For all Ellen's dithering, when she made a decision there was no stopping her.

There was no danger of heads turning as the door opened, or of voices being subdued, for the girl in her ill-fitting clothes looked as badly dressed as most of the teenagers in Crantsford, if not better than some. And mercifully she seemed clean enough and had nothing skewered through her nose or eyebrows. Hermione picked up one of her glossy holiday brochures and shuddered at the thought of some of the youngsters in the town who apparently had more bodily parts pierced than a pin-cushion.

'This is Jo-Jo,' Ellen said brightly.

'Hi,' the girl said awkwardly. She looked older than she had outside, but paler.

Hermione lowered her brochure. 'Well, Jo-Jo,' she said, 'this would seem to be your lucky day. There are still plenty of meringues left on the trolley over there, I see.'

'I'm not big on meringues,' Jo-Jo said, stowing a large rucksack under the table and sitting on the edge of the chair – she had the look of being ready for flight, just in case.

Hermione raised an eyebrow. 'Correct me if I'm wrong, but in my day it was beggars who couldn't be choosy.'

'And even in your day I'm sure that beggars suffered from allergies. I get a rash from egg whites, if it's any business of yours.'

Hermione instantly warmed to Jo-Jo. She loved a dash of hostility and this girl had it in spades. That was the trouble with being old: too often you were treated with reverence and respect, nobody ever told you to shut up. It was amazing what you could get away with once you got past sixty. Ellen was one of the few people who wouldn't let her get away with too much nonsense. The same was true of Matthew, who had always been blunt and to the point. Last week he had been especially blunt. He'd called Hermione to ask how she was and when she had asked after his current girlfriend he'd replied tersely, 'Mind your own business, I don't want to talk about it.'

'Pot of tea for three?' asked the waitress with the pinny.

Both Hermione and Ellen looked at Jo-Jo, each suspecting, each dreading, that she would want something different – something more expensive.

'What?' she said, when she realised she was being stared at.

'Tea or coffee?' Ellen urged.

'Earl Grey would be great.'

'Expensive tastes for one so impoverished,' Hermione muttered. Both she and Ellen exchanged looks of concern. They only treated themselves once a month to this luxury of having morning tea in town, a luxury comprising a couple of cream meringues – justified on the grounds that they could not make them successfully at home – and a pot of the Patisserie's cheapest tea. Never did they squander money on the more expensive teas that the tearoom's proprietor, Miss Astley, kept in large Chinesy-looking tins on the glass shelf above the rows of cups and saucers. It was out of the question: neither had money to throw so recklessly down the drain.

'Normal tea will be fine,' Ellen told the waitress. If Jo-Jo was going to take her for a ride it would be a very cheap ride.

The order was completed with the addition of two meringues and a modest hot cross bun for Jo-Jo, and was brought to the white-clothed table with bustling speed and efficiency that spoke of Miss Astley having impressed upon her staff that time was money.

It was only when Jo-Jo had wolfed down her bun before Ellen and Hermione had even reached for their pastry forks that Ellen realised quite how hungry the poor girl was.

'Would you like another one?' she asked, overcome with shame.

Jo-Jo nodded and then she fainted.

Chapter Two

'I'm all right,' Jo-Jo mumbled weakly. 'I'm all right.'

'Sure you are,' responded Ellen, kneeling on the floor beside her. 'People go around fainting all the time.' She tried to ease the girl into a sitting position. 'Let's get you back onto your chair and do something about trying to get your head between your knees. I think that's what you're supposed to do.'

'No!' said Jo-Jo, her voice suddenly more forceful. She pushed Ellen's hands away from her. 'I told you, I'm fine. Now leave me alone.'

'Is anything the matter?' It was Miss Astley, a solid chunk of a woman with too much eye-liner and a short navy-blue skirt slightly concertinaed below the curve of her pot-bellied stomach. She was accompanied by the large pinny, who must have summoned the great lady from her den at the first sign of trouble. An audience of curious onlookers were casting surreptitious glances over their china cups towards the scene of the commotion.

'Nothing that a glass of water won't put right,' Hermione answered smoothly, straightening the table-cloth and picking up a knocked-over bowl of sugar cubes.

'Would that be still or carbonated?'

Hermione gave Miss Astley a withering stare. 'I think you'll find tap water is generally still.'

There was nothing else for Miss Astley to say and,

giving Jo-Jo a reproachful look, she turned away and stretched her lips into the professional smile that she reserved for her less troublesome clientele.

'I really don't know why we bother coming here,' Hermione said huffily, in a voice designed to be heard some several yards away.

Ellen ignored Hermione's stage-managed attempt at pique. She was watching Jo-Jo retrieving her rucksack from under the table. 'What are you doing?' she asked, when the girl got to her feet.

'Look, you've done your bit for society and I've had something to eat, so that makes us quits and happy all round.' She moved towards the door. 'And thanks,' she added, sounding as if she meant it.

'But you can't go yet,' Ellen called after her. 'You need to have something else to eat, you need . . .'

'Let her go,' Hermione said. 'After all, what else do you want to do? Offer her a bed for the night?'

Ellen watched Jo-Jo step outside onto the street. She couldn't bear the thought of abandoning her and leaving her to the mercy of a way of life that would inevitably turn her into little more than a depressing statistic.

There but for the grace of God go I, she thought miserably.

The girl slung her bag over one shoulder, looked first to her left along the narrow road, which would take her to the bottom of Lower Market Street, and then to her right, which would lead her up the hill towards Church Walk and eventually onto the main road out of Crantsford. While she seemed to weigh up which road to take a group of women appeared and gathered round the tearoom window. They peered in through the small panes of glass to see if there were any free tables and when they finally pressed against the door and stepped inside Jo-Jo had gone.

'Perhaps now we can get on,' said Hermione, pushing her pastry fork into the crisp meringue in front of her. With one eye on her brochure, she said, 'Did you know that the temple at Abu Simbel was rescued from the floodwaters of –'

'Don't you care at all?'

'I care very much,' Hermione said slowly, her hooded eyes staring straight at Ellen. 'That's why –'

'I'm not talking about some rescued temple,' Ellen said sharply, 'and you know jolly well I'm not.'

'Whose is the glass of water?' the pinny said, once again at their table.

'You're too late!' Ellen said crossly.

The pinny looked confused. 'I'll leave it anyway, shall I?'

'Oh, do what you want.'

'My, you really are bothered by her, aren't you?' Hermione said, when the glass had been plonked down and they were left alone. 'The question is, why?'

Ellen said nothing and then she jabbed at her meringue. Small powdery chunks exploded off her plate and onto the tablecloth. 'I don't know,' she said at last. 'I really don't know. She just seemed so pathetic. And here I am, worried half out of my mind every time my bank statement slips through the letter-box, and yet compared to the Jo-Jos of this world I'm probably sickeningly well off.'

'Aha! Do I detect the first signs of some fledgling socialist tendencies coming to the fore? Tendencies which a stable marriage and comfortable middle-class background have kept at bay all these years?'

'Oh, be quiet!'

11

Hermione chuckled and looked affectionately at Ellen. 'Maybe the Jo-Jos of this world are a good influence on you. But I'd like to point out, though, that she didn't seem too impoverished. Her clothes were clean enough and there was nothing backward about her in her choice of tea.'

'Appearances can be deceiving.'

'Indeed they can,' Hermione said, casting an eye about the Patisserie.

They sat in companionable silence for a while. When they'd both finished eating, Ellen said, 'I'm fed up with having no money, I mean *really* fed up. And living here doesn't help.' She inclined her head towards Miss Astley's other customers, with their trim carrier bags of expensive goodies carefully positioned on the floor beside their chairs.

'I know,' Hermione said. She glanced down at her right hand, where up until a week ago her third finger had worn a ring that her father had given her for her twenty-first birthday. Now the heavy-knuckled finger was naked, its loose skin deeply channelled where the ring had once been. She placed her hand on her lap, out of sight, and tried to think positively: at least now there was sufficient money in the bank account to pay off the builder who had patched up the roof last month.

'So what are we to do?'

'Do, Ellen, my dear? Why, I only wish I knew. Perhaps we ought to take to the streets like our young friend. Or maybe we could set ourselves up in a knocking shop. I'm a little past my best, but heaven only knows there are enough strange men out there who might take some perverse pleasure in –'

'Don't flatter yourself.' Ellen laughed lightly, wishing that Hermione wouldn't be so flippant at times. 'But seriously, though, we have to find some way round the problem that doesn't include lying flat on our backs and thinking of England.'

'Was that what you did with Roger?'

Ellen kept her eyes down and folded her paper napkin neatly in four. There were times when Hermione had an irritating knack of aiming her arrow with unerring accuracy. Sex had certainly become a problem between her and Roger when towards the end of their marriage Roger had decided that he wanted to be more adventurous. Dressing up as a school-girl at the age of thirty-seven had not appealed to Ellen and with visions of having to perform this ritual regularly for her husband she had begun to go off the idea of sex altogether. Eventually Roger had got tired of her reluctance to play along with his flights of fantasy and had sought his pleasure elsewhere; secretly, of course, until one day he had simply announced over supper that he had met a woman who had literally made all his dreams come true. Shock and fear at losing her husband and their twenty-year marriage and the only life she'd known had driven Ellen to extraordinary limits, making her plunder the agony columns in magazines for help and advice, which all, to a single voice, urged any woman in her position to take her courage in both hands and play the tart in bed. For two miserable and agonising months she had tried it, only to find a note on the mantelpiece one morning after coming back from the supermarket. Roger had not only left her for the accommodating Charmaine, who worked as his dental nurse at the surgery, but they were leaving the country. The note had gone into considerable detail – she had always viewed that A4 piece of paper as not only a coward's way out, but as Roger's final confession – explaining that he was tired of their marriage and of capping teeth in Crantsford; he wanted a new life and was setting up home in Provence with Charmaine.

For the first six months after Roger had gone Ellen had been unable to stomach anything with a French connection. Irrationally she had blamed croissants, baguettes and Perrier water for the loss of her marriage. She also blamed Peter Mayle. For who else had planted the idea of Provence in Roger's confused brain? The writer's tales of fragrant lavender fields and garlic-smelling plumbers and good-for-nothing builders must surely have been responsible for seducing her husband away from her. But it wasn't long before she had realised that Peter Mayle and his charming come-right-in-the-end tales had had no more to do with the end of her marriage than she had.

'There's one very obvious answer to solving your financial problems,' Hermione said, sensing that she had set her friend off down the tortuous track of Memory Lane.

'Yes?' Ellen said, lifting her head to meet Hermione's faded blue eyes. 'So, what's your latest brainwave then?'

'Marry Duncan.'

Ellen prodded at the cubes of sugar in front of her with her unused teaspoon and smiled. 'I'm not so sure Duncan's the marrying kind.'

'Everyone's the marrying kind at some time or other. Have you considered him as a potential husband?'

Ellen laughed. 'Well, of course I have. He's ideal husband material. He's single, about my age and a respected solicitor with a reputation –'

'And loaded, up to his legal lawsuits,' interrupted Hermione, 'to say nothing of the gorgeous Queen Anne manor house he lives in.'

Ellen continued to play with the sugar cubes, stacking them on top of each other into a wobbly pyramid.

Without looking up she said, 'Would you be very shocked if I told you that if I ever marry again it will be for money and not for love? . . . I tried the love thing and look where it got me.'

'Seems perfectly reasonable to me,' Hermione said. 'I just wish I could do the same. Do you think there's any chance of Duncan falling for you?'

'I don't know. He's so quiet it's difficult to know what he's thinking half the time.'

'I hope by quiet you don't mean dull?'

Ellen sighed. 'After what Roger put me through I'll settle for dull any day.' She reached for her bag. 'Come on,' she said. 'Time to pay and let our fertile imaginations cool down. Oh, what's this?' She picked up a pound coin from beside the plate that Jo-Jo had used.

'Should we think well of the girl, or put it down to carelessness?' asked Hermione.

Johnny Foreigner was hot and airless and Ellen and Hermione quickly wound down the windows. Johnny Foreigner was Ellen's car, and being unfortunate enough to be French – a Peugeot 205 – it had come in for its share of abuse after Roger had run off to France and had subsequently been renamed.

'We didn't get to discuss Egypt,' Hermione said, when Ellen had negotiated her way through the one-way traffic system and paused at the lights at the top of Church Walk. As they turned green and Ellen slipped into first gear she was conscious that anybody who didn't know Hermione well might wonder if the seventy-eight-year-old woman wasn't showing signs of senile dementia with all her talk of holidays that could never be. But it was harmless enough. Whereas some people dreamed of winning the Lottery each Saturday night and revelled in

15

idle speculation as to how they would spend their winnings, Hermione simply let her mind wander from country to country, indulging herself in the harmless fantasy of exploring new territories from the safety of her armchair. Even Ellen had sometimes joined in with the game, allowing herself to be drawn into talk of a cruise for the pair of them around the Norwegian fjords. Hermione would speak of cocktail parties and sitting at the Captain's table for dinner, while Ellen contented herself with the happy thought of escaping the financial mess in which Roger had left her.

'Well, well, well,' Hermione said, with a ring of pleasure in her voice, 'and who do I spy pounding the road out of town with her thumb catching nothing but the wind?'

There was no mistaking the figure with the rucksack slung over its shoulder. The only difference now was that Jo-Jo had removed a layer of clothing and as she turned round at the sound of their approaching car a ripple of wind caught her thin white T-shirt and flattened the fabric against her young body. What Ellen had suspected earlier on the floor in the Patisserie when she had tried moving Jo-Jo was now confirmed. By her reckoning the girl had to be at least four months pregnant. She slowed the car and pulled over.

'Going our way, young lady?' Hermione asked through the open window.

Jo-Jo shifted her rucksack as though trying to hide behind it. 'I might be,' she said, pushing her long hair out of her eyes as the warm spring wind whipped it up from her shoulders.

'Well, hurry up and get in, and let's have no more nonsense from you. We'll sort out the details later, but if you play your cards right I'm sure my well-meaning

friend here will provide you with a bed for the night.'
Hermione turned and faced Ellen. 'That was what you
had in mind, wasn't it?'

Chapter Three

'Shall I drop you off?' Ellen asked Hermione, knowing full well the answer.

'There's no hurry,' the older woman replied. 'I'll toddle home later.'

Yes, thought Ellen, why go home now when things were just getting interesting?

'Is she your mother?' Jo-Jo asked Ellen, catching her eye in the mirror from the back of the car.

'You'd think so, wouldn't you?' Ellen said, with a sideways glance at Hermione.

Hermione humphed. 'What rubbish. I'm infinitely better than any mother. Have I ever made demands on you or made a nuisance of myself?'

'Never, thank goodness.' Ellen smiled. She indicated left to leave the main road. There were three signs at the top of the small unadopted road they turned into. The smallest one was a dead-end sign and beneath it was another – Beggarman's Lane. The irony of her address never failed to make Ellen wonder at the way her life had turned out. The most obvious sign was a large, well-positioned cream board with green lettering on it spelling out the words Spring Bank Dried Flowers, and in one corner there was a simple depiction of a jug containing an arrangement of blooms. The sign still looked brand new although it had been in position now for several months. For Ellen it was yet another reminder of the many changes she'd been forced to accept. Sometimes she resented the sign – that was on a bad day when her anger for Roger could not be stifled; on other days she would indulge in a little back-patting and allow herself the luxury of imagining herself as Businesswoman of the Year. The reality was quite different, of course: she had yet to reach a point where she could even pay herself a regular salary.

There had been no rain for over a week and as Johnny Foreigner bumped its way down the steep incline of the potholed lane a gauzy cloud of dust was left hanging in the air behind the car. The narrow lane curved gently round to the left and brought them to a tiny white-rendered cottage with a low, sloping roof and a front door that was painted black; either side of the door was a window and a matching pair above. It was the archetypal house painted by every primary-school child who had ever picked up a brush – all it needed to make it complete was a splodgy yellow sun wearing a smily face in the top right-hand corner.

Directly opposite the cottage was a grassy bank, dotted with daffodils, which fell away to a stream, and beyond this there were trees bordering the edge of a field where local people walked their dogs. On the face of it, it looked a dream hideaway cottage, but for Ellen there had been times when it had been more like a nightmare – the cottage from hell, she'd called it when she'd moved in and discovered just how damp and dilapidated the place was. Wet rot and dry rot abounded, but these were defects she could tolerate; they were small fry compared to the more obvious horrors that had demanded her immediate attention. She had spent weeks scraping off the mould from the kitchen walls and twice as long in ridding the entire cottage of the foul stench of urine, the source of which was the minuscule bathroom on the first floor. The previous occupant had been a man who had lived alone in the house – and died in it – for nearly half a century and whom Ellen was sure had never acquainted himself with even the most basic of household cleaning products. She had cursed him daily for his lack of hygiene, especially his inability to aim anything into the toilet, preferring instead, it seemed, to leave his mark like a tom cat on the filthy sodden green and yellow lino that partially covered the bathroom floor.

But at least all the cursing and constant elbow grease had taken her mind off Roger.

When Roger had done his disappearing act, Ellen had had no idea of the mess he'd left behind him. She'd been aware of the second mortgage that he had taken out on their home – had even been a party to it, as joint owner of Orchard House – understanding that the money borrowed from the bank was to enable Roger to expand his recently acquired dental practice. What she hadn't been aware of was that when she had signed the papers giving her agreement to this transaction she had also given him *carte blanche* to borrow further amounts of money. Within days of his disappearance she had discovered that over the previous year Roger had been spending money secretly like a drunken sailor home on leave. It was mind-boggling how much he'd spent on weekends away in Amsterdam and Paris with Charmaine. But worse was to come: Roger had developed a drug habit, which had not only drained away their savings to nothing but also the hope of making him responsible for the debts he'd left behind.

Ellen still didn't know what had shocked her more – that Roger had been leading a double life, or that she had been stupid enough to believe in all the dentistry conferences he had suddenly felt so compelled to attend.

And while trying to come to terms with the emotional trauma of the loss of her marriage, she was forced to sell her home – her lovely dream home – find a new one and a way of earning a living.

She parked the car alongside the barn where over a wide, studded door hung a similar sign to the one at the top of the lane – Spring Bank Dried Flowers.

'Here we are,' she said, unnecessarily.

Jo-Jo got out first. Ellen and Hermione watched her wander across the thin strip of road to the sloping bank. She dipped her hand in the water. 'It's freezing!' she yelled back at them, as if they were in some way to blame.

'Are you sure you know what you're doing?' Hermione asked Ellen, as they walked towards the cottage. 'She'll make a dreadful house guest.'

'I like that. It was you who invited her to come back with us.'

'I was only voicing what was already in your mind.'

Ellen ignored this truth and unlocked the cottage door. It was pleasantly cool inside and she hung her bag on the back of the door where she kept her coats – gone were the days of a cloakroom the size of a small bedroom. She mentally slapped her wrists: Orchard House was long gone and Spring Bank Cottage was her new home. She looked about her at what doubled as her sitting room and dining room. Hanging from the two beams that ran the length of the cramped room were enormous bunches of dried flowers – a clever device for covering up the ominous cracks in the ceiling. Either side of the fireplace were two armchairs she'd covered with yellow and blue fabric bought from the market in Crantsford – last year's colours but a classic in its own right, the stallholder had insisted. She'd made scatter cushions from contrasting fabric and used these to make a pretty feature of the window-seat that overlooked the front garden and the stream beyond. To the left of the window she'd managed to squeeze in one of the few remaining pieces of furniture from her marriage: a large dresser that had stood perfectly in the kitchen at Orchard House. Here it dominated the small room like a towering oak tree in a tiny walled garden. She should have sold it, along with the other pieces of furniture that had had to go, but sentiment had got the better of her. Opposite the fireplace and nestling against the wall was a chunky pine table; this was where she ate her meals, struggled with her paperwork and sometimes fell asleep.

'So what exactly do you intend doing with her?' Hermione asked, settling herself into one of the arm-chairs.

'Jo-Jo, you mean?'

'Who else?'

Ellen sat on the window-seat, and peered out through the square panes of glass. Jo-Jo was lying on the grassy bank, her trousers rolled up and the sleeves of her T-shirt pushed up to her armpits. She looked so at home lying among the daffodils; so childlike. Ellen suddenly longed for her own child.

At the age of nineteen Simon would hardly like to be described as a child, and coming to the end of his second term away at college he was now more of an adult than Ellen felt herself to be at times. They had always been close and if she let herself dwell on how much she missed him she felt wretched at the thought of being separated from him . . . She'd already lost so much.

'She's pregnant,' she said, returning her attention to Hermione.

'Does that make a difference?'

'Oh, Hermione, she's so young to have fouled up her life already.'

'So it's better to wait until you're older, is it?'

'You know what I mean.'

'I do, but it's only your opinion that she's made a mess of things. She might not think she has. How old were you when you had Simon?'

'That's different. I got married as soon as –'

'How old?'

Ellen shrugged. 'Twenty, as well you know.'

The point made, Hermione moved the conversation on. 'I suppose you'll keep her here for tonight and then persuade her to go to some kind of authority-run place tomorrow. Who do you think we should get in contact with?'

'Perhaps we should be trying to persuade her to go back to her parents.'

'Don't even think about it,' said an angry voice from the open doorway.

Ellen stood up awkwardly. 'Would you like a drink?'

Jo-Jo nodded and followed Ellen to the kitchen.

Ellen took a carton of orange juice down from a shelf beside the cooker and snipped off the corner with a pair of scissors. Juice spurted over the work surface.

'My gran was always doing that.' Jo-Jo laughed unexpectedly, her features instantly softening. She turned away and picked up a cookery book, *Easy Meals For One*.

Ellen wanted very much to pursue this tiny piece of accidentally offered information, but the expression on Jo-Jo's face told her that it would be an unwelcome intrusion. And, anyway, what right had she to pry into Jo-Jo's life? She would give her a bed for the night and tomorrow she'd set about organising a more permanent base for her and that would be that. By this time tomorrow she would have done what Jo-Jo had described at the Patisserie as her bit for society. She handed the girl her glass of orange juice. 'Would you like a biscuit?'

'I'd prefer a sandwich.'

'Of course.' How utterly stupid she was being. Here she was handing out well-meant crumbs of hospitality when what this girl really needed was a damn good meal inside her. The absurdity of what she'd instigated now hit her. Just what had she thought she was doing, acting like Lady Bountiful on the streets of Crantsford, offering food and then a bed for the night? Had she gone completely round the bend?

'Cheese and pickle okay?' She hoped it was. It was either that or a few sad-looking lettuce leaves and the tail end of an out-of-date cucumber.

'That'd be great and . . .'

Ellen waited for her to carry on. 'Yes?' she said, when the silence became uncomfortable.

Jo-Jo swallowed. 'I just wanted to say thank you. There's not many who'd do this. I mean, I could be a drug-crazed psycho for all you know.'

'You mean you're not?' called Hermione from the sitting room, where she was flicking through her travel brochures. 'How very disappointing.'

Jo-Jo and Ellen looked at each and both smiled. 'Is she for real?' Jo-Jo whispered.

'And some.'

Ellen made two rounds of sandwiches for Jo-Jo and they joined Hermione in the sitting room. While Jo-Jo ate, Hermione kept up a rapid fire of questions to which

24

Jo-Jo either shrugged her shoulders in response or lied blatantly with an inscrutable expression on her face. When Hermione asked her where her family lived she made it obvious that she had had enough and in a bored voice said, 'I am not of this planet.'

To which Hermione replied, 'And just how do you go about getting yourself pregnant on your planet? The same way we earthlings do, with the tried and much-tested act of sexual intercourse?'

Jo-Jo froze. She looked accusingly at Ellen. 'I knew you'd guessed,' she said.

'So why the secrecy?' asked Ellen gently. 'In a matter of weeks you'll find it even more difficult to conceal the fact that you're pregnant. Is the baby the reason you've run away from home?'

'The baby's a way out,' she said, cramming the last of the sandwiches into her mouth. 'A blessing, you could say.'

'Well, I'm glad you've been blessed so abundantly,' Hermione said drily. 'Ellen, my dear, this could be the answer to all our problems. We'll get ourselves pregnant and then run away and all our troubles will be over. I don't know why the idea hadn't occurred to us before.'

Jo-Jo scowled and wondered why she'd allowed herself to be talked into accepting help from these two women. The younger one was okay but the older one had to be a head-case. Still, a proper bed for tonight would be better than another night spent in that churchyard. It felt like weeks since she'd slept in her own bed, whereas it was only yesterday that she'd left home. Her mother had discovered the pregnancy-test kit in her bedroom, which she'd forgotten to throw away, and then all hell had broken loose when her step-father had been told. She had known her mother would be too weak to stand up for her, she had expected that – two nervous breakdowns and a decade of tranquillisers had kept her firmly under her husband's thumb. Maybe when she got herself sorted she'd write to her mother, just to let her know she was okay. Or perhaps it would be better to ring when *he* was out at work. She felt sad at the thought of her mum in that miserable house all alone with nothing but the telly for company.

'You mustn't mind Hermione,' Ellen said softly. 'She's an old lady and we have to humour her.' She frowned at Hermione. Hermione frowned back and stuck out her tongue.

Jo-Jo laughed. 'You're a right pair, you really are.' After a few seconds she said, 'It's no big deal why I left home. I just don't get on with my step-dad, that's all. He likes to push people about. Mum isn't able to stand up to him, but I won't put up with it . . . and never will. I'm not going back.'

'He sounds a delightful man, your step-father,' Hermione said. 'Perhaps we should arm ourselves and plan a rescue attempt for your mother.'

Ellen ignored Hermione and leaned towards Jo-Jo. 'What about the baby's father? Does he even know that you're pregnant?'

'He knows all right, but he doesn't want anything to do with it, or me. It wasn't like we were together . . . It wasn't serious.'

Hermione noted the twisted hands in the girl's lap and decided that, for now, enough questions had been asked.

An hour later, when Jo-Jo had wallowed in a bath and had been instructed by Ellen to take a nap in Simon's tiny bedroom, Hermione gathered up her holiday brochures and said it was time she was going.

'I'll run you back,' Ellen said, already reaching for her keys.

'You'll do no such thing. My legs are more than capable of making the short walk home. I'll give you a ring in the morning to see what you've decided to do with our young friend.'

A few minutes after Hermione had left, the phone rang.

'Ellen, it's me, Duncan.'

'Hello, Duncan.' She wanted to add, 'We were only talking about you earlier', but remembering what the conversation had been about she thought better of it. 'How are you?' she said instead.

'I'm fine. Look, I was wondering if you're not working tomorrow whether you'd like to come over for lunch.'

'Oh.'

'Is that a no?'

'No. I mean, yes. Yes, I'd love to. You just surprised me, that's all.' This was the first time Ellen had been invited *home* and the tempting picture of an elegant Queen Anne house shimmered enticingly before her eyes.

'We always like to have people round on Good Friday – it's a bit of a thing Mother has, roast lamb and a table of guests to share it with.'

The Queen Anne house instantly vaporised and was replaced with the far from pleasant image of the indomitable La Carter. 'What time shall I come?' Ellen asked, squeezing her eyes shut to block out the vision of Duncan's mother about whom she had heard so much from Hermione.

'It's twelve for twelve thirty, but don't worry about driving, I'll come and pick you up.'

Ellen replaced the receiver in its cradle and smiled. Of course Hermione had been right this morning in the

Patisserie – she had done a darn sight more than merely consider Duncan as a potential husband. What fool wouldn't? But was there really any chance of winkling the eligible Duncan out of his tightly fitting bachelor shell?

Chapter Four

As Hermione walked home the thought occurred to her that perhaps she shouldn't have left Ellen alone with a person they knew so little about, but crossing the main road to join the Crescent she dismissed this as absurd. Jo-Jo may have tried earlier to come across as bolshie and street-wise but there was a naïvety and overall honesty to her bearing that gave one no reason to suspect her capable of taking an axe to her good Samaritan and making off with the family silver and credit cards.

Much good it would do the girl anyway, for Hermione knew better than anyone how hard up Ellen was these days. Her dried-flower business was still in the early stages of getting off the ground and Hermione suspected that it would be a while before Ellen's financial position improved dramatically.

She was now halfway along the Crescent – a road that bore no resemblance to the shape suggested by its name, but which was a quiet through road and home to some of the largest and most interesting houses in Crantsford. Most of the properties had been built at the turn of the century for the wealthy local industrialists of the era, but nearer the main road where Hermione was now walking stood a few recent additions. Built to individual designs and constructed of Cheshire brick, the modern properties blended in with their surroundings pleasantly enough, and in Hermione's opinion they deserved nothing like the outrage that had greeted their arrival from some of the more conservative-minded inhabitants of the Crescent.

She slowed her step as she drew level with one of the newer homes on her right – Orchard House. She stood still and cursed Roger under her breath.

Ellen and Roger had moved into Orchard House a month after the builders had moved out. Hermione had seen the removal van arrive late in the afternoon when she had been on her way back from Crantsford – in those days she had thought nothing of walking into town for her shopping, but recently her legs and back had started to object and she now used the local bus service or relied upon Ellen's generosity to drive her to the shops. Which was how she had got to know Ellen. It had been raining one morning when Hermione had set off with her basket and umbrella and as she'd come to the end of the Crescent a small red car had pulled up alongside her. An attractive fair-haired woman had wound down her window and asked Hermione if she wanted a lift into Crantsford. 'I'm still finding my way around,' she'd said, as Hermione had climbed into the passenger seat, 'so shout if you think I'm going the wrong way.'

They had taken to each other instantly and had quickly settled into a comfortable routine of tea and cake while listening to the afternoon short story on the radio in Ellen's luxuriously fitted kitchen. Afterwards they would give their verdict on the writer's talent, or lack of it, until it was time for Ellen to start thinking about feeding the men in her life, Simon and Roger.

Simon was the kind of son for whom any mother would willingly suffer. Tall, fair, well-mannered and heartbreakingly good-looking, he was also the kind of boy for whom most girls would willingly suffer. Hermione was sure that Simon's father's absconding to

France just as he was about to sit his A-levels, had upset him more than he would admit but, all credit to the lad, he'd not only kept his head and sailed through his exams but had been there for his mother in moments of crisis. For one so young he was particularly clear-sighted and self-possessed, but with none of the arrogance usually associated with these qualities. It was hard to imagine how any father could have turned his back on such a delightful son.

Hermione was not by nature a vindictive person, but she felt sure that she would never forgive Roger for what he had put Ellen and Simon through . . . or for the disruption to her own life. She missed Ellen now that she worked full time and lived just that little bit further away. Ellen usually had only one day off a week – Thursday – and it wasn't enough for Hermione. She wanted things how they used to be when she'd had Ellen all to herself. Damn Roger! He'd spoilt everything. And damn him for making her realise what a selfish person she was becoming in her old age.

She moved along the road until she came to the Lodge, set back some thirty or so yards from the pavement. Early-flowering cherry trees lined the curving driveway and Hermione could see that even though the blossom was barely a week old there was already a sprinkling of delicate pale pink petals lying on the lawn beside the smooth black tarmac – this, too, had only made its appearance last week and gave the impression of having been laid by an experienced carpet-fitter.

The Lodge was one of the oldest properties in the Crescent and during the past six months it had been the focus of much speculation. It was by far the largest and most elegant of the houses in the road and had stood empty for almost a year before a buyer was found. Now it was in the process of being transformed into what had been advertised in the local press as 'A retirement home of distinction for the distinguished'. Rumour had it that the alterations and building work were nearing an end, and certainly there had been far fewer comings and goings of noisy tradesmen's vehicles just lately which would support this theory. In more recent days there had been quieter visitors to the Lodge. Several spotlessly clean cars had made appearances, bearing men in suits and brightly coloured ties as well as a woman with a scarf tucked artfully around her neck. They all carried brief-cases and were too engrossed in what they were discussing to notice Hermione peering through the hedge at them as they walked the grounds comparing notes and nodding energetically into their mobile phones. She had named them the Management.

When planning permission had been sought for the change of use of the house the residents in the Crescent had all been assured that they would not be affected or inconvenienced in any way. Hermione had often wondered in what way anyone would think they could possibly be inconvenienced. Was the Management worried that the residents of the Crescent would be offended by the sight of a dead body being removed from the Lodge, and were they even now devising some discreet method of disposal of their future clients when they were no longer a viable proposition?

She pressed on towards Laburnum House, turned into the gravelled driveway and automatically stooped to tug at a clump of dandelions. She flung them, roots and all, into a massive rhododendron bush, its swelling buds on the verge of unfurling and showing tantalising glimpses of brilliant pink flowers, peeping out from beneath their protecting wrappings. She carried on round the house, through the courtyard and to the back door where she let herself in.

The telephone was ringing, but by the time she'd made her way through the garden room – stepping round and over discarded wellington boots, secateurs and gardening gloves – before reaching the kitchen and finally the hall, the ringing had stopped. Perhaps she should sell another piece of jewellery and buy herself a mobile phone. She laughed at this improbable idea and went to look for Botticelli and Giotto.

She found them in the sitting room, curled up in her favourite armchair, asleep in the sunlight flooding through the south-facing bay window. The large panes of glass were almost opaque with neglect. Neither of the cats stirred when Hermione approached, until she clicked her tongue at them. Giotto, black and white with a completely white face, opened his eyes and stretched out his front paws. Then Botticelli lifted his mackerel-striped face at the disturbance and he, too, stretched. Together they jumped to the floor and rubbed themselves against Hermione's legs, lifting the hem of her skirt with their heads, purring rhythmically.

'Good boys,' Hermione said, commandeering the arm-chair. She picked up the faded needlepoint cushion on which Giotto had been sleeping, and which she'd made almost twenty years ago, repositioned it into the small of her back and sank gratefully into the old chair. She was tired, and putting her exhaustion down to the surprisingly warm temperature of the day she closed her eyes and permitted herself a late-afternoon doze.

She dreamed of the Lodge next door and of rows of upright chairs that tilted forwards at the touch of a button, sending the occupiers sprawling to the floor.

*

Duncan dropped into second gear and approached Crantsford Hall carefully through elegant cast-iron gates, the spearhead tips of which were painted gold. He drove slowly along the cobbled driveway, brought the car to a stop alongside the garage block and hesitated a few moments before turning off the engine. He rested his head against the restraint and closed his eyes to concentrate better on Mahler's 'Kindertotenlieder'. He felt enormously happy. Not only did he have his new BMW at last – he'd waited patiently for more than three months for this particular model – but he had the prospect ahead of him of four days off work during which time he planned to play several rounds of golf and see Ellen.

When the CD came to an end he reluctantly opened his eyes, gathered up his briefcase and the evening paper from the passenger seat, locked the car, taking care to set the alarm, and strode over towards the house. He let himself in through the heavy oak door and walked across the stone-flagged floor.

'Is that you, Duncan?'

He ignored the question and placed his briefcase neatly beside a bow-fronted chest of drawers, straightened an out-of-place tulip in the vase on top, glanced briefly at the mail waiting for his attention on a large silver plate, then sought out his mother. He found her in the dining room at the other end of the Georgian table apparently attending to the oak panelling with a feather duster.

'What on earth are you doing, Nadia?'

'Please don't you use that tone of voice with me, Duncan, not after the day I've had. I've been let down. Mrs Harmen hasn't been in today. Not so much as a phone call. Not a word. Nothing. I'm completely worn out and I've a good mind to cancel lunch tomorrow. It'll be a miracle if I can get out of bed in the morning after all

34

the cleaning I've done today, never mind put a meal together. You'll have to ring round and explain to everybody. Tell them I'm ill. They might even send flowers.'

'Don't be ridiculous,' Duncan said, balling his fists behind his back. He was furious that his good mood had been so roughly taken away from him, and, recognising that his mother was playing the part of helpless-woman-gone-to-pieces, he said, 'I need a drink.' He turned away and marched to the drawing room where he spun the top off the whisky bottle, poured himself a good measure and tossed it back. He didn't know which had angered him most, his mother or his near loss of control just now.

By the time Nadia joined him he'd drunk another glass of whisky and had calmed down sufficiently to say, 'Don't worry about tomorrow, everything will be fine. You can lie in and I'll see to lunch.'

She smiled. 'What would I do without you, Duncan?'

'What indeed?'

Hermione could hear ringing. A vague persistent ringing. After a while it stopped, but then it started up again by which time she was fully awake and aware that it was the telephone she could hear. She hurried out to the hall and picked up the receiver.

'Where on earth have you been?'

'Asleep, as a matter of fact.'

'What, all afternoon?'

'Matthew, is it really any of your business what I choose to do –'

'I'm sorry, I was concerned, that's all. I tried this morning and earlier this afternoon. Are you sure you're okay?'

Hermione smiled. 'I'm fine, really. In fact, I've had quite a day.'

'So what have you been up to? Ram-raiding the local post office?'

'Matthew, you really are one of the most irritating and rude men I have the misfortune of knowing.'

'It's your own fault. As my godmother you should have played a more active role in my upbringing.'

'Yes, forty-two years ago I should have drowned you in the font!'

Matthew laughed. 'So that's all the thanks I get for ringing to see how you are and to ask if I can come and stay with you on Saturday.'

'What, the day after tomorrow?'

'Is there a problem?'

'Well, I had thought I might go hot-air ballooning for the Easter weekend, but I suppose I could put it off until another time. Why are you coming?'

'To see you.'

'Rubbish. When you come to see me you never ring, you just arrive. Why is this visit different? Why the advance warning?'

'If you must know I've been asked to do a commission for some neighbours of yours, the Buchanans. What are they like?'

'I'll let you work him out for yourself, but she's sweet, a bit of a Dizzy Nora.'

Matthew groaned.

'And they've more money than you'd ever know what to do with. Now if you've nothing more to tell me I'm in dire need of the lavatory. Goodbye.'

'Hermione.'

'Yes.'

'Take care, won't you?'

'Matthew, the day I can't manage the loo is the day I shoot myself.'

'I didn't mean that, you silly old woman.'

'I know. I just don't like people being sentimental these days.'

'I'll see you on Saturday, then. Late, probably about ten. I'll eat on the way. 'Bye.'

Chapter Five

When Ellen woke up she could hear music, a faint trickle of sound coming from downstairs. For a split second she thought that Simon must have arrived home in the middle of the night and that he was in the kitchen beneath her making himself a gigantic sandwich, the radio blaring beside him. 'It helps me concentrate,' he'd say, in his typical youthful fashion, whenever she turned the volume down in her typically parental way.

But realising that her bedroom floorboards weren't actually pulsating to the beat of something fast and furious, Ellen abandoned the idea that it was Simon downstairs and decided that Jo-Jo was up and about.

Ellen hadn't seen anything of Jo-Jo all yesterday evening. She'd slept right through from what was supposed to be a late-afternoon nap till now. The poor girl must have been exhausted to have slept so long.

Ellen pushed back the duvet, got out of bed and padded downstairs. She found Jo-Jo in the small narrow kitchen. She was already dressed, in the same clothes that she'd been wearing yesterday. She was getting herself something to eat while listening to the radio and swinging her narrow young hips. She looked as if she didn't have a care in the world.

'Hello.'

Jo-Jo started and turned round. 'I'm sorry,' she mumbled guiltily, her mouth full of what Ellen took to be

38

toast and Marmite, judging from the things spread over the work surface and the smell from the toaster. 'Did I wake you?'

'You did, but I should have been up anyway. How are you? Did you sleep well?'

'I slept brilliantly and I feel great. Well, great for a pregnant runaway. I helped myself to some bread, do you mind?'

Ellen shook her head. 'Have another slice of toast while I make us some tea.'

'No,' Jo-Jo said. 'You go and sit down and I'll make you some breakfast.' She hesitated and then laughed. 'Bloody hell, I sound just like I do at home.'

'What do you mean?'

'It's what I have to do with Mum. Sometimes she's like a child and you just have to treat her like one.'

Ellen cleared the table in the sitting room while Jo-Jo filled a tray of breakfast things and carried it through. 'You're very domesticated for your age,' Ellen said, slightly amused at the situation.

Jo-Jo shrugged. 'I've been doing it for years. Or, rather, I've been covering up for Mum for years. My step-father can't stand it if things aren't done the way he likes and Mum's so far gone she hasn't got a clue about organising a meal or the house. So when I finish school I pick up something from the shops and shove it in the oven and peel a few veg. Then all Mum has to do when he gets back from work is serve it up for him.'

Ellen was shocked. 'But how long has that been going on?'

'Ages. Well, for as long as I can remember.'

Ellen didn't have the nerve to ask how Jo-Jo thought her mother might be coping without her.

They ate in silence for a while until Jo-Jo said, 'I'll

39

wash up for you when we've finished and then I'll get going, see if I can find a hostel or something.'

After a pause Ellen said, 'Yes. I suppose that would be best.'

Jo-Jo looked up at her. 'Best?' she repeated, disappointed. She had thought, had hoped, that maybe she could . . . Oh, but what was the use? She'd got a bed for the night and something to eat, what more could she expect? This wasn't some fairy-tale where the poor little runaway lands on her feet in the land of plenty and ends up marrying a handsome prince – or even, to be politically correct as Alan would insist, ends up with a person of above-average means and well-enhanced looks.

Ellen dusted the crumbs of toast off her fingers and then pushed her plate away from her. 'Best all round,' she said at last, her voice firm and determined. 'After all, I've done my bit for society, I've contributed my two penn'orth to the kitty for the great unwashed. Nobody could accuse me of not having helped.' She didn't like the sound of the words coming out of her mouth, but she had to distance herself from Jo-Jo and her problems. She had enough of her own.

She started gathering up the mugs and plates, crashing them onto the tray. 'Well, what else can I do?' she asked, her eyes anywhere but on Jo-Jo's face.

'You could let me stay, until I get myself sorted?' Jo-Jo whispered, hardly daring to ask. 'I could help you. I – I can cook quite well.'

Ellen sank into her chair. 'But I can't afford to have you here. I can only just keep a roof over my own head and occasionally Simon's, never mind anyone else's.'

'How about just for the weekend?'

'Go home, Jo-Jo,' Ellen said, exasperated. 'Just go

home and sort out this awful mess with your parents. Get social services involved, get –'

'Anyone so long as it's not you, is that it?'

'That's not fair.'

'No, but then, so they tell me, life isn't. Now if you don't mind I'd like to stick to my agreement. I'll wash up and then go, and you needn't ever think of me again.'

'Oh, don't be so dramatic.' Ellen relented. 'Put that tray down, and heaven help me for my stupidity.'

Jo-Jo did as she was told.

'You can stay here over the Easter weekend but then on Tuesday we're going to have to find you a more permanent place in which to live. Don't interrupt, I haven't finished yet. And I'll let you stay these next few days on the condition that you ring your mother and let her know you're safe. Agreed?'

Jo-Jo nodded.

'And perhaps you should see a doctor. I don't want you fainting on me again.'

Jo-Jo gave another little nod.

'Good. Now, get cracking with that washing-up!'

Ellen followed a smiling Jo-Jo to the kitchen.

The phone rang. It was Hermione.

'So how's our little runaway? Not left town with all the silver, I hope?'

'No,' replied Ellen, watching Jo-Jo squeeze a long thin yellow snake of economy washing-up liquid into the sink. 'Not so much!' she cried out, alarmed at the extravagance. 'Sorry, Hermione, what did you say?'

'I'm ringing to make sure you haven't been robbed in the night.'

'Only robbed of my senses. I've been emotionally blackmailed into letting her stop here over the weekend.'

Hermione cackled. 'Now tell me why that doesn't come as a surprise.'

'Because I'm emotionally weak, I suppose.'

'Don't be so absurd. You've got more about you than any of that weak, wishy-washy lot yesterday who walked straight past Jo-Jo pretending not to notice her.'

'I don't recall you giving her anything. Does that make you weak and wishy-washy?'

'No, merely as tight as Giotto's bottom. And I'm referring to my cat's hindquarters, not to the great Italian artist's derrière, which, given the age he lived in, doesn't bear thinking about.'

Ellen smiled, thinking that if Hermione ever went round the bend nobody would ever notice. 'Hermione,' she said, looking at her watch, 'I'm going to have to go as I'm going out in a couple of hours and I've got to get ready. Hair to wash and act to clean up.'

'Duncan, I presume?'

'Yep. He's invited me for lunch at no less a place than Crantsford Hall.'

Hermione whistled. 'Time to meet the folks, is it? Oh, oh. So what are you going to wear? Nothing too racy, I hope.'

'No fear, not with La Carter there.'

'Now, Ellen, don't blow it. Just sit at the table nodding your pretty little head like one of those awful toy dogs in the back of a car. And if you keep your mouth shut she'll like you even better. And don't, whatever you do, say you've been ill recently. Nobody's allowed to be ill except La Carter. Got that?'

Ellen laughed. 'How do you know so much about her?'

'Old money, Ellen. It's the *entrée* to most evils, especially an old witch like Nadia Carter, and I'm referring to the days when I did have more than two and six to my name. But never mind all that. Go and tart yourself up while I have a quick word with Jo-Jo. And, Ellen . . .'

'Yes?'

'Try not to think of Daniel and the lion's den.'

Chapter Six

Duncan arrived early, just as Ellen had thought he might.

She'd learned that much about him during the time he'd acted for her during her divorce. He'd always been ready at least five minutes before any of their appointments in his neatly presented beamed office in Church Walk Mews and had been painstakingly conscientious in his dealings with her.

Her first visit to his office had been almost as unbearable as reading the note Roger had left on the mantelpiece. She had arrived far too early for her eleven o'clock appointment and, sitting in the small waiting room, she had watched a variety of smartly dressed men and women passing to and fro through an open door – the other partners who made up the practice of Church Walk Mews Solicitors, she had assumed. At five to eleven Duncan had come for her in the waiting room. 'Mrs Jacobs,' he'd said briskly, holding out his hand, 'Duncan Carter. Shall we get on?'

He was younger than she had expected, but she had only spoken briefly with him on the telephone a couple of days previously. From the sound of his voice she had anticipated someone in his early fifties with thinning hair and a tired suit with faint pinstripes and shiny creases. But in reality it was difficult to pin an exact age on Duncan Carter, for his thick black hair, neatly cut and swept to one side, gave him a youthful, boyish appearance, which was immediately at odds with the mannered style in which he spoke and moved about his office. His suit was fashionably single-breasted and fitted his tall slim body perfectly, and his shoes, classic lace-ups, were as black as his hair while the toe-caps had a lustre matched only by the polished desk behind which he positioned himself. He motioned to a comfortable chair, waited until she was sufficiently settled, then removed his jacket and spent a few seconds straightening it on the back of his own chair, before sitting down, picking up his fountain pen and finally facing her.

For almost an hour she had listened in numbed silence to explanations of maintenance orders, decree nisis and decree absolutes while watching him methodically run his thumb and forefinger slowly up and down the sides of his pen, again and again. 'It's going to be a bumpy road for you,' he said kindly, when at last he seemed to run out of things to say, 'but not an impossible one. Just remember, my job is to smooth out those bumps for you. Do you have any questions?'

'How much will all this cost me?' had been the only one.

'My fee is one hundred pounds an hour,' he'd answered, without batting an eyelid.

One hundred pounds an hour! 'In that case I'll have a cup of tea. Or is that extra?'

Tea in delicate bone-china cups appeared within minutes. 'Mrs Jacobs,' he said, when they were alone again and he had passed her a cup and saucer across his desk, 'forgive the impertinence, but please don't let the issue of money cloud your long-term view.'

Advice that fell on stony ground, for ever since Roger had left all she had thought about was money. Did she have enough that month to pay the electricity bill or fill the car with petrol? Could she afford to splash out on real chocolate digestives instead of making do with the red and green labelled biscuits in the barrels at the supermarket, which were always broken and covered with a curious brown substance masquerading as chocolate that stuck tenaciously to the roof of her mouth like gum?

From the window she watched Duncan park what appeared to be a new car alongside the barn. She remembered him saying some months ago that he'd ordered a BMW. She smiled to herself, realising now why he had offered to pick her up.

He came towards the cottage and she congratulated herself on picking out the right outfit – a pale pink linen skirt and jacket she'd had for years but which never failed to lift her spirits, and which she had felt sure would complement what Duncan would be wearing. She had second-guessed him well. He was dressed in smart grey flannels with a navy blazer, white shirt and tie, and she had to admit that together they made an attractive couple. She let him ring the bell – it wouldn't do to let him know she'd been pacing the room waiting for him – and then very quietly chanted to herself, 'One two three, give him time to wait for me,' before opening the door.

'Duncan,' she said, in a voice that she hoped contained just the right amount of pleasure at seeing him. 'Come on in while I find my bag. Would you like a drink?'

'No thank you,' he said politely. She watched him move awkwardly into the little room. It was the first time he'd stepped inside Spring Bank Cottage. On their previous evenings out together they had arranged to meet up at the restaurants Duncan had pre-booked for dinner – these invitations had only materialised once her divorce had been finalised: while she had still been a client and a married woman Duncan had not made the slightest hint of an advance towards her. He was clearly a man of principle.

'You've done this up very nicely, Ellen,' he said, stooping slightly to avoid knocking the arrangements of dried flowers hanging from the ceiling. 'It's charming. You've made it quite your own.'

'I'm still trying to get used to it,' she said, gathering up her bag and a large bunch of daffodils that she'd picked from along the river-bank earlier that morning, 'but after Orchard House this seems so –'

He raised his hand in the air. 'Ellen, I've told you before, the past is irrelevant. It's where you are now that's important and where you think you might be going.'

She thought of Crantsford Hall and smiled. 'Perhaps you're right, Duncan. Shall we go?'

As Duncan pulled out onto the main road at the top of Beggarman's Lane he glanced sideways at Ellen and thought how attractive she was looking today. He noticed, too, her long legs just inches away from the gear stick.

'What a lovely car,' Ellen said, conscious that Duncan was scrutinising her. 'It's new, isn't it?' she added, doing her best to inch her skirt down discreetly, but it was having none of it and seemed determined to stay right where it was.

He smiled and pressed his foot down on the accelerator a touch more. 'It arrived yesterday. Do you like it?'

'It's beautiful,' she answered. 'It must be wonderful to drive.'

'It is,' he agreed, and took a corner fast enough to feel

the pull. He then had to brake sharply as he came up behind an ancient Allegro, flat out at twenty.

Ellen had a pretty good idea what was coming next – after all, Duncan had the perfect right to be a racing driver *manqué*, just like any other man with a new car. She held her breath as he swerved round the Allegro and then accelerated at such a rate that her head was forced back against the head restraint and kept there for some moments. As they came into the speed-restricted area at the top of Church Walk Duncan slowed down. He took the fork in the road that directed the traffic away from the town centre, headed in a north-easterly direction towards Mobberley and once they were clear of any speed restrictions his foot went down again. Within a matter of minutes they were in open countryside and he was slowing down to swing the car through a pair of cast-iron gates. They turned a bend in the cobbled driveway and Crantsford Hall stood before them, resplendent in the bright midday sunshine, slightly raised above a lawn planted out with clumps of yellow and white daffodils, their delicate heads bobbing in the gentle breeze.

'How long have you lived here?' Ellen asked.

'We moved here when I was ten, but I've had stints away of course – boarding school, college, a couple of years in London and then for a while I had my own place over in Alderley Edge.' He paused for a moment before adding, 'But when my father died so unexpectedly it made sense to move back here to keep an eye on Nadia.'

He parked the car next to a dusty Range Rover and a metallic grey Jaguar. 'Good,' he said, switching off the engine. 'Everyone else has arrived.'

They entered the house through a large oak door, which Duncan held open for her.

48

'Sounds like they're all in the drawing room,' he said. And sure enough, as they passed a series of closed panelled doors and grim-looking oil paintings of what looked like eighteenth-century grandees, they came to a room where the other guests were standing around, glasses in hand, making noisy small-talk. Ellen didn't recognise any of them, but she recognised their type – the honkers and brayers, as Hermione called some of Crantsford's worthies.

An extremely large woman came forward. She wasn't fat, but everything about her seemed oversized, shoulders, hands, feet, even eyes. She was colossal. If Ellen wanted to be generous, and she wasn't sure she wanted to be, she would say the woman was big-boned – like a dinosaur! Ellen disliked her on sight.

'Nadia,' Duncan said, 'this is Ellen Jacobs. Ellen, this is my mother.'

'Well, get out of the way so I can see her,' Nadia said impatiently. She was anxious to view this guest of Duncan's, especially as he hadn't mentioned anything about inviting anybody else for lunch until a couple of hours ago. All legs and blonde hair, she thought dismissively, after paying the scantest of attention. Where *did* Duncan find them?

Ellen handed her hostess the large bunch of daffodils. 'Though having seen your garden I feel a little silly giving you these,' she said, with a light laugh.

'Delightful,' Nadia said, without even looking at them.

Sensing his mother's disapproval, Duncan intervened. 'Why don't you put those in water, Nadia, while I introduce Ellen to everyone?'

Reluctantly Nadia did as she was told. In the kitchen she threw the daffodils in the sink, took a gulp from the glass of sherry tucked behind the jars of herbs and spices

49

in the alcove above the cooker and hurried back to the drawing room, just in time to catch the last of the introductions being made. Henry and Cynthia Koval were having their glasses refilled and the Winstanleys – Maurice and Phyllis – were shaking hands with Ellen.

'Jacobs,' Henry said loudly, coming back towards Ellen. 'That name rings a bell. Bugger me if I can think why.'

'You always say that,' Cynthia drawled. 'Ignore him, Ellen. He thinks he knows everyone in Crantsford.'

'Do you play golf?' asked Maurice who, Ellen decided, had the look of a man who certainly knew his way round a clubhouse bar as well as a bag of clubs, if his weather-beaten face and purplish red hooter was anything to go by. 'Is that how you met Duncan?'

'No,' Ellen said, amused. 'I'm no golfer.'

'Ellen and I met in a professional capacity,' Duncan said, passing round a tray of olives and cashew nuts.

'Got you,' Maurice said. 'You're one of those clever types, aren't you? I knew it the moment you opened your mouth. I said to myself, she's not just a pretty popsie on legs. So you're in the legal profession as well, are you?'

Popsie! Any more talk like this and she'd pop him right in the eye! 'Actually,' Ellen said, straining to keep a polite smile on her face, 'Duncan was my solicitor. He acted for –'

'Come on, Maurice,' Duncan interrupted. 'You're not wearing a wig and gown today.'

'A wig and gown,' Ellen repeated, helping herself to a couple of olives. 'Does that mean you're a barrister or a transvestite?'

'Ellen, my dear,' Nadia said in a voice awash with condescension, 'Maurice is a judge. You must surely have heard of Judge Winstanley.'

50

And, as though to rub her nose in it even more, Nadia placed Ellen next to Maurice-the-red-nosed-judge for lunch, which was served in an enormous oak-panelled dining room with a polished oak floor and stone fireplace the size of a single bed. The room must have been north-facing and was freezing, and Ellen stared reproachfully at the empty fireplace.

Conversation around the table fairly skipped along with talk of birdies and handicaps and, even more exciting, the Winstanleys weren't renewing their AA membership after being kept waiting for more than thirty minutes on the hard shoulder of the M6 in February when their Jaguar broke down. Ellen let their voices drone on while she contented herself with imagining how, as mistress of Crantsford Hall and with a limitless budget, she would bring this cheerless room to life. The drab, sludge-green curtains would be first to go and in their place she'd put up sumptuous drapes with plenty of warm tonal shades to the fabric, probably reds, golds, anything that would add some warmth to the room. Next she'd have a log fire crackling and everywhere there'd be flowers: armfuls of daffodils in the spring and in the summer masses of fragrant sweet peas and roses and anything else that would sweeten the leaden atmosphere.

'Jacobs!' roared Henry-bugger-me-Koval from the other side of the table.

Ellen jumped and sent a piece of roast lamb skidding across the table, followed by a splash of mint sauce.

'Bugger me if I haven't got it!' Henry beamed happily. 'I knew I'd get there in the end. There was that dentist chappie in Lower Market Street called Jacobs. Bugger of a dentist he was. I turned up for my appointment and he wasn't there. Buggered off to France with some totty. I ask you! I heard that he left behind him debts worse than the national borrowing rate of a third-world country and a pretty wife to pick up . . .' His words fizzled out as he looked at Ellen and saw the expression on her face. 'Oh, bugger!' he muttered, his discomfort as great as Ellen's.

Nadia saw her chance. 'Ellen, my dear. I had no idea you were *that* Mrs Jacobs.'

'Mother.'

'Don't you Mother me anything, Duncan. You really should have said something. It's unforgivable that you should have caused Henry to feel so embarrassed and to humiliate Ellen in this way. Why didn't you say that you had acted on her behalf for her divorce? Why all the secrecy?' Her enjoyment of the situation was undisguised.

'I didn't think it was anyone else's business,' Duncan said simply. He reached forward to retrieve Ellen's piece of meat from the tablecloth, slipped it onto his own plate and then carefully wiped his hands on his napkin.

'I don't feel at all humiliated,' lied Ellen, lifting her eyes from the congealed lamb in front of her. 'And, Henry, please don't worry on my account. Your description of my ex-husband is as apt as any I've heard.'

Henry mumbled something that passed for an apology, and Phyllis Winstanley said, 'Didn't you have to sell your lovely house in the Crescent?' She knew full well that this was indeed the case. She'd seen it for herself in the estate agent's window in Lower Market Street last year, and had also seen the asking price drop steadily.

Ellen nodded.

'I heard you'd recently set yourself up in your own little business,' Cynthia said. 'Terribly brave of you, and after everything you'd gone through.'

Ellen felt trapped. It was obvious that these two women knew everything there was to know about the infamous dentist, Roger Jacobs. The only missing piece to their jigsaw of gossip was that they hadn't known who Mrs Jacobs was, but now that they had the very woman herself in their midst they were clearly determined to squeeze every last detail out of her.

'What kind of business is it you do?' asked Nadia from the head of the table. 'Business lunches or interior design? I hear that's what a lot of young women are occupying themselves with these days.'

'Dried flowers,' replied Ellen, mustering what was left of her dignity. 'I have a barn in Beggarman's Lane where I sell them. I also take orders.' She glanced over to the fireplace. 'In the summer months when you're not using it, that fireplace would look wonderful with one of my arrangements.'

Nadia took this as a personal slight. 'I think you'll find that a fireplace which has a date stone of 1705 stands for itself and needs no artificial adornment.'

But Phyllis was more cunning. 'I'd love you to put something together for my sitting room. Perhaps I could come along and see your barn. Beggarman's Lane, did you say?'

'What a good idea,' chimed in Cynthia. 'I'll join you. Nadia, you'll have to come as well. You're always saying how we should support local businesses.'

'I'm surprised you're not working today, Ellen,' Nadia said flatly. 'It's the Easter weekend, after all. I would have expected this to be one of your busiest times.'

'Mother,' Duncan said sharply, 'it's Good Friday and I'm sure you'll agree that Ellen's as entitled as the next person to take a holiday if she so chooses. I think it's time for our dessert now.'

Just desserts, Ellen wanted to add.

The plates were cleared away and Duncan brought in a large trifle and the customary noises of appreciation were made. 'Bugger me,' said Henry, who had now overcome his earlier blunder and resumed his normal self, 'that looks promising.'

The mood around the table lightened.

'You'll never guess what I saw in Crantsford yesterday,' said Cynthia. 'A girl begging! In Crantsford, of all places.'

Ellen stiffened. She kept her eyes firmly on her bowl, but beside her she felt Maurice-the-red-nosed-judge pull himself up onto his judgemental high horse.

'We're being overrun with them,' he said. 'Worse than vermin in my opinion.'

'Absolutely,' agreed his wife, Phyllis.

'I think I saw her as well,' said Duncan. 'She was trying her luck in Church Walk Mews.'

Ellen remained silent and hated herself for it. She thought of Jo-Jo and hoped that she was enjoying herself with Hermione, who had insisted that while Ellen was out for lunch the girl should go to her. Dear sweet Hermione, mad as a hatter but more in touch with the real world than any of this lot with their tired old clichés. Suddenly Ellen wanted very much to go home.

As it turned out she was first to leave.

'Let's go for a drive,' Duncan whispered to her, when everyone had started decamping to the drawing room for coffee and he found her lagging behind the group. She nodded, and in the kind of voice that would brook no argument he said to his mother, 'Nadia, I'm taking Ellen home.'

Nadia made a token gesture of disappointment and everyone stood to say goodbye. Ellen thought she had better give a plausible excuse for her early departure. 'A headache,' she apologised, 'it'll soon go.' Too late, she remembered Hermione's warning.

'Headaches are nothing compared to migraines,' announced Nadia, 'nothing but an inconvenience that can be easily borne with the right mental attitude. But migraines are a completely different matter. When I have one of my sessions, I'm flat on my back for at least a week. Isn't that so, Duncan?'

Eventually they made it to the front door where they stood for a further five minutes while everyone insisted on waving Ellen off with promises made by both Cynthia and Phyllis that they would be calling on her in Beggarman's Lane before very long.

In the end Duncan took Ellen firmly by the arm and led her to his car. She felt like a bride being whisked away on her honeymoon and as they drove out of view of the house Duncan leaned over and kissed her cheek.

Chapter Seven

'Who's Duncan?' Jo-Jo asked.

Hermione looked up from the tray of sweet-pea seedlings she was potting on. She was dressed in one of her more eccentric gardening outfits – an old brown and cream kaftan with a fringe added onto the hem to give it extra length, except it didn't quite reach all the way round and there was a gap at the back. On her head was a large floppy hat that possessed a solitary pink feather, which had a habit of shifting position. Sometimes it was upright like an antenna and other times it drooped mournfully over the brim and tickled Hermione's face.

'Duncan is hopefully going to be Ellen's next husband,' she confided, with a smile.

'You make her sound like she collects them. How many has she had?'

Hermione laughed and returned her attention to the seedlings on the wooden table in front of her. 'Just the one,' she answered, making a small hole in a pot of compost with the end of a pencil. She carefully picked up a tender plant and settled it into its new home.

They were sitting on the terrace overlooking the garden, having eaten lunch, cleared away and then come outside to enjoy the afternoon sunshine. Her young companion had proved to be good company – a compulsive interrogator it turned out, which backed up the opinion Hermione had made of her yesterday, that despite the stupidity of her current predicament she was an intelligent girl with something to say for herself.

'So where's he now?'

'With any luck being driven mad by the brainless wonder he flitted off to France with.'

'You don't sound as if you liked him very much.'

Hermione thought about this. Had she liked Roger at all? Probably not, was the honest answer. More likely she had tolerated him, and only tolerated him because he was Ellen's husband. 'He was a dentist,' she replied. 'Nobody likes dentists.'

Jo-Jo laughed. 'You're just like my grandmother. She never answered my questions properly either.'

Hermione lifted out another sweet-pea plant and held it gently between her thumb and forefinger. 'No chance of this *doppelgänger* of mine taking care of you, is there?'

Jo-Jo rose from her chair and went and stood next to the low black wrought-iron railings that overlooked the rockery six feet below. 'No,' she said.

'I thought not.'

'But if she'd still been alive that's where I'd have gone.'

'I'm very pleased to hear it, and it only goes to confirm what I've long since thought – that we old folk certainly have our uses.'

Jo-Jo came and sat at the table again. She traced her finger in a mound of spilled compost on the table and formed the letter A. Hermione pretended not to notice. 'I can't always work out whether you're being sarcastic or just plain horrid,' Jo-Jo said, picking up a clay pot and obliterating what she'd just drawn.

'Don't fret yourself. You'll get the hang of it eventually.'

Jo-Jo doubted this, and decided to follow her earlier

line of questioning. 'Why does Ellen want to get married again? Isn't she better off on her own?'

'Depends what you mean by better off.'

'You're not saying she wants this Duncan for his money, are you?'

'My dear Jo-Jo, you look quite prim. But whoever said that Duncan had money? I certainly didn't.'

Jo-Jo frowned. 'You implied that he did.'

'You don't want to listen to what a rambling old woman says. Especially one as daft as me.' She shook her hands free of compost. 'Come on, let's go for a wander. The rest of these sweet peas can wait till later.'

They left the terrace and took the small path of stone steps to the right of the rockery down to the area of lawn below. 'This used to be a tennis court,' Hermione said, 'but I stopped playing when Fred Perry bowed out. I lost heart in the game.'

'Who's he? An old boyfriend of yours?'

Hermione smiled. 'Oh, the ignorance of youth. What a joy to behold.'

To their right, and behind a straggly beech hedge, was a greenhouse, and to their left, tucked into the rhododendron bushes and surrounded by a mass of yellow daffodils and primroses was a wooden summer-house with an ornately tiled roof. But Hermione ignored both of these and continued further down the garden where there were two large yews which for the past thirty years she had clipped and bullied into resembling a pair of Christmas puddings. Between them were more steps and as Hermione walked on she stooped to pick a daffodil bent at a ninety-degree angle. She snapped it off and wiped the gooey thread of sap from the stem onto the step and handed the flower to Jo-Jo.

'Will you keep the baby?' she asked unexpectedly.

58

Jo-Jo was taken aback. 'I don't know,' she said.

Hermione gave her a long, hard stare. 'You must have thought about it, though. Is it too late for an abortion?' She lowered her eyes to Jo-Jo's stomach.

Jo-Jo didn't answer but she wrapped her slender arms in front of her and covered her stomach protectively.

'Much too late obviously,' Hermione said. 'But at least that narrows your options to just the two possibilities open to you. You either keep the baby, or give it up for adoption. Do you love the father?'

'For a daft rambling old woman, you're very direct, aren't you?'

Hermione didn't respond and started walking again. 'There's a seat further down,' she said. 'Let's go on, it'll be cooler in the shade.'

They crossed another lawn and went through an arch to the wild, unkempt patch of garden that Hermione rarely visited these days. There wasn't a path and their shoes all but disappeared into the thick layer of leaves as they made their way through the wilderness that had been left to fend for itself. Fallen branches obstructed the way, with brambles and stinging nettles.

Just as Jo-Jo was beginning to wonder if they shouldn't be heading back towards the house they came across a stone seat and a statue of a young woman with her hands in front of her holding an open book. Her face was turned up, as though something in the air had caught her attention, and even with the gathering moss and years of discoloration that had taken its toll, the features were still visible and Jo-Jo could make out a familiar smile.

'She looks so happy,' she said, going straight to the statue and touching the face. She brushed away some lichen and traced her fingers over the cheekbones and proud chin.

'The man who made it was a friend and he had that effect on . . .'

Jo-Jo glanced back at Hermione. 'Is it you, when you were young? Was he that Perry bloke you mentioned earlier?'

'Just as I was beginning to think you possessed half a brain you go and spoil it. Fred Perry was one of the most brilliant tennis players this country ever produced and sadly he was never a boyfriend of mine.' She turned away and sat down on the seat. Jo-Jo joined her.

'But the man who created that beautiful statue, he *was* a boyfriend of yours, wasn't he?' she persisted.

Hermione shrugged. 'It matters not what he was, he's no longer here. Now tell me about the baby's father. Do you love him and is that the reason you want to keep the child?'

Jo-Jo considered lying but what was the point? 'His name's Alan, I don't know how old he is but he's married with two children of his own and he's my English teacher, or rather he was. Are you shocked?'

'Now what do you really think?'

'I suppose not,' Jo-Jo said, with a smile. 'You're not the shockable type, are you?'

'Thank you, I'll take that as a compliment. But this Alan character, he sounds like he might be of the shockable variety.'

Jo-Jo thought about this. She recalled the look of horror on Alan's face when she'd told him. He was taking her home after she'd babysat his children while he'd been out for the evening with his wife. He'd stopped the car in the usual place down a quiet unlit road and had started kissing her and pulling at her clothes. It never took him long. And always afterwards he'd tell her how clever she was. He would stroke her hair and say how she

60

was the best student he'd ever taught and that she was special. But he didn't that night. That night he told her she was stupid and that she should have known better. Banging his fist on the steering-wheel, he'd shouted, 'Haven't you listened to anything in school? The amount of curriculum time devoted to pastoral care and you still wind up pregnant!'

Two days later he'd spoken to her at school. 'Sorry about the other night,' he'd whispered. 'It was the shock. I'll get the money together and we'll arrange an abortion. You're not to worry about a thing.'

But the next day her mother had found the pregnancy-test kit in her bedroom and told her husband about it. Predictably he had ranted and raved about how much he'd done for her since taking her on from the age of six and what a disappointment she'd turned out – he made her sound like an employee caught with her hands in the till. And, just as predictably, she was told to leave the house. She had thrown some things into a bag, emptied the box in her drawer where she kept her babysitting money and then got a bus to the station, where she caught a train with the intention of going to Manchester. But she messed everything up and found herself on the wrong train heading for a place in Cheshire she'd never even heard of – Crantsford. As she had stepped down onto the empty platform, tears had filled her eyes: all she could think of was her mother's act of betrayal. Why had she told her step-father? After all the years of help she had given her mother, was this to be all the thanks she got?

She had phoned her mother earlier, just as Ellen had instructed, and again the betrayal was there. 'It's better this way,' her mother's pathetic voice had said. 'Better

61

that you stay away.' It was as if she was pleading with her.

'Jo-Jo?'

She looked down to see Hermione's liver-spotted hand covering her own. Gran used to do that to her when she knew she was about to cry. She swallowed hard to loosen her constricted throat, but it didn't work. 'I only went with him because I was so lonely,' she murmured. 'I wanted somebody to love me in the way Gran used to love me. He said I was special, I . . . I wanted to believe him.'

Hermione took Jo-Jo in her arms and held her tightly. 'Oh, Jo-Jo, you poor sweet child, of course you're special.'

Chapter Eight

'Were you very bored?' Duncan asked, pulling up alongside Ellen's barn.

'Not in the slightest,' she lied glibly.

Duncan suspected that this was not the truth but he let it go, preferring instead to admire Ellen for her tact. 'I'm sorry about all that fuss with Henry at lunch,' he said. 'He can be a bit of a terrier. Once he gets hold of something he doesn't like to give it up.'

'No harm done.' Ellen thought that of all the people round the table who most resembled a terrier it was La Carter who fitted the bill. 'Would you like to come in for a drink?' she asked, sensing that they'd reached the tricky stage of still sitting in the car, the engine off, and each waiting for the other to determine what happened next. She wondered if Duncan was now regretting having kissed her when they'd sailed through the gates at Crantsford Hall. It had been so unexpected that it had rendered them both silent for the following few minutes – he silent with embarrassment, she fancied, and she silent with wishful thinking. She'd been mentally stuffing her belongings into packing cases and setting up home with Duncan ever since.

He looked at the clock on the walnut dashboard. 'I really ought to get back, but, well, all right, then, but just a soft drink.'

Not much chance of anything else, thought Ellen, as

she let them into the cottage. She left Duncan prowling around the small sitting room and went through to the kitchen. She opened the fridge and found the carton of orange juice she'd opened yesterday morning, but there was little more than a dribble left in it – Jo-Jo would have to be pointed in the direction of the tap for the remainder of her stay. 'Fizzy water okay?' she called out to Duncan.

'That would be fine,' he answered.

She reached into the door of the fridge and pulled out a near empty plastic bottle. She twisted the cap and, just as she had dreaded, it gave off a tired little hiss confirming her fears that the remains of the carbonated water were way past their best. She poured out what was left into a glass and then rummaged through the contents of the fridge. Not that there was much to rummage through, just a tub of margarine, a cling-film-wrapped nugget of cheese that had all the taste of a bar of soap, and a bag of carrots – carrots were a frequent stand-by at Spring Bank Cottage, they were good and cheap, especially if you bought the pre-packed inferior variety with splits running the length of them. Hiding behind the carrots she found what she was looking for. A plastic lemon. She squirted a shot of juice into Duncan's glass, added a couple of ice cubes and hoped for the best.

'Here we are,' she said, joining him in the sitting room. She handed him his drink.

'You not joining me?'

'No,' she answered, and went and sat in the window-seat. She opened the small window behind her, hoping that the warm breeze blowing in through the window would somehow make her seem more alluring, but her efforts were wasted as Duncan continued to prowl round the room preferring to inspect her meagre possessions rather than her potential charm.

'That's a nice watercolour,' he said, pointing with his glass at the picture above the fireplace. After the dark foreboding paintings she'd just seen at Crantsford Hall, Ellen supposed that the light, airy depiction of a group of children playing on a beach would seem like a breath of fresh air to him.

'And you've some interesting china,' he continued, now addressing the assortment of jugs, plates, cups and saucers on the dresser. 'Very nice,' he added, ducking the hanging dried flowers as he moved across the room to take a closer look.

'All junk, I'm afraid,' Ellen said, getting up from the window-seat and settling herself in an armchair where perhaps her legs might be more noticeable. 'Just bits and bobs I've collected over the years, nothing of any value. I had to sell the good stuff.'

He came and sat opposite her and lifted his glass to his lips. The taste took him by surprise and he peered at the slightly cloudy water.

'It's a new variety I've just tried,' Ellen said, 'but I don't think I'll bother with it again. It's a touch too tangy for my taste.'

'Perhaps not,' Duncan said politely, waiting for his mouth to recover from being turned inside out.

'Would you prefer something else?'

He shook his head and bravely took another sip but instantly regretted this foolhardiness. He placed the glass on the hearth and smiled at Ellen. She smiled back and wondered how on earth to crank up the conversation. 'You must thank your mother for such a lovely lunch,' she said.

Duncan leaned back and crossed his legs. 'I will,' he said, and thought of the irony. He himself had cooked the meal while Nadia had lain in bed upstairs. It was easier that way. By keeping her out of the kitchen he could at least ensure that she wasn't troubling him. It also meant that she wouldn't drink as much. Even Nadia wouldn't drink in bed. For some time now he had taken to monitoring the quantity she got through and as long as he was able to do this he felt he was in control of the situation. That, of course, had been the main reason for his moving back to Crantsford Hall after his father had died. There had been no question of Nadia being allowed to live alone. With nobody there to check on her each day, there was no knowing the havoc she could cause.

'You must be very close to your mother,' Ellen said.

'What do you mean?' His tone was too sharp and at once he corrected this slip by adding lightheartedly, 'You're surely not insinuating something along the lines of an Oedipus complex?'

She laughed awkwardly. 'Heavens, no.'

But he was nettled, and not just by Ellen's comment. During lunch it was as if Nadia had gone out of her way to be as hostile towards Ellen as she could. To a lesser extent it had happened in the past, with previous girlfriends, but then it hadn't seemed important. With Ellen, it was different. He was genuinely fond of her. He didn't want this relationship spoiled.

'Ellen,' he said, suddenly understanding that if he hoped to further things with her there would have to be a degree of honesty between them. There were explanations to be made. Confidences to share. 'There's something I'd like to say to you.'

Ellen was all ears. A declaration of love, perhaps? 'Yes,' she said calmly, her mind already racing along to the nearest jewellery shop.

Duncan reached nervously for his drink. Just in time he remembered the last mouthful and lowered the glass. He cleared his throat. 'I've never actually told anyone this before,' he began.

Yes! cheered Ellen to herself. A declaration for sure – *Darling, I've never said this to anyone before, but I love you.* Not that she'd had much experience in that department. In fact, she couldn't remember Roger broaching the subject of love with her, even when she had made her feelings for him so obvious. She had loved him so much she had never once doubted that he didn't feel the same for her, and when she'd discovered that she was pregnant with Simon and they had married almost immediately, she couldn't have been happier.

'There's never been any real reason to tell anyone before,' Duncan carried on.

Yes, yes, Duncan, she silently encouraged him. You love me and want to spend the rest of your life by my side. She had chosen the ring and was tearing along the high street of matrimony towards the bridal shop.

'The thing is, I want to be honest with you, I feel it's important. And once you know, well, then I think you'll understand things better. You see . . . Nadia isn't my natural mother.'

'Oh.'

'You sound disappointed.'

'No, not at all.' She was now plodding home empty-handed, exhausted and let down.

'Does it make the situation clearer?'

'Clearer?' she asked. 'In what way?'

He got to his feet and resumed his earlier prowling. He went over to the dresser and picked up a plate. He examined the back of it and then returned it to its place. 'My parents adopted me when I was three weeks old,' he said, as though the plate inspection had been a metaphorical gulp of Dutch courage, 'and I think, as can quite often be the way, Nadia as an adoptee parent has always veered towards over-protecting me, and in return I've always been slightly over-protective towards her. She's not a strong woman and sometimes she's in need of a little shoring up.'

Shoring up! Surely he wasn't referring to that Amazonian woman with shoulders Atlas would have given worlds for?

He sat down again, part horrified at what he'd just told Ellen and part relieved. Now at least she'd understand the relationship between him and Nadia.

'Well,' Ellen said, completely at a loss as to what to say next. Clearly what Duncan had just shared with her was of the utmost importance to him. Though why, she didn't know. She was desperately trying to think of something to add to the conversation when she was distracted by the sound of something moving outside the window.

'What is it?' he asked.

'I don't know.' She went to investigate. 'What the –'

Duncan joined her and found himself looking down on two strange figures crouching in the flower-bed beneath the window. One was a young girl, who appeared normal enough, but her companion was a different matter altogether. Was it a nightdress she was wearing? Or a pair of curtains? And as for that hat! He was about to launch into a polite 'Be off with you,' when he heard Ellen start to speak at his side.

'Duncan, I'd like you to meet some friends of mine. Hermione and Jo-Jo.'

Outwardly, Ellen was all smiles and nonchalance; inwardly she was screaming like a banshee and wishing Hermione a million miles away.

But Hermione was clearly enjoying herself and, stretching her hand through the open window, she smiled

68

engagingly at Duncan. 'How do you do? I've heard so much about you.'

'How long have you been there?' he asked, suddenly mortified at the thought of his conversation with Ellen having been overheard.

Hermione shook her head and puffed at the feather on her hat, which was tickling the end of her nose. 'Matter of seconds.' She puffed again. 'No more than that. We thought we'd come and see if Ellen was back yet and when we saw a strange car parked by the barn and a window open, we thought, Aha, we'd best creep along in a stealth-like manner and check that all was well. One can never be too sure, can one?' She smiled sweetly at Duncan.

Duncan smiled back, but warily. Then he glanced at the young girl behind this strange elderly apparition and thought for a crazy moment that he recognised her. 'Do I know you?' he asked.

'I shouldn't think so,' she answered.

Duncan continued to stare at her. After a few seconds he said, 'I know who you are. You were begging in town yesterday, weren't you?'

'Begging's such an ugly word,' Hermione said serenely. 'I'm sure there must be a more politically correct phrase.'

'Yes – how about income-supplementing for the economically marginalised?' offered Jo-Jo. She turned her back on them all and sauntered over to the river-bank.

Ellen knew that there was no chance of getting rid of Hermione so easily. She had no choice but to invite her in. 'No, not through the window,' she cried. 'Use the door, and take off that silly hat. You're frightening the life out of Duncan with it.'

Hermione did as she was told and removed the offending article. 'Duncan, dear boy, please allow me to

69

put your mind at rest. I am a perfectly respectable member of the community. In fact, I'd go so far as to say –'

'Enough, Hermione!'

Duncan, too, had had enough and Ellen watched him inch his way towards the open door to make his escape.

'I think it's time I was going,' he said.

'Yes, I suppose so,' she replied, resigned to the inevitable truth that this was the end of the road as far as she and Duncan were concerned. He'd have no more to do with her now, not after he'd met her lunatic of a friend. Without doubt she'd be tarred with the same brush. 'I'll walk you to your car,' she said gloomily.

Outside they saw Jo-Jo sitting by the river-bank. She was throwing pebbles into the water.

'Is she a relative of that strange woman?' asked Duncan, as he pulled his keys out of his jacket pocket.

'Not exactly,' Ellen said cautiously.

'Solicitors don't like phrases like that,' he said, unlocking his car.

'It's a long story, Duncan.'

He looked at her thoughtfully. 'Perhaps you'd like to tell it to me over dinner next week?'

All was not lost! 'Yes,' she said. 'Yes, I would.'

'Eight o'clock, Wednesday night. I'll pick you up.'

There was no goodbye kiss, but then Ellen didn't think there would be, not with Hermione gawping out of the window at the pair of them.

When Duncan's car was out of sight she marched back to the cottage. 'And just what the dickens did you think you were doing?' she shouted at Hermione. 'You very nearly blew everything, crouching there in the bushes like a couple of second-rate spies.'

'I thought it all went rather well.'

'Rather well?' repeated Ellen, stunned. 'What on earth do you mean?'

'The poor man will be hooked, Ellen. Simply hooked with the desire to rescue you from a life of poverty and batty old women peering in through your windows. Take my word for it, he'll be back. He won't be able to help himself.'

Ellen laughed and some of her anger subsided. 'Actually, he's just invited me for dinner next week.'

'Well, there you are!'

'So why's he so hung up about being adopted, then?' asked Jo-Jo, who was now leaning in through the window. 'Why's he never told anyone about that before? It's hardly a big deal, is it?'

'She's right,' said Ellen. 'There really isn't any stigma attached to being adopted, so why would he feel the need to keep it a secret?'

'You dunderheads, you're both missing the crucial point here,' Hermione said impatiently.

'Which is?'

'Which is, Ellen my dear, why Duncan has chosen to tell his most closely kept secret to *you*.'

Chapter Nine

'So,' Nadia said, as she came into the kitchen where Duncan was clearing up the mess from lunch.

He didn't bother looking up from the dishwasher he was stacking, but carried on carefully placing the less expensive pieces of crockery into the racks – the Wedgwood plates he'd wash by hand in a moment, along with the silver cutlery.

'So,' repeated Nadia.

'I heard you the first time,' he said, still not looking up. He had no need to. He knew only too well what the expression on Nadia's face would be. Yesterday she had played the part of helpless woman and today, like a chameleon adapting to its surroundings, she'd adopted her more usual role of imperious matriarch. He knew, too, that she'd had just the right level of alcohol throughout the day to buoy her sufficiently to be thoroughly disagreeable if she so chose.

He moved over to the sink where Ellen's bunch of daffodils still lay – one or two of the flower heads were crushed beneath a large saucepan. 'You were supposed to put these in water.'

'Daffodils,' muttered Nadia.

Duncan walked the length of the kitchen to the pantry where his mother kept a selection of vases. When he reappeared Nadia said, 'Cynthia and Phyllis brought me proper bouquets with ribbons and cards.'

He made no response but carefully removed the aluminium foil from the stems of Ellen's daffodils and put them in the vase he'd chosen. He held it under the tap for a few moments and passed the flowers to Nadia. 'Go and put these somewhere,' he said, 'and make sure it's somewhere nice.'

Nadia pursed her lips and left the kitchen. She stood in the large reception hall and glanced round at the oak-panelled walls and closed doors. Which room should she choose? The drawing room? No, her 'proper flowers' were there. The dining room? No, that rude Jacobs woman had implied there was something wrong with the fireplace. The games room, then? No. Nobody ever went in there and there was no point in unnecessarily antagonising Duncan. Her own personal sitting room was certainly out of the question, which left only Duncan's study. At least then she wouldn't have to look at the flowers and be reminded of that wretched woman. Transvestite indeed!

She opened the door and walked over to Duncan's leather-topped desk – a desk that had once belonged to her husband, as indeed had the book-lined room. It was strange but she hardly missed Donald, but maybe that was because Duncan was so like his father. There were times when it was as if she was face to face with Donald himself. Duncan may not have inherited any biological genes from his father but he'd acquired so much more that he had earned the right to be described as a real chip off the old block.

She dumped the vase on Duncan's tidy desk, sure in the knowledge that despite the designs Ellen might have on Duncan, her presence in their lives would be short-lived. She knew her son well enough to know that his sense of duty would come before anything else.

She had learned years ago that holding on to what was important was all a question of balance. All she had to do was make Duncan believe that he was in charge, and by appearing incapable at times and making herself out to be a loose cannon on deck, this was simplicity itself. She was secretly very proud of the loose cannon bit and had come up with the idea during Donald's funeral last year. Standing over the gaping hole in the cemetery, the rain lashing against their black umbrellas and with so many depressed-looking people surrounding her, she had found herself wanting to be anywhere but there. When they had all moved away to the cars and she was the only one still standing there over the hole, people had thought her consumed with typical widow's melancholy. Duncan, very correctly and dutifully, had come back for her and whispered that it was time to go. But what they hadn't realised was that she had lost track of where she was and had been imagining herself in the clubhouse bar overlooking the eighteenth tee and downing a large gin and tonic. It was then that she'd realised how easy it was to fool people.

And hiding bottles about the house had proved to be the perfect method of keeping Duncan on his toes. Poor Duncan, so concerned with keeping up the appropriate appearances of their position that he was horrified he might have an alcoholic for a mother. The truth, of course, was very different, but appealing to her son's sense of propriety had been her trump card in having him reinstated at Crantsford Hall.

She went back to the kitchen, where she found Duncan up to his elbows in hot soapy water and a pile of clean plates on the draining board.

'Where did you put them?' he asked.

'In your study.'

74

Clever, thought Duncan. Very clever.

'I thought they'd remind you of *her* when you're working late at night. Isn't that the kind of thing lovers like to do?'

'I wouldn't know,' he replied evenly. 'Ellen and I are not lovers.'

'What's her background?' she pursued. 'Apart from having been married to that appalling dentist fellow.'

'I really don't think it's fair to saddle Ellen with blame by association. It's hardly her fault her husband – her ex-husband – turned out the way he did.'

'Maybe she drove him to it,' Nadia said quietly.

Slowly Duncan turned round. 'I think you've said enough.'

'Perhaps so,' she agreed, but only for now. 'I only want what's best –'

'Please,' he interrupted, turning his back on her and submerging his hand under the soapy water where Nadia couldn't see that his fists were tightly clenched, 'just please don't say that. I've heard it too many times before.'

'But it's true.'

'Why don't you go and sit down and let me finish here?'

A few minutes later, while flicking through that month's issue of *Cheshire Life* in her sitting room, Nadia made up her mind to get in touch with Phyllis and Cynthia first thing in the morning. A little trip to Spring Bank Cottage was called for.

Duncan pulled sharply on the plug and watched the water drain away from the sink. He pushed at the bits of food left behind and forced them down the plug-hole. The moment he'd decided to invite Ellen for lunch he'd

75

known what the consequences would be. He thought now of his words at Ellen's when he'd tried to explain his relationship with his mother. He'd said that Nadia was over-protective towards him and how this had brought about a mirrored response from himself, but this wasn't the whole truth.

From as early as he could remember Nadia had brought him up to believe that he was special; special because he'd been adopted and had been picked out from all the other babies available to Nadia and Donald at the time. 'No ordinary baby would have done,' she'd told him. 'We were looking for the very best because we had the very best to offer.' He'd grown up with this belief deeply engrained in his whole being, that and the idea that everything he had he owed to his parents. He couldn't remember a time when he hadn't felt beholden to Donald and Nadia, especially Nadia. His entire childhood had been shaped around the one single thought: that without his parents, he was nothing. They hadn't just rescued him from being an unwanted child, they had re-created him. As a boy it had been a heavy load to carry and as he'd grown up he had come to know that instead of there being a bond of love between him and his adoptive parents a tough, impenetrable chain of duty linked them together.

Not long after his eighth birthday he had been sent away to school, and as he'd waved goodbye to Donald and Nadia he had made the decision that from that day on he wouldn't tell anyone that he was adopted. Even at that age he was tired of feeling 'special'. He wanted to be normal. He wanted to be like the other boys in his dormitory. But he found he couldn't. Quite simply, he didn't fit in. While his contemporaries laughed and joked about their parents, he had remained on the sidelines of companionship, appalled at this apparent display of disrespect. Inevitably the other boys found out that he was adopted and he became even more isolated. He also became a target for bullying. In a strange way it didn't bother him: at least it was some sort of connection with his peers; he wasn't totally ignored.

He thought now of what he'd shared with Ellen. He'd had no intention of telling her that Nadia was not his real mother, but sitting opposite her in her cramped sitting room and hearing her words, 'You must be very close to your mother,' he had suddenly felt overwhelmed with the desire to put the record straight. He was no Hamlet with some strange obsession with his mother. He was just an ordinary forty-one-year-old man who had been brought up with a deep sense of duty and loyalty and, as habits went, especially a lifelong habit, it was unlikely he'd be able to give it up.

He didn't regret telling Ellen, but he did regret her odd friends having been there to hear their discussion.

Ellen had always struck him as such a sensible woman, which was why he couldn't understand her having such unusual friends. Throughout her divorce she'd never once overreacted to any of the bad news that he'd had to deliver. It was one of the things that had attracted him to her. After Nadia it came as a refreshing tonic to find a woman who was calm and level-headed. During his first appointment with Ellen he'd realised straight away that she stood out from the rest of his clients – there had been no histrionics, no demands for vengeful letters to be written and mercifully no tears in his office. All in all she'd been a perfect client. And just lately he had begun to believe that she could also be the perfect wife.

But there were those weird friends to consider.

'So why exactly were you eavesdropping on my conversation with Duncan?' Ellen asked Hermione, as the old woman tried to catch her reflection in the picture glass above the fireplace. She was putting her hat on, getting ready to go home.

Hermione whipped round to face her. 'Perish the thought, dear Ellen, that I would ever be accused of eavesdropping.'

'What would you call it, then? Hunkering in the bushes checking the damp-proof course?'

'Ellen, you've become really quite assertive these past twenty-four hours. What can have come over you? Is it love? Has the sight of Crantsford Hall and all its booty made you tetchy with love for Duncan?'

'I thought you said this Duncan bloke didn't have money?' Jo-Jo joined in with the questioning.

'I neither said he had money nor hadn't any,' Hermione replied, regretting the conversation she and Jo-Jo had had earlier while out on the terrace at Laburnum House. She'd known at the time that the girl had wheedled out from her more than Ellen would approve of. And as she turned to readjust her hat in the reflection of the picture she caught the expression on Ellen's face, which confirmed her fears. It was one thing privately admitting to a good friend that one had plans to marry purely for money as a way out of being strapped for cash, but it was quite another making it common knowledge. 'As I told your beau earlier,' she said airily, 'we came to see if you were back and when I saw the ostentatious car parked over by the barn I made the assumption that it was Duncan's. I then thought it best to take the precautionary measure of listening at the window to check if I was right before barging in on your romantic tête-à-tête. There, now, does that satisfy you?'

'Not in the slightest,' Ellen said.

'So *is* Duncan loaded?' Jo-Jo persisted.

Ellen glared at Hermione.

'He obviously is,' Jo-Jo said at last, when nobody answered her question. She went over to the window-seat and joined Ellen. 'But you don't just like him for his money, do you?' Even to her own ears she sounded sanctimonious.

'Ellen, my dear,' cut in Hermione, wishing more than anything that Jo-Jo would drop the subject, 'my legs are worn out, would you mind driving me home?' Her legs were perfectly all right but the conversation needed finishing and she also wanted the opportunity to talk to Ellen alone, about Jo-Jo.

Chapter Ten

Only seconds after a middle-aged couple had left, carrying with them a large box containing an expensive garland arrangement, the barn door opened again and a young mother came in with a round-faced toddler dangling from her arm. 'Don't touch,' she said to the child, 'hands in pockets.'

Ellen watched the mother and child move about the barn. Whenever anyone came in she liked to see which arrangements caught their eye. She could see, though, that the small child wasn't interested in any of the flowers: his eyes were fixed firmly on the basket beside the till, which was filled with fluffy yellow chicks and tiny chocolate eggs. Yes, it was an exploitative trick guaranteed to have the punters slipping their hands deeper into their pockets, and yes, it was devious, but if it was good enough for all the other shops in town then it was downright good enough for her.

She'd started work just after nine that morning and so far this Easter Saturday was proving a busy one, and if trade kept up for the rest of the Bank Holiday weekend then she might be able to think about paying her telephone bill before the reminder made an untimely appearance through her letter-box. She might even go so far as to treat herself to a bottle of plonk from the supermarket that evening when she went into town for her weekly late-night shopping. She usually planned it so that she got there in time to catch the marked-down food items which in theory wouldn't last the weekend on the shelves of the chilled cabinets – heaven help her if the small family-run supermarket decided to open on a Sunday as bang would go her bargain buys.

'I can't find what I'm really looking for,' the young mother said, approaching the work-bench where Ellen was putting the finishing touches to a commission for a hall table.

'What have you got in mind?' Ellen hoped that this wasn't a customer wanting a twee little wheelbarrow or a rocking chair filled with gaudy flowers. She hated making these ornaments but for reasons known only to those who bought them they were a steady seller. If she wasn't so desperate for the money she wished she could put up a sign outside the barn saying, *No miniature wheelbarrows or rocking chairs sold here – tasteful arrangements only.*

'Well, I've got one of those pretty Victorian cast-iron fireplaces in my bedroom and I'm looking for something with shades of gold and russet to match the curtains.'

'No problem.' Ellen smiled, relieved. 'If you want to bring in some measurements and a sample of the fabric I can make one specially for you. I can have it done within a week.'

'As quick as that?'

Ellen nodded and handed her a small business card. To be sure of clinching the deal she leaned over the counter and gave the round-faced child a chocolate egg. He beamed up at her and began to peel away the gold foil.

When Ellen was left alone she thought how much she enjoyed running her own business. Hindsight was a marvellous thing and it told her she should have done this years ago. After Simon had been born she had revelled in the role of mother and home-maker, and even when her friends, with children more or less the same age as Simon, had started to drift back to work she had chosen to stay at home. She was content with her life the way it was, she told her friends, who were all claiming to be liberated and fulfilled now that they were back in the saddle of the workplace – no matter that they frequently complained of saddle-sores from trying to run a home and a career. The rewards far outweighed the disadvantages, they told Ellen repeatedly. And while she was surrounded by all these heroic women, she quietly told herself that they were doing their families no good, their children would grow up delinquents through neglect, and their marriages would suffer.

How self-righteous she had been. And how very wrong.

But the real reason behind her disinclination to join the great salaried workforce was not because she was some fossilised remnant from the fifties who believed that a woman's place was in the home, but because she was crippled by the thought that nagged at her constantly: she doubted her ability to get a job, and as the years went by the doubt grew bigger, as did the cover-up. 'Who in their right mind would want to employ me?' she'd laugh over the dinner table with friends, only to have Roger's quick-fired response, 'Certainly not anyone I know.' And so it became a running joke: 'The day hell freezes over is the day Ellen goes out to work.'

But then along had come Charmaine and Roger's one-way ticket to love in Provence – not quite hell freezing over, but just as unlikely – and suddenly Ellen had had to find a way of supporting herself.

Nearly two decades of home-making was hardly material to get the head-hunters' adrenaline pumping with eager anticipation; it was unlikely to have anyone beating a path to her door to help plan her all-important career move. Night after night she had lain awake in bed, trying to figure out what to do next. And never far from her mind was the thought that her current situation served her right. She should have got off her butt years ago. It was a deserved punishment for someone who had hidden behind a husband's ability to bring home the bacon.

'We suggest your client brush up on her existing skills,' had been the phrase Roger's helpful solicitor had put forward in response to a maintenance proposal submitted by Duncan. Which had left her with precisely two mind-boggling options: child-minding or cleaning.

It was Hermione who had suggested that Ellen try running her own business. 'You're imaginative enough,' she'd said. 'Just look around your own home and see how you've made it so attractive. Do it for other people and charge them the earth.'

The idea of dried flowers had come to Ellen while spending a wet, weepy weekend with her mother, who had a passion for I-told-you-so disaster stories – she had known right from the start that Roger was a bad 'un but had never had the heart to tell Ellen so – and visiting craft fairs. That particular weekend a craft fair had been on at a nearby National Trust property and when they entered the marquee with its array of stalls Ellen had been struck by the amount of dried flowers for sale, but even more struck by the quantity of customers each stall attracted. There was obviously money to be made out of thistles and honesty, she had concluded.

She returned home and did her research. She drove around the surrounding areas of Crantsford and found, to her amazement and delight, that apart from one small shop selling the ubiquitous decorated wheelbarrows and

rocking chairs the market was ready to be tapped. She
borrowed all the books on the subject with which the
local library could supply her and sent off for as many
catalogues as were available.

Then Spring Bank Cottage with its run-down barn
came on the market and, fired up with enthusiasm – and
Hermione telling her constantly that it was fate (and
never mind that the place was falling apart and that no
one with half an inch of common sense would touch the
stench-ridden property) – Ellen told her estate agent to
pull her finger out and find her a buyer for Orchard
House. Within four months she had not only moved but
was enthusiastically opening the barn door of Spring
Bank Flowers to the inhabitants of Crantsford. She
wasn't exactly rushed off her feet in the first few weeks,
in fact she was so demoralised with the lack of interest
she almost gave up. But gradually a few customers found
their way to the barn and things began to pick up.

By lunch-time Ellen had finished a second arrangement
and boxed it up ready to deliver – another service she
offered. She had taken more money that morning than
the whole of last week put together. Hey ho, she might
even run to some decent loo paper instead of that
scratchy cheap stuff with the perforations that never
quite worked.

There were no customers now and, taking the opportunity to grab herself a break, she made a drink and went
outside to sit in the sun on the bank by the stream. She
wondered if Jo-Jo was still asleep. Teenagers were like
that – given the opportunity, they'd sleep for ever.

When Ellen had driven Hermione home yesterday, not
surprisingly Hermione had confessed to having legs fit
enough for a marathon and that she wanted to talk to her
about Jo-Jo. Ellen had listened to her friend repeat what

84

Jo-Jo had told her earlier that afternoon. Poor Jo-Jo. So mature and worldly wise on the one hand but so young and confused on the other.

They talked at length. Just how best could they help Jo-Jo? And what was the legal situation if she was under eighteen, as they suspected? Could they be accused of kidnapping? Would they be better off just informing the local authority, or whoever it was who dealt with things like this, and leaving them to sort out the rest of Jo-Jo's life?

Ellen sipped thoughtfully at her mug of tea, knowing very well that she could no more turn her back on Jo-Jo than she could welcome Roger home with a hug and a smile. Hermione had put forward the idea that Jo-Jo could move in with her. 'My house is far larger than yours,' she'd said. 'It makes sense for her to be with me,' and then she had added, 'Just until we get her sorted.'

'You're not going soft, are you?' Ellen had asked her with a smile.

'Don't be ridiculous, I'm going to get her signed up for some lucrative benefits and then insist she pays me rent.'

'Are we mad?' Ellen had asked Hermione, as her elderly friend levered herself out of Johnny Foreigner.

'I thought you'd given up rationalising.'

'I have or, rather, I'm still trying to.'

Ellen drained her mug of tea, lay back on the soft grass and wondered about this. The truth was she was still busy rationalising everything like mad, as how else would she be prepared to contemplate marrying a man – if the opportunity arose – whom she didn't love?

But perhaps love would come later.

Jo-Jo looked out of the bedroom window and saw Ellen sitting on the grass, but as a car came along the bumpy road Ellen immediately got to her feet and went back to the barn. Jo-Jo continued to stare out of the window beyond the stream and to the field the other side of the bank where she could see a woman walking an Irish setter.

She would miss this place when it was time to go, and she'd miss Ellen and that head-case Hermione even more. She'd only been here forty-eight hours but it seemed longer, longer because she felt so happy. It was as if she'd escaped to another world – there was no Mum to worry over, no step-father to put her down and no Alan. She breathed out . . . No Alan.

She thought of what she'd said to Hermione yesterday – *I wanted somebody to love me in the way Gran used to love me*. And she had. But Alan had never said he loved her. She'd offered so much of herself in the hope of him loving her. She covered her stomach with her hands. She had no idea what a baby inside you was supposed to feel like: all this felt like was a firm swelling. She tried to imagine the baby – *her* baby. Would she be able to love it? Would it love her?

She breathed out deeply again, turned away from the window and looked along the shelves of books above Ellen's son's bed. The selection was mainly science fiction, including a couple of *X-Files* books, but mostly the shelves were full of what she recognised as A-level set texts – *Mansfield Park*, *Howards End*, *Lady Windermere's Fan*, *Hamlet* and *Jane Eyre*. She picked out *Howards End* and opened it at random. There were neatly pencilled notes on either side of the printed text. She sat on the bed and started reading what Simon had written, enjoying his thoughts and comments, for she, too, had recently studied this book . . . with Alan.

Alan had joined the school last year, halfway through

the autumn term after their previous English teacher had suddenly left without explanation. He'd insisted from the start that they call him by his Christian name, and sitting on his desk at the front of the class, his thin legs swinging backwards and forwards, he'd said to them, 'Now, tell me what you know about *Howards End*. For my money the ending's wrapped up too conveniently. It's a cop-out.'

At first nobody had known what to say. This wasn't the way they'd been taught by Mr Johnson. 'Come on,' he'd shouted, 'I want our lessons to be an open forum.'

Jo-Jo had taken up the challenge. 'I don't think the way the novel ends is important,' she'd said. 'It's the way he portrays human relationships that counts.'

'Oh, oh,' he'd responded, leaping from the desk and coming towards her. 'Would you care to expand?'

She snapped the book shut and returned it to its space on the shelf above Simon's bed. She got dressed and went downstairs, hungry.

She made herself some Marmite toast, cleared up and then wondered what she should do next. She decided she should earn her keep and when she'd found where the cleaning things were kept she set about surprising Ellen.

It was such a small house that she was soon finished, but all the while she was dusting and Hoovering she kept thinking of the one aspect of her life that she'd left behind which she missed. Reading through Simon's notes upstairs had brought home to her how much she would miss her studies. Last night, on their way back from the supermarket, she'd told Ellen that before she'd found out she was pregnant she'd planned to go to university – it was to have been her escape. 'But now I've blown it,' she'd told Ellen.

'Just because you're pregnant,' Ellen had answered,

'don't think for one minute you've lost your brain.' She'd then added in a sombre voice, 'I made that mistake.'

Jo-Jo knew Ellen was right. But what was she to do? Drop out now and go to night school next year? Or could she sit the exams this summer anyway? She'd covered most of the syllabus already.

But it was all pointless. How could she do her exams when she had nowhere to live? And there was nothing that would make her go back home. Not now.

It was too late. She pushed the Hoover back into the space under the stairs in the sitting room where she'd found it and drew the pretty curtain across that kept it out of sight. She felt miserable. She'd screwed up badly. She didn't know who she hated most, herself or Alan.

Ellen was delighted. She'd sold two more large fireplace arrangements and taken another commission and it was only two o'clock. Now there was just a fussy-looking woman, examining in minute detail the baskets of hydrangea, achillea and helichrysum. Ellen decided the woman was a definite case of the three Ps – the pick up, the put down and the push off. After a few minutes she was proved right, and the woman left empty-handed, but the door opened again almost immediately and Ellen, just in the process of wiring a rose head, nearly pierced her forefinger in shock at the sight of her next customers: La Carter, with Phyllis and Cynthia in tow. The three were dressed to kill and wearing sunglasses, which, given the subdued lighting in the barn, gave them a bizarre, comical appearance – the Spite Girls, thought Ellen, Crantsford's answer to the Spice Girls. 'Hello,' she said. 'I didn't expect to see you so soon.'

'We've come to prove we're as good as our word,'

Phyllis said brightly, advancing towards the counter at breakneck speed. 'Isn't that right, Nadia?'

Nadia nodded. 'It's much smaller than I'd imagined,' she said. 'Darker, too.'

Try taking your sunglasses off, you ugly old harpy! 'Barns come in all sorts of sizes,' Ellen said demurely. 'Thank you for yesterday by the way,' she added. 'Lunch was lovely.'

'And your headache?'

'Headache?'

'Yes,' Nadia said, raising her sunglasses and moving off to make a full inspection of the shelves. 'You had a headache, don't you remember?'

'Oh, that – it was practically gone by the time Duncan got me home.'

They could go on sparring like this for ever, thought Ellen, it came as naturally as breathing. She returned her attention to pushing wires through the pile of rose heads on the work-bench behind her. Phyllis and Cynthia got the message and joined Nadia over by the shelves. When she heard the sound of the door scraping open she turned round, hoping to greet a *bona fide* customer. It was Jo-Jo.

'I've brought you a sandwich,' she said.

Ellen was touched. 'Thank you,' she said, aware that the Spite Girls were twittering at the other end of the barn. 'How long have you been up?' she asked. 'Not that I'm checking on you.'

'For ages. I read for a while and then I did a bit of tidying for you.'

'There's no need for you to do that.'

'But I might just as well, anyway. There's always the hope I can make myself indispensable. Is there anything I can do here for you?'

Ellen smiled. 'Not really, but how about you go and see Hermione? I think she has a proposition for you.'

When Jo-Jo closed the door behind her, Ellen saw Phyllis nudge Cynthia. 'Go on,' she heard Phyllis whisper, 'ask her.'

Ellen knew what was coming next.

'I hope you don't think we're being nosy, but wasn't that the girl . . . you know, the one we were talking about at lunch yester –'

'What Cynthia is trying to ask you,' interrupted Nadia, 'is whether that's the person she saw begging in town on Thursday. I've told her it can't possibly be the same girl, as what would a friend of Duncan's have to do with a good-for-nothing like that?'

'Which girl?' Ellen asked, knowing she sounded ridiculous and that her next line would have to be, 'Oh, you mean that girl.'

'The one you were talking to just now,' replied Nadia, with a look that said she knew when she was being led a merry dance.

'Oh, you mean that girl. Well, Nadia, I'm afraid you've got it totally wrong and, Cynthia, you're absolutely right. Jo-Jo is indeed the very same girl you saw in Crantsford on Thursday.'

'I knew I was right,' Cynthia said smugly. 'I never forget a face.'

'But what is she doing here?' asked Phyllis.

'She's got nowhere else to stay so she's stopping with me for a few days.'

'You mean, you took her in from off the street?' Cynthia shuddered. 'But, Ellen, what do you know about her?'

'Very little,' Ellen said, enjoying the look of shock on the three faces in front of her, 'but I'm sure the good

Samaritan didn't wait to take up character references before he offered a helping hand.'

'But surely this is taking things too far,' said Phyllis, whose idea of a helping hand was buying a book of raffle tickets at a charity coffee morning in the hope of winning a bottle of champagne.

'I think you're a fool,' Nadia broke in. 'She'll take you for everything she can get and then move on to the next half-witted person who'll take her in.'

Half-witted! Ellen's face coloured and the wire she'd been about to push through one of the roses suddenly snapped in two and dug into the palm of her hand. She hoped it hadn't damaged her marriage line.

Chapter Eleven

Hermione stepped into the pitch-dark greenhouse and shone the torch along the rows of sweet-pea pots on the wooden bench. She had never experienced motherhood but she had always supposed that this was the kind of thing mothers of newborn babies got up to: nocturnal visits to the nursery to check on their offspring for the slightest of reasons.

The young girl on the television had said the weather was going to turn cold that night with the likelihood of a heavy frost covering most parts of the country, which had had the effect of galvanising Hermione into ransacking the cluttered drawers in the garden room for the torch and then pulling on her boots.

She found some old sacking from further along the bench and carefully tucked it around the pots and, satisfied that this was as much protection as she could offer the plants, other than taking them to bed with her, she closed the badly fitting door as best she could. From further down the garden she heard a rustling sound. She flashed the torch over the black lumps of silhouetted bushes and saw the tail of something disappear out of sight. A fox, perhaps? Or one of the boys, Giotto or Botticelli?

On her way back up towards the house she paused on the steps between the two Christmas puddings and ran her hand over their shape, feeling for new growth. 'Soon be time for a short back and sides for you two,' she told them affectionately. She then walked across the lawn to the summerhouse where she sat in one of the wicker chairs. It rasped and creaked like arthritic joints under her weight, sounding loud and obtrusive in the still night air.

Hermione had never been scared of the dark. Even as a child when her elder sister had locked her in the musty-smelling wardrobe at the top of the house because she had given her measles, she had spent a couple of happy hours there asleep until their mother had instructed the maid to look for her. If Roberta hadn't been such an actress and made such a fuss of being ill, and if their mother hadn't been such a gorgeously flighty woman more intent on getting herself ready for a party that night, Roberta would have been punished. But she rarely was.

The summerhouse was built mostly of stone with vertical oak beams supporting an ornately tiled roof, and though it had been repaired many times over, it was, to all intents and purposes, the same summerhouse in which Hermione had secretly slept one hot summer night as a child. It was also where she'd first kissed Matthew's father.

She shone her torch at her watch. Nine o'clock. Matthew would soon be here. Matthew, the child she'd always considered her own. She breathed in deeply and felt the first signs of night coldness bite through her. She got up and went inside the house where she found Giotto and Botticelli curled up on the boiler in the garden room.

The room was a mess even to Hermione's indifferent eye. Like her mother, she had no inclination towards housework, but whereas her mother had lived in an era of cooks and housemaids Hermione did not. For most of her married life she had employed the services of a cleaner, and a handyman called Mutters – so-called because Hermione had never been able to understand a word he'd said – who had been a wonder with a fork and a barrow. But Mutters was long gone, as was the cleaner.

She wondered for all of three seconds about tidying up the garden room, but the sight of the overloaded shelves that sagged in the middle and the knowledge that all the cupboards and drawers were already stuffed full made her dispense with any good intentions. She placed the torch on top of a pile of seed packets sprawled over a stack of newspapers and went through to the kitchen, which was just as untidy.

Jo-Jo had commented on her untidiness earlier that afternoon when she'd called to see her. It was funny how some people just weren't comfortable in a room full of clutter. Jo-Jo was obviously one of them, for she had surreptitiously tried to move things into neat piles. 'Leave that alone!' Hermione had said, after ten minutes of sleight-of-hand movements. 'You're making me feel confused.'

'You mean I'm making you feel guilty,' Jo-Jo had responded.

'Sharp little minx,' Hermione threw back. 'Now come through to the sitting room where there's nothing for you to fiddle with. I want to put something to you.'

Poor Jo-Jo had made the mistake of sitting in the armchair that smelled of lavender – put there to cover up the less fragrant aroma of forty-five years of active service – and had a tendency to take the unwary by surprise and swallow them whole.

'How would you like to stay here with me for a few days?' Hermione had asked. 'Just until you've got yourself organised. I wouldn't like you to go running off with the idea that you've got it made. Unlike Ellen I run a tight ship here.'

'I can see that.' Jo-Jo smiled as she tried to haul herself out from the depths of the chair.

'What do you say, then?'

Jo-Jo frowned. 'Why?' she said. 'Why are you and Ellen doing all this for me?' She stood up and paced the room. 'I mean, you don't know me. You meet me on the street, you give me something to eat –'

'Correction, Ellen gave you something to eat. I didn't.'

Jo-Jo stopped moving. 'Okay, but now *you* are offering me somewhere to live –'

'Only to stay.'

'To stay, then. But why?'

'Lawks! It's come to something when a truly altruistic person such as myself can't offer –'

'Be serious!'

'How do you know I'm not?'

Jo-Jo began pacing again. 'Because . . . because I don't believe in fairy-stories – or fairy godmothers for that matter. What is it you want from me?'

'Would you believe your company?'

'No. You're too independent for that.'

'Okay, then, I admit it. I'm after your money. It's a financial nightmare running this house and I want a cut of the benefits you must be entitled to.'

Jo-Jo leaned against a large bookcase and stared at her. 'Are you serious?'

After a few moments, Hermione shook her head and laughed. 'Jo-Jo, you're going to have to learn to trust me . . . just as I trust you.'

In the end Jo-Jo had agreed to move in but only on the understanding that she helped Hermione about the house.

'We'll see,' Hermione had told her.

Alone now in the kitchen, Hermione wondered about what she had said to Jo-Jo about wanting her to stay with her for her company. Like everybody else, Jo-Jo had assumed that she was too independent to want anybody else's company. It grieved her to admit it, but they were wrong. She did get lonely. Very lonely. She missed her lazy afternoons with Ellen. There was nobody else in the Crescent half as much fun as Ellen: they were all mostly executive types and not her sort of people at all. The Buchanans next door but one in Ellen's old house were civil enough, but with two young children to occupy them they were too busy to be much interested in her. She had the feeling that the rest of the neighbourhood had dubbed her as you-know-the-eccentric-one and were probably forming a committee in case she started going ga-ga and appeared in the Crescent in nothing but her wellington boots. She smiled. Who knows? One day she might do exactly that. But not just yet. Best wait till the threat of frost had passed.

She filled the kettle, plugged it in and looked at the clock on top of the fridge. Half an hour and Matthew would be here.

No more than ten minutes from Crantsford, Matthew's car headlights picked out an Audi estate on the grass verge ahead of him. He could see a woman standing beside a man and they were both staring at a flat tyre.

Matthew slowed his car and pulled up behind the Audi. He wound down his window. 'Need any help?'

The woman came over. She was smartly dressed with dark hair pushed back from her face with a black velvet hair-band, and within a fraction of a second Matthew could smell her perfume. 'You angel of a man,' she gushed. 'My husband's a genius with a woman flat on her back but an absolute ninny when it comes to anything mechanical. Please do help us.'

Matthew got out of his car and followed the woman and her trail of perfume.

'Hi,' the genius-cum-ninny said. 'I'm afraid my wife's absolutely right. I know this is a flat tyre, but what the devil I do with it is anybody's guess. Any ideas?'

This had to be a wind-up. These people just couldn't be for real.

'Why have we stopped, Daddy?' came a faint, sleepy voice from the back of the Audi. 'This doesn't look like home.'

'Go back to sleep, Floss, there's a good girl, we'll be home soon.'

'I think you should get your children out of the car,' Matthew instructed, resigned to rolling up his sleeves, at the same time wondering whether there shouldn't be a law against incapable twits like this being allowed out to drive, let alone to procreate.

'Oh, do you think it's really necessary?' implored the wife. 'There's only the two of them and they're both so light, barely an ounce on them. I'm on at them every day to eat more.'

'Okay.' Matthew gave in. 'But you'll need to get me the spare tyre.'

The genius-cum-ninny, whom Matthew had decided bore an uncanny likeness to a young Terry Thomas, looked first at his wife and then back at Matthew. 'That'll be where exactly?'

When Matthew was tightening the last of the nuts on the wheel, the woman said, 'We're so enormously grateful to you. Are you local? Perhaps you'd like to call in for a drink one evening?'

'No, I'm not local,' Matthew said, straining to unwind the jack. 'I'm just visiting Crantsford.' He removed it, stood up and handed it to Terry Thomas.

'Well, I really insist that you call in on us so that we can thank you properly. Bonkers, darling, have you got one of our cards?'

Bonkers? Nobody, but nobody, could be called Bonkers!

'Sorry, they're in my other jacket, but we're easy to find – Orchard House, the Crescent.'

Matthew stopped in his tracks. 'The Crescent,' he repeated.

'That's right. Do you know it?'

Matthew nodded, realisation and horror dawning on him. 'I'm Matthew Collins, and you must be Susie Buchanan. We spoke on the phone.'

Bonkers looked on, confused, but his wife trilled delightedly, 'Ah, ah, ah. Too extraordinary. Just too extraordinary.'

She was right and the prospect of working in the same household as this extraordinary couple filled Matthew with dread as he followed the red Audi for the rest of the journey. Why hadn't Hermione warned him? And why hadn't he himself realised what he was getting into when he'd spoken to Susie Buchanan on the phone earlier in the week? Perhaps his judgement was going. Maybe this commission was going to be a complete disaster. They were probably expecting him to paint cartoon characters all over the children's bedrooms.

When they reached the Crescent, the Buchanans – with much tooting of the car horn and hands waving out of the windows – turned into their drive. Matthew waved back politely and drove on until he pulled into Hermione's. It was well after ten but there were still lights on. He smiled, pleased that Hermione had waited up for him, and pleased also to have arrived. Laburnum House was like a second home to him.

He found Hermione in the sitting room. The curtains were drawn, the room was lit by a single lamp and in the corner a man and a woman were making love, noisily and energetically. Matthew switched off the television and went over to Hermione, who was fast asleep, her head slumped almost to her shoulder. She smelled of 4711 cologne and Matthew could see the distinctive glass bottle tucked into the side of the armchair.

'You daft old thing,' he whispered affectionately. As a young boy he'd often given her a bottle of 4711 at Christmas and now each time he came to see her she would make a point of wearing the fragrance. He knelt and kissed her soft cheek.

She started.

'It's okay, it's me, Matthew.'

She straightened up. 'What time is it?'

'Twenty past ten.'

'You're late,' she rebuked him, and looking across the room she said, 'what's happened to the television?'

'I switched it off.'

She tutted. 'There was a film I wanted to see, one of those ones they warn you about.'

'I think you've missed the best bit.' He laughed.

She sighed and shook her head. 'That's what will be written on my gravestone – "Here lies Hermione Rowlands, sadly she missed the best bits".'

'If you think for one moment I've come all this way to listen to your self-pitying drivel you can forget it. Now, be quiet and stand up so I can hug you properly.'

'Only if you've brought me a present.'

'You're a hard woman, Hermione Rowlands.'

'That's what your father always said.'

Chapter Twelve

Bonkers was not a pretty sight first thing in the morning, and as much as Susie loved him there was no getting away from the fact that he benefited enormously from a shower followed by a shave. And only after he'd cleaned his teeth would she entertain the idea of kissing him. She could hear him now, the tap running and the sound of him intermittently brushing his teeth and singing 'I Am the Monarch of the Sea' from *HMS Pinafore*.

She sat up, positioned the pillow behind her head and glanced about the bedroom. Their suitcases lay open in front of the wardrobes that ran the length of the room and she thought of all the washing waiting for her. They'd only been away for a couple of days to the cottage in Abersoch but seemingly they'd used more clothes in those few days than they'd normally have worn in a week. She closed her eyes to the thought of filling and emptying the washing machine for the rest of day.

Bonkers had now moved on to 'Three Little Maids From School Are We'. Bless him, the man was a complete butterfly brain, switching from one operetta to another. But there again, the way the poor darling sang, the songs all ended up sounding the same anyhow.

When the bathroom went quiet she opened her eyes and saw that Bonkers was standing in the doorway. He had a small towel wrapped around his waist and was rubbing his hair with another. 'I've been thinking,' he said, peering out from beneath the towel. 'How about a party?'

'What sort of a party?'

'Just drinks and nibbles. Nothing too over-the-top. I thought we could invite a few people from work, some of the neighbours and maybe one or two parents from school. What do you think?'

'I think you're a genius.'

He came over to her and smiled. 'That's not what you told that artist chappie last night.'

She laughed and reached out to him. 'You weren't listening properly. I told him you were a genius with a woman flat on her back.' She loosened his towel and pulled him into bed. 'And so you are.'

'Sweetie, I can't find my trousers,' Bonkers said, an hour later, turning over the contents of his suitcase.

Susie smiled the smile of a woman who'd just enjoyed great sex and who was prepared to forgive her husband anything so long as he continued to please her in the way he just had. She often joked with friends that marriage to a consultant gynaecologist and obstetrician had a lot going for it – Bonkers knew exactly where everything was and what it was supposed to do. Sadly, though, his consummate skill as a lover wasn't much use when he needed to get dressed.

'Darling,' she called through to him, from the bathroom, 'there are plenty of clean pairs in the wardrobe.' She carried on brushing her hair and wondered who to invite to their drinks party. Bonkers could sort out his work colleagues, but she would choose the rest of the guests.

She went downstairs, leaving Bonkers still wandering around the bedroom in his boxer shorts, and found the girls in the kitchen. The Frosties packet was on the worktop and a trail of cereal led from it to the far end of the kitchen where the children were sitting at the table. 'Good morning,' she said, kissing them both on the top of the head, which was a bit difficult in Millie's case as she was wearing an Easter bonnet she'd made at school in the last week of term.

Floss, the elder, aged ten and the spitting image of her mother, though her hair was less dark, glanced up from her cereal bowl. 'It was Millie who made the mess.'

'You did it as well,' Millie shot back. Three years younger than her sister, she was always convinced she got the worst of everything.

'Not in the mood, girls. Simply not in the mood. You can both tidy up the mess or there'll be no Easter eggs for either of you.'

They pulled faces at one another and carried on eating in silence until their father drifted into the kitchen. He was still in his boxer shorts, but had managed to find a polo shirt and a pair of slippers.

'Daddy, what happened to the car last night?' asked Millie. 'Floss says we broke down. I don't remember that happening. Is she lying?'

Bonkers groaned dramatically. 'It was ghastly, Millie. We had a wretched flat tyre and, luckily for you, you were fast asleep and didn't wake up until we reached home.' He crunched his way across the kitchen floor, oblivious to the Frosties and the look on Susie's face.

'See, I told you!' Floss said triumphantly, then, turning to her father, she said, 'And who was that man who helped you?'

Bonkers's face was a blank. 'Damned if I can remember his name. Your mother knows all about him, though.' He went over to Susie and encircled her in his arms. 'Please, sweetie,' he whispered in her ear, 'find me some trousers.'

She laughed and shrugged him off. 'Remember we told you we were having a special painting done?' she said to the children.

They nodded.

'Well, he's the artist who's going to paint it and his name's Matthew.'

Millie frowned. 'Will he wear one of those floppy hats when he comes here?'

'Good Lord, of course he will,' exclaimed Bonkers. 'He'll wear a large brown velvet one or he shan't be paid a penny. I want a proper artist, not some fly-by-night Johnny in jeans who flicks paint at a bicycle and calls it art.'

Matthew pulled on his jeans and pushed back the faded curtains. For the first time in ages he'd had a decent night's sleep. Usually he slept for little more than a couple of hours, four at most, but Laburnum House had always had a good effect on him. He should visit more often, he told himself ruefully, if not for the pleasure of seeing Hermione, for his sanity.

He was slightly ashamed of himself for not having been to see his godmother for so long – his last few visits had been one-night stopovers *en route* for London.

He stared out over the garden below and caught sight of Hermione. She was dressed in wellington boots and a fur coat over her nightdress and was walking across the frost-covered lawn. He watched her go into the green-house and then lost sight of her behind the dirty panes of glass.

As a young boy he had practically lived in that greenhouse with Hermione. When everybody else was busy playing tennis or croquet the pair of them would escape to the humid atmosphere and smell of compost and tomato plants and anything else Hermione was growing. He had hidden in there once when his mother had been cross with him. He couldn't recall what he'd done wrong, but he could remember Hermione shouting at his mother, 'Leave the boy alone, or you'll lose him for ever.' He hadn't understood what she had meant at the time for he'd only been six years old, but her words had held a prophetic significance.

He finished dressing and climbed the stairs to the top of the house, to the boxroom directly above the room he'd slept in which also overlooked the garden. But it wasn't the view that he was interested in. Directly opposite the window and behind a couple of dust-covered small tables and a battered trunk with bits of old clothes poking out was a large wall covered in the first mural Matthew had ever painted. In style it was reminiscent of the reading books Hermione had given him as a small boy, and it was for her that he had painted it. He'd painted animals for her, lots of them: rabbits, squirrels, cats and an owl tucked into a tall oak tree that had a winding staircase leading upwards. There were frogs and ducks in a meandering stream, a dragonfly hovering above it, and in the distance, far away beyond the perfect arches of a bridge and a tiny train puffing out clouds of steam, there were specks of cows.

It was an idyllic scene and made all the more interesting by the depiction of three different characters in varying stages of their lives. In the middle of the picture was a baby in the arms of a young woman in a pale blue coat, her hair tied back and her face happy and smiling. To her right there was a small dark-haired boy pushing along a toy donkey on wheels, and in the foreground this same boy, though several years older, was crouched in the grass and peering into the water at his reflection. To the left of an oak tree was an older woman staring straight out of the picture. As a portrait it was the most interesting part of the whole painting and showed a woman confident and at ease, and smiling more for her own pleasure than for anyone else's. To her right and the other side of the tree was a man. He was tall, serious, and looked awkward with himself, his hands in his pockets, his face half turned towards the woman the other side of the tree. This same figure appeared elsewhere in the painting, older, greyer but still undeniably the same man.

Matthew had been fifteen when he'd painted the mural while staying with Hermione during the long school summer holidays. She had asked him to paint a set of portraits: of Kit, himself and of her. But when he'd said he had something better in mind, she had given him free range to do as he pleased. He'd cleared out the old box-room and set up his paints, telling her she couldn't go in the room until he'd finished. Working mostly from memory, and with the help of a couple of photographs he always kept with him, he managed to create a picture that captured the Hermione he'd grown up with, as well as his father who had made the mistake of not marrying the woman he loved. In many ways it was a sad painting, but one that he'd never regretted carrying out.

His talent for painting had come from his father, a man who had never had the opportunity to explore his own creative talents to the extent he would have liked. Kit had been an intense man of duty, but also a solitary man who had never been happier than when he'd been allowed to be alone. Matthew's mother had never understood that. Roberta had been a woman who couldn't bear to be alone and who only felt alive when she was surrounded by a gathering, the larger the better.

Matthew supposed he was the same as Kit. Now that Bridget had gone, his own company had become more important to him. He'd grown tired of trying to make the right impression on people and he was aware that these days he was becoming increasingly less tolerant of those around him.

The Buchanans came into his mind and he wondered how on earth he was going to survive them for the duration of the commission.

He returned his attention to the mural in front of him, smiled back at his father, then at Hermione, and left the room. As he went downstairs he noticed how much sadder and more down-at-heel the house had become since his last visit. On the top landing large areas of wallpaper were beginning to peel away from the walls and ominous patches of damp had appeared. Downstairs in the hall there were holes in the plasterwork. He couldn't bear to think of Laburnum House deteriorating any further, but he knew that Hermione could no longer afford to run the old place and he suspected they both knew what the solution was. He wished he had the money to help Hermione, but he hadn't.

He found Hermione in the kitchen, still in her fur coat. She turned round at the sound of his footsteps on the quarry-tiled floor.

'Is that coat for my benefit?' he asked.

'You flatter yourself, dear boy. I'm afraid my dressing gown didn't survive the rigours of the washing machine the last time I washed it, but so long as I go no further than the confines of Laburnum House I think that I shall be safe from the egg-throwing populace. And, talking of eggs, what would you like for breakfast? Kedgeree, scrambled eggs or kidneys on toast?'

He smiled. He'd seen the contents of Hermione's fridge last night and knew what was really on offer. 'How about some toast?'

They ate in the kitchen.

After a few minutes of watching him closely, Hermione said, 'You're very quiet. Why don't you tell me about you and Bridget.'

'Nosy old devil.' He reached for another slice of toast.

'Am I to presume she's given you the heave-ho and that's why you're behaving like a –'

'Actually it wasn't like that. It was me who said it was better we ended it.'

'Oh?'

'Because . . .' He twisted the top off a jar of damson jam and pulled a face at the sight and smell of a thick layer of mould growing inside. He screwed the lid back on tightly. 'Because I could see things going just the way they did with Kit and Roberta. I could see this awful pattern repeating itself.'

Hermione stared hard at Matthew. One of the great joys in her life was that he was so like his father. He had the same tall, angular body that tended to look constrained in anything other than a casual shirt and jeans. He had the same dark hair, which was just beginning to show signs of grey, and the same penetrating hazel eyes and lopsided smile that had made Hermione's heart lurch when Kit had spoken to her that special night in the summerhouse. But there was another similarity, and perhaps a more worrying one: like his father, Matthew, it seemed, had a growing need for solitude.

She had only met Bridget once – two years ago at Roberta's funeral – but that one occasion had been enough for Hermione to realise that Bridget in her extravagant black hat and high heels and endless talk of her job as a PR consultant was no more the right woman for Matthew than Roberta had been right for Kit.

'So what attracted you to her in the first place?' she said at last.

Matthew shrugged. 'Her mind?'

'You mean, you thought she'd be great in bed. And was she?'

'Mind your own business.'

Hermione laughed. 'So, you got rid of her before she drove you mad with her incessant chatter.'

'Surely it's better this way? If we'd stayed together I would have turned her into a sad, bitter woman, just like –'

'Just like your mother?'

They sat in silence for a while until Hermione said, 'My sister should never have married your father. They were totally ill-suited. Kit should have married a woman more –'

'The only woman my father should have married was you, and we both know that.'

Hermione stood up abruptly and went and looked out of the window. She watched Giotto slink across the herb garden and shake his tail at the bay tree. Matthew came and joined her.

'I'm glad you got rid of Bridget,' she said. 'I'd have never forgiven you if you'd married her.'

Chapter Thirteen

Ellen had never before seen herself as a neurotic person but in all honesty she could think of no other word to describe her current state of mind. She looked at the phone once more and willed herself to tap in the numbers that would either result in the sound of Duncan's reassuring voice speaking to her or La Carter's strident tones hammering in her ear.

It was eleven thirty in the morning and she'd already had the barn open for more than two hours and had managed to sell nothing but a measly selection of pink and white rhodanthe daisies. And all the while the phone hanging on the wall above the work-bench had been giving her the come-on – Ring Duncan, it urged her, ring Duncan ... just for a chat, pretend you want to discuss Jo-Jo's legal position. But each time she reached for the receiver she pictured La Carter snatching it up at Crantsford Hall and immediately she backed away.

Cowardice was pathetic in other people but perfectly excusable in oneself and she had made up logical reason after logical reason why she shouldn't dial Duncan's number. He'll be playing golf. He'll be busy working in his study. He'll be busy, full stop!

And just why did she want to speak to him anyway? She was seeing him in a few days' time. What was the hurry?

The hurry was that somebody else might get to him

before her. Somebody else might already have designs on Duncan, someone whom she knew nothing about. For all she knew, Duncan might have a string of lady friends he alternated between. Maybe that was why he wasn't married: he was too busy enjoying himself bouncing from one woman to another.

But then she thought of the Duncan she had come to know. Straightforward, uncompromising Duncan. A man who sat behind his desk soothing the troubled waters of so many divorces. This picture did nothing to help matters, though, for in her mind's eye she pictured countless distraught women rolling their tearful eyes at Duncan and he reaching forward with a handkerchief, a decree absolute and an invitation for dinner.

No! she told herself. Duncan was not a man to be swayed by tears. He was a man of detail who dealt in hard facts. If he was capable of falling for a weeping, wronged woman he would have married one years ago.

The phone suddenly rang, loud and shrill, barely inches away from her, and all at once she imagined a telepathic Duncan at the other end of the line declaring that he was missing her and that he couldn't wait until Wednesday, he had to see her now, there was something he wanted to discuss with her – how did she feel about a wedding ceremony in St Lucia?

This wildness of thought took all of two seconds and was squashed in less time by the sound of Simon's voice. 'Just thought I'd ring to say happy Easter,' he said, through the hiss and crackle of a bad line. 'I tried the cottage but you weren't there. Who's the girl?'

Ellen told him.

'Should I be worried?' he asked.

'What do you mean?'

He laughed. 'You're not about to turn into a crusading middle-aged hippie mother, are you?'

'Less of the middle-aged.' She laughed. 'So, when are you coming home?'

'The weather looks like it's going to break tomorrow, so we thought we'd give Buttermere a miss and drive back on Tuesday. Will there still be a bed for me?'

She explained about Jo-Jo going to Hermione's and then, hearing the sound of a car outside, she said, 'Look, I'm going to have to go. It's a customer. See you tomorrow. Drive carefully, now. 'Bye.'

Susie had meant many times to come and see where the previous owner of Orchard House had set herself up in business, but the hectic life she led had deprived her of satisfying her curiosity.

After breakfast, when she had been sorting through the mail that had come during their short stay away at the cottage, she had discovered a letter from France addressed to Mrs E. Jacobs – please forward. Delivering it by hand seemed the perfect excuse for leaving the pile of dirty clothes on the utility-room floor.

She pushed against the heavy door and stepped inside. She was immediately impressed with what she saw, and glad that she had brought her handbag with her. 'Hello,' she said, as she approached the counter. 'Do you remember me? I'm Susie Buchanan. My husband and I bought your house.'

'Yes,' Ellen responded with a stab of jealousy, remembering all too well who this woman was. 'Nothing wrong with the house, I hope,' she added, secretly hoping that the gable-end wall was cracking in two and that the foundations were slipping on a bed of sand.

'Oh, no, nothing wrong at all. The house is fine and we

just love it. But we told you that when we looked round it the first time. It was definitely a case of love at first sight.'

Ellen recalled the Buchanans wandering rapturously about Orchard House – 'Darling, do look at this . . . Ooh, isn't this hall wonderful? . . . Ooh, isn't this window sweet?'

'I've brought you this,' Susie continued. She opened her bag and pulled out the envelope.

Ellen made no effort to take it but watched it being pushed across the counter. 'Thank you,' she said reluctantly. She recognised the handwriting and knew perfectly well who it was from. She had no desire even to touch it, never mind read it.

'I suppose you're all settled in now, aren't you?' Susie said. 'I know we are. It feels like we've always lived at Orchard House.'

'Good,' Ellen said flatly.

Susie looked at her, awkwardly. She knew the reasons behind Orchard House being sold – the estate agent had furnished her with diplomatic hints of divorce – but never had the previous owner openly discussed her situation, and being new to the area, moving up from London, Susie hadn't been privy to any local gossip. During the negotiations for buying the house she had been full of admiration for Ellen Jacobs. She couldn't imagine herself being that calm if Bonkers ever did the unthinkable, and she had clung to the image of Ellen Jacobs being a strong and capable woman rising above the ashes because she hadn't liked the idea of turning anyone out of a home they so obviously loved. 'Spring Bank Cottage is terribly sweet,' she said, with a smile. 'It must have been so snug and warm in the winter.' She nearly added, and cheap to run, but stopped herself in time.

'I'm sorry,' Ellen said, 'I probably seem rude and churlish, I didn't mean to –'

'Gracious me, you didn't sound anything of the kind,' Susie said, 'and now I'm going to have a look at all your gorgeous dried flowers. You're terribly clever to have done this. I'd be hopeless trying to run a business. I'm bad enough trying to organise my own family. Takes all my concentration to bring in the milk each morning!'

Ellen watched her move away to the area where the most expensive arrangements were displayed – perhaps out of charity she might buy one.

After ten minutes of browsing Susie returned to the counter with a large red and black stained rattan basket filled with a mass of red sterlingia and lagurus. 'For the dining room,' she said. 'We've stacks of mahogany inherited from the old rellies and I've just had the most fabulous curtains made out of the heaviest brocade you've ever seen.'

'Sounds wonderful.' Ellen smiled generously, eyeing the price tag on the basket.

Susie started to delve in her bag for her wallet. 'I say,' she said, looking up with a credit card in her hand, 'I don't suppose you'd make up an arrangement specially for me, would you? I'd love a really big one for the fireplace in the sitting room to go with the new sofas we've bought.'

'If you bring in a sample of the fabric I'd gladly do it.'

'Oh.' Susie's face dropped. 'No can do, I'm afraid. I haven't any spare material and no cushions either.' Then her expression changed and she smiled appealingly. 'Gosh, I don't suppose you'd call round and see for yourself, would you?'

Ellen opened her mouth to say no, and no with a capital N, but Susie went on enthusiastically, 'I've had an even better idea. We're giving a little drinks party next weekend. Why don't you come then? Do say yes. I'd love you to see the house and all that we've done. Oh, excuse me.' She opened her bag and retrieved a bleeping mobile phone. 'Bonkers, darling, what is it?'

Ellen turned away tactfully and started to cut some of the rhodanthe daisies to the length she required for the arrangement she planned to do next, but there was no avoiding Susie's loud voice or, she suspected, the invitation to Orchard House.

'Darling, calm down. I'll be back in two ticks. I'm still at Ellen Jacobs's place and I've invited her to our party. Yes, I thought it was a good idea too. Now you'd better put a video on for the girls and then clear up the worst of the mess. But don't, whatever you do, scrub at it. Just pat gently. 'Byee.' She put the phone away and rolled her eyes heavenwards. 'Bless him, he does try.'

Chapter Fourteen

Easter was over, and predictably the Bank Holiday had been true to form and offered up a ritualistic downpour as its contribution to the end of Holy Week.

It was Tuesday morning and still the rain hadn't let up. From her bedroom window Hermione watched the rain trampling on the drooping daffodils in the waterlogged garden below. She looked anxiously at the greenhouse. It was a wonder any of its panes were still intact.

She moved away from the window and went back to making the bed. She patted and smoothed the faded silky green eiderdown into place, gently, so as not to force any feathers through the many holes. But despite her care a tiny feather did break free. It floated upwards before it finally settled on the pillow. Hermione picked it up between her thumb and forefinger and slowly stroked it against her cheek, backwards and forwards, conjuring up the memory of a similar wet day when Kit had held her and softly caressed her cheek and kissed her. But eagle-eyed Roberta had seen them in the summerhouse and later she told Hermione that she meant to have Kit for herself.

'Are you okay?'

She dropped the feather and turned to face Jo-Jo. 'You shouldn't creep up on old ladies, it's bad for their hearts.'

'I'm sorry, I didn't think –'

Hermione smiled. 'You really must stop taking everything I say so literally. What is it you youngsters tell one
another? Stay cool, get a life.'

'That's the trouble,' Jo-Jo said, coming further into the
room and running her hand over her stomach, 'I did.'

'Oh dear, we've gone all deep and profound, have we?
Well, I have just the tonic for that.' She flung open the
doors of an ugly, cumbersome wardrobe and stood back.
'I've decided to have a sort-out,' she declared. 'You can
help me if you like and by the time you've cringed and
laughed at some of my clothes you'll have stopped feeling
sorry for yourself.'

Hermione was right. Within a couple of minutes of
seeing the old lady parade around the bedroom in a
mishmash of dusty old clothes Jo-Jo was joining in the
fun. She wrapped a pink feather boa around her neck,
slapped a mauve hat the shape of a flying saucer on her
head and struck up a silly pose in front of the mirror with
Hermione.

'We look like a regular couple of old trouts.' Hermione
laughed delightedly.

'As good as that?' It was Matthew, leaning against the
door frame and staring in at them. There was a hint of a
smile on his face.

Embarrassed, Jo-Jo tugged at the feather boa. She
hadn't yet worked out whether Matthew was friend or
foe. It wasn't that he was unpleasant to her, it was just
that he seemed so stern. She had wondered whether he
was jealous of her being here with Hermione or, worse
still, suspected her of taking advantage of the old lady.

When she'd arrived yesterday afternoon he'd greeted
her and her rucksack with politeness, but nothing more,
disappearing upstairs within minutes of Hermione intro-
ducing her. Hermione was obviously very fond of him

and Jo-Jo sensed that despite his aloofness he was fond of Hermione.

'Don't stare like that, Matthew,' Hermione said. 'You're making poor Jo-Jo nervous.'

'I'd be nervous in that hat.'

Jo-Jo had forgotten the flying saucer and she snatched it off quickly. 'I'm helping Hermione sort out her clothes,' she said, by way of explanation.

He ignored her. 'I've made some lunch, if anybody's interested.'

'How marvellous it is to have guests staying,' Hermione said, still in her dusty ensemble, as she and Jo-Jo followed Matthew downstairs to the kitchen, 'especially the helpful variety. And, my word,' she exclaimed when they saw the table, 'what a spread.' There were whole-meal rolls, pâté, slices of ham, a selection of cheeses and a bowl of salad, shiny with mustard dressing.

'I decided you hadn't anything worth eating in the house,' Matthew said, pouring out glasses of wine for Hermione and himself, 'and stocked up at the supermarket. You'll find I've thrown away your antique collection of tins from the larder and replaced them with stuff which should take you into the next century without too much risk to your health.' He handed Jo-Jo a glass of orange juice.

Hermione pulled a face at the sight of the juice. 'Matthew,' she said, 'this is most thoughtful of you, but Jo-Jo is technically an adult, so stop being so stuffy and let her have some wine with us.'

'She's also technically pregnant, so orange juice it is.' He got up from his chair and went over to a small carrier bag on the draining board. He handed it to Jo-Jo. 'I thought this lot might be a good idea.'

She peered into the bag.

'Vitamins and an iron supplement,' he said, in answer to her surprised expression. 'The woman in the chemist's recommended them.'

Both Hermione and Jo-Jo stared at him. Jo-Jo tried to assert herself. 'How do you know I'm not already taking –' she glanced inside the bag again '– folic acid and –'

'Call it intuition.'

'My, you have been a busy boy this morning,' Hermione said. 'You're quite the patriarch all of a sudden.'

Matthew cut himself a wedge of Cheddar. 'And what about a doctor?' he asked. 'Have you even had so much as a check-up yet?'

'Oh, do stop fussing, she's perfectly all right, anyone can see that.'

'Hermione, she needs to register with a doctor,' Matthew said firmly. 'There are scans, blood tests and heaven knows what else she has to do. You can't just take her in off the street and forget about the fact that she's pregnant. What if something goes wrong? Don't touch that!'

Hermione started and Jo-Jo stopped in her tracks.

'I'm sorry,' Matthew apologised to Jo-Jo, 'but you're not supposed to have any soft cheese, or pâté for that matter.'

'Why on earth not?' Jo-Jo asked, disappointed, her hand and knife still poised over the triangle of ripe Brie.

'You see?' Matthew said, raising his hands in the air. 'Neither of you have got a clue about pregnancy. Haven't you heard of listeria?'

'No,' Hermione said, with a smile, 'but I've heard of hysteria.'

Jo-Jo sniggered and Matthew gave up. Why bother? It

really wasn't his problem. His problems, he suspected, were waiting for him at Orchard House where he was going after lunch.

From the road Matthew couldn't see much of Orchard House: it was set back and discreetly hidden by a large imposing brick wall, which was newly built like the house itself and stuck out, in his opinion, as stark and ostentatious. It wasn't until he was standing between an unnecessarily large pair of wrought-iron gates that he caught his first glimpse of the house and, walking up the herringbone brickwork drive in the pouring rain, he was surprised to find that he actually quite liked its exterior design, despite the architect's propensity to mock Tudor, especially in brown and white. There was a symmetry to the front aspect of the house that appealed to him, that and a tall thin Gothic window in the middle that he decided must light the hall and landing beautifully. Already his painter's eye was sizing up this area of the house as a potential canvas.

He rang the bell and almost immediately the door opened. He found himself staring down at a dark-haired girl with large inquisitive eyes – shrewd, inquisitive eyes, he decided. She said nothing, but an excited voice behind her whispered, 'Is he wearing a hat?'

The question was ignored and the shrewd-eyed girl said in an authoritative voice, 'Mummy's on the telephone.' She sounded as though she was perfectly at ease with the situation, which was more than Matthew was.

'Right,' he said. Children were strange beings to him and he rarely felt comfortable with them, especially the quiet, noncommittal, staring ones. He shifted the bag on his shoulder, turned away and looked out over the sodden lawn with its perfectly mown stripes. Thoughts of abandoning this particular commission flitted through his head. It wasn't as though he was desperate for the money. He had enough for his modest lifestyle and now that he no longer had a mortgage hanging over him, which meant that his small Lakeland cottage was secure, all he had to do was earn enough to get by, and he could do that on the paintings he sold effortlessly and regularly to the tourists who poured into the Lake District each year.

So why the hell was he standing here in the rain being scrutinised by some devil child?

'Oh, I'm terribly sorry to have kept you waiting,' Susie's voice sang out loudly from behind him, accompanied by a rattle of gold bangles from one of her wrists. 'Do come in. And thank you again for your help the other night. Come on, girls, make way for our very own Michelangelo.'

Matthew smiled politely – he suspected he'd be doing a lot of that while he was here. He stepped inside and wiped his feet on the *Welcome* doormat. He took in his surroundings. The hall was large – large enough to accommodate the beautiful grand piano facing him, a grandfather clock, several other items of furniture and about an acre of cream carpet between himself and any of these objects. Behind him was the window he'd noticed from outside: it stretched elegantly up to the floor above them, and if the sun had been shining the hall would have been filled with light. In place of natural light several large lamps illuminated the space.

'I thought you said his name was Matthew,' whispered a voice from behind Little Miss Shrewd Eyes.

'Millie, come on now, don't be shy.' Susie looked up at Matthew. 'She's been so excited about you coming to see us. She loves drawing, don't you, Millie, darling? I'm sure Matthew would like to see your pictures in the playroom.' She smiled encouragingly at him.

Matthew could relate to shyness – he'd been painfully shy as a young boy himself. He offered a smile to the small girl now peering cautiously at him from behind her more confident sister.

'Ignore her,' said Little Miss Shrewd Eyes. 'She's only attention-seeking.'

Susie laughed. 'Just listen to Floss, only ten years old but going on eighteen. I don't know what I'd do without her. She's truly the only sane member in our family. Bonkers and I very nearly didn't have children. There's madness in the family. No, honestly, mad as hatters some of them!'

Matthew could well believe it.

Coffee was suggested and served in tiny china cups and saucers along with gold-edged paper napkins decorated with cherubs. They sat in a large conservatory filled with the sickly smell of pot-pourri. Draped from a central point above their heads, and hanging in four white columns against the glass, were yards and yards of muslin – it was like being in a four-poster bed. Millie hadn't ever fully materialised and had apparently disappeared upstairs to her bedroom. Little Miss Shrewd Eyes, on the other hand, chose now to tackle her music practice.

'Fifteen minutes a day – her music teacher insists,' Susie told Matthew, and, leaning forward, her gold bangles clanking against her coffee cup, she added in a lowered voice, 'and honestly, it's the longest fifteen minutes of every day.'

Again Matthew could believe this as he listened to something completely unrecognisable.

'It's called "Mexican Melody",' Susie whispered helpfully.

'No, it's not,' came an indignant voice from the hall, 'it's "The Emperor's March".'

Matthew placed his cup and saucer and unused napkin on the glass-topped table in front of him. It was time to get things moving. 'Perhaps I could have a look at the room now.'

'Ah, yes,' Susie said slowly, making no move to get up.

Matthew inwardly sighed. He knew what was coming next.

'Thing is —'

Thing is, we've changed our minds. Yes, yes, he'd heard it all before. On one occasion the client had even changed her mind halfway through the commission.

'We've been having a think or, rather, *I've* been having a think.'

'No problem,' he said, getting determinedly to his feet. 'Just show me the wall and we'll take it from there.'

'Gosh, you must think me awfully stupid.'

As if! 'Of course not.' Unable to think of anything else to say, he picked up his bag of notebooks, pencils and photographs and started towards the door. He knew he made a wretched salesman and had always been grateful that he personally didn't have to sell his paintings back up in Coniston and the surrounding areas. These days all he had to do was deliver the pictures to the gallery owners and let them do the hard work. It was a cinch compared to this.

Still Susie made no attempt to move. 'Actually,' she said, 'it's this room I've decided on. Don't you think that wall would look absolutely sweet with one of your murals?'

Sweet! He didn't do sweet. He lowered his bag and

stared hard at the wall Susie was pointing at and which was behind the chair he'd been sitting in. He walked up to it, backed away and then went over to the other side of the conservatory where Susie was sitting. He didn't need to consider the wall a moment longer.

'What do you think?' Susie asked anxiously. He was a strange man. Almost friendly, but not quite, which was a pity if he was going to be working here over the next few weeks. Not only that, but she'd had high hopes of showing him off among her new friends in Crantsford. She'd heard about him not long after moving into Orchard House while reading a copy of *Homes and Gardens*. A house in the Lake District had been featured and in particular it showed the owners' dining room and its mural painted by a local artist called Matthew Collins, who had cleverly depicted all the members of the family at different stages in their lives. Bonkers had been all for it, saying that he never intended moving house again and wanted his family immortalised for ever – 'our own little bit of history', he'd called it.

Susie wondered if Matthew hadn't heard her, or whether this was all part and parcel of the floppy-velvet-hat syndrome; you could be as rude as you liked and make people pay for the pleasure of your wobbly ego. She cleared her throat in the silence that had been created now that Floss's fifteen minutes of piano practice had come to an end. 'What do you think?' she repeated.

'It's perfect,' he answered, at last wrenching his eyes away from the wall. 'Have you got all the photographs I asked for?'

'I thought maybe you could have a look through the albums yourself, that way –'

'Fine,' he interrupted. Now he'd have to suffer endless holiday snaps and all those meaningless 'special moments' caught on camera that meant nothing to anyone except those involved. 'But I'll have to take the albums away with me so I can study them. I need to get to know you all as a family.'

'Heavens, you'll end up as mad as us!'

More than likely, thought Matthew. More than likely.

Ellen was just locking the barn door when she heard the sound of a car coming down Beggarman's Lane. I'm not opening up, she told herself firmly, I don't care how much money they've got stuffed in their pockets. I'm all done in. They're too late.

All the same she held back from turning the last of the locks. But when a horn the volume of the $QE2$ berthing in dock sounded she hurriedly turned the key and went to greet Simon and his rusting Fiat Uno.

She waited for him to unfurl himself from the small car, then kissed his stubbly cheek before he stood up completely and was beyond her reach. 'You smell,' she said, in the way only a mother can get away with.

'And so would you if you'd been cooped up in this car for the past three hours with Craig and Dave the Delhi Belly.'

Ellen groaned. Dave the Delhi Belly was one of Simon's oldest friends and was famous for two things: misquoting any and all of the great poets and eating kamikaze curries with life-threatening consequences for those around him.

Simon opened the boot and hauled out a backpack the size of a wheelie bin, hoisted it onto his shoulder, locked the car and followed Ellen into the cottage. After he'd showered, unearthed the horrors within the backpack and shoved them straight into the washing machine, he joined his mother in the sitting room. She was perched on the window-seat, her chin resting on her drawn-up knees. She looked worried. Instinctively he knew she had something to tell him.

'I've poured you a lager,' she said. 'It's there on the table. And, by the way, your father's written.' She watched his freshly scrubbed and shaved face closely as he picked up the glass and sat opposite her, one leg hanging over the side of the chair.

'And?'

'And . . . and I haven't had the courage to open his letter.' She carried on watching him and noticed that the hanging leg had started to bounce up and down ever so slightly.

'Do you want me to read it?'

'Do you want to?'

The leg was bouncing more vigorously now.

'Not really.'

'Why do you suppose he's written?' Ellen had asked herself the question so many times since Susie Buchanan had delivered the letter to her on Sunday. It was the first piece of personal correspondence she had received from Roger since his mantelpiece confession. Why had he written to her now? Had he put together a letter that he hoped would atone for everything he had done, as though a few cheery words could make everything right? Or was he in trouble? Had his money run out and was he coming cap in hand to her? Oh, the irony! Or maybe the sexual pleasures so willingly provided by Charmaine had palled.

But all these possibilities came nowhere near what she really hoped lay behind Roger's putting pen to paper. It was dreadful of her, but she truly wished him the very worst. A letter explaining that he was dying a slow, agonising death would just about make amends for what he'd put her through.

'I couldn't give a shit why he's written,' Simon said, his leg now perfectly still. 'And I don't think you should. He chose to go his own way, which certainly didn't include either of us, so it can stay that way for all I care.'

'He is your father,' Ellen said tentatively.

'Yeah, and Elvis was King. So what?'

Ellen gave up on the text-book ideology – phrases like 'It's me your father's divorced, not you,' never went down well with Simon. She got up and walked through to the kitchen. She was hungry and tired. Since Roger's letter had arrived she had spent hour after hour reliving the past events, turning over in her mind everything Roger had said and done . . . and everything that perhaps *she* should have said and done. It had been an exhausting couple of days.

Simon came into the kitchen. They looked silently at each other for a moment, both stinging with unresolved hurt and anger.

'Come on,' she said, acknowledging that they were both a long way off yet from making a full recovery from what Roger had done. 'I'll make us some supper while you tell me something disgusting about Dave the Delhi Belly.'

Simon shook his head. 'No way, I've had enough of that bloke.' He raised himself up onto the work surface, banged the heels of his bare feet noisily on the cupboard below and took an apple from the china bowl beside the earthenware pot of wooden spoons. 'Besides, I want you to tell me what's been going on here.'

'Well, you already know about Jo-Jo,' Ellen said as she filled a saucepan with water. She placed it on the hob and reached up to a shelf of jars where she hoped she had enough pasta shells for the pair of them. She was in luck. 'But something else has happened,' she said, opening a can of tuna and wondering how Simon might take the news, but feeling she should broach the subject before tomorrow night when Duncan would be picking her up for dinner. 'You could say there's possibly a man in the picture.'

'Anyone I know?'

'Kind of. It's Duncan Carter.'

Simon whistled.

'Is that approval or shock?'

'It's whatever you want it to be.'

She flicked a pasta shell at him. 'Clever Dick!'

Chapter Fifteen

'I've decided to get a job.'

'Just like that?'

'Yes,' replied Jo-Jo. She picked up a handful of tarnished silver-plated forks from the draining board and began to dry them. 'There must be loads of places in Crantsford where I can get work. Like that posh set-up where I met you and Ellen.'

Hermione rinsed a small cracked jug under the hot tap and smiled at the thought of the hideously pretentious Miss Astley being approached by a pregnant runaway looking for work.

'What's up? Why are you smiling like that?'

'No reason.'

Jo-Jo clunked the forks into the cutlery drawer, one by one. 'I'm surprised you haven't died of poisoning from the state of these knives and forks,' she said.

'I like to live dangerously,' Hermione said, tipping the dirty water out of the washing-up bowl and discovering the ubiquitous teaspoon hiding at the bottom. 'Are you serious about getting a job?'

'Yes. I have to do something. I can't stay here for ever just sitting about doing nothing.'

'I'd hardly say you've sat about the place doing nothing. Since the moment you arrived you've all but turned the house upside down.'

It was true. Jo-Jo had stuck to her guns and in return

for her free board and lodgings she had tidied, cleaned and polished almost non-stop.

'I can't help it,' Jo-Jo said, hanging the tea towel up on a hook beside the old Electrolux fridge and returning to the sink where she proceeded to squeeze out the dishcloth Hermione had left sopping wet behind the mixer taps. 'I've been doing it for Mum for so long it's second nature. By the way, this stinks, it needs bleaching.' She held up the cloth for Hermione's inspection, then opened the cupboard under the sink where she had already marshalled the barely touched cleaning products into an organised fashion, throwing away anything that didn't seem to bear any resemblance to the nineteen nineties.

'Does it, indeed? But have you thought that being pregnant might make you a tad unemployable?'

'I shan't let on.'

'And what about your studies?'

Jo-Jo stopped what she was doing. 'You sound as if you don't want me to get a job.'

Hermione thought about this. Jo-Jo was right, she didn't. This was a disquieting realisation. Was she really turning into a selfish old woman who, when it suited her, wanted to monopolise another person? First with Ellen and now Jo-Jo, a young girl whom she hardly knew. Was she so desperate for companionship that she was prepared to hold another person back, to thwart their plans?

'Of course you must get a job, Jo-Jo,' she said in a clipped voice. 'That way you'll soon be able to get yourself sorted and leave me to get back to my old untidy ways. This was always just a temporary situation until you got yourself on your feet.'

Jo-Jo watched Hermione go through to the garden room and then outside. Puzzled, she carried on filling the sink with water and then added some bleach. She dropped the grey dishcloth into the water and with the end of the mop prodded at the bubbles of air trapped by the stringy square of fabric.

'I shouldn't worry too much about Hermione, if I were you.'

She spun round to see Matthew coming into the kitchen. 'Do you have to keep creeping up on me?' she said, the annoyance in her voice undisguised.

'I wasn't aware that I was creeping up on you, or ever had been,' he replied. He opened the fridge and helped himself to a glass of orange juice. 'Hermione enjoys having you around,' he added, after he'd emptied the glass and set it down on the draining board.

Which is more than I do with you, thought Jo-Jo. Honestly, the man was so quiet. One minute there was no sign of him, and the next, there he was. She decided to be bold. 'Hermione likes having me here, but you don't, right?'

He stared at her closely. 'Why do you think that?'

She shrugged. 'You don't. You hardly ever speak to me and when you do you seem so disapproving . . . as though you don't trust me.'

'I'm afraid that's just the way I am.'

'So I'm right, you don't trust me.'

He smiled. 'And how many people do you trust, Jo-Jo?'

'I . . . I trust Hermione.'

'Snap. Which means that what you've just said about me is rubbish. Coffee?'

'Hang on,' she said, confused, 'I don't get what you mean.'

'I meant simply that I would put money on Hermione being a good judge of character. Now, do you want any coffee? I bought a jar of decaffeinated, which is better for the baby.'

For the first time Jo-Jo felt herself relax in Matthew's company. 'So how come you know so much about pregnancy?'

'Open any women's magazine and it's all there for any man to discover all he needs to know about women, everything from episiotomies to erogenous zones.'

'Apeasy-whats?'

'I think the sooner you see a doctor the better.'

Hermione was cross with herself.

Damn the girl!

She lifted the galvanised watering can over the pots of sweet peas and then cursed again at the sight of the tender young plants suddenly flooded under inches of water.

'I'm becoming a nasty, curmudgeonly, selfish old woman,' she said bitterly, and lowering the watering can to the ground she sat herself in her brown and orange flowered deck chair, which she kept permanently in the greenhouse.

Anger was an infrequent visitor to her door, but there was no getting away from it, right now she was furious. Manipulative was the word that kept coming into her mind and she was ashamed and disgusted with herself. What right did she have to question what Jo-Jo intended doing with her life? If the girl wanted to fly to the moon and back, what did it have to do with an old has-been like herself? It was Jo-Jo's life and she had only offered her accommodation, not interference of the *in loco parentis* variety.

Later she'd go back inside the house, apologise and perhaps start helping Jo-Jo to find a job.

No!

No, she wouldn't do anything of the kind. She would apologise for her churlish behaviour and let Jo-Jo go about finding her own job. She was not to involve herself so much . . . even if she did think the girl was wrong.

She breathed in deeply and then exhaled slowly and assuredly. 'There, now,' she said calmly, and getting to her feet, she smiled at the sweet peas. 'No need to worry,' she told them. 'The danger of any more flash floods has passed.'

When she had finished pottering in the greenhouse she wandered down to the lower level of the garden, to the area where she had taken Jo-Jo on Good Friday. The grass was still wet from all the rain and her boots made a satisfying squelchy noise with each step she took. When she reached the stone seat she found it perfectly dry from having had the sun shining on it all morning. She sat down and breathed in the smell of moistened earth. It was a wholesome smell, like freshly baked bread or washing hung out to dry, and it lifted her spirits. She breathed in some more, letting her eyes linger over the statue . . . Kit's statue.

How delighted she had been when he had asked her to pose for him, and how very cross Roberta had been when she had discovered what Kit was working on. Torn apart with jealousy, Hermione's sister had even threatened to smash the statue when it was finished.

She smiled and started to hum, quietly at first, just snatches of popular melodies, but then she moved on to one of Kit's favourite pieces of music, 'Ode to Joy'. He once said that it was the only piece of music that sounded truly joyous. She hadn't fully understood what he'd meant at the time, she'd been so young, but as the years had passed and she'd grown older, she had come to know exactly what he'd meant. There was a vastness to the great choral piece that could not be ignored, its composition as rich and as full as life itself should be, with each swell of the music singing out the joy and celebration of being alive.

Not long before he'd died Kit had told her that during his lifetime he'd only known pure joy because he'd experienced its antithesis.

She had cried when he'd said that, only too aware of the truth of his words.

'Hello there.'

Startled, Hermione swivelled her head and looked about her but she could see no one. She hoped this wasn't the beginning of the end – *voices in the head*.

'Over here.'

There it was again. Nearer this time and accompanied by a definite swishing of undergrowth. Did one hear swishing noises at the onset of senility? Voices, yes, but swishing? She stood up and went to investigate the *leylandii* hedge, which formed the boundary with the Lodge next door.

'That's right, over here. Left a bit, ah, there you are.' The voice was cheery and Hermione eventually found its source coming through a porthole-sized gap in the hedge. 'You hum very nicely. I was within a whisker of joining in, da dee da da –'

'Well, I can quite see what held you back,' Hermione interrupted. 'You're as sharp as a Bramley.'

The man laughed and then disappeared from view, leaving behind him the dreadful sound of coughing, followed by a wheezing that scraped at Hermione's own chest. A couple of seconds passed and then the face reappeared. 'Bloody pneumonia, never a dull moment. How do you do, by the way? I'm Bernard Malloy, but you can call me Bernie and I'm your new neighbour. I saw you from my window and thought I'd come and introduce myself.' A chubby hand with a chipolata of a little finger wearing a gold and diamond signet ring popped through the hole in the hedge.

'Hermione Rowlands,' she said, shaking the proffered hand, 'and I presume you're a newly recruited inmate at the Lodge. Do you intend on being a lifer?'

'I certainly hope so. It's like the Ritz here – red carpets, oak panelling, chandeliers, and a wine cellar to die for. I have great plans to drink myself to death on some of the finest wines available. And the best part is the totty.'

'The totty?'

'Practically throwing themselves at me during lunch, they were. One at a time I had to tell them, Bernie's not as young as he was.'

'Mr Malloy, you're obviously a pathological fibber of the highest order and I sincerely hope I have the pleasure of many more such conversations through the hedge, but if I'm not mistaken there's somebody calling for you. Time for your enema?'

He laughed, turned away, then reappeared. 'It's the totty I was telling you about, I've promised them a game of croquet. Ta-ta.'

Croquet, mused Hermione, as she made her way back up to the house. She hadn't played for years. She wondered where her old set was. It was probably little more than a pile of woodwormy dust, she reflected with regret.

'It's just the right temperature, isn't it?'

'Sorry?'

'The champagne,' Duncan said, taking a sip from his fluted glass.

'Oh, yes,' she said, kicking herself for having let her mind wander. When Duncan had ordered the bottle of Moët & Chandon from the wine waiter she had immediately leaped to the conclusion that they were about to slip into celebration mode. Certain things came in pairs – baths and tide-marks, ornaments and dust, cars and traffic jams, proposals and champagne. And okay, yes, she was jumping the gun, and probably by a long way, but she was now so set on the idea of marrying Duncan that she couldn't believe that his mind wasn't working on the same wavelength as hers. She was conscious, though, that certain crucial elements were missing from their relationship.

Romance was one of them.

If she was honest with herself there was a worrying lack of schmaltz to their potential alliance, but then you couldn't have everything and champagne would do very well instead.

'Now, tell me again about this girl. What did you say her name was? And what on earth possessed you to get involved with her in the first place?'

For a ghastly moment Ellen was reminded of Roger. '*Why on earth did you do that? What were you thinking of?*' These had been some of his stock-in-trade questions; an interrogating technique she'd been unaware of until it was no longer there. It was strange and frightening what you became used to.

'Why are you so against her?' she asked defensively. 'There's nothing wrong with her. Jo-Jo's the same as you or me.'

Duncan snorted. 'I've never looked for hand-outs on the street.'

Then you should think yourself lucky you've never needed to, Ellen wanted to say, but instead she drained

136

her glass and said pleasantly, 'Goodness, I'm so hungry I could eat a horse between two mattresses.'

'I think you'll have to make do with something a little more refined from La Maison d'Or.' Duncan smiled.

When he had called earlier to say where he'd booked for dinner, Ellen had been delighted – La Maison d'Or was one of the most expensive restaurants in Crantsford.

'Pulling out all the stops, is he?' Simon had said, when she'd put down the phone.

'I certainly hope so,' she'd answered, brushing her hair while kneeling on the floor in front of her bedroom mirror, which she still hadn't got round to hanging on the wall. 'I think I deserve a little pampering.'

Simon had opened the door to Duncan when he'd arrived and Ellen had watched the two men watching each other. The sitting room had suddenly seemed perilously small and several times she had asked them to sit down, but her words went unheard as they shifted their way to the right and then to the left as if performing a little dance. The conversation had been polite, Duncan opening predictably with, 'And how's the world of academia these days?'

Ellen had flinched, but if Simon had found Duncan's question pompous he showed no sign of it and, sounding every inch a clean-cut American preppy, he'd answered, 'Fine, sir, though probably very different from when you were there.'

They talked at length about Oxbridge – Simon was at Brasenose College, Oxford, and Duncan had read law at Trinity, Cambridge – and when Ellen had heard enough she stared pointedly at Simon and made the slightest of movements towards the front door. Instantly both men had done what was expected of them – Simon had wished them a good evening and Duncan had reached into his pocket for his car keys.

Ellen wondered now what was expected of her as she considered Duncan from behind her menu. Just what did he want from her? Marriage? Or one of those platonic friendships that you only read about? If he was attracted to her, and she couldn't really be sure that he was, he kept it very much to himself.

She had been attracted to him almost from the first moment, well, in that simple multiple-choice question-and-answer way: If presented with Duncan Carter, would you (a) prefer a bout of flu to an evening out with him? or (b) imagine yourself capable of fancying him?

Sitting in his office for her second appointment the thought had crossed her mind that her solicitor was a very attractive man. So why wasn't he married? had followed, lightning-fast. She had tried to ignore these distracting thoughts and forced herself to concentrate on what Duncan was explaining, only to find herself drifting back to his well-manicured hands playing with his fountain pen on his desk and his pressed shirt and silk tie perfectly knotted below a smooth clean-shaven chin. His eyes, always glancing from the papers on his desk to her face, were as impassive as any she'd seen, but concealed, she was convinced, hidden depths, but of exactly what she wasn't sure.

And she still wasn't sure what those pale greyish-blue eyes across the table conveyed. She watched him read his menu. He looked up suddenly and met her gaze. One of us should say something, she thought, something romantic, or at least clever and witty. But unable to think of anything remotely along these lines herself, other than to start enacting *that* scene from *When Harry Met Sally*, she lowered her head and returned her attention to choosing her meal. She was surprised, though, to feel her menu being pulled away and Duncan covering one of her hands with his own.

Chapter Sixteen

If Hermione had suspected herself of being manipulative earlier that day she now knew with certainty that this was exactly what she was.

She dialled Ellen's telephone number, knowing full well that her friend was out with Duncan, but it wasn't Ellen she wanted to speak to. It was Simon. She hoped he was in. It seemed an age before she heard his voice at the other end of the line.

'Simon,' she said, relieved, 'it's Hermione. How do you see yourself in the role of great wise one and mentor?'

'It'd make a change from Simple Simon.'

Within minutes she had his agreement.

The idea had come to her while she was sitting in the greenhouse after tea and reflecting on Jo-Jo who, once again, had been talking about finding herself a job.

'I could join an agency and clean for people,' she'd said. 'At least that's one thing I know I'm good at.'

Hermione had kept quiet and sought refuge in the greenhouse, and despite her resolution to leave Jo-Jo to make her own mistakes, she was determined that someone had to take charge and talk some sense into the girl. Taking the first job that came along was not the answer to Jo-Jo's problems. Someone had to persuade her to go home and return to school.

At first she had thought that Matthew might be the one to reason with Jo-Jo, but then she'd remembered Ellen mentioning on the phone after breakfast that Simon was back from the Lake District for a few days before returning to Oxford. Simon, she'd realised, was the ideal choice. He was more or less the same age as Jo-Jo and if anyone could convince her that she should return home and do her exams this summer it was him, for he was one of the most strong-minded young men she had come across. He knew exactly what he wanted from life and how to go about getting it.

Simon rang the front-door bell but when it made no discernible sound he walked round to the side of Laburnum House where he found his charge in the enclosed courtyard in the dusky half-light of early evening. She was unpegging a row of washing from a drooping clothes-line.

'Hi,' he said, 'you must be Jo-Jo.'

She peered at him over the top of an enormous bundle of washing in her arms. 'And you must be Simon,' she said, after a few moments. 'I recognise you from your mother's photographs. If you're looking for Hermione she's inside watching *Inspector Morse*.'

'Actually it's you I came to see.'

'Me?'

'Here, let me help you.' He took part of the pile of washing from her. 'Hermione thought you'd appreciate some younger company. How do you fancy a drink?'

They walked the short distance into Crantsford. It was almost dark when they reached Church Walk and the narrow street was picturesquely illuminated by replica Victorian street lamps painted black with fiddly gold bits. Most of the shop windows were lit and the shop nearest to them was a jeweller's with a minimalist display of modern pieces in chunks of silver.

They moved further along Church Walk and as they passed even more tempting shop windows Jo-Jo was reminded of the time when, as a small child, her grandmother had taken her to see *Dick Whittington* as a Boxing Day treat. She had never been to a theatre before and had sat spellbound in her squeaking, tilting seat, one hand clutching her bag of sweets and the other tucked in her gran's while taking in the lights and the sounds and the amazement of being transported from the world she knew to a strange and magical one.

Crantsford was a bit like that theatrically created wonderworld. The streets weren't exactly paved with gold, but there was plenty of conspicuous wealth about the place, including a good many flashy cars parked outside the town's numerous restaurants, whose doors were wide open on this warm spring evening with upbeat music beckoning customers inside. Jo-Jo could see people sitting at the tables, their faces cheerfully intent on enjoying themselves, while efficient waiters and waitresses carried large trays high above their shoulders.

'Crantsford's an extravagant place in which to live, isn't it?' Simon said, breaking into her thoughts.

'I suppose it is,' she said. She wanted to say that actually she quite liked it, but wasn't sure whether it was the right thing to say. She suddenly felt very young and naïve. Though Simon wasn't much older than her, he seemed so much more sure of himself. Was that what going away to university did for you?

'Let's try this one,' he said, coming to a stop outside a small pub with neat window-boxes and a row of polished brass lanterns hanging overhead. Inside the public bar Simon ordered a pint of local beer for himself and, remembering Matthew's stern face at the lunch table yesterday, Jo-Jo asked for a Britvic orange juice. They found themselves a small table and a couple of low stools.

'It's stupid,' she said, with a sigh, 'but I was just thinking how young I feel and here I am reinforcing that feeling by drinking orange juice.' She poked at the cubes of ice in the glass with her finger and then sucked it dry. 'And the irony is that in a few months' time I'm going to be a mother. What a joke.'

Simon raised his beer and took a mouthful. He lowered the glass and wiped the traces of froth from his top lip. 'How do you feel about becoming a mother?'

'The truth?'

'What else?'

'At first I thought it was the answer. A way out. But now I can see it isn't.' She fiddled with a beer mat. 'This might sound selfish but I want the old me back . . . Well, some of the old me.'

'Mum said something about home not being ideal.'

Jo-Jo shook her head. 'What a huge understatement, but that's definitely the part I can do without.'

'So which bits do appeal?'

She thought for a moment. 'I want what you've got. I want to go to university and do something for *me*. I could never harm this baby but I'm not convinced I could be the mother it deserves.' She lowered her gaze and stared into her drink. 'You probably think I'm a selfish cow.'

'Sorry to disappoint you, but no. To a certain degree we've all got the same attitude of what's in it for me? We might manage to persuade ourselves that we're being altruistic, but mostly we do things because *we* want to do those things.'

'That doesn't sound at all politically correct.'

He laughed. 'Whoever said it was?'

'Alan always . . .' She hesitated.

'Is that the baby's father?'

She nodded. 'Alan was obsessed with being politically correct.'

'To the point of not believing in contraception, I suppose?'

A tiny seed of annoyance flared within her. She had known all along that she shouldn't have relied on Alan so heavily, she should have gone on the pill, but she hadn't. And because of her stupidity she had inadvertently gambled away her future.

'Haven't you ever taken a risk?' she asked bitterly.

'Not in that department,' he answered, without even having to consider the question. He drained his glass in one long gulp. 'You see before you *el supremo* when it comes to the art of self-preservation. I worked my arse off to get to Oxford, and what with the sacrifices Mum's made to help finance me, I'm not about to let a quick moment of pleasure get in the way of my future.'

'Which is?'

'Aha, you'll have to wait and see. Another drink?'

Jo-Jo watched Simon walk over to the bar. He was much taller than any of the other men either side of him and a darn sight better-looking. She hadn't realised until now how attractive he was and as he stood with his back to her she noticed how a group of girls wearing short skirts and tiny cropped tops in the opposite corner were leaning into each other and eyeing him up and down. A few moments ago she had felt young and naïve, but looking at these girls with their minuscule midriffs and giggly made-up faces she felt ancient, like she'd lived several lives already.

When Simon returned she said, 'So what would you do in my place?'

'The truth?'

'As you said earlier, what else?'

'Okay. When's the baby due?'

'September.'

'That's easy, then. I'd go home, no matter how awful it was, and sit my exams. I'd wait for my results, have the baby, give it up for adoption and then take up my place at college. How's that?'

'That's easy for you to say because –'

'Yeah, yeah, because I'm a bloke and I don't feel the same way about –'

'No, not that. I just don't know what I'll find if I go home. You might not have noticed but nobody's come looking for me.'

'Stuff that. You'll only be there for a few months. They'll just have to put up with you and you with them. The important thing is to get yourself back to school when your term begins in a couple of weeks' time. That way you won't miss any crucial work before your exams start.'

Jo-Jo frowned. 'Are you always this bloody sure of everything?'

'Yep. It's the only way. Go for it, Jo-Jo. And, besides, what have you got to lose?'

Chapter Seventeen

Much to Botticelli's annoyance, Hermione stopped rubbing his chin. She'd just caught a glimpse of Ellen's fair hair passing by the kitchen window. A couple of seconds later she appeared in the doorway between the garden room and the kitchen.

'I know it's early, but can I come in?'

'Ellen, it's barely eight o'clock. Has something terrible happened?'

Ellen's face broke into an enormous smile. 'Quite the opposite,' she said happily. She came and sat at the table, directly opposite Hermione. Botticelli, sensing either that he was no longer the centre of attraction or that there was no likelihood of him being fed, now begrudgingly leaped off Hermione's lap and disappeared out of the kitchen to go in search of something edible in the garden.

'So it's good news, is it?' Hermione said, straightening out her rumpled nightdress and fur coat. 'I'm so glad, because I've got something exciting to tell you as well.'

'Oh?' Ellen was put out. She hadn't bargained on having to wait her turn.

'Yes, while you were out ensnaring the hapless Duncan, things were happening here. Jo-Jo's decided to do the sensible thing and go home. She phoned her mother late last night and it's all arranged.'

'So your deviousness with Simon actually came off?' Ellen tried to sound genuinely pleased, but she felt childishly piqued. She had barely slept last night, going over what Duncan had said during dinner, and she had been bursting to tell Hermione ever since. He hadn't exactly proposed but their relationship had definitely moved on. There had even been a hint of romance in the car. As kissing went it had been a little hurried, but she suspected that had been down to Duncan trying to keep his eyes firmly on the cottage. Poor man, he'd probably been terrified of an over-protective son coming out and banging on the car window, demanding what the devil he thought he was doing with his mother.

'So Simon told you of the plan I'd hatched, did he?'

'Yes,' Ellen said, dragging her mind back to Jo-Jo. 'He told me when Duncan dropped me off late last night. I must say I hadn't expected it to work. She seemed so adamant about not going home.'

'Your son's a smooth operator, Ellen.'

'Evidently.' She heard the sarcasm in her voice and was mortified. Was she *that* annoyed with Hermione for not letting her share her good news first?

'Now all we've got to do is organise Jo-Jo's travel arrangements for getting back home.' Hermione had caught Ellen's sharp tone but had decided to get to the bottom of that when she had resolved the more pressing item on her agenda. 'It's your day off today, isn't it? Do you think Johnny Foreigner's up to the journey?'

'Today?' Ellen's heart sank. Two disappointments now. She had hoped to spend the day with Simon. She saw so little of her son that she had been determined to set aside her one day off to be with him. There was also still the matter of Roger's letter to deal with and she wanted Simon's help with that, especially as he'd told her yesterday afternoon that he wanted to get back to Oxford as soon as possible to make a start on some work before the summer term got under way. As far as the letter went, it was today or never.

Hermione saw the unhappy expression on her friend's face. 'Have you made plans already?'

She shook her head. 'No, not really.'

'You're lying, Ellen, I can see it written all over your face. Is it Duncan? Is it another command performance at Crantsford Hall?'

'No! And you wouldn't be asking me that if you'd let me get a word in edgeways!'

'Goodness, Ellen, whatever is the matter? I've never seen you like this before. He hasn't rumbled you, has he? Is that what you came here to tell me?'

'No!' cried Ellen. 'No! No! *No!*' She jumped up from the table. 'I just wanted to spend the day with Simon, if you must know, but to please you I'll agree to drive to Pluto and back if it will only shut you up and give me the opportunity to speak!'

Hermione was amused. Clearly Ellen was in danger of injuring herself if she wasn't allowed her two penn'orth, and soon. But a few moments longer wouldn't do any harm. 'How very kind of you, but I think Sheffield will be as far as we need go. And as to being deprived of Simon's company, that's easily remedied. Why don't we invite him along as well? We could make a day of it. We could put a picnic together and stop off on the way. It could be like a Jane Austen excursion, except we'd have to carry all our own hampers and whatnot. Do you remember when we went to see *Emma* and they all climbed up Box Hill with an army of Sherpas? What do you think? Shall we get out our Empire lines and heaving bosoms and a selection of frilly parasols?'

Ellen plonked herself back into the chair. Hermione was a formidable player in the art of prevarication and it was really quite futile to try to score any points against her. 'The trouble with picnics in novels,' she said, in a tired voice, 'is that they're quite often turning points.'

'What profundity for so early in the morning.'

'Jane Austen and E. M. Forster were always making a drama out of a day in the country with a hamper.' And I'm going slowly mad, thought Ellen. Slowly, but ever so surely, I'm becoming as mad as Hermione. I only came to say that Duncan is making definite overtures towards me and here I am expounding on the English novel. She picked up an ancient, badly stained cork mat from the table and fiddled with the crumbling edge. She caught the blank expression on Hermione's face. 'Oh, never mind,' she muttered. 'Just forget I ever said anything. The idea's fine by me. I'll have a word with Simon.'

'Ellen, my dear, you seem quite *distrait*.' It was time to put her friend out of her misery. She had teased her long enough. 'Would I be right in thinking that you have news of earth-shattering importance to share with me?'

'You know jolly well I have. Whoops. Sorry.' Ellen pushed the cork mat away from her. It now had a hole where she'd poked her finger right through the middle.

Hermione smiled. 'Come on,' she said, 'tell me that your seductive skills have thoroughly charmed Duncan and that you're about to become the grand lady of the manor. I insist on being your matron of honour for the big day, by the way, and a regular house guest thereafter so that we can get back to afternoon tea and cake while listening to the short story on the radio.'

'If you don't be quiet you'll never hear another story again in your life,' laughed Ellen, glad to have her friend's undivided attention at last. 'Make some tea and I'll fill you in.'

Hermione did as she was told, held the kettle under the

tap and then plugged it in. 'You won't miss the best bits out, will you?' she asked, picking up two mugs from the draining board.

'Best bits?'

'Well, I presume there was more than just prawn cocktail on the menu last night.'

'Duncan isn't like that,' Ellen answered, and, conscious that she sounded both defensive and prim, she added, 'He's too much of a gentleman.'

'Either that or he's impotent, or worse still he's –'

'Hermione!'

'I hope you're not discussing me.'

Hermione greeted Matthew with a broad smile. 'Good morning,' she said, and handed him the warmed teapot. 'You're just in time to make us a pot of tea, and, no, we weren't discussing you but Ellen's future husband. Have you met Ellen before? I can't remember.'

'No,' Matthew said, uninterestedly, and immediately turned his attention to seeing to the tea.

'She's a very dear friend of mine and used to live in Orchard House where the Buchanans now live. Ellen, you'll have to excuse my godson's appalling manners but he lives alone and has lost touch with the niceties of life. I think it's an air he affects to put other people at a disadvantage and keep them at arm's length. Take no notice of him.'

Ellen had forgotten that Hermione had told her about Matthew coming to stay, and from the way in which her friend had described him throughout their friendship she had expected someone quite different. She'd had in mind someone older, someone pale and thin with an earnest face – this was based on the sensitively painted watercolours dotted about Laburnum House, which she'd always admired. But from the little she had seen of him so far she could see that she had got him totally wrong. She certainly hadn't expected such a total lack of manners. While his back was to her she took the opportunity to size him up. He was tall – but not as tall as Duncan – and he had a square pair of shoulders beneath a white T-shirt and a loose-fitting denim shirt tucked into a pair of jeans. His feet were bare. She decided he had the kind of build that would look all wrong in a suit, and that *casual* was probably what he favoured most. His hair, though, was really quite smart and looked as if it had been recently cut. It was dark brown and very fine, with a hint of grey just beginning at the temples.

Matthew brought the tea to the table. He didn't sit down as if to join them but instead leaned on the back of a chair and stared first at Hermione and then at Ellen. She turned away. It was obviously his turn to size her up.

The only thought that flashed through Matthew's mind was that Hermione's attractive friend would be a terrible waste on an impotent husband.

'When's the big day?' he asked.

Ellen looked blankly at him.

'When are you getting married?'

Ellen coloured. 'I'm not, well, not yet, nothing's definite. You know how it is.' Floundering hopelessly, she looked to Hermione for help.

But Hermione chose not to notice. 'Ellen's just being discreet, Matthew. But before you came in she was about to tell me how her skill as a Mata Hari beguiled Duncan into proposing last night.'

'I never said that,' Ellen protested. Honestly, there was no trusting Hermione to behave with any tact at times.

'Perhaps I should go and leave you to your gossip,' Matthew said.

'There's no need,' Ellen said, suddenly rising to her feet

and scraping her chair on the quarry-tiled floor. 'It's me who should go.' Addressing Hermione, she added, 'If we're going to have this picnic I'd better start making some sandwiches. What time are we setting off?'

Hermione smiled. 'Tell you what, why don't we invite Matthew to come with us as well? Do you think we can squeeze one more into Johnny Foreigner?'

'What picnic and what Johnny Foreigner?'

'Matthew, you sound almost as peppery as Ellen. We're taking Jo-Jo home to Sheffield and stopping on the way to break the journey, and Johnny Foreigner is what Ellen calls her little car.'

'We could take mine if you want. It's a decrepit old wreck, but it's got plenty of room. How many are going?'

Hermione did a quick mental head-count, wagging her forefinger in the air. 'I make that four of us, no, I'm wrong, I was forgetting Ellen's son, Simon.'

Matthew suddenly regretted his rash offer. Being cooped up in a car with a child who, no doubt, would insist on chattering the whole journey or, worse still, want to play stupid I-spy games was not his idea of fun. But it was either that or spend the day going through the Buchanans' photo albums. It was a peach of a dilemma.

Ellen walked home, down in the dumps. She was thoroughly out of sorts and thoroughly peeved with Hermione and that rude godson of hers. Between them they had spoilt her day. If Hermione hadn't rabbited on so much, and if *he* hadn't come into the kitchen when he had she would have been able to share with Hermione all about Duncan telling her how fond he was of her. 'I want you to know that you've become very important to me,' he'd said, his hand stretched out across the table and squeezing her own, 'and that there's nobody else I'd rather be with.'

She smiled happily to herself. Dear, sweet Duncan. He was so old-fashioned at times but, then, perhaps that was what she found so attractive about him. After the demands put upon her by Roger, Duncan's courteous approach to their relationship was so welcome that it made her feel safe and at ease. She was even beginning to wonder if she wasn't falling in love with him.

Everyone, even Jo-Jo, was in good spirits as Matthew headed out onto the Macclesfield road to Buxton, which would eventually take them on to Jo-Jo's home town of Sheffield. The sun had climbed high in the sky and was already hot and it made the dusty interior of the car warm and slightly smelly. There were strange and not very pleasant pongs coming from the back, which Ellen put down to Matthew's tools of the trade. She didn't know much about painting, but she presumed the cardboard boxes behind her were full of manky tubes of paint and filthy rags covered in turps, or was it linseed oil artists used? She wound down her window for some fresh air and thought that it was a shame Matthew wasn't a writer. Pens and paper were far less offensive.

In the front, next to Matthew, was Hermione. She was supposed to be in charge of map reading but she was more occupied with sorting out the position of her seat – she kept sliding it backwards and forwards, oblivious to Simon's long legs behind her. Jo-Jo was between Simon and Ellen, and with her head turned to the open window, Ellen was conscious that she was beginning to feel anxious.

Before they had set off from Laburnum House Ellen had taken Jo-Jo aside and asked her if this was really what she wanted. A part of her was worried that if Jo-Jo returned home and something ghastly happened to her it would be all their fault – it was like returning a rescued and cared-for animal to the wild, then having to trust the forces of nature. It was hard not to play God and intervene.

'Oh, yes,' Jo-Jo had answered. 'I think I knew all along what I should be doing, only I didn't have the nerve to admit it. I kept thinking what I thought would be expected of me. I tried to convince myself that I'd be happy having the baby and living off what I could, but deep down I knew it was wrong for me . . . and the baby. Simon really made me see things clearly.'

'Well, so long as you're sure. But what about your step-father? He won't have changed just because you can see things more clearly.'

'I'll just have to keep out of his way. Like Simon says, I've only got to put up with him for a few months.'

Simon says, thought Ellen, and tilting her head forwards slightly she looked across to her son. He was chatting to Jo-Jo about a book he'd read recently. She had never thought about it before but Simon was that rare person who only offered his opinion when it was asked for; mostly people were only too quick to give their advice. It was strange, though, that in the aftermath of Roger's disappearance she had never once asked Simon directly what he thought she should do. She wondered what his advice would have been, had she sought it. Come to that, what did he really think of Duncan? But did it really matter? Surely what mattered most was what *she* felt, and right now she decided she was close to falling in love with Duncan. She smiled contentedly and closed her eyes, but then wondered if it was possible to be consciously *close to falling in love*. Wasn't it more like being pregnant? You either were or you weren't? Oh, what the heck! What difference did it make anyway?

154

She opened her eyes to see where they were, only to find Matthew glancing at her in the mirror.

They drove through Dove Holes, past Sparrowpit and then onto the spectacularly steep and rocky gorge of Winnats Pass. A few minutes later Hermione gave the word and they left the car. Carrying between them an assortment of travel rugs, baskets and Hermione's deck chair from the greenhouse, they walked on until they found a secluded, sheltered spot among the gritstone boulders. Ellen spread out a blanket for the baskets and Matthew tried to position the deck chair for Hermione.

'No, not there,' she told him. 'I think here would be better – that way I can enjoy the splendid views across to Mam Tor.'

Then he offered her a travel rug for her legs but she shook her head and pushed it away.

'I haven't been here in years,' she said happily, taking an old pair of field-glasses from a mould-spotted leather case and peering through them like Jack Hawkins in *The Cruel Sea*. It was a wonder she could see anything at the speed she was sweeping the binoculars along the horizon, thought Ellen, as she settled herself on the blanket beside one of the baskets. She started lifting out the plastic boxes of food, at the same time watching Simon and Jo-Jo. They had wandered away to a large rock. Simon was leaning back against it: with one hand he was pointing out something in the distance, and with the other he was pushing his wind-blown hair out of his eyes.

From nowhere Ellen was reminded of Roger. She turned away, unable to cope with her son's unintentional betrayal. People had always said how alike she and Simon were; rarely, even as a baby, had anyone suggested that there was any of Roger in him, but of course there was, and in that simple gesture of raising his hand to his eyes she had witnessed father and son as one. Roger had always been running his hand through his hair. Angry, she hoped that he was now bald and didn't have any hair to run his hand through. She hoped that life in Provence had made it all fall out. *All of it, every last strand!*

'Good idea,' said Matthew, kneeling beside her to help open the boxes of sandwiches. 'I'm starving.'

She quickly dispelled a bald Roger from her mind and held up a large greaseproof-paper parcel tied with string. She called over to Hermione, 'What's in here?'

'Spam and chutney. I found a vintage jar knocking about. It's one of the few items to survive Matthew's ruthless desire to ethnically cleanse my larder.'

'And just how old is this vintage chutney?' Matthew asked. 'Roughly – to the nearest decade will do.'

'I know exactly when I made it,' retorted Hermione. 'Do you remember when you came to stay and broke your arm while mending the summerhouse roof –'

'But that was *years* ago –'

'Oh, do stop making a drama out of everything, Matthew, you're getting as bad as Ellen. Now, pass me a sandwich and let me get on with enjoying myself.'

Reluctantly, Matthew handed Hermione her parcel then turned to Ellen. 'Let me have something you've made, and explain why you're being accused of making a drama out of everything.'

'Search me,' she said. 'I haven't a clue what she's on about.'

'You should have heard her earlier this morning,' Hermione said, waving a doorstep and a half of a sandwich in the air. 'She was like some harbinger of doom wittering on with some such nonsense about picnics being turning points.'

'A turning point doesn't necessarily mean a change for the worse,' Simon called over. He and Jo-Jo came and joined them. 'It's actually a moment when a decisive change occurs,' he added, helping himself to something to eat.

'He's right,' Jo-Jo said. 'Like last night when I decided I had to go back home.'

'Oh,' said Hermione craftily, 'so is that what happened with you and Duncan, Ellen? Was that what you came to tell me about this morning?'

'Behave yourself, Hermione,' Matthew said, sensing Ellen's discomfort. He delved into one of the other baskets for his contribution to their lunch: a bottle of white wine picked up on the way from the off-licence in Crantsford. He deftly pulled out the cork with a penknife from his trouser pocket and poured the wine. He handed the mugs round and gave Jo-Jo the one with the smallest amount in, 'So that you don't feel left out.'

'Here's to Jo-Jo's turning point,' Hermione said, raising her mug.

'You'll keep in touch, won't you?' Ellen asked, when they'd all toasted Jo-Jo.

'She'll be too busy climbing the ladder of success,' Simon said, with a proud smile.

When everything had been eaten – except for the spam and chutney, which had been universally condemned by all except Hermione – Ellen went for a walk on her own. She was sad. During lunch she had realised that Hermione was now the last person in whom she could confide about Duncan. Her dear friend was never going to believe that over the last few days Duncan had come to mean more to her than just a meal ticket.

With a heavy heart she wandered further away from

the group until she came to a high drystone wall. She leaned against it and stared out at the uncompromising beauty of the Dark Peak. With its gritstone terrace of moorland it was more sombre and bleaker than the White Peak of undulating limestone lying to the south, but its hardness appealed to Ellen. She was no walker, no rambler of the highways and byways, but she was suddenly filled with an inexplicable urge to scramble over the wall and to walk as far as she could, on and on, basking in all that freedom and space. She wondered whether Duncan would enjoy doing the same. She tried to imagine the pair of them hand in hand, dressed in cagoules, woolly hats and sturdy walking boots.

But she couldn't.

She couldn't prise Duncan away from his BMW or his leather-topped office desk.

She heard footsteps and turned to see Matthew coming towards her. He drew level and he, too, leaned against the drystone wall. He said nothing, but kept his gaze firmly ahead of him.

'Beautiful, isn't it?' she said at last, when the silence grew uncomfortable for her.

He turned and faced her. 'No,' he said flatly. 'You're wrong. It's majestic, savage, benign, challenging and a whole lot more.'

'But not beautiful?'

He shook his head.

'Well, I disagree with you. I think it is.'

They remained in silent disharmony, each looking in separate directions until Matthew said, 'Does this Duncan know how lucky he is?'

'I beg your pardon?'

He suddenly turned, contemplated her for a moment,

then as if it was the most reasonable thing in the world, held her face in his hands and kissed her on the lips.

And before she knew what she was doing she was kissing him back.

This is crazy, she thought, feeling the roughness of the wall behind her pressing into her back.

This is crazier still, she told herself, when he had wrapped his arms around her shoulders and had drawn her closer.

But she didn't care and for the sheer hell of it she sank deeper into the pleasure of him – it was as if she had climbed over the wall and was running free.

He pulled away abruptly.

'Is that how you kiss Duncan?' he asked, his voice low, and undeniably tinged with cynicism.

She could have slapped him!

And she would have, had she not caught sight of something even more alarming than the strange expression on his face.

Back at the picnic site, there was no sign of Simon and Jo-Jo. But Hermione was still there. She was alone, and sitting bolt upright in her deck chair, her binoculars glued to her eyes, she was looking straight at Ellen and Matthew.

Chapter Eighteen

The car was very quiet as they headed towards Sheffield.

Too quiet.

Even for Matthew.

He could never be described as a loquacious man – nowadays he spent most of his time alone and had come to value the peace of mind that he derived from his solitary way of life. The sound of meaningless chit-chat was abhorrent to him, he had no mind for it – but right now he'd give anything to be able to light the touch-paper of small-talk. He badly wanted someone to speak – even a facile comment about the weather would be welcome. He even wished that Ellen's son had turned out to be the young irritating chatter-box of a child he'd earlier imagined, and not the full-blown adult now sitting quietly in the back of the car reading *The Ballad of Reading Gaol*. But it seemed as though everyone was happy to sit in silence, either reading or staring out through the windows at the passing scenery.

He desperately needed someone to speak in the belief that it would break the spell of what he'd just done. He'd done some pretty dumb things in his life, but what had just taken place took some beating.

What the hell had he thought he was doing? Audition-ing for the part of Rhett Butler in *Gone With the Wind*? If he wanted to play a romantic lead he should join an amateur dramatic society and not take it into his head to go behaving in such a foolish and juvenile manner. For the love of God he was forty-two years old and had just made a complete idiot of himself. What was worse, and much more worrying, was that he had no idea what had possessed him to do it. It was as if for a few seconds he'd lost control of his senses.

He would have to apologise. But how? Judging from the way Ellen had acted after discovering that Hermione had been secretly watching them through her binoculars, the possibility of speaking to her again, and alone, seemed about as likely as . . . as likely as Hermione pretending she hadn't seen them.

They had tidied up the picnic in silence – even Hermione had been rendered speechless and had turned her attention to trying to collapse her deck chair. He suspected that she would be saving up something special to say for when they were alone later that evening. As they'd walked back to the car, having called out to Simon and Jo-Jo that they were off, Ellen had kept as far away from him as possible, lagging behind on the pretext of either admiring the view or stooping to retie a shoelace. And in the car she'd practically glued herself to the window rather than risk so much as a glance in his direction.

'I shall miss you all.'

Matthew inwardly sighed. At last, somebody had spoken.

'I will, honestly. I'm not just saying that.'

'And we shall miss you, Jo-Jo, my dear,' Hermione said fondly, looking up from the map on her lap at which she'd been staring through unseeing eyes for the past thirty minutes. 'Isn't that right, Ellen? After all, it was you who set this particular ball rolling.'

Ellen prised her head away from the window and

smiled at Jo-Jo. She caught Matthew's eye in the mirror. 'You can always come and see us again – you're more than welcome.'

Jo-Jo smiled. 'Tell you what, I'll come back for your wedding.'

Simon laughed loudly. 'I didn't know the fabulously wealthy Duncan had even proposed. Tell me more, Mum.'

'He hasn't,' she said, 'and I think you've all got hold of the wrong end of the stick. Duncan hasn't asked me to marry him. Okay?' She put her head back where it had been against the window and stared dejectedly out at the lacklustre terraced houses that now lined both sides of the road as they entered the city of Sheffield.

'Yet,' said Simon, with a laugh.

Ellen didn't respond. Her mood was as dark and as joyless as the streets they were passing through.

Mrs Clarke had been waiting for them since nine o'clock that morning. She looked hopeless and exhausted, red-eyed and taut with nervous anxiety, her arms as tightly wrapped around her wire-thin body as if they were a strait-jacket. The air in the sitting room was blue and thick with smoke and an ashtray on the coffee table in front of the sofa was almost buried beneath a pile of ash and half-smoked stubbed-out cigarettes. There was no welcome hug for her daughter, no sign that her only child had even been missed. Ellen wanted to snatch Jo-Jo away. She wanted to bundle her into the car and drive her back to Crantsford. This woman didn't deserve Jo-Jo.

'I've been waiting so long for you to come,' Mrs Clarke whined.

Ellen watched the poor woman lower herself into the cushions of the Dralon-covered sofa – it was like watching a heavy wet sponge sink in the bath. Ellen moved towards the bay window that overlooked the surrounding houses and the road, where Matthew and Simon were sitting in the car. It was a good residential area made up of nineteen-thirties detached properties, each separated from its neighbour by a wide garden and a strip of driveway enabling the inhabitants to keep themselves to themselves – so that the likes of Jo-Jo and her mother could go unnoticed.

'I thought you'd be here hours ago,' Mrs Clarke complained again. 'I put the kettle on, but you never came. And I was so thirsty. I kept flicking the switch on the kettle . . . I think it's broken now.'

Ellen wanted to offer sympathy to the woman before her, but she couldn't. All she could see was a worn-down woman who was obsessed with one thing, and that was herself. So consumed was she by her own struggle with life that even the trivial – such as the making of a drink – had become an insurmountable task, way beyond her capabilities. Clearly Jo-Jo and her problems wouldn't get a look-in.

'And you didn't say anything about bringing people with you.' Mrs Clarke looked accusingly at Jo-Jo, then at Ellen and Hermione. 'You're not social workers, are you? My husband won't like it if he finds out –'

'Come on, Mum,' Jo-Jo said patiently, 'I explained everything on the phone. I'll make you a cup of coffee, shall I?'

Ellen motioned to Hermione to stay with Mrs Clarke while she escaped to the kitchen with Jo-Jo. She closed the door behind them. 'Jo-Jo,' she whispered, 'are you sure you're doing the right thing by coming back?'

Jo-Jo smiled. 'This is Mum on a good day.'

When it was time to leave, Mrs Clarke remained in the sitting room, lighting yet another cigarette. Jo-Jo led her friends to the front door. It was an awkward moment, standing there in the narrow hall. Behind them, a long thin mirror reflected their unsmiling faces.

'Come on,' said Hermione, 'we'd better get this over with.' She embraced Jo-Jo and slipped a folded ten-pound note into her hand. 'In case you feel like running away again.'

Ellen saw Jo-Jo's lips beginning to tremble and, frightened that if Jo-Jo cried so would she, she hurriedly threw her arms round the girl and hugged her tightly. 'You'll phone if there's anything you need, won't you? Promise?' She opened her bag and pulled out a phone card. 'Here, you'd better have this.'

Hermione and Ellen joined Matthew and Simon in the car. They waved goodbye, watched Jo-Jo close the front door and then drove away.

'I can't bear it,' murmured Ellen, her voice thick with emotion. 'I didn't think it would be so bad. Surely she would have been better off staying with us?' She suddenly turned on Hermione. 'It's all your fault!' she cried. 'You shouldn't have meddled.'

'Hey, Mum, that's not fair,' Simon said. 'It was Jo-Jo's decision to go home.'

'She was coerced!' she said defiantly, staring him in the eye.

Very calmly he said, 'How's that exactly?'

Ellen turned away. Deep down she knew that Simon was right. Nobody but Jo-Jo had taken the final step in deciding what she was going to do. 'I'm sorry,' she said with a sniff. She began hunting through her bag for a tissue. 'I'm behaving irrationally I suppose. Just ignore me.'

'I think it's been that kind of a day,' Matthew said quietly. He passed a tissue through to the back of the car for Ellen.

Forgetting herself she looked up and met his gaze in the mirror. 'Thank you,' she mumbled, then hid her face in the tissue.

'And the worst of it,' Hermione said, noting the small exchange between Ellen and Matthew, 'was that Jo-Jo's mother accused *me* of being a social worker! Imagine!'

Chapter Nineteen

Duncan parked in the office car park and wrenched on the handbrake. His mind was made up. He was going to do it. He'd been a fool to wait this long.

Late last night in his study Nadia had pushed him too far and he'd come within an inch of losing his temper with her. Their argument had started predictably enough with Nadia accusing Ellen of being nothing but a cheap gold-digger – an appalling cliché to have used – and further suggesting that he was a sitting target for such a woman.

'You know nothing about Ellen,' he'd responded calmly, 'other than what you and your gossiping friends have put together. So kindly keep your slanderous comments to yourselves.'

'But, Duncan –'

'Let me continue, I haven't finished. The very idea that you think me stupid enough to fall for such a scheme is utterly absurd. Credit me with sufficient perspicacity to recognise such a ploy!'

'Your fine words don't impress me,' she had said flatly. 'Everyone knows men are complete fools when it comes to sex. It makes them blind to what's really going on.'

He had been so annoyed that his relationship with Ellen had been debased and vulgarised in this offhand manner that he'd said, 'I think we should stop this conversation right now, before we both say things we'll regret in the morning.'

But Nadia, as ever, had been determined to have the last word and her parting shot had been, 'I should be very careful if I were you, Duncan. Sex can incite recklessness in the best of people. After all, you're the result of somebody's recklessness.'

Furious, he had leaped from his chair. But Nadia had sailed out of his study with nothing more to say. For some moments he had paced the room, expecting to be able to marshal his unruly emotions back into line, but he couldn't: he found that the confines of his study only added to the constraint he was experiencing. He had poured himself a large brandy from the decanter in the walnut bureau, opened the French windows in front of his desk and strolled out onto the terrace. Staring out into the chilly dark night sky he had tried hard to rationalise his reaction to his mother's words.

In the course of his work it was his job to use the law as a device for achieving the best possible outcome for his client; to this end he had to scrutinise, analyse and double-check everything pertaining to that case. To be a good solicitor one had to be highly attuned to motives and hidden agendas, and he considered himself to be as proficient at this as anyone could be. But at analysing his own behavioural patterns he was a non-starter. Introspection had never appealed: in his opinion, self-analysis could only be flawed. But right then, in that moment beneath the dark night sky, the question had to be asked, and answered: Why was he so furious?

The level of his anger was deplorable and disgraceful, and way beyond anything he had previously dealt with. He'd long since discovered the art of untangling himself from Nadia's grip of protection and arming himself against her possessiveness, but she'd caught him with his guard down. Never before had she referred to his illegitimacy in so cruel a fashion and her words had struck a blow so hard that he had been within an inch of striking her.

Even admitting the thought had filled him with horror. He had gone back inside the house, into his study, and had locked the French windows, knowing it was time for him to act.

And now, the following morning, he let himself into the office, fully prepared to. He was first to arrive, as he was most days. At this time in the morning the rest of the partners were either wiping regurgitated lumps of baby food off their ties or were caught up in the school run – an activity which was made to sound like an Olympic event when they finally made it into the office.

In comparison his own life seemed infinitely more agreeable, with the prospect of it becoming even more so. He picked up the mail from the mat and took it through to his office, where he placed the pile to one side of his tidy desk. Taking his fountain pen from his breast pocket, he sat down and pulled a pad of paper towards him. He began to write a list. First he wrote, *Visit florist*, followed by, *Woodward's the Jeweller's*. He was about to replace the cap on his pen when he hesitated. After a few seconds he began writing again: *Travel Agent's*. Well, why not? If a job was worth doing, it was worth doing properly.

Ellen still hadn't managed to shake off her gloomy mood from yesterday. She couldn't rid herself of the picture of poor Jo-Jo's face as they'd said goodbye. Jo-Jo deserved better.

The sound of an approaching car interrupted her

thoughts. At first she thought it might be Simon but then remembered that his old Fiat made far more noise and, anyway, he'd said at breakfast he wouldn't be back until late and it was only one o'clock. Curiosity and the desire to sell something worthwhile made her want to peer out of the window to weigh up the potential customer, but knowing that there was nothing worse than an over-keen salesperson, she carried on organising the display of garlands she'd finished making late last night.

Even when the door opened she played it cool – *one two three, give them time to wait for me* – and only when she heard the sound of the door closing did she turn round with her best smile in place.

'Duncan!'

He came towards her at a surprising speed, managing in his haste to kick over a large basket in front of the main display area. 'Ellen,' he said, quickly settling the basket back into its correct position, 'I'm not a man given over to acts of impetuosity, but I want you to come with me. Now.'

'Now?' she repeated, astonished. This was not the Duncan she knew. 'Why, what's happened?'

'Please. Just lock up and I'll explain in the car.'

'Heavens, Duncan, if this isn't impetuous I don't know what is.' She flipped the Closed sign over, turned the key in the lock and hurried after Duncan, who was already standing by his car holding the door open for her.

He drove fast and in complete silence, ignoring all her questions. She sensed that he was nervous. When he brought the car to a halt in a quiet picnic spot he unbuckled his seat belt. 'I want you to close your eyes,' was all he said.

She wanted to laugh. It was all so bizarre. 'You're not

trying to kidnap me, are you?' she called to him, as he got out and went round to the boot.

Still he didn't answer her. 'Don't open your eyes, not until I say so. I've got something for you.'

She did as she was told, but recalled Roger's words one night in bed. '*Close your eyes, I've got something for you.*' He'd disappeared out of the bedroom and when she'd been allowed to look she'd seen, just inches away from her face, two beady eyes staring at her through a terrifying black-leather mask. She'd screamed and leaped out of the bed and almost knocked herself unconscious tripping over a pair of shoes and banging her head on the dressing table. Playful eroticism, Roger had called it. Downright lethal, she'd described it, coming home from Casualty in the early hours of the morning with concussion and a couple of stitches to boot.

'There,' said Duncan. 'Now you can open them.'

She did. On her lap was the largest bouquet of red roses she'd ever seen. It was so large she could barely see over the top of the flowers. 'Duncan, they're beautiful.' She breathed in deeply, hoping the roses would smell. They did. The fragrance was heavenly, sweet and redolent of a perfect summer's day. 'They're wonderful,' she said.

'And so are you.' He slipped his hand into his pocket and pulled out a small square box. 'Ellen,' he said, his expression suddenly earnest, 'I . . . I want you to marry me.' He slowly opened the box and, like the roses, the ring was exquisite. 'Shall we see if it fits?'

Ellen was in shock. It had happened. It had *really* happened. Duncan had proposed. He had actually asked her to marry him. Oh, how she had hoped for this moment, and oh, how much mental effort she had put into rehearsing him till he was word perfect. It was too good to be true.

You're right, whispered a voice in her head, *it is too good to be true. And the sad truth is, you're not worthy to be this man's wife because you've planned it all along. And you can't plan love.*

She chewed her lip and squeezed her eyes shut. This was not what she wanted to hear.

'Ellen? Are you all right?'

She opened her eyes. 'Oh, Duncan,' she said, 'I don't know what to say. I . . .'

'Say yes. It's as simple as that.'

You're not worthy of him, hissed the voice in her head.

'Yes, I am!'

Duncan's solemn face broke into a tentative smile. 'Is that yes, you will marry me?'

'No! I mean, oh . . .' What was she doing? Of course she wanted to marry him. So why the hell was she letting some imaginary smooth-talking voice, otherwise known as her guilty conscience, push her around like this? She took a deep breath. 'Oh, Duncan,' she said, hoping to appease her high-minded conscience, 'you deserve someone so much better than me.'

Well, it's a start, but how about telling him the truth, eh? We could open with how attractive his bank balance is and then casually throw in yesterday's soap-opera scene when you were snogging a complete stranger among the rocks and boulders while supposedly admiring the view!

'Ellen. This is the first time I've ever proposed to anyone. Am I to understand that there's a level of prevarication to get through before I have my answer?'

His voice was bordering on the stern and had the immediate effect of stirring Ellen into action. Without giving another thought to the pestering of her inner voice, she waved it *adios* and said, 'Duncan, of course I'll marry you. Just name the day!' She reached out to kiss him, but he smiled and gently pushed her away.

'I'm not finished yet,' he said. He leaned through to the back of the car and picked up a large envelope from the seat. He handed it to her. 'I thought a honeymoon in Florence might be fun.'

She gazed ecstatically at the brochure. 'You've thought of everything, haven't you?'

'That's the kind of man I am – but, then, you knew that already. Now where's that kiss?'

They drove back to the barn at a less reckless speed. Ellen presumed Duncan's nerves were now fully restored to their usual composure, but hers were not. She felt sick and she was trembling inside with the sheer unadulterated excitement of what lay ahead.

She glanced down at the roses and beautiful ring Duncan had chosen for her and thought again how organised and methodical he was. She smiled. How wonderful he was, and how wonderful her life would be from now on. No more dried flowers! No more cheap broken biscuits! No more tiny damp cottage! No more worries! Oh, what joy!

'Where shall we live?' she blurted out, having just pictured them flying back from their honeymoon and trying to squeeze Duncan and all his belongings into Spring Bank Cottage.

'I thought initially we'd live at Crantsford Hall,' he said, parking the car alongside Johnny Foreigner. They both looked up at the tiny cottage. 'I thought you might like that,' he added.

He was right. Oh, boy, he was right! She leaned across and kissed him.

'It is okay, isn't it? I mean . . . I know Nadia can be a bit much, but there's plenty of room for us all until we find a place of our own.'

She kissed him again. 'It'll be fine, don't worry. By the way, how does Nadia feel about me becoming her daughter-in-law?'

His expression changed. 'Ah –'

'Duncan?'

'I wanted you to be the first to know,' he said, quite reasonably. 'But why don't you come over tonight for a drink and we'll tell her together?'

'Good idea. Oh, but I can't. I've been invited to a party – and by, of all people, the Buchanans who bought Orchard House.'

'Well, ring them up and tell them you can't come. But don't say why. I don't want everyone else knowing before we've told Nadia.'

She frowned. 'But I've sort of promised. She wants me to do an arrangement for the sitting room and I need to see –'

'Darling,' Duncan said, patting her hand, 'you don't have to worry about all of that now. Once we're married you can give up toiling away here. Now, out you get. I must get on, I've a client in half an hour.'

Ellen smiled and opened the car door. 'Poor you,' she said. 'Another ghastly divorce to get through.'

'Now don't forget, ring this Buchanan woman and put her off, and I'll see you tonight at eight.'

She watched Duncan turn the car round. She waved goodbye, unlocked the barn door and went inside. She placed the roses on the work-bench and rushed to the phone, not to ring Susie Buchanan, but Hermione. She wanted to tell Hermione the news. She squeezed the receiver tightly in her hand, willing her friend to answer it, but it kept on ringing. She waited for what seemed an age before accepting that Hermione was probably pottering in the greenhouse and would no more hear the phone that far away from the house than she would notice if it was burning down.

Disappointed, she replaced the receiver, then remembered she was supposed to be ringing Susie Buchanan. But how stupid, she didn't have the number. Oh, well, she'd close the barn for the rest of the day and call round. What did a few lost customers mean now?

Susie was on the telephone and emptying the dishwasher at the same time. 'I don't know if he'll come, Janey,' she whispered into the portable phone. 'He's a bit Heathcliffy. You know, impossibly grumpy one minute as though I've just said completely the wrong thing and at other times he can be quite charming. I think he's got a soft spot for Millie, though. Anyway, must dash, I'm up to my elbows in sun-dried tomatoes. See you tonight, 'byee. And don't worry, of course I'll introduce you.'

She put down the phone and tiptoed through to the conservatory, which was now bereft of all its muslin drapes, plants and furniture. She could see Matthew bent over a selection of photographs and a large piece of paper with a roughly drawn sketch of what was going to be their family mural.

'Cup of coffee?' she offered. He didn't hear her. 'Coffee?' she repeated, this time louder. Still he didn't hear. She rolled her eyes and wondered why she'd just spent ten minutes whispering into the phone to Janey about a man who couldn't hear her voice when she was only a few feet away from him. She turned to leave him to it.

'Thank you,' he said, raising his head from the large piece of paper, 'that would be great.'

'How's it going?' she asked, venturing a little nearer. She had hoped for at least a few daubs of paint to be on the wall in time for the party that night, but as yet all there was to show for his work were a few pencilled outlines that bore little relation to anyone she knew, let alone her nearest and dearest.

'Okay.'

'And have you thought any more about coming tonight? I've got lots of people dying to meet you.'

He shook his head. 'I really don't think –' he started to say but was interrupted by the sound of the doorbell. Susie excused herself.

Matthew returned to the safety of his work, preferring to keep as low a profile as he could if this was another of Susie's many friends who was *simply dying* to meet him. So far there'd been three who'd been at death's door. He could hear Susie's voice out in the hall. 'Come on in,' she was saying, 'no, not interrupting at all. Stay and have a chat and I'll put the kettle on.'

Through the open door of the conservatory he saw Susie ushering her guest into the kitchen and immediately he picked up his pencil and climbed up the step-ladder against the wall he was working on.

'As you can see, we've barely touched the kitchen,' he could hear Susie saying, 'so I suppose it looks much the same as when you lived here.'

He stopped what he was doing. Hadn't Hermione said that Ellen had been the previous owner? He turned his head slightly and saw Ellen with her back to him. Funny, he hadn't got her down as Susie's type.

'I won't stop long,' he heard Ellen say. 'I'm afraid I've come to apologise. I can't make it tonight, after all.'

'Oh, that's too bad,' Susie said, disappointed, but added good-naturedly, 'have you had a better offer?'

Ellen laughed. 'You could say.'

'Oh, do tell. And if it's really good you'll be excused.'

Ellen hesitated. Duncan had asked her not to say anything, but ... oh, but nothing, she had to tell somebody. You couldn't keep something like this a secret. 'Actually I'm getting married.'

'What, tonight?'

A crash, followed by a stifled cry, had Susie and Ellen rushing to the conservatory. They found Matthew lying on the floor among the step-ladders.

'Hi,' he said, slowly getting to his feet and rubbing himself down. 'So you finally got him to propose, did you? Congratulations.'

'How long have you known him?' Susie whispered, when they were back in the kitchen making coffee, having been reassured by Matthew that there were no broken bones and that he'd survived worse accidents. 'Matthew, that is.'

'Only since yesterday, though I've heard Hermione talk about him occasionally.'

'What do you make of him? No, don't answer me now, let me take his coffee to him while you go through to the sitting room, it's the second door on the ... Oh, but you know that, don't you? How silly of me.'

Ellen smiled and wandered out to the hall of what had once been her dream home. She let herself into the sitting room and braced herself. This room had been her favourite: south-facing with a wide door opening onto a patio and a landscaped terraced garden. She went over to look at the garden. She had spent weeks planting out hundreds of spring bulbs in the first few months of living in the house and she could see how Susie was reaping the benefits of her hard work. But there were tulips as well now, in neat small wooden barrels on the patio. She'd never liked tulips, they were too orderly and precise for her taste.

Turning away from the garden she felt pleasantly surprised at her reaction on being back in Orchard House. There was a marked absence of sadness or pain, no sense of regret, no thoughts of petty jealousy. It was easy to figure out why. She was on the verge of becoming Mrs Duncan Carter and her future sparkled as brightly as the diamonds on her finger.

Susie came into the room and found Ellen standing by the patio door, holding her left hand up to the light. 'May I see?' she asked, placing the tray of coffee on a polished table and coming over.

Ellen showed her.

Susie was impressed. 'How *sweet*. Now, tell me all about this divine man you're going to marry. What's his name?'

Ellen told her.

'Duncan Carter!' exclaimed Susie. 'As in Church Walk Mews Solicitors?'

'Yes, that's him. Do you know Duncan?'

'Oh, yes. Well, know of him in truth. Clever old you to have snapped him up. Sugar?'

Ellen shook her head and took the proffered cup and saucer. 'So how do you know of Duncan?'

'The mother of one of Floss's friends at school works with him. We had dinner with her and her husband just the other night and she was joking that there weren't many men left in the world like Duncan. He comes highly recommended, if you believe everything Miriam says.

Apparently the dumped wives absolutely flock to the office for his charming desk-side manner. Miriam says that for years they've joked that the reason he's never married is that he's been waiting for the perfect woman to walk through his office door. Gosh, just think where that leaves you – Mrs Perfect! How awesome.'

'I don't think it's a matter of me being perfect –'

'I think you'll find it is. Biscuit? Not home-made, I'm afraid, but the next best thing, Marks and Spencer's.' She passed Ellen a plate of shortbread and a pretty napkin. 'All I can say is that I'm only too grateful I don't have to live up to any expectations like that,' Susie continued. 'When Bonkers proposed to me he knew exactly what he was getting into. "Darling," I told him, "what you see, is what you get." He knew right from the start there were no hidden extras. More coffee?'

Ellen held out her cup and hoped that another piece of shortbread was in the offing. She couldn't remember the last time she'd bought biscuits from Marks and Spencer.

'Please, help yourself,' Susie said, pouring the coffee from a cafetière, 'you mustn't stand on ceremony here. Just make yourself at home . . .' She lowered the coffee pot and covered her mouth with her hand. 'Oh, I'm terribly sorry,' she said. 'I keep putting my foot in it, don't I? What must you think of me?'

'Don't worry,' Ellen laughed kindly. 'It doesn't bother me. This is your house now. You must forget I ever lived here.' How easy it was to be magnanimous when all was right with the world!

'Oh, but I could slap myself for my stupidity.'

'Well, don't, you've done nothing to hurt my feelings. And, anyway, it's me who should be apologising for letting you down tonight.'

'Are you sure you can't come?'

'Duncan wants me with him when he tells Nadia about our engagement.'

'I bet he does! Oh, there I go again. Me and my big mouth.'

Ellen smiled. Whoever this Miriam was, she had the greater part of Duncan's private life pretty well sewn up.

'I'm afraid I've said too much,' Susie apologised. She nibbled on a sliver of shortbread in silence for a few moments. Then she smiled. 'I tell you what, why don't you and Duncan come here after you've been to see his mother? Do say yes, it'll be such fun to see you both. And you can tell Duncan that Miriam will be here, so at least there'll be one guest he'll know.'

Ellen hesitated. Maybe it wasn't such a bad idea. That way she and Duncan wouldn't have to hang around Crantsford Hall after they'd broken the news to Nadia, especially if she took it the way Ellen suspected she might. 'Okay,' she said. 'I'll ask Duncan and see what he says.'

'Wonderful! Now all I've got to do is convince Matthew to come.' She inclined her head towards the hall and conservatory beyond. 'Bonkers's sister, Janey, is coming tonight and she's absolutely *dying* to meet him.' She lowered her voice. 'She's on the prowl for a mate ... been on her own for too long ... if you know what I mean. She's a lovely girl, just a bit highly strung. I think they'd hit it off marvellously well, if only I could get him to accept the invitation.'

'I'm sure you're right,' Ellen said, thinking that she wouldn't mind witnessing the spectacle of Matthew being chased around Orchard House by the frustrated Janey! An idea occurred to her. 'If you really want him to come, invite Hermione to the party. That way I'd put money on Matthew turning up to keep her company.' Ah! That

179

would teach him not to use that sarky tone of voice with her again – *So you finally got him to propose, did you? Ah!*

'Ellen, you're an absolute marvel. How clever you are. Now what about my flower arrangement? Shall we sort that out now, rather than later? That way tonight will be all pleasure for you and no business.'

It certainly will, thought Ellen.

Chapter Twenty

Hermione was enjoying herself. When Bernie had popped his head through the *leylandii* hedge earlier that morning and asked if she was on for a spot of ravishing, she'd told him to come back after lunch by which time she would have finished cleaning out the water butt.

There'd been no ravishing but they'd drunk nearly the entire contents of a delightful bottle of claret Bernie had brought with him. They were sitting in the greenhouse and Bernie was telling her another of his colourful stories. She couldn't recall anyone ever telling her such lurid jokes. Her background was old school, which meant that when she'd grown up young ladies such as herself were warned about the likes of Bernie Malloy. Her headmistress had repeatedly instructed Hermione and her classmates on the perils of the bantam cock who with his crowing and fine feathers would familiarise himself with their *bodily functions* and as a consequence send them all to hell. It was a confusing message, and it was years before Hermione realised that she needn't be afraid of farmyards.

Things didn't improve much, even when she married Arthur – the *bodily functions* were explored, but they weren't up for discussion. Arthur was very clear on that point. Perhaps if they had talked more they might have managed to produce at least one child. As it was, she miscarried so many times that poor Arthur grew terrified of even touching her. He was so formal, so paralysed by his inbred chivalry that he practically asked her permission before he kissed her goodnight.

They had met at a difficult time in both their lives, indeed it was a difficult time for the entire country. Britain was at war and Hermione's parents had recently died in a car accident ... and Roberta had married Kit.

After her parents' funeral, the family solicitor, a dandy of a man with a penchant for hats and cigars, explained to Hermione that her father had made several unsound investments during the past five years and, while not wishing to cause alarm, he wanted to advise her that there were sufficient funds for her to live off for the next few years if she was careful, but ultimately his professional advice was to sell Laburnum House. 'Either that or marry someone exceedingly wealthy,' he'd joked. With equal humour, even at so young an age – she was only twenty-two – she had asked him how much money he earned and would he be interested in applying for the position of her husband?

Very politely, he had declined.

Later that year, and in response to Ernest Bevan urging the female population of the country to join in with the war effort, Hermione started work in a silk factory that had been given over to producing woven cloth for parachutes. It was while she was 'doing her bit' that she had met Arthur. As a child he had suffered prolonged bouts of tuberculosis and, declared unfit to fight for King and country, he had been forced to remain at home and help his father run the family business. Hermione first noticed him when he had been staring at her through the glass window of his office, which overlooked the factory line. She had smiled at him and the following night he had emerged from his office and pretended to inspect the loom she was operating. They were married within six months and were as content as most young couples living through the fear and hardship of a war.

But Hermione had always felt as though she'd cheated Arthur: not only had she been unable to give him the son he desired but, worse, she hadn't loved him as she should have. He was a kind, decent man who had willingly solved her financial difficulties and had insisted they live where she was happiest, which was, of course, Laburnum House. He died of pneumonia, not long after his fiftieth birthday, and she suspected that he had passed away knowing that there had been a part of her that she had deliberately withheld from him. Only a small part, mind.

Her heart.

'You've got that look in your eye again, haven't you, my little Hermaseta? You're thinking, I wish that Bernie would shut up and make with the foreplay.'

'If you really want to know, I was wondering what the poor doddery folk at the Lodge make of you,' she lied.

He poured the rest of the wine into her glass and laughed. 'You reckon I don't fit in with them, don't you? That I'm not lah-di-dah enough. That it?'

'Frankly, yes, that's exactly what I think.'

He laughed again, so much so that his large round belly wobbled over the top of his trousers, but his chest got the better of him and he coughed loudly, then spluttered to catch his breath. He didn't sound at all well and Hermione was reminded again of Arthur. She wondered just how ill Bernie really was.

'It's the sex that does it,' he wheezed, reaching into his jacket pocket. He pulled out an inhaler and held it to his mouth. 'Three times a day is too much I keep telling them, but they won't listen.'

'Oh, shut up, you silly old sod.'

'Hermaseta, my little sweet,' he said, when at last he'd caught his breath, 'I'm shocked. Such language, and from one who considers me too vulgar to be socially acceptable.'

'You haven't answered my question,' she said, ignoring his look of mock horror. 'How do they view you next door?'

'How I've always been viewed.'

'Which is?'

'They throw themselves at me.'

Hermione gave up. 'Does anyone ever get any sense out of you?'

'Not if I can help it. Now, why don't you ask me some less serious questions?'

'Like what exactly?'

'Like, what shall we do tonight?'

'That's easy. While I'm enjoying an evening with Matthew, you'll be forced into eating puréed carrots before being strapped into your plastic-covered chair in the communal lounge to watch a television screen with the sound up too loud.'

He started to laugh again.

'No. Don't laugh any more,' she said. 'I don't want you dying in my greenhouse.'

'For your information,' he said, 'tonight I was planning on having prawn roulade followed by noisettes of lamb and a crème caramel to finish up with. And after dinner I had in mind a game or two of snooker. There are plastic chairs but they're out on the terrace and to my knowledge they don't have straps.'

Hermione humphed and stared at him beneath her hooded eyelids. 'Bully for you,' she said quietly.

'On the other hand, you could join me. We're allowed guests.'

'What? And give you the opportunity to show me off as some new piece of totty?'

He slapped his forehead with the palm of his hand. 'Heavens to Betsy, I've been rumbled!'

'Come on,' she said, 'let's go up to the house. I'm in need of a cup of tea – that red wine's completely dried me out.'

When they reached the garden room they met Ellen coming into the small courtyard. Hermione took one look at the expression on Ellen's face and knew what her friend had come to tell her. But instead of being delighted for her, she felt her heart sink. She suddenly had no desire for Ellen to get married, because if she did, it would mean having to share her. Or, worse still, Duncan would monopolise her to the extent that Ellen would have no time for her old friend. Appalled at her selfishness, she hurriedly introduced Bernie and led the way inside.

'Well,' she said, when she knew she had to listen to Ellen's news, 'I can see from that ridiculous smile on your face that you've got something to tell me.'

Ellen didn't speak, but she held out her hand.

Hermione whistled and Bernie leaned forward to take a look as well.

'Bernie,' Hermione said sternly, 'I suggest you keep your mouth closed while Ellen's here. She won't want to hear any of your dirty jokes, not now that she's going to be moving up in the world. She's marrying money, and lots of it.'

'Congratulations,' Bernie said, 'you're a woman after my own heart. Marrying for money is the only way to true happiness, in my opinion.'

'I'm not marrying for money,' Ellen protested. Why

did Hermione have to keep telling people that she was? She wished she'd never confided in her now. 'Duncan's a lovely man,' she continued, 'he's –'

'I'm sure he is,' Bernie cut in, 'but I bet the old oncers make him even lovelier!'

Hermione and Bernie laughed complicitly. Ellen felt annoyed and left out. She wished she hadn't come now. She refused a drink and went home to put Duncan's roses in water.

Susie tiptoed into the conservatory.

'I'm just popping out,' she said to Matthew. 'The girls are in the playroom – could you be a real sweetie and listen out for them while I'm gone? I'll be less than two ticks.' She didn't wait for a reply.

As soon as the front door closed Floss appeared in the conservatory with Millie in tow. For several minutes they stood and stared up at Matthew. From the top of the ladder he stared back at them. He tried a smile but their faces remained blank. 'No school?' he asked.

'We're still on holiday,' Little Miss Shrewd Eyes informed him, and in a tone of voice that suggested he should know this. 'We go back on Monday. You haven't done very much, have you? Dad says you'd better make a good job of it or he'll make you do it again.'

Matthew came down the ladder and moved it along a few feet. 'And I suppose your father considers himself an expert,' he muttered under his breath.

'Dad's a special kind of doctor,' Little Miss Shrewd Eyes continued.

'Yes, I know,' Matthew said, climbing back up the ladder.

'Do you know what he does?'

'I think so.'

'What, then?'

Matthew gripped his pencil and wondered how much longer Susie would be.

'Shall I tell you?'

'Do I have a choice?'

'He looks up ladies' bottoms.'

'A fascinating job in anyone's book. Isn't there anything on the television you want to watch?'

'We're only allowed to watch the television if Mum says we can. She's very strict like that.'

Not strict enough, in Matthew's opinion. 'What about your music practice?' he asked, anxious to be left alone. 'Have you done that yet?'

Floss considered this. 'Okay,' she said. And as though a satisfactory agreement had been reached she turned and left the conservatory.

Millie remained where she was. She took a step closer to the wall Matthew was working on.

'This is me, isn't it?' she said quietly, pointing to a sketched outline of a girl holding a toy rabbit in her hands.

'Yes,' Matthew answered. He came and stood beside her. 'Do you like it?'

Her small serious face looked up at him, her eyes large and solemn. 'Yes,' she nodded, 'I really like the way you've drawn Bobtail. Could you do him on a piece of paper for me? Please.'

He smiled and said he would. From the hall the unmistakable sound of 'The Emperor's March' filled the house. Matthew wondered again how much longer their mother would be.

Susie was delighted. Hermione had accepted the invitation and was bringing with her that jolly man who had been in the kitchen when she'd arrived at Laburnum House. She didn't know what Bonkers would say to all these extra guests, but he would think it was worth it if they could get poor old Janey fixed up. She just had to hope that Ellen had been right when she'd said that if Hermione was invited Matthew would agree to come.

Chapter Twenty-One

Duncan glanced at his watch.

She was late. She had never been late before, so why now, and on such an important night? He'd told her in the car to be here at eight, there could have been no confusion. Even on the phone earlier when she had called to say that they'd both been invited to the Buchanans' he had reminded her what time to arrive.

His bedroom overlooked the lawn that straddled the long strip of driveway. He went over to the small leaded window, lifted the latch, leaned out and watched for Ellen's car headlamps. But there was no sign of her. He shut the window, went over to the mahogany wardrobe and inspected himself in the mirror. He pulled at his tie, trying to straighten it, then noticed a tiny stain in the silk fabric. He yanked it off, threw it on the floor and opened the wardrobe to choose another. Lifting his shirt collar he slipped the replacement tie round his neck and carefully began to knot it.

There were to be no hitches tonight. Everything had to be exactly right.

So where the hell was Ellen?

The sooner she came, the sooner they could get this over and done with.

Downstairs in her sitting room Nadia was pouring

herself a glass of Croft's pale cream sherry from the tray on the Pembroke table behind the sofa.

'Cheers,' she said, raising her glass to her reflection in the gilt-framed mirror above the mantelpiece. She drained the glass in one and poured herself another.

In a strange way she was looking forward to the evening. 'I've invited Ellen for a drink tonight,' Duncan had told her on the phone late that afternoon, calling from his office. 'I thought it would make a pleasant evening, just the three of us,' he'd added.

She raised her glass and scoffed at the idea. Pleasant for whom?

Ellen was about to leave the house when the phone rang.

'Hi, Ellen, it's me, Jo-Jo.'

'Everything's all right, isn't it?' Ellen asked, immediately concerned, her mind flitting through a list of atrocities that might have happened to Jo-Jo since yesterday, and before Jo-Jo even had a chance to reply, Ellen had the step-father banged to rights.

'Yeah, don't worry. I'm fine, apart from being treated as a social leper by you-know-who, but I'm managing pretty well to keep out of his way.'

'And your mother? How are you coping with her?'

'The same as ever.'

'How about seeing a doctor? Have you arranged an appointment yet?'

'Way ahead of you. I had an antenatal check-up today and I'm seeing someone at an adoption agency in a couple of weeks' time. I start back at school on Monday. I can't say I'm looking forward to seeing Alan again.'

'Don't give him a thought,' Ellen told her. 'Just think about yourself. Now, take care. I've got to dash, I'm seeing Duncan and I'm already late. Oh, Simon's just walked in, do you want a word?'

She passed the phone to her son, mouthed to him that she'd see him later, grabbed her bag and rushed out of the cottage, nearly missing her footing in the dark as she hurried over to Johnny Foreigner. She drove like the wind, at the same time skidding some lipstick across her lips and smoothing down her hair. Twenty minutes late, she turned into the cobbled drive of Crantsford Hall. She'd never been late for Duncan before and, given the importance of the evening, this was probably the one time when he wouldn't make allowances for her. This thought did nothing to calm her already lurching stomach.

It had been easy to say to Duncan, in the excitement of the moment earlier that afternoon, that it would be fine living with La Carter, but there was no doubt in her mind that in reality it would be quite the opposite – a padded cell and a strait-jacket held more appeal right now. She parked Johnny Foreigner alongside Duncan's BMW and gazed up at the house.

In the dark, Crantsford Hall seemed large, looming, sinister and not at all welcoming as it had in the sunshine on Good Friday. A flicker of movement at a window on the first floor of the house caught her eye. She smiled. The situation was fast becoming a scene out of a Gothic novel: any minute now Duncan would appear in riding breeches surrounded by a pack of snarling dogs, with a wild, haunted look on his face.

She was just locking the car when the front door opened, spilling light across to where she stood.

'What happened? I was worried.'

'I'm sorry, Duncan,' she said, hurrying over to him. 'The phone rang just as I was –'

'Oh, well, never mind all that. At least you're here now. Come on inside and let's get this over with.'

So, Duncan was as nervous as she was. But instead of feeling comforted by this, Ellen was disappointed. Following him up the steps and into the house she felt let down – her lion-hearted Sir Galahad wasn't supposed to be frightened of his mother.

When Ellen and Duncan came into the room Nadia didn't bother getting up from her chair. This was her house and she would do as she pleased.

'Ellen,' she said, 'how good to see you again. This is the third time in just over a week.'

Ellen laughed and, settling in for a sparring session, began, 'Yes, it's as if I'm part of the family, isn't it?'

Duncan rattled his throat and Nadia looked on stonily. She shot a glance at Duncan. 'Another sherry for me and I'm sure you'll know what Ellen's tipple is.'

'White wine?' he offered.

If she didn't feel so sorry for Duncan being caught in the crossfire she'd ask for a cocktail, something outrageous and along the lines of a Long Hard Screw, but it was an old joke and she thought better of it. 'White wine would be fine,' she answered decorously, and as no one asked her to sit down she stood awkwardly by a handsome satinwood secretaire, ornately decorated with large marquetry flowers. She examined it for a few seconds then watched Duncan pour the drinks.

The room was silent and, in Ellen's opinion, looked as if it had been pre-set. The only light was cast from two lamps placed either side of Nadia in the corner where she was sitting: it was as if she was meant to be the focal point. If this was the case, it was working a treat. There was no avoiding the incredible big-boned hulk.

Duncan handed Nadia her sherry and then came over to Ellen. 'Please,' he said, 'sit down.'

They perched on a sofa together, directly opposite Nadia who had already finished her sherry. Like a fish, thought Ellen, watching Nadia place the empty glass on the table beside her.

'Well, this is *pleasant*,' Nadia said, her tone implying that it was anything but. 'We should do this more often, but Duncan has so little time for socialising. I pity the poor woman who ever marries him.' She laughed without humour. 'She'd see precious little of him, what with the hours he works, and then there's the golf course that takes up so much of his weekends. No. It would have to be a very stupid woman willing to put up with that, don't you think, Ellen?'

'A patient and understanding woman, perhaps,' Ellen said with a smile, willing Duncan to take his cue. Come on, Duncan, she wanted to say, get on and tell the wicked old witch!

'I think you're exaggerating, Mother,' Duncan said quietly, leaning back, crossing his legs and turning the stem of his wine glass round in his fingers. 'I don't work absurdly long hours and on average I play just one game of golf a week.'

Nadia waved aside his words with a huge hand. 'Whatever you say. Another drink, Ellen?'

Ellen had barely touched her wine – her stomach wasn't up to it. 'No, thank you,' she said politely.

'I think I'll have another sherry,' Nadia said. She looked pointedly at Duncan but he made no move. 'I said, I think I'll –'

Reluctantly he got to his feet.

Nadia frowned when he handed her glass to her. 'Are we on short measures tonight?' she asked. He topped up the glass and Ellen was sure she heard him muttering to himself.

'Duncan, you can be so churlish when you want to be,' Nadia scolded, as he stood beside her. 'A few glasses of sherry won't do me any harm.' She held the glass to her lips and drained it in one long swig.

Ellen watched, mesmerised. She wouldn't be a bit surprised if the ghastly woman didn't drag the back of her hand across her mouth and bang the empty glass down on the table and demand another – *Line 'em up, bartender!* When this didn't happen, Ellen shifted her gaze to Duncan. She was alarmed at what she saw. His whole body had turned rigid with fury, his jaw was tightly clenched in a grim, hard line and a muscle at his temple was ticking worryingly.

This was no way to announce an engagement, thought Ellen. What they needed was a diversion.

She let her glass slip between her fingers. 'Oh, I'm so sorry!' she cried. 'How careless of me.'

'Duncan, fetch a cloth,' Nadia ordered, not making a move herself.

Duncan didn't move either. His eyes were fixed on Nadia. 'No, not until you've heard what I've got to say.'

'The carpet, Duncan. It'll be ruined.'

'To hell with the sodding carpet!' he exploded. 'Ellen and I are getting married.'

They arrived at Orchard House to find that the only parking spaces available were further up the Crescent beyond Laburnum House. Duncan got out of the car and came round to Ellen's side. He hadn't spoken a word since they'd left Nadia gulping like a fish and reaching for another fix of Croft's pale cream.

Ellen couldn't get over La Carter and all that sherry. It

was truly the last thing in the world she had expected and it was probably a family secret that Duncan would have preferred to stay that way. She was saddened, though, that he was so ashamed of his mother's behaviour that he had been unable to share it with her.

Susie opened the door to them. She was dressed simply in a black dress that hugged her slim body perfectly.

'Ellen!' she exclaimed, her voice in party mode, high and shrill. 'You made it, and this must be the gorgeous Duncan I've heard so much about. Bad news, I'm afraid. Miriam and Charlie have cried off, little one's got a tummy bug.'

'Darling,' came a voice from another room and, above the sound of a sudden burst of laughter, 'any more bubbly? We're running low, getting through it at a terrifying rate!'

'I'm out here, sweetie. Ellen's just arrived,' Susie called back.

Bonkers appeared in the hall with an empty bottle in his hand. He was wearing a paisley silk bow tie with a matching waistcoat and a helpless look on his face. 'I can't find any more of this stuff. Where've you hidden it?'

'Don't be so rude, Bonkers. Say hello to our guests. You remember Ellen, don't you? And this is her fiancé, Duncan. You take them through to the party and I'll find some more champagne.'

Bonkers led the way to the sitting room where he unexpectedly clapped his hands together. 'Attention everyone,' he yelled, 'this is Ellen and Duncan. Be nice to them.'

Ellen wanted to slink under the nearest piece of furniture. This was just how she used to feel when as a small child she had been deposited at a birthday party. She wondered what Duncan was thinking, and when

Bonkers was called away to the other side of the room she glanced sideways at him.

He didn't look happy.

Was he still cross with Nadia or was he regretting coming here? Something told her they wouldn't be staying long. He caught her staring at him.

'How did she know we were engaged?' he asked, in a low voice.

Ellen frowned. 'I told her this afternoon . . . I didn't think you'd –'

'I told you not to tell anyone, not until we'd told Nadia.'

'I'm sorry, Duncan,' she said, taken aback at the sight of his clenched jaw again, 'I didn't think it really mattered.'

He stared at her incomprehensibly. 'Mattered,' he repeated. 'That it mattered is simply not the point.'

'Duncan, what's got into you?'

He seemed to consider this question for a moment, and then shook his head. 'You're right,' he said. 'It doesn't matter at all, and I'm sorry I snapped at you. Forgive me, darling?'

'Of course,' she said, relieved to see his face now returning to its normal composure. 'Let's get a drink and mingle, seeing as we've been left to our own devices.'

It wasn't long before Ellen recognised Janey, or a woman whom she took to be Janey. Duncan had found himself a hospital administrator to talk to and, bored with the conversation, she had wandered away and noticed a self-conscious-looking woman standing alone with an empty glass in her hand. She had a mass of dyed chestnut hair piled on top of her head with what looked like a stick pushed through it. From the way she was shifting her weight from one foot to the other she was either very nervous or desperate for the loo.

'Hello,' Ellen said, going over to her. 'Are you by any chance Susie's sister-in-law, Janey?'

'Yes,' she said, instantly on her guard, her eyes darting anxiously through several layers of mascara and eyeliner, 'how did you know?' She tried drinking from her empty glass.

'A lucky guess.' Ellen introduced herself.

'Oh, right, you're the woman Susie and Bonkers bought the house from. Nice place. What've you gone to – something even bigger and better?'

'I traded down,' Ellen replied noncommittally, and was glad when Janey didn't pursue the subject but said, 'I expect you know everyone here. Susie's told me about this gorgeous artist she's got working for her. Have you met him?'

'Yes, I have.'

'What's he like?' whispered Janey, moving in closer and wobbling slightly.

Ellen thought about this. It was a good question. Matthew Collins was really a bit of an enigma. He was strange, unlike most men she'd ever met. 'I'm afraid I don't know him well enough to say.'

'First impressions, then.'

Ellen laughed. 'Those are always dangerous.'

'But usually the best ones.'

Ellen's immediate opinion of Matthew was that he could be taciturn and brusque to the point of rudeness and that Hermione was right when she had said it was an air he affected to make himself superior. She was about to say this when she remembered his response to her suggestion that the Dark Peak was beautiful. 'I'd say he was a passionate man,' she said, 'the kind of man who when he feels something he feels it strongly.' She then recalled him kissing her for no apparent reason. 'He's also a bit on the spontaneous side.'

'He sounds a dream. Hey, we're not in competition, are we? I mean, you don't want him for yourself, do you?'

'Good grief, no.' Ellen laughed. She held up her hand. 'Look, I've just got engaged today.'

Janey admired the ring. 'It's an omen,' she said, suddenly sounding like Mystic Meg and staring into the distance. 'I can feel it. You're going to bring me luck tonight.' She tried another hopeful sip at her empty glass.

Only Hermione could make arriving at a party an event in itself, thought Ellen, when the Laburnum House trio eventually turned up. She was like the Queen Mother, standing in the hall for an age, escorted on one side by Matthew and her new neighbour Bernie on the other, as if waiting for all the guests to be lined up in front of her. She was dressed in a pastel floaty chiffon number – more echoes of the Queen Mum – and once she'd moved on from the hall she was determined to meet as many of Susie and Bonkers's friends as she could. 'Gracious,' Ellen heard her say after being introduced to yet another of Bonkers's work colleagues, 'and just how many gynaecologists have we here tonight, and is there a collective noun for such a gathering?'

'How about a handful?' suggested Bonkers, his bow tie now hanging limply round his neck like a string of sausages.

'Or a wombful,' put forward Bernie.

'Isn't that the strange woman I met at your cottage last week?' asked Duncan, coming over to join Ellen who was now on her own.

'Yes.' Ellen smiled. 'That's our Hermione, working the room like a real pro. Star quality or what?'

'But is she quite the full shilling, I find myself asking?'

'Oh, I doubt that. But she's been a wonderful friend to me since Roger left.'

He squeezed her hand. 'And now you've got me, darling.'

She leaned into him and kissed his cheek. 'So I have.'

'I'll go and get us another drink, shall I?'

Ellen watched Duncan go in search of the kitchen, where no doubt the bottles would be lined up on the granite worktops that she had spent weeks deliberating over when she had had the kitchen designed. It was strange being at a party in a house where she had once been the hostess. It was difficult not to rush about offering drinks and plates of food.

'You look deep in thought.' It was Matthew.

'Just remembering days gone by,' she said, when he came and stood beside her.

'In the circumstances, I think you're pretty brave coming here at all.'

'Not as brave as you.'

He stared at her, puzzled. 'What do you mean?'

'Oh, nothing.'

'Liar.'

'All right, I'll tell you. Susie's got someone lined up for you to meet. I've just met her. She's interesting in a –'

'Oh, hell!'

'There's always a chance you might like her.'

'Yeah, and I'm a Chinaman. Do me a favour and don't leave me alone with her.'

She laughed. 'You're a big boy, Matthew, you can look after yourself.'

He scowled. 'I bet it's the usual scenario. She's

divorced and hunting for a new husband and Susie's told her I'm single.'

'And if you stay as obnoxious and as arrogant as that you'll end up single for the rest of your life and you'll deserve what you get.'

'Enlighten me. What will I get?'

'A lonely, miserable old age.'

He laughed cynically. 'While you, Ellen, will be a happy kept woman. Oh, yes,' he carried on, seeing the look of anger on her face, 'Hermione's told me all about your little ploy to catch yourself a rich husband. You must be very pleased with yourself, though how you'll feel in a few years' time when you realise your mistake is anybody's guess. Perhaps it will be you who's lonely and miserable.'

Ellen was livid. 'I don't think there's anything else I want to say to you. Goodbye.' She started to walk away from him.

'The truth always hurts,' he called after her.

She came back. 'The truth,' she hissed at him, 'is that you don't know what you're talking about. Duncan and I love each other and we're –'

'Love! Don't make me laugh! I've met your precious Duncan just now in the kitchen and he looks no more capable of loving another person than he is of climbing Everest.'

'And I suppose you're an expert on both counts, are you?'

Matthew opened his mouth to reply but then thought of all the disastrous relationships in his life. 'I've climbed Helvellyn,' he said, with a slow lopsided smile spreading over his face.

Despite herself, Ellen couldn't help but return it.

'I'm sorry,' he said. 'I shouldn't have sounded off at

you like that. It's been one of those days. I don't find it easy working here, it's all the interruptions. Then when you said about Susie having got somebody lined up to meet me, it was the last straw.'

'Forget it,' Ellen said, her anger beginning to subside.

'Seeing as I've made one apology, there's – there's something else I should make amends for. I, um . . .' He hesitated and his eyes wavered from her face. He suddenly looked overcome with embarrassment.

Ellen guessed what was coming next and was curious to see how he was going to explain himself. 'Yes?' she said, helpfully.

He cleared his throat. 'You could try to make this easier for me.'

Ellen opened her eyes wide. 'How so?' she asked innocently. 'I don't know what you're talking about.'

'Yes, you bloody well do,' he growled. He pushed up the sleeves on his denim shirt then folded his arms across his chest and stared down at his shoes, his tall frame slightly hunched.

She smiled, touched by his awkwardness. 'Is it something to do with yesterday?'

'Well, of course it is. What else could it be to do with?'

'For someone making an apology you don't seem very penitent. Is this a new phenomenon for you?'

'Ye gods! You're the most infuriating woman I've ever met.'

'You should get out more.'

He rolled his eyes. 'Will you just shut up and let me get this over with. When I kissed you, I . . .' He unfolded his arms, pushed his hands into his jeans pockets and tried again. 'I don't know what came over me and I want you to know that I don't normally go around behaving like that.' He ran his hand over his chin and finally met her gaze. 'Is there anything I can do to make amends for what I did?'

'Yes,' she said, seeing Duncan coming towards them, 'don't mention it ever again.'

'Darling, sorry I've been so long, here's your wine. Drink up and let's get going, I'm bored with all this medical talk.'

'Matthew's not a doctor,' she said lightly. 'Try talking to him.'

Duncan gave Matthew a cursory glance. 'Have we met?'

'A few moments ago in the kitchen.'

Ellen saw the expression on Matthew's face. 'Matthew's a painter,' she said hurriedly. 'He's doing a job for Susie and Bonkers.'

'Wouldn't have thought Orchard House needed much decorating,' Duncan said.

Matthew had heard enough. 'I'll see you, Ellen.' He turned and collided with a woman who had a ridiculous bird's nest stuck on her head. 'Sorry,' he muttered, without even stopping. But she came after him.

'Matthew Collins?' she asked. 'Susie's artist?'

He froze. Was this the woman so keen to meet him? 'No,' he said, 'you've got the wrong man, I'm not Susie's anything.'

He walked out of the room and out of Orchard House.

Chapter Twenty-Two

When Ellen and Duncan went in search of Susie and Bonkers to say goodbye they found them in the kitchen with Janey who was clearly upset and hugging a box of Kleenex to her chest.

'Anything we can do?' Ellen offered hesitantly. She had witnessed the brief exchange between Matthew and Janey only a few moments ago and had also seen Janey literally disintegrate before her eyes and then stumble away in the direction of the kitchen. What *could* Matthew have said?

'Family problems are best left to those personally involved,' Duncan said, holding Ellen firmly by the arm and edging her back towards the door.

'She told me he was passionate,' came a reproach-ful voice from behind Bonkers as Ellen allowed herself to be propelled out of the kitchen. 'She said he was spontaneous.'

Remembering her manners Susie quickly followed them. 'Gosh,' she said, when they were out in the hall, 'I don't know what to say. Poor Janey, she's always been highly strung and she was so hurt when Matthew refused to talk to her. Apparently he was quite rude. I've no idea where he is now, have you?'

Ellen shook her head. 'Sorry, I haven't got a clue. Will she be all right?'

'Oh, heavens, yes. A good dose of black coffee and

she'll be as right as rain. She really shouldn't drink so much. And Bonkers is too soft with her, of course. It's as plain as the nose on my face that he needs to take a firmer line, but you know what men are like with their families – duty and the desire to hush everything up turns them into complete jelly babies every time.'

Ellen felt Duncan stiffen at her side and, conscious that Susie was unintentionally tweaking a raw nerve in him, she inched towards the front door and raised her hand. 'It's been lovely, Susie,' she said, 'but it's been a long day for us and we ought to be off. Tell Hermione I'll catch up with her tomorrow. Goodnight.'

As Duncan drove the short distance to Spring Bank Cottage, Ellen thought that the evening had been anything but lovely. Poor Duncan, he must have had an awful night. First Nadia and her coldness towards him and then a party at which he'd obviously felt out of place.

'I shan't come in,' he said, bringing the car to a stop outside the cottage and alongside Johnny Foreigner, which Ellen had left there after she'd driven back from Crantsford Hall with Duncan following behind. 'Like you said to your friend, it's been a long day.' He leaned over and pecked her lightly on the cheek. 'Goodnight, darling. I'll ring you in the morning.'

Duncan didn't go straight home – he knew exactly what would be waiting for him when he did get back. He wanted some time on his own, so he drove through Crantsford and then out onto the dual carriageway. It was late enough for there to be barely any traffic on the road. He turned up the volume on Mahler's 'Das Lied von der Erde' and pressed his foot on the accelerator. He felt the surge of the engine and his spirits lifted.

Cruising at a hundred and twenty-five he caught sight

of a flashing blue light in his rear-view mirror. He jerked his foot off the accelerator and hoped that he'd seen the police car before his speed had been registered. There was always the chance that they weren't interested in him anyway and that they were on their way to deal with something more worthwhile than his Highway Code misdemeanour.

He was wrong. The police car slowed behind him and flashed its lights for him to pull over into the nearest lay-by.

Two officers got out of the Ford Sierra and sauntered towards him. 'Good evening,' one of them said when Duncan activated the electric window; the other was already making a note of the number plate. 'I shan't insult your intelligence by asking if you were in a hurry, sir, but do you have any idea just how fast you were –?'

'Oh, spare me the niceties and just get on with it, will you?'

The two officers looked at each other. 'It'll be a pleasure.'

Matthew wasn't sure what had rattled him most – Ellen's gross stupidity or Duncan's patronising manner.

'What a complete and utter jerk!' he said out loud. 'And with more airs and graces than you could shake a stick at.'

He threw himself into an armchair in Hermione's sitting room and kicked off his shoes. 'What the hell does she see in him anyway?' He poked his finger into a hole in the heel of one of his Wallace and Gromit socks – a Christmas present from Bridget last year.

It had been a waste of an evening and it was the last time he'd allow himself to be talked into doing something he didn't want to do. He'd had enough of that with

Bridget. 'Parties are important,' she would say in the face of his apathy. 'It's how you build up an effective network; it's how you get on in life.' He would then be forced into spending a mind-numbing evening being bored to death by sharp-faced young men in city suits, ever more convinced that if there was one thing he didn't want, it was to get on in life. He would never be so stupid as to say that he was ambivalent about money because he wasn't – he'd had enough lean times in his chosen profession to appreciate the benefits of a steady income – but he could think of nothing worse than sacrificing oneself on the high altar of success and ambition for fear of being considered an also-ran.

It was crazy that he'd got involved with Bridget in the first place. It hadn't really been the age difference that had made them incompatible towards the end – she'd been twelve years younger than him – so much as the difference in their lifestyles. But he had come to realise that for Bridget that had all been part of the attraction. For a smart City girl based in London, a boyfriend who was not only an artist but who was older and lived in what she referred to as Melvyn Bragg country was as much a turn-on as a bit of rough for a middle-class housewife. He smiled at this comparison and at the knowledge that in the early stages of their relationship it had flattered his ego that someone like Bridget had been interested in him at all.

He heard the sound of laughter coming from the hall and then footsteps. Hermione came into the room, followed by Bernie. Matthew was struck by how comfortable they looked together: it was as if he had seen Hermione and Bernie come through that door a million times before.

'There you are, Matthew,' exclaimed Hermione, settling herself on the sofa and covering most of it with her chiffon dress. Bernie squeezed in next to her. 'You wouldn't believe the kerfuffle you've caused next door. What on earth did you do to the poor girl?'

Matthew shrugged. 'I don't know what you mean. She was perfectly all right when I left her. In fact, I even apologised.'

'Well, it couldn't have been much of an apology. The idiotic wretch was quite beside herself.'

'If you ask me,' joined in Bernie, 'she's a sandwich short of a loaf.' He and Hermione laughed.

Matthew was puzzled at Hermione's rudeness towards Ellen. It wasn't like her to be disloyal to those she was fond of. 'I wouldn't have expected you to describe Ellen as an idiotic wretch,' he said.

'Good heavens, we're not talking about Ellen,' exclaimed Hermione.

'Then who, for crying out loud?'

'Bonkers's sister, of course. Janey.'

'I didn't even know he had one,' Matthew said dismissively, 'and I've certainly never met her.'

'But you must have. She said you were beastly to her.'

'Then she's got the wrong man, either that or she's off her head.'

Bernie chuckled. 'My money's on the latter.'

Matthew frowned. 'Is this some kind of wind-up, or have you both been drinking too much next door?'

'Neither,' Hermione said firmly. 'In fact, Bonkers is so cross he's talking about withdrawing the commission.'

'What?' Matthew said, exasperated. He wasn't bothered about losing the work but he was bothered by what people were saying about him. 'I was there less than half an hour and the only woman I spoke to was Ellen.'

'Not a woman with lots of hair piled up on top of her head?'

'There was a woman like that,' Matthew said slowly. 'She wanted to know who I was . . .'

'And?'

'I lied. I said I wasn't Matthew Collins. But that was all. Then I came home. From the way you're talking, anyone would think I'd attacked her.'

'She'd probably have made less fuss if you had!' joked Bernie.

Matthew stood up. He pushed his hands inside his trouser pockets and hunched his shoulders. 'Well, that's her problem. I'm off to bed.'

'Time I was going as well,' said Bernie, getting to his feet.

'Yes,' yawned Hermione, 'you'd better rush back in time for Matron to tuck you into bed.'

'Now there's an idea.'

After Bernie had left, Matthew offered to lock up and bring Hermione a mug of warmed milk. He knocked on her bedroom door and went in. She was in bed with an old Aran cardigan draped over her shoulders and she was brushing her long white hair. He was so used to seeing it pinned up on her head that he was surprised at how long it really was. She looked older, though, and slightly diminished, not the Hermione he knew.

'You're staring at me,' she said, putting the brush on the bedside table and taking the mug from him.

'Sorry.' He sat on the edge of her bed.

'Something on your mind?' she asked.

'No, not especially.'

'You sure?'

'Drink your milk and mind your own business.'

208

She raised the mug to her lips and stared at him over the rim. 'So what did you apologise to Ellen for?'

He stood up and walked over to the chest of drawers opposite the bed. It was covered in bits and bobs of cheap jewellery and old pots of cream and powder. A thick layer of dust dulled everything to the same peppery hue, except for the necklace Hermione had been wearing for the party. He picked up the string of amber beads. It had been a present to her from his father and she usually kept it hidden in a drawer because, as she had told him years ago, it was the only thing in the house of any real value – sentimental value, that was. He had teased her at the time that she thought so little of his paintings at Laburnum House.

'Did it have anything to do with you kissing Ellen during the picnic?' Hermione asked, catching his eye in the mirror above the chest of drawers.

This was the first time Hermione had referred to what she'd seen through her binoculars and the wonder was that it had taken her this long to get round to quizzing him. He came back to the bed and sat down.

'Maybe,' he said.

She humphed. 'And what's that supposed to mean?'

'I said some other things to her as well . . . I think I went too far.'

They gazed at each other for a moment. 'Well, go on, then,' Hermione said. 'Tell me what you said or I shall never sleep tonight.'

'I . . . Now, just a moment, Hermione,' he said, getting to his feet again, 'I'm not some silly schoolboy having to report my every move.'

'Then stop acting like one. If you fancy yourself in love with Ellen, do something about it and do it before it's too late.'

He scowled and went and stood at the end of the bed. He rested his hands on the brass rail. 'Who said anything about love?'

Hermione smiled at him beneath her hooded eyes. 'I saw you, Matthew, through my binoculars. I saw the way you held Ellen and the way you kissed her. I don't know what Ellen thought about it but I've a pretty good idea what was going through your mind at the time. Now, come back here and sit by me. We need to discuss what you're going to do.'

He banged his hand on the bedstead. 'Nothing!' he exploded. 'I'm going to do absolutely nothing because she's determined to marry that prat of a solicitor and live out the rest of her life in hypocritical splendour!'

'Don't be such a defeatist, Matthew.'

'But it's true. You told me yourself that her intention was to marry for money and that's exactly what Duncan can offer her.'

'Then make her realise that it would be better to marry for love.'

He shook his head violently. 'Love be damned! It's ready cash she wants.'

'No, Matthew,' Hermione said. 'Ellen isn't as mercenary as that. It's security she's looking for, and she truly believes Duncan will provide her with that.'

'Then she's a bloody fool.'

Hermione smiled. 'Quite possibly, but before you condemn her completely why don't you calm down and let me tell you what Ellen has gone through. Then maybe you'll understand why she's so keen to marry Duncan.'

Chapter Twenty-Three

Janey was all contrition. 'I'm sorry,' she croaked, concentrating all her efforts on lowering her cup of black coffee. When the cup was safely installed in its saucer she risked a bleary-eyed glance at Susie across the breakfast table. 'I'm sorry,' she repeated.

Susie carried on reading about the average niacin intake from a bowl of Raisin Wheats.

'What more can I say?'

Susie raised her eyes from the cereal packet. 'But it's not as though it's the first time, is it?' she said. She was trying to be stern, but it wasn't easy. She and Bonkers had discussed Janey for some time when they'd eventually collapsed into bed, just after three in the morning, hours after the last of their guests had left but only minutes after Janey had finally calmed down. Bonkers had agreed that something had to be done, but he hadn't come up with any solutions to the problem.

According to Bonkers, Janey had always been one for the dramatics. At the age of eleven she had been sent away to school in the mistaken belief that life as a boarder would be a great leveller. In Susie's opinion boarding school helped only those who were already level-minded, like herself: she'd thoroughly enjoyed her time away from home as a child. But sending a crackpot like Janey off to a school hundreds of miles from home might be convenient for those left behind breathing continuous sighs of relief, but for the poor soul in question – and not to mention the poor souls cooped up with said crackpot – life had been bound to be anything but a bed of roses. Bonkers's stories of Janey away at school were legionary. There were tales of Janey running away, tales of Janey smuggling a pet rabbit into the dormitory, only to forget about it tucked away in her trunk and then discover it days later, stiff and smelly. There were tales of Janey starving herself and, the worst of the lot, was the story of Janey making herself sick by drinking a glass of salty water before breakfast every day and pretending that she was suffering from morning sickness.

Susie knew as well as the next person that these acts of insubordination had all been cries for help and she felt genuinely sorry for her sister-in-law but, really, it could not go on. Janey was twenty-nine years old, and it was time for her to start acting in a responsible adult manner.

'Janey,' she said firmly, 'you're a dear sweet girl and you know how fond Bonkers and I are of you, Millie and Floss too, but last night was the final straw. Bonkers agrees with me. You need help in sorting out your muddled life.'

'What kind of help?' Janey whispered. 'Men in white coats?'

'There you go again, Janey, overreacting.'

'Well, what do you mean?'

'Ever thought that you might be . . . well, you know –?'

Janey looked blankly back at Susie. 'Might be what?'

Oh Lord, how did one go about this bit? How did one tactfully suggest that one's sister in law was a touch barmy, that she was about as stable as a two-legged stool. 'Look, Janey,' she said, steeling herself, 'have you ever considered some kind of counselling?'

Janey's face crumpled. 'You think I'm doolally, don't you?' And seeing Bonkers coming into the kitchen, she struggled to her feet and went to him. She was crying now.

'Susie thinks I'm crazy,' she bawled into the shoulder of his dressing gown.

'Of course you're not,' he said, patting her reassuringly on the back.

Bonkers gave Susie a helpless stare and Susie returned it with a but-you-agreed-we-had-to-do-something expression.

An hour later Janey had packed her overnight bag and was preparing to drive home to her flat in Chester, where she said Dionysus would be waiting for her with nothing more accusing to strike her with than his slightly smelly litter tray.

The atmosphere in the hall when the goodbyes were being said was cold and unforgiving, and when Janey had gone Bonkers followed Susie into the kitchen. They had been so occupied with Janey last night that the clearing up from the party was still waiting to be done. Empty bottles jostled for space with plates and dishes of uneaten party food, and everywhere they looked there were screwed-up napkins and dirty glasses, hundreds of them.

The breakfast dishes were now adding to the chaos, and Susie pushed up her sleeves ready to tackle the mess. She was cross, though. Very cross. Rarely was she ever seriously angry with Bonkers, but today she was. She sensed him standing behind her.

'You could help,' she said, bending down to open the bin. Well, why shouldn't he? It was his sister's fault that this lot was still here this morning.

'What shall I do, sweetie?'

She banged the lid down on the bin. 'You can stop calling me sweetie for a start!'

Bonkers took a step back. 'Susie, whatever is the matter?'

She turned on him. 'It's you. You and your silly sister. I was just getting through to her when you walked in and totally undermined me.' She mimicked his voice, '"*Of course you're not.*" Well, pardon me, but I don't share that opinion and you agreed in bed that it was time we did something. You agreed and then reneged just at the crucial moment.'

Bonkers laughed. 'I say, Susie, you don't think you're taking this whole thing a touch too seriously, do you?'

'It's not funny!'

'Yes, it is.' He came over and hugged her. 'Dear sweet little Susie. I've never seen you so uptight before. Why don't you go into town and cheer yourself up and let me sort out this mess?'

Susie contemplated this proposition. Trusting Bonkers to do anything in the kitchen was something she seldom did but, on the other hand, some new shoes would be nice.

Simon had finished packing up his car and Ellen watched him coming towards the barn.

'All done?' she asked, as he came in.

'Yep, including all the things you said I'd forget.'

She smiled. 'So when will I get to see you again? Not that I'm putting any pressure on you.'

'That's one thing you never do, Mum. But I guess it won't be for some time. It's going to be a hectic term.'

'Mm . . . All those summer balls and fun and games on the Cherwell, no doubt.'

'I was talking about work, Mum.'

'Come on.' She laughed. 'Let's get you on your way.'

They walked over to the bursting Fiat in the warm sunshine. It had rained in the night but now the clouds were little more than fluffy specks in the sky and a bright sun shone down, picking out the wisps of golden weeping willow trailing the surface of the stream.

'I suppose you'll be putting this on the market soon, won't you?' Simon said, gazing around him.

'I guess so,' she said.

'Shame.'

'Simon?'

'Nothing.' He opened the car door.

'Oh, no, you don't,' Ellen said. 'You're not leaving until you've explained what you meant just now.'

'It's no big deal.' He shrugged. 'I just quite like this place. It's got something about it.'

'You're right,' she agreed. 'Wet rot, dry rot and any other crumbling-house disease you'd care to mention.'

'Come on, Mum, where's your soul?'

'Oh, I'm all out of that.'

'Well, don't be. And just because you're marrying some rich bloke who can give you anything you want, don't go thinking that the things for free in life don't matter any more.'

She stared at him, shocked. 'Simon, is that how you see me?'

'It happens to the best of people.'

'But –'

'Cheerio, Mum. I'll give you a ring some time next week.'

Ellen watched him drive off and wondered how it was that some of the most important things people had to say were often relayed as postscripts to a conversation. Had Simon done it deliberately? Had he kept back his heavily weighted statements for when it was too late to discuss them properly?

He hadn't said all that much about her marrying Duncan. She'd tried to get him to talk about it late last night when Duncan had dropped her off after the party at Orchard House, but all she'd managed to get out of him was that he hoped she would be happy.

This noncommittal response worried her. It wasn't so much that she needed Simon's approval to go ahead, it was more that she couldn't bear his indifference, which in her opinion was the next best thing to disapproval.

'It's your life, Mum,' he'd told her. 'If he's the right man for you, then go for it.'

But that wasn't what she wanted to hear. She wanted him to say, 'Duncan's a really great bloke and I can see how much he loves you.' That was the confirmation and reassurance she was after, not this go-ahead-you're-a-grown-woman-free-to-make-your-own-decisions routine.

It was most frustrating.

Going back into the barn she heard footsteps on the gravel beyond the cottage. She turned to see Matthew coming along the lane. When he saw her he waved. She wondered what he wanted. After their conversation at Orchard House last night she thought they'd said all they were ever likely to say to each other. To her surprise she found she was pleased that this was not the case. There was something comfortably familiar about the sight of him as he strolled across the car park. She supposed it was the casual way in which he dressed. As on other occasions when she'd seen him he was wearing faded jeans and a loose-fitting shirt tucked in at the waist with the sleeves rolled up to his elbows.

'I met the postman at the top of the lane and thought

I'd save him a trip,' he said, when he drew level. He handed her a bundle of mail.

'Thank you.' She watched him stare over towards the cottage, and then at the bank and the stream. He seemed lost in his own thoughts.

When he returned his attention to her he said simply, 'It's a nice spot here.'

What was this? First Simon and now Matthew going on about what a bijou residence she had.

He caught the expression on her face. 'But I suppose you'd prefer to be back at Orchard House, right? May I see inside the barn?'

'Feel free.' She stepped aside to let him pass. She followed him inside and went over to the bench where she was preparing a garland of herbs and dried flowers for a customer's kitchen. She flicked through the pile of letters Matthew had just handed her and was about to condemn them all as bills when the last one showed itself as another letter from France – Roger must have found out her address.

She stared at the letter, unprepared for this second assault from Provence. The first still lay unopened on the kitchen window-sill: she had never got round to summoning up the courage to read it. Now it would have a companion.

'Not all bills, I hope,' Matthew said, coming over to her.

'No,' she replied. 'Though I wish they were.'

'Bad news?'

She bit her lip. 'Probably.' She tapped the offending envelope on the counter. 'It's from my ex-husband.'

'Oh.' Matthew wasn't sure what to say. After his conversation last night with Hermione, when she'd told him all about Roger, he'd come here this morning with the sole intention of trying to make his peace with Ellen and prove to her that he wasn't the curmudgeonly devil – Hermione's words – he had so far made himself out to be. The last thing he'd expected to happen was that he'd end up acting as a messenger boy for her ex-husband. 'What do you think he wants?'

'I've no idea.'

'Open it and see.'

She frowned.

'Come on, what's the worst it could say?'

'That he's sorry and wants to come back,' she almost whispered.

'And is that an option you'd consider?' He held his breath. It was bad enough knowing that he was competing against Duncan the Incredibly Wealthy One, without having the complication of an ex-husband also vying for a position in Ellen's heart.

'Of course not,' she snapped. 'I never want to see Roger again as long as I live.'

'Brilliant!'

She looked at him.

'I mean, it's good that you know your own mind so clearly. So why not simply get it over with and see what the letter says?'

'Trouble is, there's another in the kitchen. It came a few days ago.'

'And you've not read that either?'

She shook her head. 'I wanted Simon to do it for me but it got forgotten, what with Duncan and our engagement, and now he's gone.'

Matthew thought about what Ellen had just said. If she'd asked Simon to read the first letter it probably meant she didn't want to bother Duncan with it. Was this his chance to absolve himself by stepping in and offering his services? 'Would it help for a stranger to read the letters for you?'

She raised her eyes from the envelope in her hand. 'Meaning you?'

'Why not?'

'I wouldn't describe you as a stranger exactly.'

'What would you describe me as?' *Shit!* He couldn't believe he'd just said that. Just what the hell was happening to him that he was going around talking like some clever-arsed character out of a book?

'I don't know,' she answered, with a cautious smile. 'You don't seem a stranger exactly, not now, but you are strange. You do odd things like kiss women whom you've only just met.' She expected him to turn away embarrassed and to hunch his shoulders and fold his arms like he had at Orchard House. But he didn't.

'If you think I'm going to apologise again for that, you're wrong,' he said. 'It's not something I make a habit of.'

'The kissing bit, or the apologising?'

His face broke into his lopsided smile. 'Both,' he said.

'I seem to remember you saying last night that I was the most infuriating woman you'd ever met, so why the sudden desire to help me?'

'And if you recall our conversation correctly I also asked if there was anything I could do to make amends. I'd like to help you . . . if you'll let me.'

Ellen considered his offer. She lowered her eyes to the envelope in her hand. She was tempted. Very tempted. It would at least get it over and done with. All he had to do was read through the sheets of paper and tell her there was nothing to worry about. Except she knew in her heart that it wouldn't be as simple as that.

219

'You could always ask Duncan?' Matthew said, sensing her indecision and deciding to test her.

'No,' she said briskly. 'I don't want to bother Duncan, he's far too busy. And anyway it wouldn't be right, would it? Not my fiancé reading my ex-husband's letters.'

'I suppose not.'

'I need someone objective, someone . . . someone detached from me.'

Matthew hesitated. Her words were uncomfortably reminiscent of a conversation between him and Bridget one night in bed. 'I never feel I'm with the real you when we make love,' she'd said. 'You keep yourself so private at times, even at the most intimate of moments. It isn't good to be this detached. You must learn to give something of yourself.' She'd been quite right in her little lecture. He doubted whether he'd ever revealed the real him when he had been with her.

'I think you'll find me suitably detached,' he said, his voice perfectly neutral.

Ellen ran her hand through her hair. It was make-your-mind-up time. 'Oh, come on, then,' she said, remembering that these days her life was supposed to be spontaneous and free of self-doubt. 'Let's go over to the cottage right now and you can help me sort out Roger once and for all. And then you can laugh at me for my stupidity.'

Chapter Twenty-Four

Ellen watched Matthew's face intently, scrutinising his every eye movement for clues to what Roger had to say for himself. Of course, it would have been easier to have read the letters herself, but that would have taken more courage than she possessed right now. Coward that she was, she didn't even have the nerve to see how many lines Roger had scribbled.

'Well?' she asked at last, aware that Matthew had gone very quiet. 'What does he say? Has he run out of money?'

Matthew composed his face. 'It would seem so,' he said simply.

'And?'

He lowered his eyes and started folding the letter with great care.

'That can't be all. Surely there's more.'

'There is, but I don't think you should bother yourself with it.'

'He's not coming back, is he?'

Matthew shook his head.

'Has he asked for money?'

'Like I said, don't even think about it.'

It was no good. She had to know. 'How much? How much is he asking for?'

'Does it make any difference if he's asking for ten pounds or a thousand pounds?'

She didn't answer at first, but went over to the

window-seat and straightened the cushions. 'Does he say why he needs the money? Is he ill? Is that it?'

Matthew's face hardened. 'Yes, I'd say he was ill, quite sick in fact.'

Ellen thought of all the times she'd wished for Roger to fall victim to some incurable disease. 'On a scale of one to ten, how ill would you say?'

Matthew stared at her. He was at a complete loss as to what to say or do. All he knew was that through the need to ingratiate himself with Ellen he now found himself in an impossible situation. He should never have come here this morning. He should have thrown some things into a bag while he was not wanted at Orchard House over the weekend, gone for a drive and found himself an interesting view to paint. But no! He'd been arrogant enough to think that all he had to do was show a little sympathy towards Ellen and she'd be bowled over by him. Whereas the truth of the matter was that he was now caught up in something he was sure she would rather he knew nothing about. He glanced down at the letter in his hand. If only he could get rid of it without Ellen reading the contents. But how? And there was the other letter as well.

'What's wrong, Matthew? He's . . . he's not dying, is he?'

'If you want my opinion, you should have a ceremonial bonfire,' he waved the letter in his hand along with the unopened one, 'and then forget about him.' He tried to sound casual, flippant, even.

'But you haven't answered my question,' Ellen persisted. She was beginning to be slightly annoyed by Matthew's evasiveness. 'Is he or is he not dying?' Having wanted Roger dead it was unnerving to consider the possibility that her wish might come true. She remembered Hermione telling her that the danger about wishing for something was that sometimes that wish was granted – 'Careful what you wish for,' she'd said in the past.

Matthew still hadn't answered her.

'Oh, this is hopeless,' she said. 'Give it to me and let me see what he's got to say for himself.'

'No!' But he wasn't quick enough. Ellen snatched the letter out of his hands.

'I just need to know,' she said. 'Then I can put this behind –' But her voice broke off as she began to read Roger's familiar handwriting and took in his message.

Matthew saw the disbelief on Ellen's face, then the horror and finally the humiliation. Last came the realisation that he, too, had read the same offensive words. She slowly screwed up the letter into a tight ball. She didn't look at him.

'He must have been drunk when he wrote it,' Matthew said pragmatically.

Still she didn't look at him.

'Or, like I said, he's sick. Sick in the head.' He placed the second letter on the dresser behind him and reached out to Ellen. He touched her shoulder lightly. She stiffened. 'Forget him,' he said gently. 'He's just trying it on. You have to be strong and ignore the letter. Blackmail only works when the victim is weak.'

'But why?' she murmured, turning her head away from him, unable to look him in the eye. 'Why's he doing this to me? Hasn't he done enough already?' She began to cry. 'He took everything I had,' she sobbed, 'he humiliated me and threw me away . . . and now this.' She covered her face with her hands. 'Why?'

Unable to bear the sight of her suffering, Matthew took her in his arms to comfort her. It was an instinctive response and he didn't think twice about it. He held her tightly, willing her hurt to pass. He knew, though, that it wouldn't be as easy as that. Roger must have hurt Ellen badly in the past and from what his vile letter said he had every intention of continuing to do so. Matthew's heart went out to her, every inch of him wanting to protect her. Without thinking what he was doing he stroked her shoulders, slowly, reassuringly, gradually working his hands up towards her neck and then running his fingers through her fine hair. But suddenly he was conscious of his heart slamming inside his rib-cage. He caught his breath and swallowed and with the greatest of effort kept his hands from moving any further. Very slowly, though, Ellen lifted her head from his chest. Don't do that, he thought, just don't look at me. Not now.

Oblivious to his unspoken words she gazed into his face. He swallowed again but knew he was trapped, held by the expression in her sad misty blue eyes and by his desire for her. He recalled now the moment a few days ago when he'd quite literally lost his wits and kissed her. It was the same now. He was no more in control of his emotions today than he had been that day of the picnic. He lowered his head to her lovely upturned face and kissed her fleetingly on the mouth. Finding no resistance he kissed her again, gently parting her lips with his tongue, and when she kissed him back and he felt the pressure of her hands linked around his neck and the sway of her body moving against his, he dared to dream that she might feel for him just a fraction of what he felt for her. He wanted to make love to her and he could think of nothing but the joy that their love-making would bring him and when Ellen started unbuttoning his shirt he knew with certainty it was what she wanted too.

They didn't speak and they didn't stop kissing, not even when they fumbled to get out of their clothes and slipped breathlessly to the floor clutching each other.

Their love-making was clumsy and frantic and at one stage they were both helpless with laughter as they bumped their heads on the leg of a chair. Afterwards Matthew realised that never before in his life had he been so consumed with the act of simply loving a woman . . . and never before had he given so much of himself. But when he turned to look at Ellen there were tears in her eyes.

They both heard the sound of an approaching car but it was Ellen who reacted first.

Immediately she was up on her feet and scrambling into her clothes. With one leg in her jeans she hopped over to the window.

'I don't believe it,' she cried, 'it's La Carter! Quick, get dressed and get out of here. No, second thoughts, stay where you are and don't move, not until I get back.'

If it wasn't such an anticlimax to what had just taken place Matthew would have laughed. Disappointed, though, he watched Ellen finish dressing and then launch herself out of the cottage. He pulled on his trousers and wandered through to the kitchen. He made himself some coffee and, while waiting for the kettle to boil, threw Roger's letters in the bin and wondered what would happen next between him and Ellen.

If he was honest it didn't bear thinking about.

Taking his cup of coffee with him he went upstairs to see if there was any chance of a shower.

Ellen was struggling to keep her composure while Nadia hurled one heavily loaded statement at her after another.

'*When* you marry Duncan,' she was saying, 'you must realise that you're not just marrying any old man. Duncan has his peculiarities.'

'Yes,' Ellen said, barely listening. She was too preoccupied with peering out of the window over to the cottage to be bothered with what Nadia had to say – there were also one or two thoughts running through her head demanding her attention, her immediate attention!

She couldn't believe what had just happened. She would have to talk to Matthew, and talk to him seriously. It was madness what they'd just done. It was a heat-of-the-moment thing. These things happen.

But never to her!

Oh, in heaven's name, never to her!

She snapped her eyes shut and tried not to think of the expression on Matthew's face when his hands had lingered over her body. She blamed herself entirely. He'd only been trying to comfort her but the effect of his arms around her had been so potent that suddenly every bit of her had ached to be touched. It had been so long since anyone had held her, really held her. When he'd kissed her she had been staggered at the intensity of her reaction. All her senses had been thrown into disarray and she'd wanted nothing but to make love with him. She had never before experienced a need so acute. Sex with Roger had been a very serious business and had always been planned precisely around his needs. Even in the early stages of their marriage it had never been a spontaneous act of love where they'd collapsed to the floor clamouring for each other. And towards the end of their life together his desire and passion had been squashed altogether by obsession and fantasy as he'd concentrated on forcing her to conform to the current role he fancied.

She chewed her lip, bringing to mind Roger's letter. She had forgotten about the photographs he'd taken of her and now he was threatening to send them to Duncan if she didn't send him the money he wanted.

'Ellen, you're not listening to me, are you?'

She turned and faced her future mother-in-law. She offered a conciliatory smile. 'I'm sorry, it's just that it's been a busy morning.'

Nadia gave the empty barn a contemptible stare. 'I see no customers, Ellen.'

'I've got a lot of orders to be getting on with,' Ellen parried.

Again the same stare but this time it was aimed at Ellen.

It hadn't passed Nadia's notice that Ellen was looking decidedly dishevelled. Her face was flushed and her hair didn't look as if it had been brushed since she had got out of bed, and her shirt was creased as though somebody had been sitting on it, and worse still the buttons had been done up incorrectly and one side was longer than the other.

Then it dawned on Nadia. *That* was why she had seen Ellen tearing out of the cottage and racing across to the barn to meet her. She had been otherwise engaged.

So Duncan had lied. He'd said he was going to be playing golf this morning, whereas in fact he had been coming here to get up to heaven knows what with Ellen. Well, she'd teach the pair of them a lesson.

'Oh!' she cried, putting her hand to her forehead. 'I feel quite faint. It must be the lack of air in here. I don't suppose I could rest for a few moments in your lovely little cottage?'

'No!' Ellen almost screeched.

Aha! thought Nadia. It was just as she suspected. She reached out to the counter for support. 'I think it's one of my migraines.'

Ellen was horrified. 'Perhaps if you go outside for some fresh air you'll feel better.'

She led Nadia to the door and the awaiting cure. Immediately Nadia said that the sun was too strong. 'Just let me sit in the cool of your sweet little cottage,' she implored. 'And maybe a glass of water would help.'

Ellen felt like Snow White. 'Sure you're not trying to palm off a juicy red apple?' she wanted to ask. 'Why don't you go and sit on the bank and I'll bring you some water,' she said, with a flash of inspiration.

'I don't think so,' Nadia said pithily, giving Ellen a baleful expression and smoothing away an imaginary crease in her expensive Jaeger skirt. She then set off towards the cottage at a surprisingly brisk pace for one so faint.

Ellen dashed after her, glancing up at the cottage windows for any sign of Matthew. 'It's such a lovely day, isn't it?' she said loudly, hoping to alert Matthew. 'Really beautiful,' she shouted.

Nadia smiled to herself. This was fun. The look of panic on Ellen's face was a picture and no doubt the expression on Duncan's face when she routed him out would be equally interesting.

'Oh, look,' she exclaimed, pushing against the front door, 'it's not locked. You really should be more careful, Ellen, you never know who might come calling.'

Oh, how true!

The sitting room was empty and the relief showed only too plainly on Ellen's face. Nadia quickly sized up the interior of the cottage. The only other room downstairs was the kitchen and she could see from where she was standing that it was empty, which left upstairs. 'May I use the bathroom?' she asked.

Ellen could feel herself sweating. She was pretty sure

she was hyperventilating as well. Any more of this and she'd pass out. 'How about that glass of water?' she tried.

'Ellen,' Nadia said in a voice that clearly indicated that she would brook no argument, 'I think I'm going to be sick, I need the bathroom *now*!'

Ellen had no choice but to lead the way upstairs. Perhaps Matthew had hidden himself up there when he'd heard their approaching voices. Oh, please, let him be hiding under a bed, or in a wardrobe, anywhere but the bathroom.

It was when they were standing on the tiny landing directly in front of the bathroom that Ellen heard a sound so distinctive that she nearly toppled back down the stairs.

Somebody had just pulled the plug out of the bath!

She gripped the banister beside her, but Nadia smiled triumphantly and reached out to open the door.

Chapter Twenty-Five

While Ellen gulped and Nadia clutched at the silk scarf knotted at her neck, Matthew reached for a towel and tied it around his waist.

'This is Duncan's mother,' Ellen squeaked.

He nodded at Nadia, then flashed one of his lopsided smiles at Ellen.

'It was good of you to offer the use of your bathroom while Hermione's is out of action,' he said. 'Are you having problems with your plumbing as well?' he asked Nadia.

Ellen smiled inanely but Nadia had steam practically coming out of her ears and was already stomping off down the stairs. Hurriedly Ellen followed. When she caught up with her in the sitting room Nadia turned on her.

'Don't think for one moment that I'm taken in by that little charade,' she hissed. 'I shall tell Duncan what's been going on here the minute I see him.' She moved to the front door and glared at Ellen one more time. 'I knew you were up to no good the moment I set eyes on you. I warned Duncan, but he wouldn't listen and now he'll have to.' This was said with great satisfaction.

'Nice woman,' Matthew said, coming downstairs and joining Ellen in the sitting room when the front door had been slammed shut and the china on the dresser had stopped rattling. He was fully dressed now and bracing himself for an angry outburst from Ellen. She would have to take it out on someone and it might just as well be him.

But she didn't turn on him. Instead she moved across the small room to the window-seat where she dropped down and stared forlornly out through the panes of glass at Nadia's car disappearing along the lane.

'I knew it was too good to be true,' she said gloomily, resting her head against the window and drawing her knees under her chin. 'And now I'm stuck here for ever. No money. No future. And no bloody Marks and Spencer's shortbread! He was my escape from all of this,' she cried. 'Now I'm going to end up a lonely old lady shuffling around Woolie's with a plastic mac and one of those horrible string shopping bags.'

'Oh, stop exaggerating. Of course you're not going to end up like that.'

She turned and faced him, her eyes tinged with a dark hue. He realised too late that he'd been too sharp with her.

'And what would you know?' she said angrily.

He moved across the room. 'Look,' he said gently, kneeling beside her, 'why do you think you have to escape? What you've got here is –'

She pushed him aside and walked away. 'You wouldn't understand, you don't know anything about me.'

'I think I do,' he said. 'Hermione told me how difficult it's been for you since you've been on your own.'

'So,' she said hotly, the colour rising in her face, 'Hermione's been gossiping about me, has she?'

'Hermione doesn't gossip,' he snapped defensively. 'She was trying to make me understand why you had decided to marry Duncan. That was all.'

'I'm marrying Duncan –' She broke off. 'Correction, I *was* marrying Duncan because I . . . because I . . .'

'You can't say it, can you?' he challenged, crossing the room to her. 'You can't bring yourself to say that you love Duncan because you don't.'

'What rubbish! Of course I love Duncan. There, I've said it.'

He scowled and pushed his hands into his pockets.

Weariness got the better of Ellen. 'What does it matter, anyway? Nadia's probably already told Duncan about you being here in my house.'

He looked up at her. 'And what about me, Ellen?' he said softly.

'You?'

'Yes,' he replied evenly. 'Shouldn't we talk about us and what we just did? Or have you decided to block that out conveniently?'

'No!' she cried. 'No, I don't want to talk about us.' Anger now replaced her weariness. 'It's all your fault that I'm not marrying Duncan. If you hadn't come here this morning none of this would have happened. I should never have let you read Roger's letter.'

'But you did.' He reached out to touch her. 'Look, Ellen, I want you to know –' But he got no further.

'And where's Roger's other letter?' she demanded. 'Where have you put them?'

'I put them both in the bin,' he said firmly, 'where they belong.'

She marched out to the kitchen and he saw her flip off the lid. He watched her tear open the envelope and slide out a sheet of writing paper. He caught a glimpse of a photograph, but turned away to allow Ellen the privacy she deserved. He heard the sound of ripping followed by a stifled moan. He went to her, but she pushed him away.

'No!' she shouted, tears streaming down her cheeks. 'Don't touch me! Just leave me alone. I wish you'd never come! Can't you see the harm you've done already? If you hadn't interfered over those awful letters we wouldn't have . . . Oh, please, just get out!'

He knew it would be useless to argue with her – anger and hurt were making her irrational – so he did as she asked.

When he reached Orchard House in the Crescent he paused and considered the comparison between this house and the one in which Ellen now lived. He knew which he preferred, but he could well understand how difficult it must have been for Ellen to leave this large, elegant house for something so much smaller, especially when it was through no fault of her own. He thought of the man to whom she had once been married. Surely Roger couldn't always have been such a bastard, for how else would Ellen have stayed with him for so long? He tried to comprehend what must be going through Roger's mind to make him turn on someone whom he must have loved once. Or perhaps he hadn't ever loved Ellen. People married for the strangest of reasons. Like his own father. He had never understood what had possessed a man like Kit to marry a woman like Roberta. They were as different as . . . as different as Ellen and Duncan.

Hell, the woman had lousy taste in picking husbands!

He was still standing in front of Orchard House when he heard the sound of his name being called out. It was that wretched Bonkers.

This he did not need. A bollocking from a ranting Terry Thomas, whose sister he had supposedly insulted, was the last thing he was prepared to put up with right now.

'Now, look here,' Bonkers said, slapping towards him

in a pair of flip-flops, 'I think we need to have a word or two.'

Matthew fixed him with a long, hard stare. 'Yes,' he said savagely, seized with the urge to add, '*go ahead, punk, make my day.*'

Bonkers cleared his throat. 'It really won't do,' he said. 'I can't possibly let you go around offending a member of my –'

'You're right.'

'Don't interrupt, please. I simply can't allow you to get away with –'

'You're absolutely right.'

'Now, look here. I wish you'd let a chap get his words out. I'm trying to tell you that –'

'Yeah, and I'm trying to tell you that I agree with you. I'm obviously – and to use your tiresome vernacular – a bounder of the worst order and shouldn't darken your door again. Which is fine by me, so I won't. And to make everything all right I won't even charge you for wasting my time. How's that? Reasonable enough, *old thing*?'

Bonkers's jaw was dangling somewhere on a level with his collar-bone. He struggled to speak but all that came out of his gaping mouth was a croaked, 'Yah. Thanks.'

'Don't mention it,' Matthew said, through clenched teeth. He turned and went.

Bonkers slapped his way back inside Orchard House with a feeling of dread. He had the feeling that when Susie got back from town there would be hell to pay. He had only meant to extract an apology from the fellow and bluster a few threats of disbanding the commission – just to show who was boss, that kind of thing – but now this had happened and Susie would be so disappointed not to have her painting.

He stood in the kitchen and looked at all the mess from

last night, which he still hadn't got round to clearing up –
he'd been having a doze in the sitting room while the girls
were playing upstairs. He'd better get on or Susie would
be doubly furious with him.

Laburnum House was empty. Matthew went outside to
the garden to find Hermione. But there was no sign of her
stooped figure pottering among the overgrown herba-
ceous borders. Nor was she in the greenhouse.

He sat in the summerhouse in an old wicker chair and
stretched out his long legs in front of him. Coming away
from Orchard House he'd made up his mind what he was
going to do. There was no point in him hanging around
any longer. He'd lost the Buchanan commission, and
despite what he felt for Ellen, there really didn't seem
much to be gained from staying on in the hope she would
calm down and see sense. No, he might just as well push
off home before he made an even bigger fool of himself.
When Hermione turned up from wherever she was he'd
tell her he was going and then get on his way.

He tried to comfort himself with the thought that he
could be home by early evening, and if the weather held
up for tomorrow he'd have a day painting from his boat
on Coniston Water. And with a bit of luck Coniston
would be relatively peaceful with most of the tourists
chasing daffodils up at Dora's Field.

Hermione had just thrashed Bernie at croquet and she
was now relaxing comfortably on a sun-lounger on the
terrace at the Lodge. Apart from one or two residents
who weren't up to the trip, the rest had been taken into
Manchester to see a matinée performance of the hit show
Grease at the Palace Theatre.

'Not such a bad place, after all, is it, my little

Hermaseta?' commented Bernie, picking a slice of orange from his tall glass and sucking the juice out of it.

'If you like that kind of thing,' she conceded. As much as it pained her, Hermione had to admit that she was impressed with the Lodge. The Management had transformed what had once been a large, scruffy, rambling old house into a magnificent property. There was an atmosphere of ease and elegant country home about the place that reminded Hermione of a lifetime ago when Laburnum House had had money lavished freely on it.

Bernie had insisted on giving her a guided tour when he'd invited her over for a game of croquet and she had wandered through the rooms aghast at the opulence of so many crystal chandeliers hanging from the high ceilings. She was impressed by the quantity of antique furniture everywhere and the delicate side tables dotted about the place offering an assortment of magazines and pretty glass bowls of wrapped sweets. There was even a library, which would have delighted the heart of any avid reader, and a snooker room that was already suitably stamped with the smell of cigars and brandy. And housed in a new extension was an indoor heated pool in the shape of a kidney – admittedly it was small and Hermione didn't much care for the look of some of the hoisting tackle hanging from the ceiling – but it was a pool all the same. There were several Jacuzzis – in which she could well imagine Bernie with a female resident for company – and everywhere there was the smell of lavender polish as well as the more luxurious fragrance of cut flowers beautifully arranged in expensive vases.

It was stylish. It was wholesome. It was comfortable. And it was a million miles away from the image Hermione had had in her mind of what the Lodge would be like.

Where was the whiff of disinfectant to cover up the sad smell of urine-soaked chairs and mattresses? Where was the pong of institutional cabbage and poached cod? And where, she wanted to know, was the hum of death and decay? Surely that should be lurking somewhere among the sumptuous brocade curtains and ankle-deep carpets? But try as she might – just to prove that she'd been right all along – Hermione could not find fault with the Lodge. Even the annexe, which had once been the stable block and which was now the medical wing, didn't look too sinister. Bernie had caught her eyeing a couple of oxygen tanks and he'd joked that they were for the Monday-morning scuba-diving lessons.

Joking apart, the Lodge had a lot going for it.

'How much does it cost?' she asked, staring out at the well-kept lawn and croquet hoops. 'To live here, that is. How much gelt?'

Bernie chuckled. 'Thinking of shacking up with me?'

She turned her gaze on him. 'I could do a lot worse.'

He laughed again and rattled his chest. 'They don't take any old codger,' he wheezed.

'They took you!'

It was late afternoon and a low sun was casting beams of soft light through the small windows of the barn; dust motes danced in the rays.

Ellen was waiting for the phone to ring, as she was convinced it would. Surely Nadia must have spilled her poisonous beans to Duncan by now. So why hadn't he phoned? Or was he, perhaps, never going to speak to her again? Was she to be consigned to the silent-reproach treatment and never given the opportunity to say that she was sorry? Because she was, and sorrier than she could say.

It had been a sad, depressing afternoon, despite there having been a steady flow of customers, none of whom had left empty-handed. On any other day she would have been delighted with the amount of money deposited in the till, but today it meant nothing to her. She wanted Duncan and the life she'd thought they would have together, not this life that had been thrust upon her.

At last the phone rang. She reached out to it straight away. Please let it be Duncan, please, oh, please, let it be Duncan. But she hesitated. What if it was? What was she going to say to him? How was she going to deny what his mother had seen with her own eyes? A naked man in her bathroom!

The phone carried on ringing, loud and shrill, demanding her attention. She snatched it up.

'Spring Bank Dried Flowers,' she said, trying to sound normal, even businesslike.

'Ellen?'

It *was* him!

'Ellen?'

She swallowed hard. 'Yes, Duncan, it's me.'

'You're very faint, you're going to have to speak up.'

She struggled to say something. Anything. 'How are you?'

'I'm fine. Now look, I'm on my mobile in the car. Can I come and see you? There's something we need to discuss.'

Her legs buckled beneath her. So Nadia *had* told him and he was playing it cool right to the end. He was coming to watch her squirm while she confessed her sins. How ironic, the solicitor who had once acted for her was now to be her judge and jury.

'Can't you . . .' her voice broke, 'can't you tell me on the phone?'

'No. I want to speak to you properly. It's important. I'm at the lights at the top of Church Walk, I'll be with you in less than two minutes.'

She was shaking when she saw his car appear in the lane. She watched him lock the car methodically and activate the alarm. The BMW pipped and winked its lights behind his back as he strode over to the barn. Her throat was dry and she had no idea how she was even going to speak to him let alone what she was going to say. She stayed on her side of the counter and pretended to be counting the money from the till.

'You look upset, Ellen,' he said, when he came in and stood opposite her. 'And I would imagine it has something to do with Nadia coming to see you this morning. Am I right?'

She nodded, wishing he'd just get on with it. Any minute now he'd pull out a barrister's wig and lean his elbows on the counter and make a proper job of cross-examining her.

And how did she plead?

Guilty. She was as guilty as hell. She didn't know what had possessed her, but yes, that morning, in a crazy moment she'd ripped off her clothes and made love on the floor with someone other than her fiancé.

'Ellen,' he said, reaching out to take her hands in his, 'I'm so sorry for what my mother's put you through today. She obviously came here with the sole intention of causing trouble between us. I know what she's up to and I want you to know that it's not going to stop me marrying you. Not ever. My mind's quite made up.'

Ellen didn't know whether she was hearing right. But hang on. Was this some subtle court-room trick for catching out the defendant?

'Nadia told me some ridiculous story about finding a naked man in your bathroom this morning.' He shook his head disparagingly. 'I know she's against me ever marrying but to sink to these depths is so unseemly and, to be honest, she's to be pitied. But you saw what she was like last night. And in a way I'm glad you know what I have to put up with. I've given her a good telling-off and she's under clear instructions to stay away from you.' He came round to her side of the counter and slipped his arm around her waist. 'Darling,' he said, 'I want you to know that there's no danger of Nadia ever coming between us.'

PART TWO

———

August

The Song of the Nightshade Fairy

My name is Nightshade, also Bittersweet;
Ah, little folk, be wise!
Hide you your hands behind you when we meet,
Turn you away your eyes.
My flowers you shall not pick, nor berries eat,
For in them poison lies.

Cicely Mary Barker

Chapter Twenty-Six

The estate agent – Call-Me-Trudi from Harker and Company – walked purposefully from room to room. Every now and then she would stop and nod. 'Delightful,' she would say. Often this was followed by an enthusiastic reference to a *charming double aspect* or *an interesting recessed fireplace*. An *airy outlook* was another favourite expression, as was *flexible accommodation*. And as for the *tremendous potential*, well, there seemed no end to it. But when the young woman, with her clipped voice and matching suit, started talking about the old Belfast sink with its wooden drainer in the garden room as though it was a national treasure, Hermione wondered whether the pudding wasn't being over-egged. In her opinion the old sink was only fit to be ripped out, put in the garden and used as a trough for alpine plants. Highly sought after, my foot!

Hermione let Call-Me-Trudi climb the stairs alone to the top of the house. It was not that she lacked the energy to follow the young woman, it was more that she didn't want to see the look of recrimination on Kit's and Matthew's faces staring back at her accusingly from the wall in Matthew's attic room.

Once she had made the decision to sell Laburnum House, she had known it was the right thing to do, although it had taken the best part of the summer to take the plunge. Her accountant had greeted the news by getting to work on something he called a spread-sheet, which would outline how the proceeds from the sale could best be allocated to enable Hermione to meet the cost of the next stage in her life. She had kept her plans to herself, confiding only in Bernie, and the Management of the Lodge, who had discreetly pointed out that they couldn't guarantee a space for her just yet as they were currently full.

'So the bottom line is that I have to wait until somebody dies,' she had said bluntly to Bernie, very much to the point after speaking to the Management. This was a chilling thought, and brought home to her just what the Lodge was all about. And while driving into town in his ancient Jag for an afternoon treat of tea and scones at the Patisserie she told Bernie that she'd changed her mind. 'I have no intention of waiting for somebody to die so that I can merely fill their space. Talk about dead men's slippers!'

'You're being morbid,' Bernie had said. 'We're all going to snuff it,' he went on, placatingly. 'Look at me. It's only the sex, drugs and croquet that keeps me going.'

During the summer months, Bernie had proved an ideal companion, encouraging her to spend less time talking to her sweet peas, which were now climbing the wigwam of canes in the garden and flowering rampantly, and more with him. He was honest and direct with her, which were qualities to which she had always warmed, and he told her on numerous occasions that she was clearly round the bend to live out the remainder of her life permanently worrying about maintaining Laburnum House.

'Sell the bloody place and live a little!' he shouted at her, late one starry night while they were sitting in the summerhouse drinking a bottle of claret from the Lodge's wine cellar. 'It's controlling you, sucking you dry of every last penny. Never mind all that sentimental tosh about your life being wrapped up in it, it's a whacking great investment just waiting to be used for a better purpose than keeping you here in solitary confinement. Sell the place and go off on one of those holidays of a lifetime you keep reading about.'

She had known he was talking sense and as she'd stared back at the pale disc of moon above their heads she'd thought how odd it was that she had indeed lived such a solitary life. She had never intended it to be that way.

Not so long ago, when Jo-Jo had stayed with her, she had admitted to herself for the first time that she was lonely. The feeling had crept up on her over the years and it wasn't until Ellen had moved in next door and then moved out that she had realised how much she valued another person's company.

And now dear Ellen, who had been so much a part of her life, had practically disappeared. Nowadays all her spare time was spent with Duncan. Hermione suspected that Duncan didn't like the idea of his future wife having a life other than the one he wanted for her. But so be it. So often that was what marriage was like. Her own brush with matrimony had been much the same. Even poor Arthur had wanted to shape and direct her life, and to a certain extent she had willingly gone along with him – in the hope of easing her conscience. Sadly, it hadn't worked. The plain truth of the matter was that she should never have married Arthur. She had only accepted his proposal because Kit had married Roberta and she couldn't bear the idea of being alone.

There had also been an element of wanting to hurt Kit,

to prove to him that she could live quite happily without him. She had been wrong.

In the summer of 1940, he had appeared at Laburnum House one sunny day. He was on leave, his face ashen and clouded with the reality of war, his body aching with exhaustion. He'd greeted her parents in the garden with a stiff formality that she hadn't recognised, and right away she sensed that something was wrong. All the excitement and anticipation that had been building up within her, since he had telegraphed the previous evening to say that he would be calling on his way up to Cumberland, vanished and was replaced with a heart-stopping fear that something dreadful was about to happen. They had sat around a white-clothed table on the lawn, politely drinking tea and passing plates of sandwiches to one another, a warm summer breeze gently ruffling their hair and clothes. They had spoken in stilted tones of the Nazi swastika now flying from the Eiffel Tower and of the two million Parisians fleeing the city. But Hermione had known that there was worse to come in the hesitant flow of conversation. On one side of her was Kit, his melancholy hazel eyes lowered – not once did they meet her own – his slim body nervously taut, his hands occupied with the buttons on his uniform. On her right was Roberta, cool, languid and relaxed, with a contented smile stretched right across her face.

By the time Kit had left Orchard House later that afternoon to resume his journey further north, their combined futures were set. Roberta was two months pregnant and was to marry Kit just as soon as he was able to request more leave. That night, just before bedtime, Roberta had taunted Hermione. 'Do you remember that day when I caught the pair of you in the summerhouse?' she said. 'I told you then that I intended to have him for myself. Aren't you jealous?'

Jealousy didn't come into it. Hermione was heartbroken. She had fallen in love with Kit and believed that in his quiet, undemonstrative way he loved her. When and *how* had he made love to Roberta?

Four months after Roberta married Kit she gave birth to a stillborn daughter. In the following year Hermione married Arthur.

'My word but it's hot up there,' exclaimed Call-me-Trudi, coming back down the stairs and fanning herself with her file.

Hermione smiled sympathetically. At this time of year it was as hot as stink in the attic rooms and that part of the house was a haven for bad-tempered flies that buzzed and crashed against the windows and at anyone who came near. 'How about we get down to business?' she said briskly. 'How much will I get for the house and what's your commission?'

'Well, now,' the young woman said, her hand resting on the balustrade, 'I haven't seen the garden properly, but you mentioned on the phone that in all it covers nearly two acres. That will have to be verified, of course, but I think we can safely say we're in a ball park of around four hundred and fifty thousand. Was that about what you had in mind?'

'Call it four hundred and fifty-five,' Hermione said. She had done her homework earlier that week, trawling Crantsford for its numerous estate agents who had all valued the house at roughly the same figure. But now was the clincher. 'And what ball park are we in for your commission?'

'We normally charge –'

'You can sell it for one and a quarter per cent,' Hermione said impatiently, not wanting to hear the same old spiel again, 'and naturally that's on a no-sale-no-fee basis.'

'Naturally.'

Hermione led the way back downstairs. Call-me-Trudi retrieved her briefcase from the kitchen table and handed Hermione her card. 'I'll go back to the office and put all this in writing. And don't worry, we'll have it sold in no time. In fact I can think of one particular buyer who'll snap your hand off the moment I let him know this is available.'

Actually, Trudi thought, unlocking her car door and slipping her slim body in behind the wheel, she'd be glad to get rid of that particular buyer. He was always on the phone pestering for anything new on the market and nothing was ever to his liking. Well, this one would be ideal. It was in one of the most sought-after areas in Crantsford and would suit him down to the ground.

Duncan closed the file on Conley versus Conley and placed it on the shelf behind him. He was nearing the end of that battle. It had been one of the more enjoyable cases because Mr Conley had stupidly thought that he could tuck away his money and plead poverty. The majority of people were too thick to hide large amounts of money successfully as any financial transaction left behind it an incriminating paper trail. It was a satisfying feeling, knowing that he had outmanoeuvred Mr Conley.

When he left law college he had not intended to specialise in divorce work, but had soon discovered he had a flair for it. One of the more pleasing aspects of his work was watching the way a case progressed. When a client initially approached him – and nine times out of ten the client was a woman – they would be lost and bewildered by the situation in which they found themselves and would come to him not just for legal advice but for emotional support. It wasn't a matter of simply steering his clients through the complexities of the latest divorce laws, it was more a case of enabling that person to realise that there really was life after divorce. Rarely did he fail.

Yes. All in all it was satisfying work, which was just as well for the past few months had been more trying than he could have believed. Nadia had always been a difficult woman, with her childlike way of playing games with him, but since his engagement to Ellen she had become impossible to live with, which was why it was so important for him and Ellen to find a place of their own. He had quite sensibly ruled out their living at Crantsford Hall with Nadia, understanding that no matter how short a time it might be, he would not risk his marriage getting off on the wrong foot.

Years of working with the detailed precision of the law had made him a patient, methodical man, but for the first time in his life he was impatient to get on. He wanted to marry Ellen but he would not do so until he had found the right house. He wanted their new life together to be exactly right. There would be no half measures.

He reached for another file – Moss versus Moss – and wondered whether things would have been different had his father not died so precipitately. One thing was for sure, the old man would have approved of Ellen. He'd had a fondness for pretty blonde women, which probably explained why Nadia had taken such a dislike to Ellen. He wondered if it was a genetic thing that he favoured fair-headed women but then checked himself. His father had *not* been his father.

It wasn't often that he caught himself out in this way and he slammed Moss versus Moss down on his desk. The file knocked over a cup and saucer beside the telephone and a puddle of cold tea spread towards the papers. He leaped to his feet, grabbed the file and began to mop up the mess with his handkerchief. He cursed loudly and threw the tea-stained square of dripping linen into the waste-paper bin. Too angry now to focus his mind on the proposed maintenance order for Mrs Moss, he pushed back his shirt cuff and looked at his watch. It was almost lunch-time.

On the way out of the office he left instructions with his secretary that he'd be back in time for his two-thirty appointment. He drove out of the car park and joined the queue of traffic at the top of Church Walk where the road was being dug up for the second time that year. The weather was hot, very hot, and the busy pavements were full of sun-tanned bodies in skimpy T-shirts and shorts. A mother stepped out in front of his car and steered a heavily laden pushchair across the road. Among the carrier bags of shopping hanging from the handles Duncan caught sight of a small red-faced child wearing a pair of silly sunglasses and holding a dribbling ice lolly. Further up the road, one of the workmen, the one with the pneumatic drill, stopped what he was doing and mopped his brow. He was shirtless and his sunburned body glistened with sweat.

Duncan turned away and switched on the air-conditioning. He drummed his fingers on the steering-wheel, turned on the radio for the *News at One* and tried to dispel his anger. After getting caught speeding back in April he'd been conscious that never again was he to allow his temper to get the better of him when he was behind the wheel of his car. But it wasn't easy, what with

Nadia being so unreasonable and not being able to find exactly the right house. It had been a difficult few months.

He pressed the horn. Surely the silly old duffer of a driver in the Metro in front could see that the lights had changed to green. He sounded the horn again and as the Metro inched forward he revved the BMW's engine, waited for the road to widen and then overtook.

His mood swings were on the increase and they worried him. He knew it was the pressure he was under, not only in his private life but in his work – they were a partner down in the office due to an extended maternity leave – and the only remedy, it seemed, was Ellen. She was the one person upon whom he could depend. He could turn up at her place no matter what time of day and she would be there for him. He counted himself a lucky man. Not a day passed without him thinking how fortunate he was to have Ellen in his life. They were so right for each other, so compatible. In everything.

Even when it came to sex.

Sex could be so divisive and, in his experience, was more often than not the main cause of marital breakdown – most of the clients for whom he acted bore the scars of their partner's adultery. He was well aware of the myriad pleasures derived from this one simple act of desire, but he was even more sensible to what a powerful and dangerous weapon sex could be.

At first he'd been wary of taking this all-important step with Ellen because . . . because if he was painfully honest he didn't think he was much good at it. It was a shaming thing to have to admit, but it was the one area in his life in which he lacked confidence. Which was probably why he hadn't put much effort into prolonging any relationship in the past. Sex had never been a priority for him and over the years it had become little more than a perfunctory act. He had no way of knowing if Ellen minded his lack of bedroom zeal for they hadn't ever discussed their love-making – a post-mortem on his performance was the last thing he wanted to encourage – but he sensed that, like himself, she had no inclination towards entering a sexual marathon each time they went to bed.

He swung the car into Beggarman's Lane where at the top of the road a For Sale board was nailed to a tree. He bumped slowly along the dusty, potholed road and pulled into the car park. Straight away he saw that Ellen's Peugeot wasn't there. He locked the car and went over to the barn. There was no sign of Ellen. Next he tried the cottage. He crashed the knocker against the door. But there was no response and the sound reverberated loudly in the emptiness of the hot, still afternoon.

Annoyed and let down, he drove back to the office. A message was waiting for him on his desk. He rang the number and asked to speak to Trudi Jennings.

Chapter Twenty-Seven

Crantsford station was busy. The one forty-five train from Manchester was due in at any minute, and waiting for it was a party of foreign-exchange schoolchildren, who were occupying the four wooden benches that lined the platform with its pretty hanging baskets of geraniums, petunias and tumbling nasturtiums. The children were French, noisy, exuberant and slightly intimidating, and despite the continuing heatwave, which was now into its second week, they were all dressed in jeans, thick-soled boots and sweatshirts. Ellen found herself wondering if they were from Provence and that maybe they found an English summer's day chilly in comparison to the dry heat of home.

She moved along the platform to find a quieter space and chided herself for thinking of Provence. Provence meant one thing and one thing only: Roger.

Since April she had received a further three letters from Roger and she had paid him over five hundred pounds – five hundred pounds she could ill afford. She knew it was cowardice on her part for giving in to him but what else could she do? She had to keep it from Duncan. She didn't want him knowing what had gone on before in her life – she wanted nothing from her past to sully her future. What she had with Duncan was so different to her life with Roger. Duncan was devoted to her; he was dependable and sincere, but most of all, being with him brought her the sense of reassurance and security she so badly craved. He made everything seem right and the very fact that his restrained approach to their sleeping together was the complete antithesis to Roger's made her even more convinced of their compatibility.

She smiled, thinking that there would be some who would view Duncan's temperance towards sex as being odd . . . somebody like Matthew perhaps.

The smile disappeared from her face. She hadn't heard anything from Matthew since that dreadful day back in April when she'd lost her head after reading Roger's vile letter. He'd disappeared back to the Lake District that evening and for that she was eternally grateful – seeing him again after what they'd done would have been intolerable. She had wondered whether he'd ring her or even write, but there had been no communication, none at all. Again she was glad. And again she knew that this was cowardice on her part. The thought of Matthew knowing what Roger had made her do filled her with shame. Oh, it was all very well saying that what people got up to in the privacy of their bedrooms was their own business and perfectly acceptable, and that was true . . . when it was between two people who both wanted it, but she hadn't. She had only done it to try to secure the love of her husband. And now he was throwing all the pain and humiliation of that episode back at her.

She glanced down at her hands and saw that they were clenched, the knuckles showing through her skin, sharp and white. How ugly they looked. She felt ugly too. She relaxed her fingers and heard the sound of an approaching train. Jo-Jo's train.

The phone had rung early that morning, forcing her to get out of bed before seven o'clock on her one day off and making her sound grumpy as she spoke into the receiver. But the moment she heard Jo-Jo's voice her mood changed.

'Is everything okay?' she'd asked anxiously.

'Not really,' Jo-Jo had replied tightly. 'Mum's been taken into hospital, a psychiatric ward. Nobody knows how long she's going to be there. She tried to kill herself . . . I only went out for a short while and when I got back she was . . . Oh, Ellen, she was in the bath and there was so much blood.'

'Who's there with you?' Ellen asked firmly. 'Who's looking after *you*?'

'No one. And I don't need looking after. I'm fine.'

Ellen had heard Jo-Jo speak like this before, at the Patisserie when her brave words had covered up a cry for help. 'Right,' she said. 'Have you still got that money Hermione gave you?'

'Yes, but –'

'Pack yourself a bag and get on the next train to Manchester. Give me a ring from there when you know what time you'll be arriving at Crantsford. Got that?'

'But, Ellen, I can't leave her like this. It doesn't seem right.'

'Your mother's in good hands for now, Jo-Jo,' Ellen said gently, 'and for a few days I think you deserve the same.'

Although Jo-Jo didn't speak, Ellen could feel the relief flooding down the line.

'And remember to leave a note to let people know where you are,' she continued. 'You're not running away this time, you're staying with friends.'

The train pulled into the station. The group of French children surged forward and Ellen stayed where she was. Doors began opening, passengers stepped down and

255

pushed their way through the noisy mêlée. Ellen saw Jo-Jo struggling to get through the crowd and went to her. They hugged and when Ellen pulled away Jo-Jo was close to tears.

'Come on,' Ellen said, 'let's get out of here.'

Johnny Foreigner was waiting for them in the station car park and Ellen opened the door for Jo-Jo to get in. She was astonished to see how enormous Jo-Jo was and she tried to remind herself that it must only be a matter of weeks before the baby would be born.

Jo-Jo noticed Ellen staring at her. 'I'm huge, aren't I?' she said, with an embarrassed smile.

'That's pregnancy for you.' Ellen laughed lightly. 'How many weeks have you got?'

'Four, but I don't think I'll last that long. I feel ready to explode here and now.'

At Spring Bank Cottage they sat on the bank in the shade of the willow tree. The grass beneath them was parched dry and only a trickle of water remained of the stream where shiny pebbles glinted in the dappled sunlight. A dragonfly skimmed across the water and on the other side of the stream hogweed, waist high with flower heads the size of dinner plates, towered over ferns and nettles and deadly nightshade. Jo-Jo fanned herself with a large dock leaf. It was good to be back.

'Heavens above,' exclaimed Susie, from the sun-lounger on which she was lying. She was flicking through last Sunday's colour supplement, which she hadn't had time to read until now. She clicked the chair into a vertical position and sat upright.

'What is it, Mummy?' asked Millie, raising her eyes

from the picture she was drawing of the back of the house.

'It's Matthew,' Susie said, showing her daughter the magazine. 'Look, two whole pages about him. Come and see.'

Millie came and stood by her mother. Her reading wasn't up to the large blocks of tiny print but she smiled when she recognised Matthew's face staring back at her. 'Is he famous now?' she asked.

'I don't know, but he's probably very much in demand.'

Millie didn't know what her mother meant by *very much in demand* but she continued to stare at Matthew's face. She remembered how she had liked the way he smiled, not that he'd smiled very often. He wasn't smiling now either. He looked rather cross. 'Why didn't he ever finish our painting?' she asked. 'Didn't he like us?'

'It wasn't that exactly,' Susie said absent-mindedly, recalling how she'd come back from the shops that day back in April and not only found the kitchen in as big a mess as she'd left it but that Bonkers had taken it upon himself – and to use his words – to relieve Matthew of his duties. Their very first full-blown argument had followed, with Bonkers sticking to his guns and saying that there was no way he'd let the man back into *his* house. She had sulked a good deal for the rest of the day and had even given him the cold shoulder in bed that night.

'Why don't we ask him to come back?'

Susie lowered the magazine and smiled at her younger daughter. 'Would you like that?'

Millie nodded, her eyes large and appealing. 'He was nice. If he came back he might draw Bobtail for me. He said he would.'

'I'm afraid your father will need some convincing on

that score,' Susie said doubtfully, but all the same she couldn't help wondering what the consequences would be if she contacted Matthew herself and then presented the whole thing to Bonkers as a *fait accompli*. Would he really be able to turn down the opportunity of owning a work of art that would be so well thought of, not to mention highly admired and the envy of all their friends? She glanced back at the magazine and carried on reading the article, reassuring herself of Matthew's worth.

When she finished the piece she began to wonder whether there was any real chance of tempting Matthew back to Crantsford.

Matthew had always thought that Coniston Water was the most striking of all the sixteen lakes in the Lake District. The surrounding wooded fells, lush and green, came right down to the water's edge and were backed by gentle moorland – it was a sight that never failed to inspire him in his work.

Along the eastern shore was Fir Island together with Peel Island, which had been the setting for Arthur Ransome's *Swallows and Amazons*, but the main focal point of the landscape was the Old Man of Coniston, a peak deeply scarred with quarries and mines, and it was this that Matthew was painting from his old wooden dinghy.

It was said of his work that he captured the spirit and serenity of the Lake District and while he had no pretentious views about painting, and in particular of his own ability to paint, he believed he had a natural affinity with the landscape that enabled him to reflect on paper and canvas what was there for all to see. Completely self-taught, he was a great advocate of teaching oneself to observe with the greatest of accuracy – 'To see clearly is poetry, prophecy and religion – all in one,' John Ruskin had written, and over the years this had been like a creed to Matthew.

For a moment he put down his paintbrush and turned his head to view the impressive house behind him. It was Brantwood, where Ruskin had made his home for the last twenty-nine years of his life and where Matthew often lingered over the sketches and watercolours that had inspired him so much as a young boy.

He returned to his painting, giving all his concentration to it. His hand moved deftly, not once did he hesitate. Occasionally he would look up and shield his eyes against the glare of the sun on the water and focus on some part of the massive fell. He would hold the image in his mind, then lower his gaze and simply allow the paint from his brush to reproduce what was in front of him.

He worked quickly and was soon finished. He packed up his box of paints and brushes, then pulled out a bottle of beer from the small cool-box in the bow of the clinker-built dinghy. He snapped off the bottle top with his penknife and drank half of the beer in one long gulp. He had been so absorbed in his work that he'd forgotten how hot it was. He looked at his arms, where the sun had deepened the colour of his already tanned skin to a dark mahogany, and caught sight of his watch. It was nearly six o'clock and, looking across the water, he saw that apart from one or two sailing dinghies further up the lake and a man walking a dog along the shore, he was alone. He finished his beer and stared up at the empty blue sky and listened to the water lapping gently against the hull of the boat.

It was a mistake, for in that moment when his body

relaxed and his mind had nothing on which to focus, his thoughts immediately strayed to Ellen.

For four months now he'd spent each day trying to get her out of his mind. He'd deliberately not even phoned Hermione for fear of the temptation of asking how Ellen was – he didn't want to hear that she was now married . . . that she was happy. What right did she have to be happy when she'd made his life such hell?

He tidied away his things and started rowing for the shore, pulling hard on the oars to rid himself of any lingering thoughts of Ellen.

When he'd left Crantsford he'd had no idea of what lay ahead. He'd had no comprehension of the misery in store for him. He had stupidly thought that by running back to Coniston his problems would be left in Cheshire, but he of all people should have known that this wouldn't be the case. When he'd unloaded his car and opened the door to his Lakeland slate cottage he had merely brought his own personal damnation with him. He couldn't sleep that night, couldn't rid himself of the memory of making love with Ellen, and after lying awake for most of the night he'd padded downstairs to his studio and sketched her face – he could see her in his mind's eye as clearly as if she was sitting with him in his studio. He'd finally turned out the light, just as the first signs of an apricot dawn began to creep over the sky, and had gone back upstairs to bed leaving his studio littered with a dozen or so frustrated attempts at capturing the woman he loved.

Love? He must be mad.

How could it have happened? How could his life have been so dramatically turned upside down by a woman he barely knew? And how the bloody hell had he allowed it to happen?

When he reached the shore he rolled up his jeans,

slipped off his canvas shoes, stepped into the cool water and began to haul the small boat across the shingle. He tied it to a stubby wooden post where his nearest neighbours kept their own rather grander vessel, gathered up his things and started for home.

Several messages were waiting for him on his answerphone.

'Hi, this is Joy Reynolds from the Cumbrian Tourist Board. We'd like to discuss the possibility of you doing a range of postcards of the area. I'll call back some time tomorrow.'

The second was from one of the gallery owners in Windermere.

And the third was from Susie Buchanan.

He glowered over the machine and listened to what she had to say.

Chapter Twenty-Eight

Hermione opened the door.

When Call-me-Trudi had telephoned just a few hours after leaving Laburnum House to say that she had a client who was keen to view the property that very evening, she had been taken by surprise, not just by the woman's apparent efficiency but by the name of the client. Duncan Carter.

Ever since the night of the Buchanans' party Hermione had wanted to sit down with Ellen and do some serious talking with her. But the chance had never presented itself. Ellen was either busy at the barn or she was with Duncan, and as it was Duncan Hermione wanted to discuss it hardly seemed appropriate to invite them both round for a drink in order to tell her friend that she thought she was making a monumental mistake.

It irked Hermione that she had encouraged Ellen to set her sights on Duncan. How flippant she had been that day at the Patisserie when they had discussed him as the means of solving Ellen's financial difficulties. It was bad enough suspecting that he was the wrong man for Ellen, but quite another accepting that part of the responsibility for the match going ahead lay fairly and squarely at her door.

It wasn't just that Hermione had taken a dislike to Duncan. It was more basic than that. If she wanted Ellen to marry anyone, she would prefer her to marry Matthew.

In the early stages of Ellen's divorce, it had never occurred to Hermione to consider Ellen and Matthew as a potential couple. She supposed it was because she had been convinced that Matthew was going to repeat history and make the terrible mistake of marrying the wrong woman – Bridget. It had been a case of her worst fears coming true. Hadn't she dreaded Roberta's siren-like charms luring Kit away from her, and hadn't it happened?

She had no idea what Matthew was up to now but she knew him well enough to realise that his sudden disappearance from Crantsford was nothing to do with a pressing engagement as he'd made out. 'Pressing engagement, my foot,' she'd told him. 'You're running away.' He hadn't risen to the bait but had carried on slinging his few pieces of luggage into the back of his car. 'I'll ring you,' he'd said. Another lie. There had been no calls, none of his usual weekly check-ups on her well-being, just a silence that spoke volumes. Damn the boy.

And damn Duncan Carter and all his money.

'Mrs Rowlands?'

Hermione brought herself back to the present and stared at the lofty figure standing in the doorway. He was holding out his hand.

'Duncan Carter, we have met before, it was some months ago at –'

'Good evening,' she said curtly. She was disappointed to see that he was alone – she had hoped that Ellen might come as well. Then it crossed her mind to have some fun. Just a little sport. She would play the part of eccentric old lady.

'I'm so glad you could come,' she said, adopting the voice of Dame Edith Evans playing the monstrous Lady Bracknell. 'It's this way, come on through. Have you left your bag of tools in the car? But how clever of you to think that you could manage without.'

Duncan tilted his head to one side. 'I beg your pardon?'

She hauled him over the threshold and tutted. 'No, no, dear boy, this won't do at all. You'll have to hurry along or else I shall miss this evening's episode of *Dixon of Dock Green*, I do so like that bit when he says, "Evening, all." ' She bent her knees accordingly and pretended to lose her balance. She reached out to Duncan for support.

'Perhaps I've called at a bad time,' he suggested, doing his best to release himself from Hermione's surprisingly firm grasp as she began to propel him at speed through the house. Barking! She was completely barking! He'd thought so the first time he'd met her.

They came to a stop in what he took to be the dining room. He tried to concentrate on the reason why he was there in the first place and started checking out the size of the room and then its architectural features, such as original plaster cornices and the like. His eyes came to rest on an interesting watercolour above the fireplace, a landscape of water and softly rolling hills in the gloomy half-light of dusk, but before he had a chance to take a really good look he found himself being dragged across the room.

'There, now, just look at the shocking picture on that. You can't see a thing, can you? I don't understand it, it was fine last night.'

He followed the old woman's gaze to a sturdy chest of drawers. Good grief! Clearly she was so ga-ga she thought this was a television.

'Well, go on then, have a twiddle with those knobs and see what you can do.'

'Look,' he said, trying to gain control of a situation that was fast slipping away from him, 'I think you've made a mistake. I'm not a television repair man, I'm –'

'Aren't you? But you certainly have the look of one, dear boy.' She saw him bristle. 'Why not have a go for me anyway? I'm sure all you've got to do is play around with those knobby things.' She forced him nearer and made him bend down. 'There, now,' she said. 'You twiddle away to your heart's content while I stand back and tell you when the picture is clear.'

There was nothing else for it but to do as she said.

Behind his back Hermione was struggling to keep a straight face as she watched Duncan in his expensive suit get down on his hands and knees and start turning one of the loose wooden knobs on the old chest of drawers. 'Try left,' she said, just managing to choke back a snigger, 'yes, that's it, oh, that's much better. How clever of you. If you're not a television repair man then I really do think you should give some serious thought to a career move.'

Duncan got to his feet and considered the possibility that this woman's madness might just work to his advantage if he decided to make an offer on the house. That's if he ever managed to see round it.

'I'll show you out now,' Hermione said mischievously. She was watching Duncan's face closely, and could see him wondering how best to proceed.

'If there's nothing else for me to fix, Mrs Rowlands, I'd like to view the house. That's why I've come.'

Ten out of ten, she thought. Most men would have been only too ready to make their escape. Credit where credit was due. 'Well, why on earth didn't you say so in the first place?'

She saw him relax.

But she wasn't finished yet. 'Let's start at the top of the house,' she suggested, thinking of all the flies. 'Now, tell me, what did you say your name was?'

'Duncan Carter, I'm engaged to a friend of yours –'

'You're not Duncan as in Ellen's *Duncan*, are you?' She smiled engagingly. Gone was Lady Bracknell, now she was everybody's favourite sweet old auntie with a jelly for a brain.

He nodded.

'But we've met already, haven't we?' She giggled. 'At Ellen's little cottage, and at the Buchanans' party. How silly of you to have forgotten.'

As they climbed the stairs to the top of the house Duncan loosened his tie. He noted the damp patches, the cracks in the plaster, the peeling wallpaper and the general state of neglect, and for each negative point he notched up he mentally knocked five thousand pounds off the asking price. He'd soon have it down to a more realistic figure.

As soon as the estate agent had given him the address of the property he'd known that no matter how bad a state the house was in, it would be right for him and Ellen. But he was no fool. He was more than aware of the colossal amount of money it would take to turn Laburnum House into the home he desired.

'It must be quite a drain on your resources, keeping a great big old house like this going,' he said sympathetically, hoping to appeal to an old lady's emotions as well as opening up the way for future wranglings. He ducked out of the way of an angry bluebottle as they entered the first of the junk-filled attic rooms.

'Terrible,' she answered. 'Shockingly expensive. You

wouldn't credit how much it costs. I wouldn't recommend anyone to buy this old barn of a place.'

He laughed politely and swiped the air as another fly buzzed at him. He moved towards the escape route. 'Shall we?' he said, his hand on the doorknob.

He found the other attic rooms just as disgusting as the first: dusty, crammed full of boxes and large pieces of ugly furniture, and yet more flies. 'You've a lot of memories stored up here,' he said tactfully.

'Rubbish,' she said.

He looked at her.

'I mean, it's all rubbish waiting to be turfed out.' She started for the stairs.

'What about that room?' He pointed to a door, which was closed.

'Oh, it's full of junk just like the other ones. There's no need to go in there.'

'I think I ought to see all the rooms, don't you? I'm really quite interested in the property.'

'Surely not?'

'I'm sorry?'

Just as Hermione had made up her mind at the front door to have some fun at Duncan's expense, the past rose to her mind and she knew she could not, *would not*, sell her beloved home to – of all people – Duncan Carter. And under no circumstances was she going to allow him to pry into the one room of the house that meant so much to her; a room that would mean absolutely nothing to him. He'd probably wallpaper over Matthew's painting the moment completion took place.

'What does Ellen think about living here?' she asked.

'I haven't discussed it with Ellen yet,' he said, wanting to add, if it's any of your business. After he'd left Spring Bank Cottage and gone back to the office and made his call to the estate agent, he'd been too busy to ring Ellen and had decided in the end to view Laburnum House on his own and surprise her with the news that he'd found the perfect home for them.

Hermione stared at him, her eyes small, dark and piercing. He shifted uncomfortably beneath her gaze.

'I can't imagine that Ellen would want to live so close to Orchard House,' she said. 'Don't you think it would be a little insensitive to expect that of her?'

'Ellen's not a woman to be swayed by sentiment,' he said firmly. 'Now, if we could get on, I'd like to see the rest of the house.'

'I've changed my mind,' she said, her voice brisk and businesslike. 'I don't want to sell it.'

Duncan breathed in deeply and took a step towards Hermione. 'But *I* want to buy it,' he said slowly.

Hermione noticed Duncan's hand gripping the newel post of the handrail. She also caught a look of something in his face that she didn't much care for. She turned away from him and started going down the stairs to the next floor. 'Then I'm sorry to have wasted your time,' she said over her shoulder, glad to have put some distance between the two of them, 'but I'm sure you'll find something much more to your taste, maybe even to Ellen's.'

She held open the front door for him and as he crunched his way across the gravel to where he'd parked his car she called after him, 'Oh, and by the way, thank you so much for fixing the television for me.'

Duncan drove the short distance from Laburnum House to Spring Bank Cottage. 'Bloody stupid old woman!' he swore, as he turned into Beggarman's Lane. 'How dare she make a fool of me?'

It was when she had stared at him through those hooded eyelids on the top landing that he'd realised that, far from being round the bend, Hermione Rowlands was as astute as any person he knew. Television repair man indeed!

He saw Ellen sitting in a deck chair in the front garden of her cottage, but she wasn't alone.

'How long is *she* staying?' he asked Ellen, when they'd gone inside the house leaving Jo-Jo stretched out on a blanket enjoying the last rays of the evening sun.

'I'm not really sure,' Ellen said, disconcerted. Duncan was clearly angry and, while she had become adept at soothing his temper, she sensed that it would take more effort than usual to pacify him. 'What is it?' she ventured. 'A problem at work?'

'No.' He turned and faced her. 'I've just been to see a property which I thought would be ideal for us, but the owner was inexcusably rude and for no good reason suddenly decided that the house was no longer for sale.'

'Oh,' was all Ellen said. Duncan had viewed dozens of properties over the past few months and none of them had been to his liking. They had either been too small or in the wrong area, or worse still, in terms of adding to his frustration, had been snapped up by some other purchaser.

'And the worst thing is she's a friend of yours,' he said accusingly. 'It was that dotty Hermione Rowlands.'

Ellen was stunned. 'But I didn't even know she'd put her house on the market. Where is she thinking of moving to?' As she heard herself speak, her conscience pricked. How long was it since she'd spent any time with Hermione? Hermione, who had been so kind and loving after Roger had left her.

'That's not the point,' Duncan said. 'She was rude to me.'

Ellen frowned. 'She has a strange sense of humour, she's what you'd call fey –'

'I don't think you're listening to me, darling.'

'Okay, okay,' she said soothingly. 'I'll have a word with her.'

'And while you're about it make sure you convince her that I'm serious about the house.'

'But, Duncan, is it really what we want?' Ellen didn't think it was. Quite apart from what lay next door but one, she couldn't see herself living in Hermione's house. She would feel like an intruder. 'It's going to take a lot of putting right,' she said.

'I know,' he said, and seeing the unsure look on Ellen's face he said, 'darling, it'll be perfect for us and the sooner we can exchange contracts the sooner we can get married. Don't you want that?' He kissed her on the forehead. 'Why don't you go and see the batty old dear and work your charms on her? I want Laburnum House for *us*, darling, and soon.'

'I wouldn't call Hermione a "batty old dear",' said a cross voice from the doorway. It was Jo-Jo and, coming into the sitting room, she gave Duncan a chilling stare.

'You have quite a habit of listening in to other people's conversations, don't you?' Duncan said, his voice as cool as the look he gave Jo-Jo.

The phone rang and Ellen went into the kitchen to answer it. She threw an anxious look over her shoulder at Jo-Jo and Duncan.

'What brings you back to Crantsford?' Duncan said. He moved across the room and made himself at home in an armchair beside the fireplace. He didn't look at Jo-Jo:

for some strange reason he found the sight of her large, swelling body unpleasant.

'Ellen invited me to stay with her, if it's any concern of yours.'

'Ellen is very much my concern,' he said, resting his elbows on the arms of the chair and steepling his fingers in front of him.

Jo-Jo didn't reply. She was busy trying to work out why she disliked Duncan so much.

'So why are you here? The father-to-be giving you a hard time?'

She looked him directly in the eye. 'If you must know, my mother just tried to kill herself.'

'Oh,' he said, taken aback, 'I'm sorry.' But then he went on, 'So why are you here? Surely, in the circumstances, a daughter should stay with her mother and not go rushing off –'

'Look,' she said angrily, 'butt out of my life, will you? You know nothing about me, so just –'

'That was my mother on the phone,' Ellen interrupted, coming back into the sitting room. 'She wants us to go and see her at the weekend, Duncan. She's suggesting Sunday.'

'I'm playing golf,' Duncan answered. 'It'll have to be another time.'

'Oh,' Ellen said, disappointed, and aware of the tension between Jo-Jo and Duncan she wondered how to resolve it. 'I thought I'd do some fish kebabs for supper. Why don't you join us, Duncan?'

'No, thanks,' he said, suddenly springing to his feet. 'I wouldn't want to be in the way here.'

She walked him to his car. 'You could have stayed,' she said. 'You wouldn't be in the way.'

He shook his head. 'I don't think your pregnant tearaway likes me very much.'

'She's not a tearaway, and I have the impression that you're not so keen on her.'

He placed a finger on her lips. 'Nonsense.' He smiled. 'I just don't like having to share you. I want you all for myself. It's a weakness I have.'

She kissed him, pleased that his good mood was fully restored.

He got into his car and lowered the window. 'Now don't forget to go and see that woman about Laburnum House,' he said. 'If anyone can talk her round you can.'

Ellen waved him off.

From the sitting-room window Jo-Jo watched Duncan's car bump along the track. When Ellen came back into the cottage she was still wondering what it was about Duncan that made her feel so uncomfortable.

Bonkers couldn't believe his ears. He threw down his Jeffrey Archer novel. 'You've done what?'

'Oh, don't get all steamed up and overreact. I'm doing this for all of us. Surely you can see that?'

Bonkers goggled. 'That's a good one! How do you make that out?'

'Now you're just being churlish.'

'No, I'm not!'

Susie came over and joined him in bed. 'It's an investment.'

'Pah! And what happens to our investment if we move from here?'

'You said yourself you didn't ever want to move again. If I remember your words correctly, you said, "I'd rather have my testicles . . ." '

'On the spur of the moment one says these things.'

'Yes, and on the spur of the moment I've invited Matthew to come back and finish the mural.'

'Then you can pay for it yourself!'

Susie smiled at him.

'I'm serious,' he said, picking up Jeffrey Archer from the folds of the duvet and finding his page. 'If you want that ill-bred chap here in this house, you can jolly well pay for it yourself! You can have a scaled-down version of the Sistine Chapel for all I care, just so long as you don't expect me to hand over any money to that hoodwinking fellow.'

'But how? Works of art don't come cheap and I don't earn any money.'

'Well, then, sweetie, there lies your dilemma.'

'That's not fair!'

Bonkers smiled. 'You sound just like Floss.'

Matthew said goodnight to Hermione. He put down the phone and went and sat outside in the garden. It was dark, but still visible in the inky night sky was the blurred outline of the Old Man of Coniston. He lit the two large candles on the wooden table and poured himself another glass of red wine from the bottle he'd opened earlier.

He knew that the decision he'd come to a few hours ago with a delighted Susie was a foolish one. It was the decision made by a man no longer in control of his senses. The moment he'd heard the sound of Susie's tinkling voice at the other end of the line he'd waved goodbye to reason and had made mindless chit-chat in order to ask the one question he'd dared not put to anyone before.

'And how's Ellen?'

'Gosh, to be honest I don't really know. I've not seen her for weeks, she seems to have disappeared.'

273

'Too wrapped up in married life, perhaps?'

'Oh, no,' Susie had said. 'She's not married yet. Though to be honest with you, and this is strictly *entre* the *nous* of us, I hear that it's Duncan who's dragging his feet because he's such a fuss-pot and can't find the right house in which to set up home.'

Matthew was so delighted with the news that he had wanted to blow Susie a kiss down the phone, but instead he'd said, 'When shall I come and start work? Day after tomorrow?'

'Golly, that would be wonderful. And I know this is terribly cheeky, but you couldn't possibly stay next door with your godmother again, could you? Only I don't think Bonkers –'

'Don't worry, I'll ring Hermione and square it with her.'

The squaring of which had just been completed. Hermione had greeted the news of his visit with her usual aplomb. 'Didn't you find enough of the family silver to filch on your last stay with me?'

'I'm hoping to come away with gold this time,' he'd replied ambiguously.

Hellfire! What a crass thing to have said, he thought now, as he sipped his wine and stared through the flickering candlelight into the darkness. If that was what love did to you, then surely he was better off without it!

He drained his glass and set his mind to figuring out how best to convince Ellen that she was marrying the wrong man.

Chapter Twenty-Nine

Ellen awoke to the sweet smell of honeysuckle.

All spring and summer long the determined shrub had been steadily climbing its way up the front of the little cottage, stretching its tendrils and fragrant flowers towards Ellen's bedroom window. It was now sending out exploratory leafy shoots to investigate her alarm clock on the window-sill as well as the framed photograph of Simon as a baby.

With only a cotton sheet covering her, Ellen raised herself up. She parted the cream lace curtains, leaned against the sill of the tiny open window and breathed in the luscious fragrance.

It was a wonderful way to wake up and for once she didn't curse the fact that her bedroom was so small that the bed was jammed up against the wall – she had meant to get rid of the double bed when she moved out of Orchard House but the idea of sleeping in a single had seemed such a retrograde step that she'd hung on to it, despite the nuisance it had made of itself by taking up most of the space in the tiny room.

She looked at the alarm clock by her elbow. It was only half past seven but already the early-morning sun was hinting at another scorching summer's day. She leaned a little further out of the window, allowing the sheet to slip away from her. She plucked a pink and yellow flower from the honeysuckle and breathed in its scent. It was heavenly and for the first time in months she felt a strange sense of calm come over her.

Life was good.

Really good.

She smiled, lay back on the bed and twirled the flower between her thumb and forefinger. But as she closed her eyes a completely different sensation began to creep over her. Words like yearning and longing and passion came into her mind. She shivered – though she was far from cold – and her stomach took a flying leap as she turned the page of her sensory diagnosis and moved on to a more down-to-earth description of how she felt.

A woman has her needs, was her conclusion.

She smiled. It was some weeks since she and Duncan had slept together and even longer since she'd experienced the truly spontaneous desire to make love; she was unprepared for her body to take things into its own hands and invite her erogenous zones out to play.

Except it wasn't so long, was it? There had been that crazy moment downstairs on the floor with Matthew.

But she refused to dwell on this memory and turned her thoughts to wondering if she was beginning to recover from what she had allowed Roger to do to her.

For a time she had been convinced that the shame and humiliation Roger had bequeathed her might stay with her permanently. She wondered now if the aftermath of his sexual predilections would have been less painful if she had had the courage to share it with somebody. But she hadn't. She had told no one, because no matter what all the magazines and tabloids had to say about sex, it was still taboo among people to talk about what they *really* got up to in their bedrooms.

As far as Ellen was aware, her friends and acquaintances were more than willing to discuss size, quality and quantity but not one had ever shared anything of a more intimate nature. Over the years there had been the usual jokes around the dinner table about men always wanting *it* and women preferring freshly laundered bedlinen and a good book. There had been tales of *coitus interruptus* with the appearance of curious small children in the bedroom, or even stories of the family Dalmatian appearing under the duvet and poking its cold wet nose where it wasn't wanted. But not once had there been any shared confidences of a husband wanting his wife to dress up on a nightly basis like something out of St Trinian's.

But no, she mustn't think of Roger, she really mustn't keep reminding herself of the past. She was now an intelligent woman who listened frequently to *Woman's Hour* and knew about the liberating joy of sex and all its equal opportunities.

It was just a shame that Roger hadn't had his surgery radio tuned in to Radio Four and listened to Jenni Murray while tinkering with his patients' mouths, because maybe then he wouldn't have been so selfish or treated her as some object for his own gratification.

The real shame, though, was that she hadn't stood up to him.

Ellen and Jo-Jo had breakfast in the garden, and sitting in a deck chair with a plate of toast balanced on her huge stomach Jo-Jo was relaxed and happy. She sipped her orange juice thoughtfully and watched a pair of young sparrows having a mud bath in the lane.

'I love it here,' she said. 'It's so simple and uncompli-cated. Do you know what I mean?'

Ellen thought about this and decided there was an element of truth in what Jo-Jo had said. 'You mean, there are no frills? What you see is what you get?' She pulled a face.

'What's up?'

Ellen shook her head. 'Somebody said that to me recently. I wish I could remember who it was and in what context.'

'It was probably Duncan.'

Ellen caught the tone of sarcasm in Jo-Jo's voice. 'You don't like Duncan very much, do you?'

Jo-Jo turned away and looked at a robin perched on the sagging wire fence on the other side of the stream. 'Not particularly,' she said.

'Why?'

Jo-Jo returned her gaze to Ellen. 'Because he doesn't like me.'

'That sounds petty for someone as smart as you.'

Jo-Jo shrugged and bent forward to put her empty plate on the little table beside her. She suddenly winced. She straightened her back and rubbed her stomach. 'I keep forgetting I can't do things like that any more.'

Ellen looked at Jo-Jo's swollen body. 'You've barely spoken a word about the baby since you arrived.'

'That's because there's nothing to say. It's all arranged. Everything with the adoption agency is set up, all I've got to do is grow even fatter and somehow find the energy to give birth. Do you know? They even try to match the parents-to-be with what they think the baby will look like. Amazing.'

'So you've not had any second thoughts, no doubts?'

Jo-Jo shook her head. 'None. I know what I'm doing is right, and when you know that, you don't have any doubts.' She watched Ellen's face closely. 'I suppose that's how you feel about marrying Duncan, isn't it? You know that it's the right thing to do.'

278

'I hadn't really thought of it in those terms, but, yes, I suppose it is like that.'

'And is that because you think he can give you the security Roger took away?'

Ellen sucked in her breath. She carefully placed her empty cereal bowl on the small table between her and Jo-Jo and poured herself some more orange juice. 'As one grows older security becomes more important,' she answered, in a measured voice, 'your priorities change. But I wouldn't expect you to understand that, not at your age.'

Jo-Jo decided to try a different tack. 'What does Simon think about Duncan?'

'They get on well enough.' Ellen had the uncomfortable feeling that Jo-Jo was building up to something.

'And Hermione?'

'Look, Jo-Jo, it's me who's marrying Duncan, not Simon, and certainly not Hermione. Okay?'

'Okay, okay.' Jo-Jo returned her gaze to the wire fence and the robin who was still surveying the scene.

Ellen got to her feet and picked up the breakfast things. 'I need to get on,' she said. 'I want to see Hermione before I open the barn. I'll tell her you're here, I'm sure she'd like to see you.'

Jo-Jo watched Ellen go back inside the cottage. If she didn't feel so grateful to her for inviting her to stay she would have been honest with her just now when they were discussing Duncan.

In bed last night she had finally worked out what it was that she didn't like about Ellen's fiancé.

She didn't trust him.

The water butt was empty and, despite the ban, Hermione was screwing the end of her old hose pipe onto the outside tap. She looked up when Ellen came round the corner of the courtyard.

'Long time no see,' she said. But instead of being delighted at seeing Ellen, she felt cross with her friend for having stayed away so long. She felt childishly put out, as if she wanted to pay Ellen back. 'But I'm afraid I can't stop,' she said, 'I have to water these tomato plants or there'll be no chutney this year to take us into the millennium.'

Ellen took in Hermione's slightly frosty welcome as well as her wellington boots beneath a faded cotton summer dress and a straw hat that was beginning to unravel itself. 'How are you?' she asked.

'Well enough. And you?'

'Fine. I hear you've put your house on the market.'

Hermione turned on the tap and fired a jet of water at the first of the tomato plants. Its tender leaves trembled beneath the ferocious downpour and a clutch of small red tomatoes dropped to the ground. Hermione tried to adjust the nozzle on the end of the hose but only managed to soak herself in the process.

'I didn't know you wanted to move,' Ellen continued, making sure that she kept a safe distance between her and the hose.

Hermione gave up on watering the tomatoes. 'Well, you wouldn't, would you?' she said curtly. She turned off the tap.

Ellen was mortified. Hermione was so cross with her. Where had their friendship gone? The last thing in the world she wanted was this cold hostility from her dear friend.

'Hermione, I know I've been busy all this –' she started to say, but she got no further.

'I need to wash my hands,' Hermione interrupted.

Ellen felt nothing but sadness as she followed Hermione inside the house. She watched the old lady wash her hands at the sink in the garden room.

'You look troubled, Ellen,' Hermione said, drying her hands on the sides of her dress. 'Like you've got something to say, which is probably what brought you here in the first place.'

'I have, as a matter of fact.' There was so much to say, but Ellen was so saddened and choked with guilt for having neglected Hermione all these weeks that she found herself unable to articulate what she really felt. She badly wanted to apologise but the thought of a rebuff from Hermione was too much, so she decided to take the coward's way out. 'It's about the house,' she said, in a small voice. 'Duncan's really serious about making an offer.'

Hermione narrowed her eyes. 'And he's sent you here to make me change my mind, has he? To soften me up? Is that it?'

Ellen picked up a clay pot from an overcrowded shelf and smoothed away some dried-on soil from its discoloured surface. 'He said you were rude to him.'

'I suppose I was.'

They stared at each other.

'Why?'

'I'm not sure why,' Hermione lied. 'It just struck me as an amusing thing to do at the time. Did he tell you about the television?'

Ellen looked puzzled. 'What television?'

Hermione suddenly laughed. 'No, I don't suppose he would have. Come on, let's go and sit in the garden and I'll tell you what I did to your darling Duncan. It was terribly amusing.'

It was just like old times.

Except it wasn't.

'I haven't got much time,' Ellen replied stiffly. 'I've got to get back to open the barn.' She replaced the clay pot on the shelf. If Hermione had been making fun of Duncan it was her job to make Hermione know that it wasn't on. And if there was any apologising to be done, it was quite obvious that it was down to Hermione.

'Oh, Ellen,' cried Hermione, 'just listen to yourself. What on earth has happened to you? You used to be so much fun, but now you've turned into as boring and stuck-up a person as that fool of a man you intend to marry!'

'He's not a fool, and he's not boring!'

'But you agree he's stuck-up?'

'Oh, you're impossible!'

They glared at each other defiantly. Then Ellen turned to leave. There seemed nothing else to say. It was only when she reached home that she remembered she'd forgotten to tell Hermione that Jo-Jo was back in Crantsford.

Hermione was more upset than she cared to admit. She hated the idea that Ellen had only visited her to carry out Duncan's bidding, and when Bernie popped round a short while later he could see that she was very much out of sorts.

'Well, my little recalcitrant Hermaseta, are you going to tell old Bernie what's troubling you, or are you going to sulk for the rest of the day?'

'Nothing's troubling me,' Hermione said, pushing him out of the way to peg out the washing.

'What a temper you have on you this morning, Grandmama.' He chuckled. 'And what attractive undies you have.' He flicked at a pair of her sturdiest knickers on the line.

'Oh, go back to your harem and leave me alone.'

'Not until I've had the truth from you.'

Hermione pursed her lips and carried on with what she was doing.

Bernie went inside the house and ransacked the kitchen for something cold to drink. He found nothing so went back outside to Hermione. 'Get your wellies off and come with me.'

'Why?'

'Because I've asked you to.'

'No!'

'Hermione Rowlands, if I was twenty years younger and you were three stone lighter I'd put you over my knee. Now do as you're told and come along.'

Hermione compromised. She went next door to the Lodge but kept her boots on. Bernie took her up to his suite, forced her to sit in the comfortable chair overlooking the croquet lawn, fetched an ice-cold can of lager from the fridge in his neat kitchenette and waited for her to speak.

He waited a long time.

'I've just lost a friend,' she eventually capitulated in a small voice, 'a very good friend.'

'Who?'

'Ellen. It was awful. She came to see me and we were both so horrible to one another.' She sniffed and hunted for a tissue in her pocket. 'It's that wretched Duncan,' she continued. 'Ever since they've been engaged it's been a case of divide and conquer. It's terrible to see someone change so dramatically. She's going to end up just like him. He's not at all the right man for her.'

'And what precisely is wrong with him?'

'Don't you remember him at Susie and Bonkers's party?'

He shook his head. 'Not particularly. Should I?'

'He's a bloody great snob and he wants to buy my house.' She told him about last night.

Bernie laughed and nearly risked his chest when she described how she'd made Duncan get down on his hands and knees and retune the chest of drawers.

'That wasn't at all kind of you.' He chortled.

'But that's the sort of man he is, he brings out the worst in me.'

'Oh, Hermione, whatever shall I do with you?'

'Don't patronise me,' she snapped.

'But you won't cut off your nose to spite your lovely old wrinkled face, will you?' Bernie asked, the laughter in his voice now gone. 'If he offers you a fair price, you will accept it, won't you?'

'Must I?'

Bernie took her hands and placed them between his own. 'Oh, yes, Hermione,' he said softly. 'Indeed you must.'

Chapter Thirty

Susie knew that Bonkers would have forgotten that it was his sister's birthday the day after next and as she herself had only remembered that morning she decided she'd have to go into Crantsford and choose something.

'Girls,' she called through to the playroom, 'we've got to go shopping.'

Floss's predictably scowling face appeared at the door. 'It's too hot to go out,' she said.

'It's too hot to do *anything*,' Susie said, 'but we need to buy a present for Auntie Janey. It's her birthday on Sunday. So hurry up and find your sandals. I want to get on.'

'I'm not going out,' Floss said. 'Shopping's boring.'

'Only because you make it so by constantly moaning.'

'*I* don't moan,' joined in Millie, appearing in the hall with her sandals in her hands and sensing that for once she might be better at something than her elder sister. '*I* like shopping.'

'Well, I don't. And I'm not going out!'

Susie was determined not to lose her temper. 'I know,' she said. 'How about we go to Spring Bank Dried Flowers and choose something for Janey there? We could walk and maybe Ellen will let you paddle in the stream. What do you think?'

Within no time at all they were crossing the main road

that went into Crantsford and walking along Beggar-man's Lane. The road was dry and dusty and it was lined on either side with an out-of-control hawthorn hedge. Grass had grown almost shoulder high in places and it was interspersed with hogweed, and buttercups, stinging nettles and daisies, bindweed and the occasional spiky pink foxglove. The girls paused for a moment and played with the bindweed, pressing the base of the snowy-white trumpet-shaped blooms between their fingers and firing the delicate flowers at one another.

There were quite a few cars in the car park and the door of the barn was wide open. It was welcomingly cool inside. Susie caught sight of Ellen behind the counter with a queue of people waiting to be served. She waved discreetly and moved about the shelves trying to find something suitable for her sister-in-law.

'This is pretty, Mummy,' said Millie, pointing at an enormous arrangement. 'Would Auntie Janey like that?'

'I was thinking of something a little smaller,' Susie said – cheaper, too.

'It's boring in here. I'm going outside,' Floss announced. 'Coming, Millie?'

'Stay together,' Susie called after them. 'No wandering off.' She returned her attention to a small arrangement of red roses in a dear little earthenware pot. She couldn't really imagine Janey with something quite as sophisti-cated as this in her flat – she was more into a couple of twigs stuck in an empty wine bottle – but even so, a present had to be bought so it might just as well be this. And, besides, it wasn't too expensive.

Ever since Bonkers had told her that she personally would have to foot Matthew's bill she had been racking her brains as to how to go about this. The first thing she had decided was to economise on certain items, secretly, of course, and siphon off the money saved to go towards paying Matthew. She would cut back on brand names, maybe even stop buying the fillet steaks they liked so much. Their nightly bottle of wine would have to stop, as would those expensive dips with ready washed and chopped crudités. She would have to convince Bonkers that they needed to watch their weight and that she had devised a diet for them. But even so, a few little economies here and there wouldn't go anywhere near the full cost of Matthew's bill. What she needed was a job. Something part time and not too taxing, which would pay her lots of money. She couldn't really go back to being a secretary, which was what she had done before she'd had Floss, as she'd need to do some kind of refresher course and there wasn't time for that. It was *now* that she needed money, not in six months' time.

'Hello, Susie.'

Susie looked up from the pot of roses in her hands and saw that the barn was empty. 'Ellen,' she said, going over to the counter, 'how are you? Business looks like it's picked up nicely for you.'

'It certainly has,' Ellen agreed. 'It's been like this for some weeks. I'm so busy on the counter I haven't got enough time for making the arrangements, and if I don't make them I've nothing to sell. Ironic, isn't it? Just when it seems I don't need to work, the business is booming. I've even been approached to supply arrangements for the show houses on that new estate being built over at Holmes Chapel.'

Susie was impressed. 'And have you had much interest from anyone to buy the business?'

Ellen shook her head. 'No. I don't understand it. I thought there'd be any number of women in Crantsford who might see this as a bit of a hobby for them. But, then, I suppose buying the cottage as well isn't that attractive a proposition.'

'Why don't you sell it separately?'

'I probably will in the end, but to begin with Duncan thought we'd try our luck selling it as one. Do you want to buy that?'

'Please.' Susie put the pot of roses on the counter. 'It's for Janey. I'm not sure it's really her, if you know what I mean.'

Ellen smiled and saw Millie and Floss come in through the open door.

'Can we have an ice cream, Mummy?' asked Millie.

'Sorry, darling, you'll have to wait until we get home. There's a couple of Feasts in the freezer if you haven't eaten them already.'

'I'm thirsty,' added Floss.

Susie turned back to Ellen, handed over a ten-pound note and waited for her change. 'You know, that wouldn't be a bad idea,' she said.

'What wouldn't?'

'Selling refreshments – teas and coffees, sticky buns and all that stuff.'

'And ice cream.' Millie smiled over her shoulder and went outside again with her sister.

'You'd do a roaring trade here,' continued Susie. 'You could have tables and chairs with pretty umbrellas overlooking the stream. I can just see it, it would be perfect. You'd become a tourist attraction with coach parties –'

Ellen laughed. 'I can't quite see a coach managing to negotiate Beggarman's Lane.'

'Well, maybe not, but it's worth considering, don't you think?'

'But you're forgetting, I'm selling up.'

'Oh, yes,' Susie said absent-mindedly. She was turning over the glimmer of an idea. 'You won't be bored, then, when you give up work?'

'I shouldn't think so,' Ellen replied, though she did have to admit that now she had been working so hard for the past year she couldn't imagine herself sitting around in a large, empty house twiddling her thumbs, waiting for Duncan to come home. 'I expect there'll be plenty for me to do when Duncan and I are married. Setting up home can be pretty time-consuming.'

Susie looked about the barn and at the depleted shelves, and decided to give the glimmer of an idea an airing.

'Ellen,' she said, 'I don't suppose you'd consider taking somebody on to help you out over the next few months, just until you've found a buyer?'

Ellen listened to what Susie had to say. Frankly she wasn't sure. Hadn't Susie once said it took all her concentration to bring in the milk? 'But why, Susie, why do you want a job?'

'Why does anyone want a job? I need the money.'

Ellen was startled. Susie and Bonkers had always given the impression of being very comfortably off – they certainly hadn't made any attempt at haggling over the asking price of Orchard House. And dressed in her Versace jeans and Lacoste polo shirt, with Ray-Ban sunglasses pushed back on the top of her head, Susie looked the least likely person to be saying that she was strapped for cash, unless . . . unless she'd got herself into a pickle with her credit cards and didn't want Bonkers to find out.

'I'd love to help,' she said, 'but there doesn't seem much point with the business being up for sale.'

Susie was desperate. With the chance of earning some

real money so very nearly to hand, she wasn't going to give up easily. 'Just keep me on until a buyer turns up. You said yourself a few minutes ago how busy you've been, and if I work here just a couple of days a week you might even be able to take a bit more time off to get yourself ready for your wedding.'

Ellen was tempted. But would it work? Susie and her working *together*?

'But what about the girls? How will you manage with them?'

'Easy. Mummy only lives over in Plumley, she'd love to have them. Oh, please, say yes. It is for a good cause.' She decided to tell Ellen exactly why she needed the money. 'I really want Matthew to finish that painting for us, and it would serve Bonkers right and show him I'm a force to be reckoned with.'

'Well,' Ellen laughed, 'I suppose we women must stick together. When do you want to start?'

'I'll have a word with Mummy as soon as I get home and then I'll ring you back. Golly! I can't wait to see the expression on Bonkers's face.'

Ellen watched Susie rounding up Floss and Millie from the stream and hoped she wouldn't regret the decision she'd just made.

Though what she might regret even more was seeing Matthew again.

If he was going to be at Hermione's for the next couple of weeks, as Susie had just told her, she couldn't imagine there not being at least one occasion when they would meet. It also meant that his being back in Crantsford would force her to confront what they had done that day in April. When he had disappeared so suddenly he had taken with him the guilt of her betrayal of Duncan, but now he was returning he would be bringing it back for her to face.

She suddenly wished wholeheartedly that she and Duncan were married. At least then she'd feel safe, because if there was one thing Matthew made her feel it was completely *un*safe. There was a recklessness about him that seemed to rub off on her.

'I've heard tell that there's a man in your life.'

Nadia lowered the dented EPNS silver teapot and fixed Phyllis Winstanley across the table at the Patisserie with a long hard stare.

'Is that so?' she remarked.

Phyllis exchanged a smile with Cynthia Kovel.

'Come on, then, Nadia,' Cynthia urged. 'You can tell us. What's he like?'

Nadia resumed pouring her tea. 'I should think you know well enough as I've no doubt you've thoroughly researched the entire subject and exhausted all sources of likely information, namely Crantsford Golf Club.'

'As if!' laughed Phyllis, helping herself to another macaroon from the tiered cake-stand.

Nadia laughed too. She had wondered how long it would be before her *little secret* would be out. To summarise: Nigel Wade was new to Crantsford; he was a sixty-five-year-old widower who had taken up golf late in life and was, according to him, trying to make up for lost time. They had met after a ladies' tournament – which Nadia had easily won – and during the presentation she had found herself standing next to him in the bar. The club membership secretary, Magnus Jefferson, had made the introductions and had left them to their gin and tonic while he went to deal with a telephone call. The following week they played a round of golf together and several weeks on they played again and had lunch afterwards in the clubhouse. Nigel was a retired business-man who led a busy life with his large family – four children and a horde of grandchildren – and was frequently away on what he called 'loose ends of business' down in London. That was all she knew about him.

'And what does Duncan make of –'

'Duncan doesn't know,' Nadia interrupted Cynthia.

'But why ever –'

'There's absolutely no reason why I should report my every move to my son,' Nadia asserted. 'Just because he lives in *my* house it doesn't make him my keeper.'

'Well, of course not,' Phyllis said, backing off from what was obviously a sensitive issue. She and Cynthia had often remarked on the strange relationship Nadia had with her son. 'A bit love–hateish, I'd say,' she'd often commented to Cynthia, 'especially now that he's decided after all these years to get married. I expect she's taking it a bit hard. Feelings of rejection and betrayal are probably near the surface in that rambling old house.' She and Cynthia had spent many conversations speculating on Nadia's future after Duncan's marriage. Would she sell Crantsford Hall? Would she heal the rift between her and Duncan? Would she ever consider marrying again?

'Why don't we have a dinner party?' Cynthia suggested, thinking that this would be the perfect way to smoke out Nadia's friendship with Nigel Wade. 'We haven't had a get-together for ages. Come on, girls, fish out your diaries and let's fix a date here and now. Nadia, you could bring Nigel along.'

Nadia raised an eyebrow. 'You know what I like about you, Cynthia?' she said, reaching for her handbag. 'It's the way you approach everything so honestly and directly. There's not an ounce of guile in you, is there?'

Matthew was stunned by the For Sale board.

When they had spoken on the phone last night Hermione hadn't mentioned anything about putting Laburnum House on the market. When had she taken this important step, and what had made her do it? Had her health deteriorated in the last couple of months and the house finally become too much for her? Or were her finances in a worse state than he'd imagined? He cursed himself for not having kept in touch throughout the summer.

He slammed the boot of his car and carried his luggage round to the courtyard where he found Hermione watering a row of tomato plants.

'You're early,' she said.

'And you're breaking the law.' He kissed her and went to turn off the tap. 'Come inside and tell me what's going on.'

'I'm not sure I like the tone of your voice, Matthew,' she said tetchily, 'especially as you're the second man to try pushing me about today. I'm not some silly child who –'

'Then stop acting like one and give me a break. Why didn't you tell me you were selling Laburnum House?'

'How could I?' she flung back at him. 'You haven't phoned me all summer. And anyway it's my house and I'll sell it if I want to.'

She sounded tired. Reproachful, even. And standing in her old boots in the corner of the courtyard with a limp hose in her hand and the low evening sun glinting off the puddles she'd created, she looked like a small defeated child. To his horror Matthew saw her eyes fill with tears. He went to her and put his arms around her shoulders.

'I'm sorry,' he said. 'I didn't mean to sound off at you like that. It was the shock of seeing the For Sale board. Please, come and tell me all about it.'

He led her slowly round to the back of the house, down the steps and across the lawn to the greenhouse where they had always gone when there had been anything serious to deal with. It was where they'd gone when Kit had died. They'd spent nearly all night in there consoling each other.

The sun had moved round and the greenhouse was in full shade, but even so, it was still warm and muggy inside. Matthew sat Hermione in her old deck chair and he opened as many windows as possible – some were beyond it, so rotten was the wood.

'Looks like you've had quite a party in here,' he said, eyeing a row of wine bottles under one of the slatted benches. He held one up. 'Pouilly Fumé,' he read from a label. 'I'm impressed.'

'It's Bernie,' she said, 'he's leading me astray.'

'And is it Bernie who's encouraged you to sell Laburnum House?'

'In part, but only because I've finally had enough of it all. I'm an old woman, Matthew. I want a rest. Is that so much of a crime?'

He came and sat next to her. 'It's nothing of the sort. So what are you planning on doing?'

She told him about the Lodge.

'Makes good sense to me,' Matthew said, after listening to her, 'but I don't think it's selling Laburnum House that's upset you, is it? You seem quite clear on that. What else has happened?'

She explained about Duncan coming to view the house

and what she'd made him do and then how she'd refused to sell to him. 'I think I may have been a little cruel to him,' she conceded.

Matthew laughed. 'What I wouldn't have given to see that! You're priceless, Hermione, really you are.'

'But it's the consequences of what I did that are so appalling. Oh, Matthew, if you'd seen how Ellen and I treated one another this morning. We were like strangers. And I'm sure she only came here on Duncan's say-so to try and make me change my mind. I haven't seen her all summer, and then hey presto! here she is on my doorstep telling me off for being rude to Duncan.' Hermione shook her head and tears filled her eyes again. 'And what I'm most cross about is that I'm to blame. I encouraged her, Matthew. I as good as said, "Go and prostitute yourself for an easy life of riches." I just wish I could undo all the harm I've done. I've spent most of today thinking about going to see her and making her understand what a mistake Duncan is. Because he is, I know it.'

Matthew leaned back in his deck chair. He sat thoughtfully for a few moments before speaking. 'I've given Ellen a lot of thought since April –' He broke off and shook his head. 'You can't imagine what an understatement that is.'

She reached out and squeezed his hand. 'I think I can.'

'Anyway, the only conclusion I've reached is that I don't think anyone but Ellen herself can decide whether or not she marries Duncan. If you or I point out why Duncan isn't right for her she'll dig her heels in even more. Remember when I was ten and I wanted to climb that old apple tree at the bottom of the garden beyond Kit's statue and you kept telling me how dangerous it was and that I wasn't to go anywhere near it? Well, you made me want to climb it all the more.'

'Yes,' she smiled, 'and a branch gave way just as I said it would and you nearly broke your neck. I remember only too well. Roberta never stopped blaming me for that.'

'The thing is, I don't think we ever grow out of that childish desire to prove our independence,' Matthew continued, 'and it will be the same with Ellen.'

'So what can we do? I don't want her to break her neck, Matthew.'

'She won't . . . I'll see to that. But first of all, and for your own peace of mind, I think you should go and apologise to Ellen, Duncan as well if you can bear it. At least then you'll have your friendship back, and that's what's really upset you, isn't it?'

She nodded. 'But what about you and Ellen?'

He sighed and ran his hand through his hair. 'I'm giving it one more shot. That's why I'm here.'

'I thought so. Or, rather, I hoped so.'

'I must be out of my mind. I don't know what it is about her but she's driven me almost insane this summer.' He explained why he'd left so unexpectedly on his last visit. He told her about Roger's letters and him and Ellen making love and then Nadia Carter arriving on the scene.

Hermione was shocked. 'Why did she never tell me about what Roger had done?'

'I don't think it's an easy subject to bring up when you've been made to feel so utterly ashamed of yourself.'

'Poor Ellen. Poor confused Ellen. No wonder she's so desperate to marry Duncan. She wants to build as big a barrier as she can to keep that blasted Roger out of her life. I see now why she agrees with everything her new lord and master says. She came so close to losing him back in April that now she'll do anything to keep him sweet.'

'That's right,' Matthew agreed. 'There's nothing like the threat of losing something to make you value it more highly . . . even if it isn't worth hanging on to.'

'So what should I do about Laburnum House? If Duncan makes an offer, should I turn it down?'

'Please don't think about sacrificing your own happiness on my account,' Matthew said firmly, 'I'd never forgive myself if you did that.' He caught an odd faraway expression in Hermione's face. 'What is it?' he asked.

'I'm not sure, really. I was just remembering Duncan's face when I told him I'd changed my mind about selling the house. There was something in his eyes that was quite disturbing.' She gazed at Matthew. 'I'm not easily scared, but in that split second of a moment I was.'

Matthew knew that Hermione was not a woman given over to flights of fancy and this description of Duncan worried him.

It was late and outside Jo-Jo's bedroom the faintest of breezes was blowing gently through the trees, rustling leaves and making the gingham curtains slide to and fro above the window-sill at the end of her bed.

She had done nothing all day but sleep, and with only a few weeks left of her pregnancy she knew she was growing ever more tired. The worry of her mother's attempted suicide had also added to her exhaustion. She had phoned the hospital after breakfast when Ellen had gone to see Hermione and she had spoken to the nurse who had been on duty when her mother had been admitted. Her mother was now in a ward with two other women of about her own age and who, for their own differing reasons, had reached a similar point in their lives. And they were probably all married to monsters like her step-father, Jo-Jo concluded. What was it with men who felt the need to dominate those closest to them? Did they do it because their wives and girlfriends were such easy targets? She felt the baby move inside her, so strongly that she had a picture in her mind of the baby being a girl and punching the air with a small defiant fist in response to her thoughts. That's right, Jo-Jo told the baby, don't make yourself an easy target . . . not like me.

Initially when she'd returned to school, Alan – who during the Easter holidays had decided to start wearing his hair in a weedy little pony-tail – had ignored her, which was an amazing feat in itself, since he was her English tutor and she had lessons with him in small groups of twelve several times a week. Then, after nearly a fortnight when he had avoided her at all costs, he'd approached her in the corridor and said that if she had any plans to blackmail him he would simply deny everything, call her home life into question and reason that she was a born trouble-maker with an unstable background.

'Oh, very politically correct,' she'd thrown back at him. 'Worried about the Child Support Agency knocking on your door and waking your wife up to what a sad loser you are?'

From that day on the man had walked about the school in dread of bumping into her. Surprisingly enough, the rest of the staff, including the headmaster, had been sympathetic towards her. She had anticipated being turned away from school, with allegations flung at her from all directions that she was a bad role model for the younger children, but not a word had been said. Even her classmates, whom she had dropped when she and

Alan had been seeing one another, drew near again. They were curious. What was it like having *something* growing inside you? And who was the father? She had joked that she'd been abducted by aliens and had had sex with an Agent Mulder lookalike. Which, with hindsight, would have been more fun than what had really happened.

She closed her eyes ready for sleep and then remembered that her A-level results were due out on Monday. She fell asleep with her fingers crossed.

Chapter Thirty-One

Susie had told Matthew not to turn up until she called him. 'Bonkers won't be leaving the house until ten-thirty,' she'd whispered on the telephone yesterday evening, 'but just in case he's running late, or we've had a drama over breakfast, best come when I've given you a little tinkle. The girls are so looking forward to seeing you again.'

As Matthew rang the doorbell he somehow doubted that Little Miss Shrewd Eyes was waiting with bated breath for his reappearance at Orchard House.

He heard somebody on the other side of the door struggling with the lock. When the door opened Millie stood before him. She smiled shyly, her toy rabbit, Bobtail, in her hand.

'Hello,' she whispered, 'Mummy's on the phone.'

Was she ever off it?

'Have you brought all your paints?'

'Of course he has,' answered Little Miss Shrewd Eyes from behind her sister. 'Or why would he be here? Let him in, then.'

They took him through to the conservatory.

It was like an inferno. The French windows were wide open but there still wasn't enough air; a fiercely hot sun was blazing through the glass. Matthew thought of the stifling day ahead of him. Already he was sweating. He began to set out his things on the floor and stared up at the wall. He was relieved to see that his sketches were still intact – at least that idiot Bonkers hadn't defaced his work, or taken a pot of paint to it. He smiled to himself, doubting that Bonkers would be capable of doing even that much.

'Matthew, you're here!' exclaimed Susie, joining him at last. 'Oh, what a treasure you are! Sorry about all that subterfuge. But it's rather exciting, really, isn't it? I suppose this is how people having affairs feel. Gosh, not that I'm suggesting anything. But, honestly, I thought Bonkers would never get on and leave this morning. He only has to do the occasional Saturday at the hospital and I thought for one ghastly moment that perhaps I'd got the dates wrong.' She paused for breath. 'Shall I just leave you to it?'

'Yes, that would probably be the best thing,' he said quickly.

She came back ten minutes later. 'You'll be needing these, won't you?' She gave him the step-ladders.

Half an hour later she reappeared again. 'You must be dying of thirst.' She handed him a glass of mineral water.

And then it was lunch-time.

Within twenty minutes of getting back to work after a chicken sandwich and a can of lager, she popped her head round the door once more. 'You will say if you need anything.'

It was hopeless. Completely hopeless! Would he never be left alone?

Oh, Ellen, you'd better be worth all this!

Hermione kicked off her boots and slipped her hot feet into an ancient pair of leather sandals; one of the straps was hanging by a thread and it looked as if it would be lucky to see the summer through. She glanced in the mirror above the sink in the garden room and smoothed back her hair, then noticed that her hands were muddy from pulling up new potatoes. She turned on the tap and started washing herself. If she was going to call on Ellen then the least she could do was look clean and tidy.

The phone rang.

'Mrs Rowlands? Hi. It's Trudi . . . Trudi from Harker and Company.'

'Hello,' Hermione responded, a little cautiously. She was half expecting a ticking off for having frightened away a potential buyer.

'The good news is we've received an offer.'

'And the bad news?'

'I'm afraid the offer is well below the asking price.'

'And, um . . . who's made the offer?'

'Mr Carter. He's just called into the office.' At the other end of the line Trudi crossed her legs and her fingers. 'He mentioned something about a little awkwardness between the two of you on Thursday evening when he viewed the property. Something about you having changed your mind and not wanting to sell.' She held her breath. Please, God, don't let this be true. Let it be some stupid mix-up. She gripped the phone tightly, as well as the thought of the one and a quarter per cent commission so very nearly in the bank.

Remembering Bernie's insistence that she mustn't cut off her nose to spite her face and what Matthew had told her in the greenhouse, she said, 'Gracious! What can the silly man have been talking about? Of course I want to sell. How much is he offering?'

Trudi let out her breath, uncrossed her fingers and legs and leaned back in her chair. 'Now, we have to bear in mind the sluggish state of the market –'

'That's not what I heard on the news a couple of weeks

ago. More houses were sold last month than in any previous –'

'But national averages don't really give the full picture when it comes to specific county –'

'Just tell me what he's trying to rip me off for, will you?'

'He's offering three hundred.'

'And what?'

'No, that's it. Three hundred thousand.'

Hermione's derisive laughter filled Laburnum House, as well as the purple-and-green-carpeted offices of Harker and Company.

'What do you want me to tell him, Mrs Rowlands?'

'You're a sweet young girl,' Hermione said drily, 'and I don't think you're up to the message I'd like to pass on to Mr Carter.'

'I don't think we want to be too hasty,' Trudi said patiently, leaning forward in her chair – elderly clients really were the most awkward, they had no idea how to play the market. 'We've got him hooked so let's try and nudge him up to a more suitable figure, shall we?'

'Nudge him! The man needs spearing with a harpoon!'

'Shall I tell him that –'

'You can tell him to increase his offer to a more realistic figure or not bother. Goodbye.'

Hermione put the phone down and decided she'd better hurry along to Ellen and see if she could make peace before Call-Me-Trudi had a chance to report back to Duncan and he had had an opportunity to whinge at Ellen.

She was halfway down Beggarman's Lane, and just pausing to admire a Red Admiral quivering its beautiful wings on a bindweed bloom, when she saw a familiar figure lumbering slowly towards her.

'Jo-Jo! What are you doing here? And, my word, just look at the size of you!'

Jo-Jo smiled and ran her hand over her thin cotton dungarees. 'Fit to burst, eh?'

Hermione kissed her. 'When did you arrive?'

'The day before yesterday.' She told Hermione about her mother and Ellen inviting her to stay. 'I didn't fancy being on my own with my step-father. I couldn't face the idea of all those silent, resentful stares.'

Hermione's heart warmed towards Ellen. She may have got herself wedged under Duncan's thumb, but at least she'd done the right thing by Jo-Jo. A shame she hadn't seen fit to let her know their young friend was back in Crantsford, though.

As if picking up on her thoughts, Jo-Jo said, 'What's up between you and Ellen? She came back dead miserable after seeing you yesterday.'

'It's a little complicated, but I've come here to apologise to Ellen. We've had a small disagreement.'

'Would it have anything to do with Duncan?'

'How very perceptive of you. Now, come along, it's far too hot to stand here gossiping. Where are you off to?'

'I was on my way to see you, so you've saved me a trip.'

They walked towards the barn. Several cars were parked outside.

'Oh dear,' said Hermione. 'I had hoped to catch Ellen on her own. I can hardly eat humble pie in front of a lot of strangers.'

'Don't worry.' Jo-Jo laughed. 'I'll mind things while you two patch up your differences out here.'

'Perhaps you could go inside and tell Ellen I'm here. Would you?'

When Ellen came out she smiled hesitantly at Hermione. 'Jo-Jo says you want to talk to me. Shall we go over to the cottage?'

Hermione shook her head. 'The bank looks as though it would be agreeably cool.'

They sat in the shade of the willow tree. At first neither seemed to know what to say. Ellen played with a long piece of grass, while Hermione fiddled with the strap on her sandal, like a small child worrying at a loose tooth. Then it came away suddenly in her hand.

'Oh dear, now I'll have to pay a visit to Oxfam.'

Ellen raised her eyes from the blade of grass. 'We used to love our rummages in Oxfam, didn't we?'

Hermione smiled at Ellen. 'Do you remember when I bought that handbag and we found a ten-pound note in it?'

'Yes, we went straight out and blew it on tea and cakes at the Patisserie.'

They fell silent again.

'I'm sorry, Ellen,' Hermione said at last. 'I'm sorry I was rude about Duncan and that I made a fool of him.'

'And I'm sorry too. I've neglected you badly these past few months, and that's unforgivable.'

Hermione shook her head. 'Nothing's that bad, Ellen.'

'I know you don't really like Duncan,' Ellen said, 'and I know he can appear a little prosaic, but it's just his way. He's what you'd call a man of form and order. I don't think he's used to people making a joke at his expense. And things are difficult at the moment between him and Nadia, she's making it very awkward for him. That's why he's so desperate to find the right house so we can get married.'

Hermione was finding it hard not to speak her mind. More than anything she wanted to shout at Ellen that Duncan was no more the right man for her than Donald Duck was. But she'd promised Matthew she'd play it his way, which meant she had to keep her mouth shut.

'Ellen,' she said, 'did you know that Duncan has made an offer on my house this morning?'

'No,' she answered. 'No, I didn't.'

'The thing is, it's too low, so ... so I've turned it down.'

'Oh.'

'You have to see it from my point of view. I need to get as much as I can because I'm hoping to move into the Lodge.'

'The Lodge? But I thought you hated the idea of old people's homes. You've always been so rude about them.'

'Believe me, this is no ordinary nursing home. This is de luxe retirement accommodation. And it's not something I'm rushing into. I've thought about it all summer.' She flicked at an ant crawling up her bare ankle. 'I'm tired of carrying the burden of Laburnum House on my shoulders. I want a rest and after all these years of making do with buttons I think I've earned the right to a bit of pampering.'

'Does Duncan know you've refused his offer?'

Hermione looked at her watch. An hour had passed since Call-Me-Trudi had phoned. 'Probably by now, yes,' she said.

Ellen sighed. She wasn't looking forward to her next conversation with Duncan.

Chapter Thirty-Two

'I shan't be able to make it,' Duncan said from the pantry, where he was supposed to be looking for a new jar of coffee. Instead he was checking up on Nadia's cache of sherry bottles. To his surprise he'd drawn a blank, which meant that she was probably getting sneakier and was hiding them somewhere other than behind the old flour bin on the top shelf.

He emerged from the pantry and found his mother sitting at the refectory table reading the *Daily Telegraph*.

'You've forgotten the coffee,' she said, glancing up from the sports page and looking at his empty hands.

'We've run out,' he said.

'Don't be ridiculous. Of course we haven't.' She got up from her chair and went to the pantry. 'What did I tell you?' she said, reappearing almost immediately with a new jar of Nescafé. She handed it to him and returned her attention to her newspaper and an American lady golfer with a sun visor and a mouthful of large, immaculate teeth. 'I'll have mine black, please.'

'Black?'

'Yes, that's what I said, Duncan. Your hearing going as well as your eyesight? Oh, and only one spoonful of sugar.'

Duncan placed the jar of coffee on the work surface beside the kettle. If he didn't know better he'd say that Nadia was on some kind of diet. She had taken to eating just half a grapefruit for breakfast each morning instead of her usual two slices of toast and large bowl of Fruit 'n' Fibre. There was also an alarming amount of rabbit fodder in the fridge.

'You haven't answered my question,' Nadia said, raising her eyes. 'Why can't you make dinner next Saturday at the Kovels'? Cynthia has gone to the trouble of inviting Ellen.'

He unscrewed the lid from the Nescafé jar, then took a knife from the cutlery drawer and stabbed at the seal. 'I've got a Law Society dinner in Manchester,' he said.

'No, you haven't. I've already checked with your secretary.'

He flung down the knife and faced her. 'You really have no right to pry into my private life.'

'And does that work both ways?' she asked. She gave him a curious look.

'I don't know what you mean.'

'I think you do.' And, in a voice Duncan didn't recognise as his mother's, she went on, 'There's a special reason why I'd like you to go to the Kovels' on Saturday. I want you to meet a friend of mine. His name's Nigel.'

It was a few seconds before Duncan had taken in this information. 'What do you mean, a *friend*?'

'I should think I've made myself quite clear. Nigel and I have struck up a relationship, if you must know.'

Duncan moved away and stood at the head of the table where he normally sat. He rested his hands on the back of his chair. 'Nigel,' he repeated, 'and just who on earth is he? Sounds like some kind of car salesman with a name like that.'

At the other end of the table Nadia carefully smoothed out her newspaper. She closed it, folded it in half and then in half again. When she'd finished she said, 'If you want to know anything about Nigel I suggest you come to Cynthia's next Saturday.' She got to her feet. 'And on second thoughts I shan't bother with that cup of coffee, it's later than I thought. I'll be out for most of the day.'

'Why? Where are you going?'

'I'm having my hair done.'

'Again? You only went the other day.'

'Well, I'm having it done again.'

'What time will you be back?'

'When I'm ready.'

She swept out of the kitchen and Duncan considered the potential consequences of what his mother had just told him.

The idea of Nadia remarrying had never occurred to him. Not in his wildest dreams had he thought it a possibility.

He barely had time to gather his wits before the phone rang.

His mood was not improved by the news from the estate agent. Hermione Rowlands had turned down his offer.

For the next hour he mooched angrily about the house. He knew there was no point in going to see Ellen. It was Saturday afternoon and she'd be far too busy to talk to him, so he went into his study and took out his temper on the errant Mr Yates of Yates versus Yates by dictating a stinging broadside on the dictaphone for his secretary to type up first thing on Monday morning. He rattled off a further series of letters and at six o'clock he rang Ellen at the cottage, but all he got was her belligerent house guest.

'Is Ellen there?' he asked.

'Yes.'

'Well?'

'Well, what?'

'Can I speak to her?'

'Don't you mean, *may* I speak to her?'

'Are you doing this deliberately?'

'Doing what deliberately?'

'Oh, for goodness' sake, just tell Ellen I want to speak to her.'

A few minutes passed and then he heard Ellen's voice.

'Hello, Duncan,' she said brightly.

'I want to come and see you. I'll be there in about a quarter of an hour.'

Ellen thought it best, given the mood she suspected Duncan was in, if Jo-Jo wasn't around when he arrived.

'Why don't you go and see Hermione?' she said, going through to the kitchen where Jo-Jo was in the middle of one of her cleaning sessions. 'I'm sure she'd love to see you again.'

Jo-Jo stopped what she was doing and put down the dishcloth. 'Is it *him*? Is he coming here?'

Ellen nodded. 'I think he's a bit upset about Hermione refusing his offer, and it might be best if I see him alone. Do you mind?'

'Course not.'

Not long after Jo-Jo had left the cottage, Duncan's car appeared in the lane. Ellen braced herself. If only she could persuade him to buy a different house.

She plied him with a glass of wine from a bottle she'd stuck in the small freezer compartment of the fridge as soon as she'd put the phone down and hoped it was sufficiently cold to mask the fact that it was cheap and not what he would normally favour. She tried to tempt him to sit outside in the garden, but he declined.

'No, I'd rather stay inside.'

While he paced the floor she settled herself on the

window-seat, grateful for the slight breeze that blew in from the open window. She waited for him to speak.

'I just can't believe she's done this. I thought you were going to have a word with her. Didn't you go and see her?'

They were off.

'I did, Duncan,' she said calmly. 'In fact, I've seen Hermione twice since we spoke, but I can't make her do something she doesn't want to do. Nobody can. Can't you increase your offer?'

'But I've offered her far more than the house is worth, she won't get a better –'

'Then perhaps we should look elsewhere.'

He stopped pacing and came and stood in front of her. 'Ellen, I don't understand you. Don't you want Laburnum House?'

She reached out to him. 'Not really,' she said in a quiet voice.

He stared at her, stunned. 'Why ever not?'

'Because . . . because it just doesn't seem right. It's Hermione's house and always will be.'

'Well, I disagree. I think it's perfect and I'm not going to back down just because you've got some silly sentimental notion about it. Besides, I want to get married. I'm tired of waiting. Just think, we could be man and wife and living in our own house in a matter of months. Don't you want that?'

She smiled and thought how lovely it would be to have everything sorted out, to be rid of all this conflict and for Duncan to be back to his old self. 'Of course I do. More than anything.'

'So why don't we both go and see the old lady? Let's ring her now and see if she'll play ball. Come on, Ellen.'

Ellen did as he asked.

'What a good idea,' Hermione exclaimed, at the other end of the line, when Ellen put Duncan's proposition to her. 'And there's no time like the present. Why don't you pop round in about an hour's time? Bernie's here, so is Jo-Jo, but then you know that – oh, and Matthew's here as well. We'll have a little party, shall we?'

When she put Hermione's idea to him Ellen knew it wasn't quite what Duncan had in mind.

'Is nothing ever straightforward with that damned woman?' he asked.

She laughed and found herself looking forward to the rest of the evening.

Ellen took Duncan round to the courtyard at the side of Laburnum House where they were confronted with two lines of washing drying in the low evening sun. As they tried to slip underneath, Duncan caught a blazer button on an item of Hermione's underclothing, the peg flipped off and the bra hung suggestively from his sleeve just as Matthew appeared.

'Hi,' Matthew said, noting the embarrassment on Duncan's face. 'You look well, Ellen.' He didn't attempt to kiss her, as she'd suspected he would, and he even kept his hands firmly by his sides – it was as if he was keeping any physical contact between them to an absolute minimum, as though he was as reluctant as she to repeat what had gone before.

'Hermione will be down shortly,' Matthew said, 'she's just changing.' Then he turned to Duncan, who had now dealt with the offending piece of washing. They shook hands.

'Do you remember me this time?' Matthew asked.

Ellen caught the edge to Matthew's voice, but Duncan

seemed unaware of the sarcasm. 'Didn't we meet at the Buchanans'?' he replied.

'Brilliant memory you've got,' Matthew said generously, giving Duncan a matey slap on the shoulder. 'Why don't you come on down to the garden?' he said to them both. 'Bernie and Jo-Jo are just warming up.'

'Warming up?' repeated Duncan warily, as Matthew led the way.

'We've decided to hold a croquet party. Any good at the game, Duncan?'

Duncan relaxed and smiled. 'As a matter of fact I used to be. I played for my college.'

Matthew smiled as well. 'I thought as much.'

They found Jo-Jo and Bernie sitting either side of a large covered drinks table in front of the summerhouse, and further down the garden the croquet hoops were ready and waiting. Jo-Jo was sipping orange juice while Bernie was mixing himself a Pimm's. He was wearing cream-coloured trousers and a cream shirt with the sleeves rolled up, and looked very much the part, even down to the cravat at his neck.

'Ellen,' Bernie exclaimed, 'how lovely to see you again and how very beautiful you're looking. I'm so looking forward to roqueting you into the bushes.'

Duncan rolled his eyes. But then he caught sight of Hermione coming across the lawn from the house. She was wearing a lime green shell suit with matching sweatband around her head and large trainers.

'Isn't this fun?' she called out, with a happy smile on her face. 'I thought I'd dress up, as we're having a sporting party.'

Ellen smiled back, recognising the shell suit as one of Hermione's impulse buys in Oxfam last year, along with the trainers.

'It was Matthew's idea,' Hermione carried on enthusiastically. 'He came across my old croquet set in one of
the attic rooms and suggested we gave it an airing. Now,
how's everyone for drinks? Bernie, how many of those
have you had?'

'Not enough, my little Hermaseta.' He chuckled and
started to pour two more tall glasses of Pimm's, one for
Ellen and one for Duncan.

Duncan waved his aside. 'I'll stick to soft drinks for the
evening, I'm driving.'

'Not staying at Ellen's for a night of passion, then?'

'Hermione!' warned Matthew.

Hermione looked innocently about her. 'My dears, I'm
so sorry, but a natural assumption to make in this day
and age, don't you think? Shall we partner up and get
on?'

Duncan took a step closer to Ellen.

'Oh, no,' said Hermione, with a laugh. 'Duncan,
you're going to play with me – that way we can mix
business with pleasure. Ellen, you go with Matthew, if
you can bear to be parted from your beau, and Bernie,
you and Jo-Jo will make a delightful pair of rotundities
together, Tweedledum and Tweedledee.'

'What sort of game are we going to play with six?'
Duncan enquired. 'I've only ever played association
croquet.'

'Oh, how dull for you, Duncan,' said Hermione, 'but
it's never too late to learn something new. Now, come
along with me while I explain the house rules.'

Everyone put down their glasses, fell in step behind
Hermione and Duncan and wandered over to the starting
hoop where they picked up their mallets and chose their
colours.

'But these aren't the proper colours,' Duncan said,

mystified. 'We should have only four balls, red, black, yellow and blue. This is most unorthodox. I've never seen a purple or an orange ball in play before.'

'I agree,' replied Hermione, 'it is unorthodox, but then that's how we do things at Laburnum House. This way we all get a ball each. It's much more fun than having to leave people out.'

'Well, seeing as you're the expert, Duncan, why don't you go first?' suggested Matthew.

'I wouldn't say expert, exactly.' He bent down and placed his black wooden ball the required distance from the hoop. He spent an inordinate length of time flattening out the dried grass and lining himself up, then taking several little practice swings.

Matthew had to fight back the urge to laugh.

'It's years since I've played,' Duncan said, after hitting the ball clean through the hoop. It ended up half-way to the next, perfectly placed, and he marched after it to take his next shot.

'I've picked myself the ideal partner, haven't I?' commented Hermione. 'You next, Ellen.'

Ellen missed.

So did Jo-Jo.

Matthew and Bernie also missed the target, but Hermione cleared it easily and moved on to join Duncan.

Duncan took his next shot. The ball shot through the hoop. 'Amazing how it all comes back,' he called, to the small group still huddled around the first hoop.

Seeing Duncan happy for the first time among her friends, Ellen began to relax a little. It didn't help her game, though. Jo-Jo and Bernie were now chasing after Duncan and Hermione and she and Matthew were left behind.

'Shall we cheat?' he whispered.

She laughed. 'It's rather humiliating, isn't it, when you can't get beyond first base?'

'Tell me about it!' he muttered, thinking of him and Ellen, and with a surreptitious nudge of his foot he lined up her red ball for her. 'Go on,' he said, 'nobody will ever know.'

She tapped the ball and smiled happily when it passed through the metal hoop. She took her next shot and waited for Matthew to do the same. They stood side by side and watched across the lawn as Duncan took a vicious stab at his ball and sent it crashing into Jo-Jo's.

'Do you think Hermione will reconsider Duncan's offer?' Ellen asked Matthew.

'Do you think he'll increase it?'

'He might, though don't let on I said so. It's just that I know he wants the house so badly.'

'And do you?'

She pretended to practise her swing.

'Ellen?'

She raised her eyes. 'No,' she said, 'not really. But if it's what Duncan wants . . . if it will make him happy –'

'And what about your happiness?'

'But I am happy.'

'Come on, you two,' shouted Jo-Jo, from the other side of the second hoop. 'It's your turn, Ellen.'

Ellen stood astride and began to make a small swinging movement with the mallet in preparation for hitting the ball with as much force as she could. She held her breath to help her concentrate. She sensed Matthew moving behind her. 'Keep still,' she said.

He moved again.

'You're putting me off.'

He came and stood beside her. 'Ellen, will you marry me?'

Ellen's red ball shot off at an angle and went hurtling under the drinks table, out the other side and straight into the summerhouse.

'Ellen, please –'

'I heard you the first time,' she said faintly, already moving away to retrieve her ball.

'Matthew, it's your go,' called Bernie, leaning nonchalantly on his mallet.

Without any finesse Matthew whacked his ball in the direction of the summerhouse.

'Not having much luck over there, are you?' shouted Duncan, who was nearing the third hoop.

'How right you are,' muttered Matthew. 'Well,' he said when he'd caught Ellen up, 'aren't you going to answer me?'

'You know very well that I'm marrying Duncan, so why are you doing this?'

She got down on her hands and knees at the furthest end of the summerhouse and began hunting for her ball among the chaos of seed trays and broken flowerpots and old gardening tools. She found it under a wicker chair alongside Matthew's.

'Here,' she said, rolling his ball to him as he crouched next to her.

He ignored it and taking her hand he raised it to his lips and kissed her palm.

'Stop it, people will see.'

'Let them, I don't care.'

'Well, I do. I've got everything to lose if we're seen.'

'And I've got everything to gain.'

She tried to snatch her hand away from him, but he held on tightly and kissed her palm again, brushing his lips against her skin. Her heart began to pound and a spark of something shot from her hand all the way up her arm.

'Please don't do that.'

He did it again.

'Matthew, stop it.' She was horrified at the effect he was having on her body – it was going to be the sitting-room floor all over again if she didn't do something. And fast.

'No. Not until I've convinced you that I've asked you to marry me because I love you.'

His face was merely inches away from her own and as she gazed into the darkening depths of his hazel eyes she saw such an intense expression of love in his face she knew he meant what he said.

'I'm marrying Duncan,' she whispered, desperate to hang on to what reason she still had.

'Ellen, I can't let you do that. I can't stand back and see you marry somebody else. Can't you see how much I care for you?'

The look in his face was too much for her and, frightened at what he might see in her own face, she summoned all her strength and lowered her gaze. She slowly withdrew her hand from his. 'Please, Matthew, don't do this to me . . . or yourself.'

'I don't seem to be able to help myself,' he muttered despondently. 'You make things bloody difficult for me.'

'I'm sorry, but it's not my intention.' She handed him his ball. 'I think we should get back to the others.'

'Yes, and pretend to everybody else that none of this has happened, like we've pretended so well that we never made love on the floor in your –'

She raised her hand to stop him. 'Matthew, please. It was a mistake. I'm not proud of what I did.'

'You should be. You were quite beautiful that day.'

She looked away, embarrassed. 'You won't make trouble, will you?'

His face darkened. 'I'll be the model of discretion, Ellen. Don't you worry about that.'

'Good.'

'Well, that's that, then,' he said flatly.

'So, there'll be no more proposals of marriage?'

He shook his head.

'No more kissing?'

'Stop torturing me, Ellen. I've made a big enough idiot of myself without you rubbing it in. And if you dare to suggest we be friends, God help me, I'll kill Duncan with my own bare hands and enjoy the moment.'

Ellen smiled, and in the ensuing silence they both heard the crack of wood against wood and the sound of Duncan's triumphant voice saying, 'I think that makes me the overall winner!'

It was late when they walked back to the cottage. The sky was dark and the air was thick and warm; insects hovered over the stream and several bats circled the barn.

Duncan was happier than Ellen had seen him in a long while, but he had every reason to be pleased. Not only had he won all three games of croquet that evening but Hermione Rowlands had agreed to his revised offer on Laburnum House.

'Now there's nothing to stop us from marrying,' he said, when Jo-Jo went on ahead and let herself into the cottage.

'No, nothing at all,' she murmured, staring out into the darkness.

Chapter Thirty-Three

Monday morning and Duncan was back in control.

It was as if the greatest of weights had been lifted from his shoulders since Saturday night and already one of the younger partners had the conveyancing of Laburnum House well in hand and Howard, an old friend, was arranging to carry out a full structural survey on the property. If all went well there was no reason why they couldn't exchange contracts within the month, which meant that within the month he and Ellen could be married.

They had decided to have a registry office wedding as neither wanted any fuss, or the complication of finding a vicar prepared to marry a divorcée. Naturally Nadia had opposed the idea when he had first mentioned their plans back in April, but just recently, he now realised, she had barely opened her mouth about his forthcoming marriage. Knowing his mother as well as he did, he'd put down her attitude to her having decided to play things from a different tack – he'd been the recipient of her silent disapproval several times. But now he saw how wrong he'd been. Nadia hadn't been rude about him and Ellen for the past few weeks because she was no longer interested in what he was doing. She was much too preoccupied with Nigel – *Nigel!* – to meddle in his affairs.

He gave a short laugh. No wonder there had been such

a propensity of lettuce and grapefruit in the fridge at Crantsford Hall, as well as so much time spent at the hairdresser's. He'd even caught Nadia preening herself in front of the mirror in her sitting room yesterday afternoon.

It was laughable.

And, quite frankly, next Saturday couldn't come soon enough. He had decided to accept the Kovels' invitation for dinner next weekend as, really, it was too good an opportunity to miss. He'd even suggested that Nigel should come for drinks before they all set off to Henry and Cynthia's, so at least then he'd get a good sighting of the man who most surely planned to shuffle his feet under the table at Crantsford Hall.

He'd tried doing a bit of detective work at the golf club yesterday lunch-time but had only unearthed what Nadia had already told him: that Nigel Wade was a widower, had recently moved to the area and had joined the club to start a new life for himself. Magnus Jefferson had hinted that he doubted whether there would be any bother over club fees being paid. 'Pretty comfortably off, I should think,' he had said confidentially in the bar, 'judging from that car he's got. Would you believe there's a nine-month waiting list for that model?'

Duncan knew all about waiting lists – he'd waited three months for his BMW, whereas Magnus drove an off-the-forecourt Toyota Corolla.

His thoughts were interrupted by his secretary bringing in some letters for him to sign. He read through the first one – Yates versus Yates, the one he'd dictated on Saturday afternoon.

'This can't possibly go out, Gail,' he said sharply. 'It'll have to be done again.'

He screwed it up and threw it into the bin, furious that

he had allowed his professionalism to be jeopardised by his private life.

While waiting for Susie to turn up on her first morning at the barn Ellen thought of Duncan and how pleased he was with himself.

She thought also how downhearted she was.

She had tried to put it down to tiredness, that and the pressure she and Duncan had been under these past few months, but she knew that this wasn't entirely the case. Her low spirits were directly attributable to the purchase of Laburnum House. She didn't want to live there.

But Duncan did.

They'd spent yesterday evening together at a restaurant in town and he'd spoken eagerly about the plans he had in mind for Laburnum House.

'If we knock through from the garden room to the kitchen we'll be able to create a decent-sized room more like the kitchen at Crantsford Hall. And one of the first things to go will be that decrepit summerhouse. Honestly, darling, it's a disaster waiting to happen. Did you notice how the tiles are practically ready to slide off? Catch one of those on your head and you'll surely know about it.'

'I rather like Hermione's old summerhouse,' she'd said.

'Oh, Ellen, we'll replace it with a much smarter one.' He'd reached out across the table and patted her hand. 'Now what about our honeymoon? I thought a week in Florence followed by a few days in Venice, or Rome. I've always wanted to see the Vatican and the Sistine Chapel. Maybe we could even go along to the Scrovegni Chapel in Padua and see those Giotto frescos the art historians are making all the fuss about. I like real art, not this pretence at it that we're bombarded with these days. What's that Matthew's stuff like?'

She had thought of the simply drawn sketches and evocative watercolours dotted about Laburnum House, and of the precocious but sensitively painted mural upstairs in the attic that Hermione had shown her one day. 'He's good,' was all she'd said, reluctant to say any more about a man who, the previous evening, had said that he loved her.

But now, as she waited for Susie, Ellen allowed herself to think of Matthew.

Several months ago Susie's sister-in-law had asked her what she thought of Matthew. At the time she had described him as passionate and spontaneous. Well, he was certainly both those things, she hadn't been wrong there. But there was something else about him which she'd never encountered in anyone before. When you were with him, you were *with him* and nobody else. It was as if he had an overwhelming presence that demanded your attention. And certainly after she'd spent any time with him she always came away feeling as though she'd been mentally mugged. He was much too much of a demanding character for her, and deep down she had the sneaky suspicion that perhaps he went around falling in love with women all the time. Maybe it was all part of his nature to make grand gestures of love like the one he'd made to her on Saturday night.

She was sure that when Matthew spoke of love he had passion in mind. Wildness, too. And lust and abandonment. But love for her had to be something much more contained. It had to be safe. It had to be secure. It had to be contentment and certainty.

That was why she was marrying Duncan.

Any woman who married Matthew would have to

cope with a daily routine of ups and downs. It would be a lifetime of uncertainty and she'd had enough of that. More than enough.

'Gosh, late on my first day, sorry, Ellen.'

It was Susie and she was dressed for action in a smart pinstripe suit with a nipped-in waist that Ellen would have died for. She looked as if she'd be quite at home behind a large black desk with a day of hiring and firing ahead of her.

'Is the suit okay?' Susie asked, noticing Ellen's gaze.

'It's fine. I'm envious, it puts my T-shirt and jeans to shame.'

'Oh, I wouldn't say that. Now, what do you want me to do?'

'Let's start with the till, shall we?'

Susie was a surprisingly fast learner and by mid-afternoon she had mastered the complexities of the till and had most of the customers' eating out of her hand. Secretly Ellen had thought she would turn out to be a dead loss and that she'd be bored within an hour, but she had been proved wrong, and could see only too well what an asset Susie might turn out to be. She had a real talent for convincing people that they couldn't possibly leave the shop empty-handed, and while she was selling coals to Newcastle Ellen was able to catch up on the backlog of orders that had been steadily growing in number.

Ellen also had to admit that it was quite fun having somebody to work with in the barn.

Matthew had Orchard House to himself. Susie had explained to him about her new job, starting at Ellen's barn, just as she was flying out of the door with Floss and

Millie. 'I've got to get the girls to Mummy's,' she said. 'Just help yourself to anything you need. 'Byee.'

Never had Orchard House felt so good.

He opened the French windows in the conservatory, stared thoughtfully up at the mural and decided to start work on Bonkers. It would have been the easiest thing in the world to caricature him as a bumbling fool but Matthew knew better than to do that.

He rolled up his shirtsleeves, set out his brushes, prepared his palette and started work, his eyes occasionally flicking from the photographs of Bonkers to the wall.

By three o'clock Matthew's neck and shoulders had almost seized up from standing in the same position for so long. He was also hungry. It was time to stop for a break. He put down his palette, opened his rucksack and pulled out a foil-wrapped package of sandwiches. He munched hungrily and wandered from the conservatory out into the garden.

There was a comfortable-looking sun-lounger on the patio but he ignored this and went and stretched out on the grass. He stared up at the Wedgwood blue sky, then closed his eyes. Straight away he flicked them open. He hadn't slept for the last two nights and he knew if he stayed there a moment longer on the grass he'd fall asleep.

He got to his feet and reluctantly went back inside the house to the stuffy heat of the conservatory. His sandwiches finished, he went in search of a cold drink from the fridge in the kitchen. He found a bottle of still mineral water, poured himself a glass and returned to the conservatory to start work again. It was best that way – it was only when he was working that he didn't think of Ellen.

He hadn't intended to say any of the things he'd said to

her on Saturday, but after four months of agonising over whether he would ever see her again he had been unable to stop himself from telling her he loved her.

But it was over now, that was abundantly clear. He'd done everything he could to convince her of his feelings. Maybe she did love Duncan, after all, and he'd been wrong all along, arrogance had got the better of him and turned him into the kind of bare-chested medallion man who thought he was too good an opportunity to pass up.

Hermione and Jo-Jo were sitting on the terrace. Hermione was doing her best to coax her young friend to go inside the house and ring her school.

'But I'm too scared,' Jo-Jo said. 'What if I've failed? What will I do then?'

'You'll simply do the exams again. Now come on, there's no point in putting it off. The sooner you know your results, the sooner you'll have a smile back on that lovely face, which is tanning by the minute in all this sun.'

'Will you come inside with me?'

'I'll even hold your hand.'

Hermione watched Jo-Jo dial the number from the pad of paper in her shaking hand. It was a while before she was put through to the right person. As they waited Hermione was almost as nervous as Jo-Jo.

'Yes, this is Jo-Jo Clarke, I'm ringing about my A-level results . . . Yes, I'll wait . . . Hold on, I've dropped my pencil.'

Hermione handed it back to her and then watched Jo-Jo scribble across the paper.

They were both crying and dancing a little jig about the

kitchen when Bernie knocked on the back door. 'Steady on, you two, you'll do yourselves a mischief.'

Jo-Jo couldn't speak. Hermione gave him the news. 'It's her A-level results. An A and two Bs! Isn't she brilliant?' Hermione hugged her again. 'I'm so proud of you.'

Jo-Jo gasped and suddenly clutched her stomach. She collapsed onto the nearest chair. 'Oh dear, I think this is too much excitement for the baby.'

Immediately Hermione was concerned. 'It's not started, has it?'

'Don't be silly,' Jo-Jo said, breathing deeply. 'I've got three weeks to go yet.'

'Even so, it might have decided to come early. Perhaps you should –'

'Shut up! I'm fine.'

'Do as the little lady says, Hermione, and calm down. If she is about to produce this child the last thing she needs is you fussing like a mother hen.'

'Will you both shut up!' shouted Jo-Jo. 'I am not in labour!' She laughed and waved the pad of paper with her results scribbled on it. 'But I am free,' she said happily. 'This is my ticket to the rest of my life.'

'And talking of which,' Bernie turned to Hermione, 'have you instructed your solicitor about the sale of your house?'

'Yes, yes, yes,' Hermione said impatiently. She didn't want to think of that right now. Jo-Jo's good news was a welcome diversion from dwelling on what lay ahead.

She had decided to sell to Duncan on Saturday night because she knew that if she wanted to take the step of moving out of Laburnum House and into the Lodge she had to think only of herself. It was too bad that by accepting Duncan's revised offer she was condoning a marriage of which she strongly disapproved. But, as Matthew had said, it was down to Ellen herself to realise that.

'I can't believe we've taken so much money,' Susie said, goggling at the day's takings neatly set out on the counter, ready to be bagged up and taken to the night safe in town.

Ellen thought how strange it was that Susie of all people should be saying this. Surely this, to her, was petty cash?

'It never used to be as good as this,' Ellen said, slipping the rows of pound coins into a money bag. 'When I first started out I was lucky to make this amount in a week.'

'Well, I think you're brilliant,' Susie said. 'You should be proud of yourself to have achieved so much. And if it was me I wouldn't give it up just because I was getting married. I'd want to keep it as a symbol of my independence. Give me my time again and I'd jolly well make sure I had a decent education instead of all that silly stuff I was force-fed at the school I went to. Do you know? Mummy admitted recently that she and Daddy only sent me there and then to the Swiss finishing school to equip me to find the right kind of husband.'

'I thought that attitude went out with the dinosaurs.'

Susie laughed. 'Heavens, no.'

'So what about Floss and Millie? What kind of future have you in mind for them?'

'Not the same, that's for sure. Floss is sharp enough to be a politician, and Millie, well, Millie is the dreamer of dreamers and never happier than when she's got a pencil in her hand and is drawing. Which reminds me, if we've finished here I should get on home. Mummy said she'd drop the girls off and I want to see how much Matthew's done of the painting.'

'Yes, that's fine. I'm practically finished myself. I've just got to take this lot into Crantsford and then I'm going to see Hermione.'

'I'll give you a lift if you like.'

They locked up, deposited the money in the night safe, then headed back towards the Crescent. When Susie had parked her car outside Orchard House she invited Ellen in.

'Why don't you come and have a peep at the painting?'

They found Matthew in the conservatory. He was half-way up the step-ladder and staring hard at a section of blue sky that he was working on in the top right-hand corner of the wall.

'Matthew!' exclaimed Susie loudly, which made him start. 'Just look how much you've done! It's beautiful, truly it is.'

He turned and faced her.

Then he saw Ellen. He quickly returned his attention to the wall.

'What do you think, Ellen?' Susie asked. 'Isn't he just the most divine person imaginable to have created this? And, golly, there's Bonkers . . . and there's me!' She rushed forward to take a closer look. 'You've got Bonkers's expression just right, as well as making him even more handsome. Clever you.'

While Susie carried on admiring the picture Matthew came down the ladder.

'Susie's right,' she murmured. 'It is lovely.'

'Thanks,' he said, and at a loss to say anything else he started packing up his things.

'Mind if I take a look at the garden?' Ellen asked Susie.

'Of course, go ahead.'

Matthew watched Ellen go outside. He wanted to follow her but he forced himself to stay where he was. He could hear Susie chattering on but all his thoughts were wrapped up in Ellen.

'I hope we won't become like a pair of Dorian Grays.' Susie laughed.

'Oh, I expect so,' Matthew replied absent-mindedly, wiping his hands on a piece of cloth sticking out from his jeans pocket.

Susie frowned and turned to face him. He was staring through the open French windows and there was an expression of such longing on his face that she did a double take and followed his gaze.

Well, well, well, she thought.

Chapter Thirty-Four

The following Saturday, while Jo-Jo was having tea in the garden at Laburnum House, Matthew offered to take her to see a film. 'Come on,' he said, flicking through the local paper for the entertainments' page, 'we're the only ones not doing anything tonight. What shall we go and see?'

Jo-Jo leaned over his shoulder and read what the cinema in Crantsford had to offer. 'How about that?' She pointed to what was described as *the* summer box-office hit starring Sandra Bullock.

'A romantic comedy,' said Matthew in disgust, 'you've got to be joking.'

Hermione glanced up from the holiday brochure she was reading. 'Isn't there something more along the lines of *Death of an Extremely Dull and Pretentious Solicitor?*'

Jo-Jo looked first at Hermione then at Matthew, who immediately turned away.

It had occurred to her back in April that Matthew had the hots for Ellen – it was the way he'd stared at her during the picnic that had made her wonder, and also the way he'd kept trying to get a look at her in his rear-view mirror when they were in the car later – but what she hadn't been able to work out was whether or not Ellen was aware of this.

She decided to tackle Matthew later that evening when they were alone. She might even have a word with Ellen.

She shifted in her seat as the baby did what felt like a pirouette inside her. She breathed out deeply and closed her eyes.

'You okay?' Matthew asked.

She nodded. 'But I reckon I'll have to go back home pretty soon. I want the baby to be born at the hospital I'm booked in at.'

'And have you got somebody who's going to be there with you?' Hermione asked.

Jo-Jo gave her a blank look.

'I think it's called a birthing partner,' Matthew said helpfully.

Jo-Jo gave a snort of derision and fanned herself with one of Hermione's brochures.

'But you must,' Hermione said emphatically. 'You simply can't go through this alone. If need be, one of us will be there with you.'

'Give over, will you? From what the midwives have told me there's no chance of being alone anyway. There'll be that many people fussing around me the last thing I'll need is somebody else getting in the way.'

Hermione wasn't convinced and she gave Matthew a something-will-have-to-be-done look.

Duncan was amused at his mother's reluctance to tell him anything about Nigel Wade, other than to say that he was fond of crushed ice and a slice of lime in his gin and tonic.

Well, *Nigel*, thought Duncan, as he cut through the middle of a small shrivelled lime, all is about to be revealed.

He looked at his watch and saw that it was exactly ten minutes past seven, which meant that not only was his mother's fancy man late but so was Ellen – Ellen he could forgive, but not a man who had such affected drinking habits.

The doorbell rang, but before he'd had a chance to wipe his hands Nadia had beaten him to it. He joined her in the hall just as she was opening the door to both Ellen and Nigel, who had arrived at the same time.

This was the first time since April that Nadia had seen or even spoken to Ellen, and Duncan had warned his mother to behave. He watched her face closely as their guests stepped over the threshold. He also weighed up N. Wade, Esquire.

He'd half expected to see an inferior version of his moustachioed military-bearing father, but the man before him couldn't have been further from his expectations. Nigel Wade was small – doubtless he had an ego like Napoleon or Hitler – excessively tanned, wearing much too much aftershave, which went hand in hand with his crushed ice and lime, and – sin upon sin – he was wearing an open-necked shirt.

Duncan thought he looked exactly like the kind of man who would go on a golfing holiday in the Algarve.

He held out his hand. 'Good evening,' he said. 'I'm Duncan and you seem to have met my fiancée, Ellen, already.' He gave Ellen a discreet peck on the cheek.

'Indeed I have, Duncan, and what delightful taste in women you have. A beautiful girlfriend and a charming mother. What a fortunate young man you are.'

Duncan cringed and watched in disbelief as his mother was kissed smack on the lips. She metamorphosed into a giggling schoolgirl, slipping her arm through Nigel's and taking him through the house and out into the rose garden where earlier that afternoon she had instructed Duncan to set out the table and chairs.

'What a lovely man,' whispered Ellen. 'How long's that been going on?'

'A darn sight too long, in my opinion,' Duncan replied drily, his mind even more set on turning up what he could about this midget-sized Romeo.

By the time they had joined the others in the rose garden, Nigel was already very much at home, pouring drinks for him and Nadia and discussing Nick Faldo's latest run of bad luck.

Bernie arrived at Laburnum House just as Hermione had finished watering the tomato plants. She was dressed in her best going-out-for-dinner skirt and blouse with Kit's necklace and her faithful old wellington boots. When she saw Bernie she turned off the hose.

'You look tired,' she said critically. 'What have you been up to?'

'A day given over to the pleasures of the flesh takes its toll,' he replied. He kissed her cheek.

'You don't fool me,' she said. 'You look pale and about ten years older since yesterday.'

'Pining for you, my little Hermaseta, that's what it is. Now hurry up and get out of those bloody awful boots and let me take you into Crantsford for an evening of good food and my scintillating company.'

They drove into town and after spending nearly fifteen minutes chasing a parking space they eventually reached La Maison d'Or where Bernie had booked a table. They were greeted in a manner that made Hermione wish she still had on her rubber boots.

'Why have you brought me here?' she hissed, when they were placed like ornaments at their table.

'Behave yourself or while you're having your coffee I'll

sneak out through the Gents' window and leave you with the bill to pay.'

'And I shall simply pretend to have a heart attack and I'll be carried out in style.'

Bernie laughed but his face suddenly contorted with an expression of acute pain as he tried to catch his breath. He slipped his hand into his jacket pocket and pulled out his inhaler.

'How often are you having to use that now?' Hermione demanded.

'Mind your own business,' he gasped.

'Very well. And when you've finished dying I'll have the lobster with brandied mayonnaise followed by the fillet of pork parcel.'

'More mange-tout and baby corn, Ellen?'

Ellen declined and carefully placed her knife and fork together on her plate. 'That was beautiful, Cynthia,' she said diplomatically, having just forced herself to eat a slab of overcooked rump steak. She was cross with herself for having been too cowardly to admit that she no longer ate beef. Another principle bites the dust, she thought gloomily.

'I hope you have room for dessert. Nadia, how about you? Any more?'

Nadia also refused.

'Nadia's watching her weight now,' laughed Phyllis, casting her eyes across the dinner table at Nigel. She was still trying to disguise her shock at her friend's apparent pulling power. On the face of things, Nigel was quite a catch. He was still pretty good-looking for a man of his age, which she surmised was slightly younger than Nadia, and he had more hair than Maurice and Henry had between them and it was silvery white in a way that complemented his tanned face. For a widower he even had good dress sense, though if she were to be at all critical he was perhaps a little on the casual side. There was, of course, the matter of him being a touch small, but what he lacked in physical stature he certainly made up for in his charming manner – in that department he was a giant. But for the life of her she couldn't understand what he saw in Nadia. A man such as he would be quite able to attract a young woman half his age. One saw it all the time in the wine bars and restaurants in town: white-haired man in open-necked shirt with a blonde piece propping him up.

'Or maybe she's lost her appetite altogether. Love does that,' smirked Cynthia from the other end of the table, interrupting Phyllis's thoughts.

Ellen almost felt sorry for La Carter, but she needn't have, for Nadia stepped in to scotch any further mischief from her friends.

'Cynthia,' she said, in a dangerously silky voice, 'you have something in your right nostril that needs attending to.'

Cynthia's embarrassed face disappeared behind a napkin. She then scuttled from the dining room on the pretext of fetching another bottle of wine and an awkward silence fell upon the diners.

Ellen found herself wishing she was at home, stretched out in a deck chair in her little front garden with a glass of wine in her hand, watching the sun slowly sink away. Then she reminded herself that Laburnum House would soon be home, and imagined sitting in Hermione's charming old summerhouse. She had determined that she would have to convince Duncan that nothing should be done to spoil it in any way. She looked to her right where Duncan was sitting next to her. He was staring across the table at Nigel, who was trying gamely to crank up the conversation around the table.

Henry-bugger-me-Kovel, who was under orders from his wife to undertake a proper sounding-out of Nadia's new golfing partner, responded with, 'So how long have you been living here in Crantsford?'

'Ooh, it must be getting on for nearly six months now,' Nigel replied.

'Bugger me, six months and our paths haven't crossed at the club. Who'd have thought it possible?'

'But I haven't been a member for as long as that.'

'So what's your line of business?'

Yes, thought Duncan, visibly leaning forward in his chair. Just what is your business? Other than digging out a suitably wealthy replacement for your dead wife. He had been most disappointed that before coming here to the Kovels for supper all he'd managed to glean from their drinks in the rose garden was that Nigel Wade seemed little more than a monumental golf bore.

'Oh, I've done nothing more than dabble,' Nigel said, with a light laugh, and taking a sip of his wine he reached out and patted Nadia's hand beside his. 'Ask Nadia,' he added. 'She'll tell you what a dull fellow I am.'

Despite themselves, everyone looked expectantly at Nadia, except Duncan, who kept his eyes firmly on the hand still covering his mother's. He was sickened by the display of cheap and easy affection in front of him and, worse, he knew a prevaricator when he saw one. He'd dealt with enough wrigglers from the truth in his time as a solicitor to know precisely which way the wind was blowing tonight, and this one was practically gale force in its obviousness.

'Dabbling,' he repeated coolly. 'You're not giving us much to go on.'

Ellen was surprised at the way Duncan was treating Nigel, especially as the man might turn out to be a godsend by taking Nadia off their backs.

'I think Nigel's just being modest,' she intervened.

'Quite possibly,' Duncan said coldly.

The two men stared at each other across the table. Then suddenly Nigel threw back his head and laughed robustly. 'Nadia, what a wonderful job you've done raising this fine young man. See how he's got your interests so close to his heart. He views me as nothing but a scheming bounty-hunter.'

Nadia started to laugh and soon everybody around the table joined in, except Duncan. Cynthia reappeared in the dining room, bringing with her another bottle of wine.

'Have I missed something?' she asked, rubbing the end of her nose nervously.

'Yes,' answered Maurice-the-red-nosed-judge, 'young Duncan's been putting Nigel here in the witness box.'

Again everybody laughed.

Duncan forced a smile to his lips but Ellen sensed him tense and hostile beside her. She wished somebody would change the subject, but the others were warming to it.

'Go on, then,' encouraged Maurice good-humouredly. 'You'll have to put us all out of our misery.'

'Bugger me, yes,' agreed Henry, 'especially Duncan. The poor boy needs to know if his mother's safe in your hands.'

Nigel smiled and, very slowly, drained his glass. Then, just as slowly, he said simply, 'Well, Duncan will have to wait and see, won't he?'

Hermione was lightheaded from too much wine and as she unlocked the garden-room door and let her and Bernie in she had no desire for the evening to end.

'Brandy?' she said, as Bernie followed behind her.

'Are you trying to get me drunk and seduce me?' he asked, catching her wrist and turning her round to face him.

'And there was I thinking that that was what you were up to with me.'

He held her close to him. 'I wish I'd met you sixty years ago, my little Hermaseta.'

She rested her head against his shoulder and sighed. 'Sixty years ago I wouldn't have looked twice at you.'

'Oh,' he said, lifting her face up to his, 'so who was the lucky man? Your husband or some other undeserving wretch?'

She slipped out of his arms. 'It's a long story, but come upstairs with me and I'll tell you all about it.'

'Now there's an offer I can't turn down.'

They took a small bottle of brandy and two glasses to the top of the house. Bernie struggled for breath when they reached Matthew's attic room. He puffed on his inhaler and sank gratefully into the old leather sofa opposite the painting. Hermione watched him closely and resigned herself to the uncomfortable truth that Bernie's health was deteriorating. She felt annoyed with him. Why couldn't he be honest with her? Why keep up the silly pretence? Pride, she supposed, as she poured the brandy and took the glasses over to the sofa and sat next to him. When it came down to it she was no different herself. All these years she'd lived alone, battling to keep Laburnum House and her independence, believing these things to be more important than anything else, to the point of excluding life itself.

'You've gone quiet on me,' Bernie said, raising his glass to Hermione's. 'Care to explain why you've dragged a poor old man up two flights of stairs?'

'So suddenly you're a poor old man?'

He grinned. 'I thought I'd try appealing to your sympathetic nature in the hope of eventually luring you into bed. That's if I can manage the stairs back down again.'

'I don't suppose there's any chance of you being honest with me, is there?'

'Heavens to Betsy, no!'

'I thought not.'

A few moments passed before Bernie said, 'Was there something specific you had in mind, in the honesty department, that is?'

She shrugged and sipped her brandy.

Bernie watched her. 'And have you thought any more about the proposal I put to you over dinner?'

'You proposed a lot of things to me over dinner.'

'You know what I'm talking about.'

'I do?'

'You do,' he said firmly.

She smiled. 'As a matter of fact, I have.'

'And?'

She lifted her head and met his gaze. 'I'd love to. The answer's yes.'

Bernie chuckled. 'I must be going deaf as well as infirm. I could have sworn I heard you say yes.'

'You heard all right.'

'Well, bless me. But is there a catch? Will the heavenly Hermione declare that −'

'Bernie Malloy, will you kindly shut up. I've merely agreed to accompany you on a cruise on the Nile the minute that twit Duncan Carter has paid up my money and −'

'Oh, be quiet yourself and give me a kiss. I've waited long enough.'

They finished the bottle of brandy and leaned companionably against each other and, while staring bleary-eyed at the painting in front of them, Hermione told Bernie about Kit.

She told him everything, how they'd met one summer when one of Roberta's many boyfriends down from Oxford brought him to the house one day. There had been an instant but shy attraction between them. They had become friends – not lovers – enjoying each other's company, knowing there was a rare level of understanding between them. There were times they were together when they barely spoke to each other, simply because there was no need. They would go for long walks up on the Edge where Kit would paint the hedgerows of gorse and red campion and delicate pink dog roses. On one occasion they drove out to Winnats Pass with a picnic and the heavens opened up and they were forced to take shelter among the rocks with a travel rug over their heads for more than an hour before finally making a run for the car.

It had been an idyllic summer.

But the following year war had broken out, bringing with it the end of Hermione's dreams. She hadn't seen Kit again until another year had passed, which was when he and Roberta announced unexpectedly that they were getting married. Years later Kit had told Hermione that he had met Roberta in London just twice when he was home on leave. The first time had been quite by chance, but the second had been by design, on Roberta's part, when they met at a party where a lot of people had been drunk, including Kit. He and Roberta spent the night together and when she told him she was pregnant, seven weeks later, he had immediately offered to do what was expected of him.

It had been a night of excesses for which he paid dearly, he admitted to Hermione in a letter a short while after Matthew's birth in the mid-fifties.

It was a long time before Hermione was able to forgive Kit, or Roberta, for what they'd done, but gradually the pain lessened until she allowed herself the luxury of enjoying the love she still felt for Kit, and the love he had for her, even though she was now married to Arthur and a different life was expected of her.

As the years slipped by, Roberta became more and more highly strung and unpredictable and despite the unhappiness of her marriage was determined never to give it up. She saw her marriage as a possession and she viewed Kit and Matthew in the same way – though Matthew she was prepared to share. 'You can never have Kit,' she told Hermione one day, 'but I will let you have Matthew when it suits me. You can be his godmother. He can be a reminder of what you missed out on.' Cruel words, and Hermione was never sure whether they were a reference to her inability to have children or a jibe at her being allowed to lavish love on her godson but not on his father.

When Kit finally asked Roberta for a divorce, not long after Arthur had died, she refused to listen to him and tried to kill herself. Afterwards Kit was desperate with guilt and so was Hermione. From that moment on they both knew they could never be together; neither of them wanted Roberta's death on their conscience.

'I think that's the saddest thing I've ever heard,' Bernie said, when Hermione fell quiet.

'Please don't tease me.'

'But I'm not.'

'You mean for once you're being serious? Good grief, Bernie Malloy, the shock's too much for me, I need the

342

loo!' She got to her feet with a smile. 'Bladders just aren't what they used to be.'

'Speak for your own.' Bernie snorted. 'Mine's fine.' He settled himself back into the sofa, yawned and watched her leave the room.

Hermione slowly tottered her way downstairs. She really shouldn't have drunk so much. She went into the bathroom and fumbled for the light pull. Afterwards she went down the next flight of stairs to the kitchen and made some coffee. Better sober the old fool up before I send him next door, she thought.

'Sorry I was so long,' she said, when she had climbed the stairs again and pushed open the attic-room door with the edge of the tray.

'Bernie!'

She put the tray down on an old trunk and rushed to him. He was slumped to one side of the sofa, his face contorted with pain, his eyes wide, bulging, but unseeing. One of his hands was tightly fisted and was held close to his chest, the other was gripped around his inhaler. His breathing was terrifyingly laboured and the sound of his lungs fighting for oxygen filled the small room. Hermione pushed the inhaler to his mouth. She pressed on the top as she'd seen him do so many times. She waited for his breathing to slow, but it didn't. She squeezed the inhaler again and started pulling at his tie and the top button on his shirt. But it made no difference.

'An ambulance. I must call for an ambulance.'

At the sound of her words Bernie's eyes focused on her and, as though summoning the last ounce of energy that was left in his body, he tried to move his pale lips. He was trying to tell her something. She moved nearer to him, her face almost touching his.

'Yes, Bernie, what is it?'

His voice was barely audible, little more than a whisper above the painful scraping sound of his worn-out chest. 'I think it's goodbye time,' he whispered hoarsely.

Hermione covered her face with her hands. 'No,' she murmured, 'please no.' But even as she spoke the room went quiet and Bernie's pain-racked body relaxed. He closed his eyes and very slowly his head tilted backwards.

Tears streamed down Hermione's cheeks. She brushed them away, but more tears came and splashed onto her hands now clasped tightly round Bernie's. She began to shake.

'No!' she cried in anguish. 'You can't do this, Bernie. You can't die. Don't leave me. You mustn't! Please don't leave me all alone.'

But it was no good, her dear sweet friend could no longer hear her. Bernie was dead.

She knelt on the floor beside him and sobbed.

Chapter Thirty-Five

Matthew dropped Jo-Jo off outside Ellen's cottage and waited for her to go inside before he turned the car round and drove back to Laburnum House.

There was no sign of Hermione and, assuming she must have gone straight to bed after her meal out with Bernie, he went upstairs to check on her. When he reached the first floor he saw that lights were on at the top of the house. He climbed the second flight of stairs, two at a time, his pace quickening with the uneasy feeling that something was wrong.

He found Hermione in the attic room on the floor, her body motionless, her head resting against Bernie's knees, but as she turned to look at him, he saw the sadness in her face and understood straight away what had happened. He gently raised her to her feet and steered her away from Bernie and held her to him.

'He's dead,' she murmured. 'He died just over an hour ago.' She looked up into Matthew's face, her own wet with tears. 'He was in such pain and I couldn't do anything for him. I only left him for a few moments, and when I came back he was . . .'

'Hush, hush,' he soothed, gently stroking her wrinkled cheek. He knew there was nothing he could say, all his words would be futile in the face of such grief; the best thing he could do was comfort Hermione with love and tenderness, just as he'd done once before.

'I'm going to put you to bed next and then call a doctor,' he said softly. 'Do you think you can manage the stairs?'

She nodded and moved stiffly from his arms. 'You'd better speak to somebody at the Lodge, they'll need to know what's happened.'

'Don't worry, I'll see to everything.'

Matthew woke early. It was a little after five.

Sunlight streamed through the large bay window in his room – he had forgotten to draw the curtains when he'd finally got to bed after dealing with poor Bernie. The doctor had given Hermione a sleeping pill and she had fallen asleep almost immediately, but he himself had lain awake for most of the night recalling his father's death nearly twenty years ago in the very same attic room in which Bernie had died.

In the autumn of 1978 Kit had asked Hermione if he could come and stay with her while Roberta was away on one of her bridge holidays. But what none of them knew was that Kit was ill. He was dying. He had been told six months previously that he had cancer of the liver and that with the right treatment he might just manage to see the year out. But Kit told no one of this. He kept his fate to himself – until he arrived at Laburnum House in October to stay with Hermione. Even to this day Matthew had no idea how Hermione had taken the news, for it was something she had never shared with him, but she did tell him that for two wonderful days she and Kit were able to live as they'd always wanted to, as man and wife. Then they had called Matthew and asked if he would come and spend a few days with them, they had something to tell him.

346

How shocked he'd been when he had found out that his father was dying.

'But why didn't you tell me sooner?' he'd asked Kit, deeply hurt that he'd been kept in ignorance.

There had been no answer for him and Kit had died the following evening while hunting for some old photographs in the attic room.

They discovered later, in a letter his father had left for Hermione, that Kit had deliberately stopped taking the medication that had been helping to prolong his life so that he could die in the way he wanted to, and when. 'It will be the best way to go,' he'd written, 'to be with the two people in the world I love most.'

Poor Hermione, thought Matthew as he got out of bed and went over to the window. He hoped the shock of Bernie's death wouldn't stop her from selling up and moving into the Lodge. If anything, she needed even more to be rid of Laburnum House: it held far too many memories for one person to carry alone.

Leaning on the window-sill he stared out onto the garden below and caught a flash of movement in the greenhouse.

So Hermione was up already.

Jo-Jo couldn't sleep. It was as if her body was too small now for the baby, which seemed to be wriggling and pushing her insides about as if it was trying to make more room for itself.

She was hot too.

She kicked back the sheet on the bed, raised herself to a sitting position and lowered her feet to the floor. She breathed in deeply and then exhaled slowly. She did this several times before standing up – it was what she did each morning to stop herself from feeling dizzy. She went over to the window and stretched her back and shoulders. She rubbed her stomach through her oversized T-shirt and wondered how much longer it would be before her body would be her own again. Maybe it was selfish of her, but she longed for the baby to be born and for her new life to start.

She went carefully down the narrow stairs to get herself a drink and found Ellen hunched up on the window-seat. She was looking out over the garden through the open window.

'Can't sleep either?' she said, as Ellen turned to face her.

'Nope,' Ellen said. 'I was too hot. There's some tea in the pot. Shall I pour you a cup?'

'That's okay, I'll do it.'

When she went back into the sitting room she joined Ellen by the window.

'I've decided to go home tomorrow,' she said. 'I think I ought to, don't you? I don't want to risk going into labour here.'

'You're probably right. But can you hang on until the evening? That way I can drive you home and you won't have to mess about with the train.'

'Sure. That would be great.'

'So how was the film last night?' Ellen asked. 'You were sound asleep when I got back.'

'Not bad. It was one of those romantic comedies. Not really Matthew's kind of film.'

Ellen smiled. 'How was he?'

'To be honest I might just as well have gone on my own. He barely opened his mouth all evening and had a face on him as miserable as sin. He wasn't a lot of fun to be with.'

The truth was she'd wound him up good and proper.

348

During the short drive into Crantsford she'd started pumping Matthew for a reaction to Ellen, dangling her name in front of him in just about every other sentence, until finally he brought the car to a halt in the car park at the back of the cinema, snatched on the handbrake and asked her what the hell she thought she was up to. She'd felt like a small child being told off and had meekly got out of the car and queued in silence with him for their tickets in the foyer of the cinema. But one thing she was sure of: if she'd rattled him to that extent then she'd been right in her suspicions that he did fancy Ellen.

'He's a moody so and so, isn't be?' Ellen laughed. 'It must be the creative genius in him.'

'Or maybe it's because . . .' But Jo-Jo lost her nerve when Ellen's eyes met hers.

'Or maybe it's what?' Ellen said slowly.

Oh, what the hell! 'Perhaps he's miserable because the woman he's got the hots for doesn't fancy him.'

'What makes you say that?' Ellen asked warily. She rose from the window-seat and went into the kitchen.

Jo-Jo followed her. She decided to press the point. What did it matter anyway? She was going home tomorrow and had nothing to lose. 'The funny part is I reckon it's you he's mad about. What do you think?'

Ellen spun round. 'That's not funny, that's just plain stupid.'

'Do you really think so?' asked Jo-Jo thoughtfully. She could see from the expression on Ellen's face that she had struck a chord. Maybe Ellen had known all along about Matthew, and maybe Ellen felt the same, only . . . only there was Duncan to consider.

'I think the stupid bit in all of this is you marrying Duncan,' she said, deciding to seize the moment, 'especially as nobody in their right mind would love a sad effort like Duncan, not when there's somebody else who's so much more –'

'That's enough!' cried Ellen. 'Jo-Jo, you've no right to talk about Duncan like that.'

'Why not?'

But Ellen's response was interrupted by a knock at the door. She went to answer it, relieved that the heated discussion between her and Jo-Jo had been brought to such a timely end. But when she opened the door she stepped back, not just in surprise, but in sheer unadulterated horror.

It was Roger.

Chapter Thirty-Six

If this had been a Victorian melodrama she would be clutching her bosom and slipping gracefully to the floor, and right now that didn't seem a bad way to avoid the shocking sight of her ex-husband standing on the doorstep.

Scruffy and unshaven, gaunt and hollow-cheeked with eyes darkly rimmed, he was dressed in creased jeans and a grimy shirt with sleeves tightly rolled up to the elbows. He was barely recognisable as the man with whom she'd spent nearly twenty years of her life; the man whom she had once loved and who had always cared so deeply about his appearance.

'Well,' he said, 'aren't you going to say anything? No long-time-no-see clichés?' He took a step forward and came into the cottage.

His intrusion had the instant effect of bringing Ellen to her senses. Here was the man who was the cause of everything wrong in her life; this was the man she had learned to hate.

'Out!' she shouted at him, appalled at his arrogance in thinking that he could just barge into her home like this. 'I don't want you here. Ever.'

'Oh, come on,' he said, with an easy smile that incensed her even more, 'there's no need to overreact, especially since you've been so generous to me, these last few months. I really did expect more of a welcome. Who's your friend?'

Ellen had forgotten that Jo-Jo was standing behind her. Jo-Jo came forward and, in a heavily loaded voice, said, 'Much more to the point, who the hell are you?'

She spoke with all the conviction of a soap-opera actor, which was how Ellen was beginning to view this whole thing.

It was unreal, Roger turning up here so unexpectedly. It was as if the situation was being manipulated by some omnipotent scriptwriter who was burning the midnight oil and playing God with his characters, moving them off-stage at the stroke of his pen, only to have them come back on when it was time to turn up the pace and move the plot along.

And there was more to come.

Behind Roger and through the open door she stared in disbelief at the sight of yet another character making his appearance. It was Matthew!

With the slightest of movements she shook her head at him, hoping he'd interpret the gesture as a polite way of her saying, 'Get lost, I've got enough on my hands as it is, without you adding to the mayhem.'

From beside her Jo-Jo directed another question at Roger.

'It sounds like Ellen doesn't want you here, so why don't you push off back to the stone you crawled out from?'

Roger smirked. 'Ellen's just surprised,' he said lightly. He came further into the room. 'A drink would be nice. How about it, Ellen? You used to make great coffee. Some breakfast wouldn't go amiss either.'

Jo-Jo looked wide-eyed at Ellen. The penny had dropped. 'Tell me this isn't Roger,' she said, horrified.

Ellen nodded helplessly. She was at a loss as to what to do, now that Roger was inside the cottage. 'Please, Roger,' she said, 'you've done so much already, why can't you leave me alone?'

Roger shrugged. 'I'll think about it.' Casting his eyes about the cottage, he said, 'Small but cosy, and you've even got your own little business. You've done better than I have out of the divorce. But hey, guess what, Charmaine's pregnant, I'm going to be a father all over again.'

'Simon will be delighted,' Ellen said acidly.

There was a flicker of something in his face. Remorse, perhaps?

'How is Simon?'

'What would you care? You just dumped us both and ran.'

'Shit, Ellen, can't you let the past go? Do you have to keep positioning everything? Things happen. Lives change.'

'Mine certainly has,' she threw back at him. 'And while we're on the subject, my *new* life doesn't include an ex-husband turning up unexpectedly and demanding a welcome cup of coffee.'

'You're right, Ellen. You're so right. So why don't we cut to the chase and I'll tell you what I've come for and then you'll see no more of me? How about it? Have we got a deal?'

Ellen gazed at him disbelievingly. Not only did he not look like the Roger she knew but he didn't sound like him either. Who was this stranger, sounding for all the world as though the only company he now kept was with boardroom hustlers?

Jo-Jo said, 'Don't listen to him, Ellen, he's going to ask you for money, it's written all over his face.'

'Bright friend you've got.'

'I know that, Roger. And the answer is no. I'm not giving you any more money. You've had all you're going to get out of me.'

'Now that's so disappointing.' He smiled and went over to the dresser. 'I remember this.' He picked up a willow-pattern plate, tossed it in the air and then caught it. 'Funny how things stay with you.'

'But there's nothing particularly funny about you, is there?'

It was Matthew. He came straight into the room, took the plate out of Roger's hands and placed it carefully on the dresser. He glanced across to Ellen. 'Everything okay?' he asked.

But before she had a chance to reply, Roger let out a loud, caustic laugh. 'And this must be Duncan Carter, the husband-to-be.'

Ellen opened her mouth to correct him, but Matthew held up his hand and stopped her. 'Jo-Jo,' he said, 'would you go upstairs, please. I want to have a private word with Roger . . . if that's all right with you, Ellen?'

Jo-Jo disappeared to the tiny landing upstairs where she hovered on the top step, hoping to hear what Matthew was going to say.

Roger spoke first.

'So, Duncan,' he said, 'what is it you want to talk to me about?' He settled himself in an armchair and waited expectantly. 'How can I help you? Do you want to know what marriage to Ellen will be like, is that it? But if you don't mind me saying so, that's not very gallant of you.'

Matthew ignored Roger and sat himself in the arm-chair opposite him. 'I'll come straight to the point,' he said. 'I know all about the disgusting letters you've written to Ellen. In fact, I've read them and I've seen the

354

photographs, and as a solicitor I think you'll find me more than ready to take the necessary action in preventing you from causing my future wife any further unhappiness. I presume that's why you've turned up here, to see what you could extract from her. Am I right?'

Ellen held her breath and Roger squirmed in his seat. One of his eyelids began to twitch and no longer did he look the cocky chancer he had a few moments ago. Beads of sweat were gathering on his forehead and he licked his dry lips nervously. He stood up abruptly and ran his hand over his stubbly chin. 'I don't need much. Just enough to –'

'Forget it.'

'What's a few thousand to you? I know you can afford it. You're loaded, you and your mother.'

'Whether I can afford it is immaterial. You're not scrounging off me or Ellen. Is that clear?'

Roger appealed to Ellen. 'How about it, Ellen? Couldn't you find it in your heart to lend me a bit of cash, just until I've –'

Matthew leaped to his feet. 'Don't even think about it! You've had everything you're ever likely to get from Ellen. Now, get out of here.'

'Picked yourself a regular champion, Ellen, haven't you?' Roger said, with a sneer. 'Well, I suppose there's nothing for it but to be on my way. But who knows? I might be back.'

As he started to move towards the door, Ellen said, 'Before you go, Roger, tell me how you knew about Duncan and me?'

'What's it worth?'

'It's worth you getting out of here with both arms resembling their current state,' Matthew said.

Roger laughed. 'That's really not the kind of talk I'd

expect to hear from a solicitor. But it just goes to show that beneath all that well-polished veneer of respectability you and your mother affect you're just as vulgar and yobbish as the next man.'

'Just tell me,' Ellen said.

'Well, why not? You've a spy in the camp up at Crantsford Hall, Duncan. Your cleaner has an easy tongue when it comes to tittle-tattle and has unwittingly shared your daily goings-on with any number of folk in Crantsford – Charmaine's sister for one. By the way, how's your mother's drinking these days?'

Roger's exit was as sudden as his arrival. Ellen watched him walk along the lane away from the cottage.

'I don't know what to say,' she said, when he was completely out of sight. 'I can't get over how changed he is. He looked so pathetic. So wasted.' Her face suddenly brightened with a radiant smile. 'But you were wonderful, Matthew. I couldn't believe it when you pretended to be Duncan. Thank you. I mean it, really.'

'That's okay.' He went over to the mantelpiece and picked up a framed photograph of Ellen and Simon. He stared at it for a few moments, then put it down. 'I hope he doesn't bother you again but, out of interest, how much have you given him so far?'

She turned away, embarrassed.

'Look, Ellen, I don't want to pry, but when I was outside I heard you say you wouldn't give him any more, which means you must have given in to his blackmail. Why, in God's name?'

'I didn't know what else to do.'

He swung her round to face him. 'Why didn't you just tell Duncan? He's a solicitor, he would have dealt with it.'

'I didn't want Duncan knowing about . . . well, you know. It's . . . it's something we don't discuss.'

A creak of floorboards above their heads reminded them both that Jo-Jo was still upstairs on the landing and that she was probably listening to their conversation.

'I think we need to talk privately,' Matthew said. He took Ellen by the elbow and led her outside, to the bank, where he made her sit down. 'Now, explain to me exactly why you didn't tell Duncan about Roger's letters.'

'Matthew, do you have to be so high-handed? I'm very grateful for you helping me just now with Roger, but this is really none of your business.'

'I disagree.'

'How can you say that?'

'Ellen, anyone who cares about you would say it was their business to help you.'

'Oh, please, don't start all that up again.'

'Start what up?'

'You know.'

'No, I don't, you'd better spell it out for me.'

'Don't be obtuse.'

He smiled. 'Does it really bother you so much that I care for you?'

She plucked a long stem of grass and chewed it.

'I'll take that as a yes, shall I?'

They sat in silence and Ellen was reminded of the day when she had first met Matthew and the moment when they'd stood side by side in silence as they'd leaned against the drystone wall. Except now she no longer felt awkward in his company. There was even an element of enjoyment creeping into their conversations, as though every exchange between them was like a verbal game of ping-pong with their wits acting as bats driving the points home. She braced herself ready for the challenge ahead and served the ball to start the match.

'You said you'd behave.'

'So I did. But if I promise to make an extra effort at curbing myself will you talk to me as . . . as a friend?'

'I thought you didn't want to be friends.'

'I've changed my mind.'

'So what kind of friend do you want to be?'

'How about you forget that I'd willingly hurl myself under a stampede of wildebeest for the chance of gaining your love and talk to me like – like you would with Hermione?'

She smiled. 'You don't know what you're saying. A conversation with Hermione is like dancing with a snake.'

They both laughed and Ellen turned over on to her front and stretched out on the grass. Matthew lay alongside her. After a few moments he said, 'What did you mean when you said it's something we don't discuss?'

She inclined her head towards him but didn't answer him.

'Is sex a problem between you? You know, actually doing –'

She smiled.

'What's so funny?'

'I don't know.'

'Yes, you do. Tell me.'

'I suppose I'm finding it slightly amusing that you should be interested in, of all things, my sex life with Duncan.'

'Given a choice I'd rather discuss *our* sex life.'

She smiled again. 'I'm sure you would.'

'Can I ask you a question?'

'You've done nothing else.'

'One more, then?'

She nodded.

'Why did you cry when we made love?'

'I didn't.'

He reached out and stroked her arm. 'You did and I want to know why.'

She shifted her arm away from him. 'It was probably because I knew it was wrong, what we'd just done.' Which wasn't exactly true. She had cried because what had passed between them had been so exquisite – she had never known a more fulfilling moment. It had made her realise that all her married life she had put up with something that had been so utterly second rate.

'I suppose it was . . . if you really loved Duncan.'

'But I do.'

'Then prove it to me. Since I've known you I've not seen any evidence that you love the man.'

'I don't know how you carry on when you're in love but not every relationship has to be chock-full of grand gestures and stomach-churning sugary sentiment.'

'I agree, but then I didn't have in mind silly *Love Is* cartoons or messages left on the fridge. Am I allowed another question?'

She sighed. 'Go on.'

'It's quite a personal one.'

'And the others weren't?'

'Did you *ever* have a good, loving sex life with Roger?'

'Heavens, you're obsessed!'

'Well?' Matthew pressed.

'Is this the objective friend wanting to know, or the flattened body under the wildebeest?'

'The objective friend,' he lied.

'Then I suppose the answer is no,' she said simply. 'No,

I didn't. And isn't it obvious? Isn't that why all men are unfaithful? If they can't get what they want at home they look elsewhere.'

'I wouldn't know, I've never been unfaithful.'

'Well, Roger was and he went off because he found someone able to satisfy him in a way I was unable to. I . . . I wasn't enough for him, I suppose. I didn't enjoy sex when it was make-believe, when I had to be something I wasn't. It just didn't feel right.' She looked up at him. 'He made me feel so inadequate.'

'Believe me, Ellen, there's nothing inadequate about you. The problem was all Roger's, not yours.'

She thought about this. How easy it was to accept blame when it was so freely thrust upon one. Not once had she questioned Roger's ability to perform in bed, only her own. 'I think I'm just beginning to realise that.'

'Good, because whatever it was that Roger felt towards you it wasn't love. How could it have been? When somebody really cares for a person the last thing they want to do is hurt or humiliate them. Now answer me this, and tell me the truth. Are you marrying Duncan because sex isn't all that important to him and you think that with him you'll be spared any further humiliation?'

She lifted her head. 'Why on earth should I answer a question like that?'

'Try it and see.'

'You're an arrogant swine, aren't you?'

He smiled. 'I did just save you from a fate worse than death.'

She shook her head. Why the hell shouldn't she tell him the truth? There was no shame in it. 'Okay, then,' she said, 'I'll admit it. I'm marrying Duncan because he's not obsessed with sex and never in a million years will he hurt me in the way Roger did. Satisfied now?'

'So you see him as safe?'

'Yes,' she agreed. 'He's wonderfully safe . . . unlike you.'

He raised an eyebrow. 'If by safe you mean dispassionate and cold and lacking the desire to make love to the woman I adore, then certainly I agree, I'm not safe.' He reached out and gently traced his hand along the line of her jaw. 'You know exactly how I feel about you, Ellen, so there's no point in repeating myself, but if Duncan wasn't around and I asked you to marry me, would you then?'

'No.'

He looked hurt. 'Am I really that bad?'

She pursed her lips and turned away from him. 'You've broken your promise. You're no longer behaving yourself.' She got to her feet. 'And I've got work to do. I need to open the barn.'

He stood up too. 'In that case I'd better get on and give you the bad news, which is why I came here so early in the first place. Bernie died last night, and I hoped you and Jo-Jo might be able to spare some time to be with Hermione. She's more upset than she's letting on.'

Susie was more than delighted to take charge for the morning. 'Gosh! Me in charge, just imagine,' she said happily. 'Of course you must go off and look after dear old Mrs Rowlands, I'll be fine here.'

Ellen hoped she was right: Sunday was usually the busiest day of the week.

By eleven thirty the day was hot, sticky and airless, the same as it had been for some days. Ellen and Jo-Jo took the steep incline of Beggarman's Lane at a slow pace. They crossed the busy Crantsford road and then walked along the Crescent in the shade of the chestnut trees. It had been hot for so many weeks now that the leaves had started to drop and lay scattered on the pavement, crisp and yellow.

'I was lucky,' Ellen said. 'When I was expecting Simon we had a lousy summer. This heat must be awful for you.'

Jo-Jo paused for a moment. 'You're right,' she puffed, 'it is, and why on earth women put themselves through this time and time again I'll never know. I can see why you only had Simon.'

They passed Orchard House where they saw Bonkers herding Floss and Millie into the car. He waved to Ellen and promptly dropped his keys.

The back door was open at Laburnum House and Hermione was throwing a pile of old newspapers into a large dustbin.

'Time to start clearing the decks ready for you and Duncan,' she said flatly, when Ellen and Jo-Jo stepped into the garden room. She hurriedly brushed away her tears. 'Goodness, Jo-Jo,' she said, in a more concerned voice, 'you look worn out. Come into the kitchen at once and sit down.'

'Don't start fussing,' Jo-Jo warned, wiping the sweat from her forehead, 'I'm fine. It's just this dreadful heat. I feel like I'm being cooked alive.'

Despite Jo-Jo's remonstrations Hermione made her sit in the kitchen where it was relatively cool. She fetched her a glass of water. 'Now don't move, not until I say so. I'm sure I've got some ice somewhere in the freezer.'

'Why don't you let me do that?' Ellen said kindly.

'Just because Bernie's died and I'm upset, don't go thinking I've lost all my capabilities,' Hermione snapped. She covered her face with her hands. 'I'm sorry,' she said, 'it's just that –'

Ellen went to her. 'It's all right,' she said, wrapping her arms around Hermione, 'I know how fond you were of him. He was a lovely man and you've every right to be sad.'

Hermione leaned into Ellen. 'He was stupid and rude and he said the silliest of things, but I miss the old rascal already. He made me laugh ... and he gave me the courage to question things I'd long since thought I had the answer for. Oh, Ellen, I shall miss him so much, he was one in a million. Truly he was.'

Duncan received the news with a mixture of annoyance and pleasure.

'Thanks, Howard,' he said, into the phone. 'I really appreciate you doing the survey so promptly and letting me know on a Sunday how you got on.'

'No problem, I'll get the typed report to you by Tuesday. Best of luck. I'm off for a round of golf now.'

'What – in this heat? You're mad.'

'Just think of the tan I'll have. See you.'

After he'd put down the phone Duncan looked at the notes he'd made. He contemplated the first four points: replace roof, replumb and rewire throughout, employ a specialist firm to eradicate wet and dry rot. There were a further ten points but they were of a secondary nature. Howard had suggested that, by the time the shouting was over, he'd be looking at a repair bill in excess of forty thousand pounds.

He leaned back in his chair and swivelled it round to gaze out of the window. The lawns at Crantsford looked worse than he'd ever seen them – there was barely a hint of green. He wondered how long it would take for the dusty grass to recover from the drought. The forecast had given rain later that day with severe storms predicted for most of the country, bringing an end to the humid muggy atmosphere they'd been suffering for over a week now. And according to Maurice, at the golf club last night, there was even a danger of flash floods.

But the weather was of little importance to Duncan right now. His two main priorities were to sort out Laburnum House and his mother.

What a ghastly little man that Nigel Wade was. And what an opportunist. Question was, where would it leave him if Nadia was stupid enough to marry the man?

Shortly after Donald had died, Nadia had made a will but she had never revealed its contents and had had it drawn up by a rival firm of solicitors in town. He could only guess at what she'd decided to do with the house and all her money. But now that *Nige* was on the scene, it was just possible that things could change.

He had no ready answers for this particular problem so he decided to shelve it until he was in a better position to do something about it – he'd always been of the belief that if sufficient information was not to hand, the right solution would never be found.

Instead he turned his thoughts back to Laburnum House and decided to call Hermione Rowlands directly, rather than leaving it to the estate agent to tell her that he was lowering his offer.

He dialled the number. Matthew answered.

'Hello, this is Duncan Carter. Is Mrs Rowlands there, please?'

Matthew recognised Duncan's voice immediately. 'She is, but I'm afraid she's not available.' This wasn't exactly the truth but he didn't want Hermione bothered by the likes of Duncan when she was so upset.

'Oh.'

'Perhaps I can help you, Duncan, this is Matthew.'

Duncan thought for a moment. It was always best to negotiate directly, but really there wasn't much time. Everything was now set for him and Ellen to be married on the twelfth of September, which was exactly three and a half weeks away. But even so, just because they had set a date he wasn't going to lose out financially. He had to hope that the Rowlands woman was keener to sell than he was to buy.

'Is it about the house?' prompted Matthew.

Duncan took the plunge. 'As a matter of fact, yes. Perhaps you'd like to pass a message on to Mrs Rowlands. It's bad news, I'm afraid. The survey report has been rather damning and the list of repairs is extensive and runs into tens of thousands, and . . . and in view of this I need to review my offer.'

'How many tens of thousands?'

'Approximately sixty,' lied Duncan.

'Approximately,' repeated Matthew derisively. 'What would you say *exactly*?'

'Sixty-five,' Duncan said coolly, doodling a picture of a house on the bottom of his note-pad.

'Go to hell!'

The phone went dead and Duncan's fountain pen skidded across the sheet of paper neatly dividing his house in two.

'Who was that?'

'I thought you were in the garden, Hermione,' Matthew said, straightening the receiver in its cradle.

'I was, but I came in for another glass of water for Jo-Jo. Was it Duncan?'

'How did you guess?'

She smiled. 'It must have been the friendly way you

said goodbye to him. What did he want, apart from the woman you love?'

Matthew pushed his hands into his trouser pockets. 'Hell, Hermione, do you have to be so direct?'

'I'm sorry.'

'Oh, forget it. Ellen's delightful fiancé is trying to lower his offer by sixty-five thousand.'

Hermione whistled. 'Is he, by Jove?'

'I did the right thing, didn't I?'

'You most certainly did. Now come and join us outside. We're in the summerhouse in the shade.' She tucked her arm through his. 'And I want to thank you for bringing in the cavalry to cheer me up. Ellen's been telling me all about Roger's appearance at the cottage this morning. Fancy you pretending to be Duncan. Pardon the expression but it sounds to me like you were quite the rooster.'

Chapter Thirty-Seven

By late that afternoon the air was as thick as treacle and the sky was as black. Threatening storm clouds had gathered and they were casting an eerie darkness over the garden of Laburnum House.

Hermione's earlier rush of energy and settled mind had evaporated and now she felt weary and overcome with sadness again. Ellen had hinted several times already that she needed to get back to the barn, but each time she mentioned relieving Susie, Hermione insisted that she stay just a little longer.

'Please don't go yet,' she said gloomily, sitting back in her wicker chair in the summerhouse. 'It's like old times having you here. It's like it used to be, before . . .' But her voice trailed away.

'Before what?' asked Ellen gently.

'Before everything, before Roger and Duncan . . . and Bernie. Why don't you give Susie a ring and see if she can cope another hour without you?'

'I've got a better idea,' Jo-Jo said. 'I want to go back to the cottage for a shower so I could check on Susie and if there's a problem I'll get her to ring you.'

Although Hermione was reluctant to part with any-one's company, she saw that if she let Jo-Jo go she could at least keep Ellen with her for a few hours more.

'Do you want a lift back?' Matthew asked from behind

his easel a few yards away, where he was working on a painting of the summerhouse.

'Don't be daft,' Jo-Jo said, struggling to her feet and smoothing down her cotton dungarees, which had ridden up between her legs. 'It's only ten minutes, if that.'

'But it's so hot,' Hermione implored. 'Why not let Matthew –'

'I'd rather walk. I feel like my body's seizing up.'

Ellen walked up to the house with her. 'Tell Susie to close the barn, will you?' she said when they reached the courtyard, and she handed over the keys of the cottage. 'I feel awful that I've left her alone practically all day. Just get her to lock up and I'll sort everything out in the morning. Are you sure you're okay?'

Jo-Jo tutted. 'Stop fussing. I'll see you later.'

When Jo-Jo reached the barn her whole body was wet with sweat: she could feel it trickling between her swollen breasts. She was also conscious of a persistent dull ache in the lower part of her back, which had been with her since breakfast-time. She supposed it was the baby getting into position for the big event shortly to come. It didn't cross her mind that she might be in labour.

She passed on Ellen's message to Susie and then puffed her way over to the cottage where she gratefully let herself in and slowly climbed the stairs. As she started running the shower and stripped off her clothes, a loud crack of thunder boomed overhead and rattled the small window in its rotting frame. She opened it. A large fat drop of rain splashed on the end of her nose. Rain at last to clear the air, she thought. Suddenly the sombre sky was lit up as a dramatic flash of lightning streaked angrily across it like a magical piece of graffiti. A few seconds later more thunder crashed and rumbled overhead.

Jo-Jo closed the window and stepped into the shower. The water was cool and refreshing, but while the storm gathered momentum outside the pain in her back steadily increased.

Duncan thought his timing would be perfect as he swept out through the gates at Crantsford Hall. Ellen would be just locking up the barn and he'd be able to talk to her about Laburnum House. He needed to make her realise that it was now down to her to convince Hermione Rowlands that what he was offering for her property was a fair price. Nobody in their right mind would be stupid enough to buy Laburnum House at anything more than he was offering. The trouble was, as he well knew, he wanted the house too much. Everything about it was perfect for him and Ellen – apart from the neglect and the current owner – which meant, of course, that he was at a disadvantage in terms of sitting round the negotiating table. It would be so much easier if he could simply walk away. But he couldn't. His mind was set and he was determined that nobody, least of all an old woman, was going to get the better of him. He would outmanoeuvre her if it was the last thing he did.

Another crack of thunder roared overhead and the rain increased. Duncan flicked the wiper blades on full and they dashed frantically to and fro across the windscreen in a futile attempt to keep it clear. The car in front had now slowed to a snail's pace and would have been invisible, had it not been for its rear lights, which glowed faintly red like hot coals, in the deluge of torrential rain pelting down and making Duncan's expensive car sound horribly like a tin can.

He pulled off the main Crantsford road and turned into the potholed Beggarman's Lane. Amazed, he saw that it barely resembled a road any longer, it was more like a river. Muddy water was gushing down the small hill, cascading into the stream at the bottom, which for the past few weeks had almost run dry. He bumped and splashed his way to the car park and, seeing no sign of light or movement over in the barn, made a dash to the cottage. He cursed it for not having a porch and he hammered on the door.

'Ellen,' he shouted, 'it's me, Duncan, let me in.'

He thumped on the door and called out again, but his voice was swallowed up by the crash of yet more thunder. Within seconds he was drenched. He bent down and pushed open the letter-box.

'Ellen,' he yelled, 'are you there?'

He saw a figure coming towards him wrapped in a towel. He breathed a sigh of relief. She must have been having a bath or a shower, that's why she hadn't heard him. But when the door opened he saw his mistake.

'Oh,' he said, when he saw Jo-Jo clutching a towel around her. 'Well, let me in,' he went on, 'I'm getting soaked standing out here.' He pushed past her. 'Where's Ellen?'

'She's not here.' Jo-Jo slammed the door shut.

He swung round. 'So where is she?'

'She's at Hermione's.'

'And?'

'And what?'

'When will she be back?' he demanded.

'I've no idea.'

'Then I'll wait.'

'I'd rather you didn't.'

'I beg your pardon?'

'You heard.'

Duncan stared at Jo-Jo, then turned away from the sight of her. He went and stood by the fireplace. He ran his hand over his wet face. 'I don't know how you've wormed your way into Ellen's life, but let's get one thing entirely straight between us. When I marry Ellen next month she'll never see you again. Is that clear?'

'Isn't that for Ellen to decide?'

'No,' he said, his eyes dark and steely. 'Ellen's too good-natured to see you for what you really are. Now get me a towel, I'm wet through.' He began pulling at his shirt and unbuttoning it. 'Well, go on! What are you still standing there for?'

She took a step nearer to him. 'Two things. First, you don't ever tell me what to do, okay? And second, you can stop treating me as though I'm nothing more than a pile of shit.'

He laughed at her. 'But that's exactly what you are.'

'The hell I am!' She lashed out at him with her hand, but he caught hold of her wrist. He stood for a moment contemplating her and all at once her open hostility towards him made him question himself. Why not just let his anger go? Why not, just for once, say and do what he really felt? Why should he have to keep struggling to control himself?

'Let go of me, you bastard!'

At first he didn't hear her, but then, very slowly, her words sank in. 'What did you say?'

'You heard me, you bastard, now let go of me.'

He gripped her wrist even harder. 'Apologise!'

'No!' She kicked out at him and somehow managed to break free. She crossed the room and clutched her towel around her. She stood behind one of the armchairs, frightened at what he might do next. She could see that both his hands were tightly clenched. He started moving towards her.

'Apologise for what you just called me,' he said, in a dangerously low voice.

'Okay, okay,' she said nervously, 'I'm sorry.'

He stood still. But her apology wasn't enough to stop what was happening inside him. The resentment he'd experienced as a child for being different – for being unwanted – had finally broken free and suddenly *it* was in control. The misery of being bullied at school because he'd been a misfit swam before his eyes. He felt the terrible burden of it and wanted to be rid of it, once and for all. He moved towards Jo-Jo.

'You're a tart, Jo-Jo, aren't you?'

She gripped the back of the armchair.

'Answer me.'

'No! No, I'm not.'

'Yes, you are. You're a waste of space.' He was standing beside her now. 'Look at you, still a child and pregnant. I bet you don't even know who the father is, do you?' He prodded at her shoulder.

She wanted to get away from him but he was too close. She was trapped. He prodded her again and his touch sent a sharp pain searing through her body. She gasped and clutched her stomach.

'How many did you sleep with? And what does it feel like knowing you're producing a child without any chance of a future?'

'It will have a future!' she shouted at him.

At the sound of her words the room lit up with an explosive flash of lightning followed by a spontaneous clap of thunder and her body tightened with the most excruciating pain. It was so awful she wanted to fall to the floor, to curl herself into a tiny safe ball. But she wouldn't let him see her weaken. She had to stay strong.

He pushed his face closer to her and laughed derisively. 'And tell me, what kind of future can *you* offer *it*?'

'I'm giving the baby up for adoption,' she managed to say. Then as swiftly as the pain had consumed her body it went, leaving her with the strength to fight back. 'You're adopted, aren't you, Duncan?' she said, her voice level and quite calm.

He drew away from her but didn't speak.

'Yeah,' she said, seeing a way to get the better of her tormentor. 'I'd forgotten that you were adopted. And I reckon you don't like it, do you? Because maybe, just maybe your natural mother was how you see me, and where does that leave you, Duncan? I'll tell you, Mr Airs and bloody Graces, it makes you nothing but a bastard!'

Too late she realised her mistake. Instead of making Duncan back off, her words had the opposite effect. She had totally misjudged him.

She felt the blinding crack of his hand against the side of her face and then nothing.

Duncan stumbled out of the cottage and ran wildly through the rain to his car. He crashed the gears and rocketed away, but the car stalled just as he reached the steepest and narrowest part of the lane. He cursed and turned the key. Nothing, just a weak apology of the engine stuttering to spring into life, and with the torrent of water still gushing down the lane the car began to slide slowly backwards. He snatched on the handbrake and then tried the engine again. Nothing. He thumped the steering wheel again and again, and then, looking back towards the cottage, he began to shake.

What in God's name had he done?

He was horrified at the anger that had unleashed itself in that small room. Horrified that he, of all people, had been unable to check it. It was like a Jekyll and Hyde experience. One minute he'd been in control and the next he'd lost it. Shame overcame him and he bent his head over the steering wheel and wept.

When eventually he pulled himself together he realised he couldn't stay where he was. He had to get away.

He abandoned the car and by the time he had staggered up the hill to the main road and reached Church Walk Mews and let himself into the office, he had managed to re-create in his mind the events that had just taken place.

The girl had provoked him.

They had had words.

She had attacked him.

He had merely defended himself.

She had been fine when he left her.

Hermione's eyes sparkled.

'I can't remember a thunderstorm like it,' she said, gazing out of the sitting-room window and over the water-logged garden.

Ellen didn't share Hermione's enthusiasm for the weather. She was worried about Jo-Jo. They had tried ringing the cottage to make sure she was okay only to find that the lines were down.

'I'm going to see if Jo-Jo's all right.'

Hermione came away from the window. 'Good idea, Ellen, I'll come with you.'

'Don't be ridiculous, Hermione,' Matthew said. 'I'm not having you out there in this weather. I'll go with Ellen.'

Hermione pulled a face. 'I always miss out on the fun.'

'I'd hardly call this fun,' Matthew said, when he opened the back door in the garden room. As he stepped outside, the ancient cast-iron guttering above the door-way gave way and an ocean of water poured over him.

Ellen laughed but Matthew caught hold of her hand and pulled her under the broken piece of guttering so that she, too, ended up soaked to the skin.

'You pig,' she spluttered, pushing back her wet hair from her face.

He smiled. 'It's called a baptism by fire. Now it doesn't matter how much it rains, we can't get any wetter.'

They found Duncan's abandoned car near the top of Beggarman's Lane. They pressed on and knocked at the door of the cottage. There was no answer. They pushed against the door but it was shut.

'Well, unless she opens the door we can't get in,' Ellen shouted above the boom of more thunder. 'I gave her my keys and the other set's hanging up in the kitchen.' She pounded on the door again. 'Maybe she's having a nap.'

Matthew peered through the sitting-room window.

'Oh, no, she's not, Ellen, she's on the floor!'

They smashed one of the small panes of glass and climbed in through the window.

Jo-Jo was unconscious. Her right cheek was swollen and bruised and blood was beginning to congeal in the corner of her mouth.

'Jo-Jo,' Ellen said loudly, down on her knees beside her. 'Jo-Jo, can you hear me?'

Jo-Jo could hear her name being called. It was a distant voice. A voice she hadn't heard in years. She could barely hear it from where she was playing at the bottom of the garden. But there it was again. It was Gran and she was calling her in for tea. She was standing on the back step, her arms outstretched, waiting for her best little girl to run to her. She ran all the way up the garden but when she got to the house it was Hermione waiting for her. 'There now,' Hermione said, 'come inside and wash your hands, your tea's on the table.'

But now somebody else was calling her name. Over and over.

Jo-Jo . . . Jo-Jo . . . Jo-Jo.

She forced her eyes open. A pink blob swam before her. 'Hermione?'

'No, it's me, Ellen.'

'Ellen?'

'Yes, and Matthew's here as well. Can you tell us what happened?'

'I . . . I don't know, I was in the garden with Gran. No, I wasn't. I was here . . . and so was Duncan, he was –' But she broke off and her face twisted with pain. She let out a loud cry and drew her knees up then slowly released them, taking small shallow breaths.

'I don't believe it,' muttered Matthew, standing behind Ellen. 'She's in labour!'

The contraction passed and a faint smile spread over Jo-Jo's face. 'I'm glad you told me that, Matthew, I would never have guessed.'

'Right,' said Ellen purposefully, doing her best to disguise the panic rising within her. 'Do you think you can move?'

'Yeah, sure,' Jo-Jo replied, 'no problem.' She lifted her head but the room started to spin. 'Er . . . actually, no, I don't think I can.'

'Okay,' Ellen said. 'Just stay there and don't do anything.' She got to her feet and motioned for Matthew to join her in the kitchen. 'I think we'd better call for an ambulance.'

'You're forgetting, the lines are down.'

She grabbed the phone from the wall. It made no sound. 'Damn! Now what?'

'We'll use your car to drive her to the hospital.'

She shook her head. 'Not with Duncan's car in the way, we won't. Oh, Matthew, what are we going to do?'

'Right,' he said, breathing out deeply and trying to keep calm, 'there has to be a way.' He ran his hands through his hair and paced the floor in the tiny kitchen. 'Okay. This is what we'll do. You stay here and look after Jo-Jo, and I'll go and see if I can get into Duncan's car to let the handbrake off. With a bit of luck I'll be able to roll it back down the lane. Then we'll drive her to hospital.'

But when Matthew went out into the pelting rain he found the car locked. Undaunted, and even taking a certain sense of pleasure in what he did next, he picked up a large stone from the muddy ground and smashed the driver's window. He reached in to open the car door. Immediately an alarm went off, loud and piercing, and as soon as he sat in the car and released the handbrake and tried to move the steering wheel he realised it was no good. The wheel had locked and the angle at which the tyres were pointing meant that the car would only move a few inches before it hit a tree, which would still leave the lane impassable.

He darted back to the cottage.

'It's no good,' he whispered to Ellen in the kitchen. 'I can't move the car. How long do you think we've got? Labour can go on for hours, can't it?'

Ellen chewed on her lip. 'I wouldn't like to say. The contractions are coming quite fast.'

Matthew groaned.

'I know!' she said, her face instantly brightening.

'Bonkers! Run up to Orchard House and get him to come here.'

'But what use would that fool be?'

'Don't be so bloody dense, Matthew. He's a gynaecologist. He knows more about delivering babies than we'll ever know. Now go and fetch him. And be quick.'

Chapter Thirty-Eight

When Bonkers opened the front door at Orchard House Matthew's relief was profound. He would never have imagined it possible to be so relieved at the sight of a man whom previously he had written off as an idiotic buffoon.

It was a while before he could speak – his running days had long since passed him by – and while trying to regain his breath he stood in the hall of Orchard House dripping water onto the cream carpet, while Bonkers looked anxiously at the rapidly developing puddle.

'We need your help,' he managed to say at last. 'It's Jo-Jo, a friend of Ellen's, she's in labour and we can't get her to a hospital and . . . and we don't know what to do. Please will you come?' He could hear the desperation in his voice, but then as if by magic he saw the man before him undergo a complete character change. Superman couldn't have whizzed into his underpants any faster.

Explanations were made quickly to Susie, who was busy with the girls in the kitchen gathering candles in case the power went, and a call was put through to the emergency services on her mobile. They were out of the house within minutes, with Matthew unable to keep up with Bonkers who was sprinting effortlessly towards Beggarman's Lane, his medical case in his hand. When Matthew managed to catch up with him, Bonkers, who wasn't even out of breath, said, 'Can you talk me through what's happened so far?'

Matthew couldn't have talked his way through anything right at that moment. 'Ask Ellen when we get there,' he panted.

Ellen let them in. Bonkers went straight over to Jo-Jo and knelt on the floor beside her. Her head was now on a pillow and she was covered with a blanket which Ellen had fetched from upstairs. 'Can you fill me in?'

'I think she's got concussion. She keeps complaining of dizziness and she's been sick a few times.'

'And the contractions?'

'Every few minutes.'

He opened his case. 'It's too dark in here, I need more light.'

Ellen and Matthew jumped to attention and crashed into each other as they moved about the room switching on lamps.

'Now, Jo-Jo,' Bonkers said, in a lighter tone, 'do you think I might possibly take a peep to see how everything's getting along?'

She nodded and then grimaced.

'Another contraction?'

She squeezed her eyes shut.

'In that case, we'll wait a few moments, shall we? Hold my hand and squeeze as hard as you can. That's it, Jo-Jo, well done. Now keep the breathing going, nice and slowly, you're doing fine. There now, you handled that splendidly.' He released his hand from her slackened grip. 'Sure you haven't done this kind of thing before? No? You do surprise me, but while we've got a moment, shall I have a quick shufti?'

Ellen and Matthew were mesmerised. Bonkers was marvellous. His words had a wonderfully hypnotic quality to them, which meant that not only was Jo-Jo more relaxed now, so were they. Matthew had the feeling that at some time in the not too distant future he might even apologise to Bonkers for having misjudged him.

Jo-Jo gave birth to a wailing girl just minutes before there was a knock at the door announcing the arrival of the ambulance, which was waiting for them at the top of the lane. A stretcher was brought to the cottage and it was only when Matthew, Ellen and Bonkers walked alongside Jo-Jo that they realised the storm had passed.

'Did it rain much?' Jo-Jo asked, sleepily, as the ambulance crew tried hard not to lose their balance on the muddy sloping path where Duncan's car was still in the way.

'Can't say I noticed,' Matthew said, with a laugh. 'How about you, Ellen?'

But Ellen wasn't listening. She was lost in her own thoughts. She was thinking of Duncan and what Jo-Jo had told her while Matthew was fetching Bonkers.

Later that evening Ellen drove over to Crantsford Hall.

'I'm afraid Duncan isn't here,' Nadia said. 'I thought he was with you,' she added. 'He left here hours ago just as the storm started up.'

Ellen explained about Duncan's abandoned car in Beggarman's Lane. 'And there's something else I'd like to discuss with you.'

'In that case you'd better come in.'

Ellen followed Nadia through the house and to a small, light room that overlooked the sunken rose garden where only last night she had sat with Duncan drinking gin and tonic – the memory appalled her now. Through the French windows she could see that the roses had taken a beating from the torrential downpour and only the tightest buds remained intact. The rest of the blooms formed a scarlet carpet on the sodden flower bed. Tiny pools of water had gathered in the petals and they glistened in the low evening sun that was filtering through the last remaining storm clouds.

'Sit down,' Nadia said. 'So what is it you have to tell me?'

Ellen wished that there was a drink on offer, but in the absence of any Dutch courage she was forced to rely on her own.

'Does it sound feasible to you that your son has a darker side to his nature?' In view of what Jo-Jo had told her at the cottage, this question was absurd and it was as much as Ellen could do to restrain herself from resorting to the same level of violence on Nadia that her son had used on Jo-Jo.

Nadia tilted her head and considered Ellen's words, her eyes keenly alert. Very slowly she leaned back in her chair. 'Get to the point.'

Ellen did. She told her what Duncan had done to Jo-Jo. 'He left her lying on the floor, Mrs Carter, unconscious and bleeding.'

Nadia's face remained impassive.

'And I suppose as his mother you'll defend him, and even convince yourself that Jo-Jo is lying. Well, let me tell you,' Ellen rose to her feet, 'the hospital will testify to the injuries inflicted on her.'

Nadia cleared her throat. 'Am I allowed to speak?'

'There's nothing you can say. It's probably down to you that he's turned out the way he has. If you hadn't bullied him he'd –'

'Sit down and let me have my say,' Nadia intoned. 'Duncan's behaviour is not my responsibility. Do you understand? I am not answerable for his character defects.'

'Then who the hell is?'

'He is, of course, and his natural parents.'

'His natural parents? You can't be serious.'

Nadia leaned forwards. 'Donald and I gave Duncan everything we possibly could. He wanted for nothing –'

'Except your love, perhaps,' Ellen said.

Nadia waved this comment aside with one of her large hands. 'That's just the kind of predictable, facile conclusion I would have expected from someone like you. But let me ask you this, was it love *you* were offering Duncan?'

Ellen hesitated. 'I . . . I would have given him what he needed.'

Nadia laughed nastily. 'As I thought. And now, I suppose, you're breaking off the engagement. That's the thing with your kind of love, easy come, easy go. Will this girl go to the police?'

'That's up to her,' Ellen responded coolly.

'But you could persuade her not to?'

'Never! Duncan deserves what he gets.'

'If it goes to court Duncan will run rings around her. He's a respected man of position, it'll be her word against his.'

Ellen sprang to her feet. 'He's nothing but a bully and so are you! And what the hell that nice man Nigel sees in you I'll never know.'

Nadia also stood up. A strange smile spread over her face. 'I thought I gave rather a convincing performance with that pathetic little man. It certainly took you all in – Cynthia, Phyllis, you and Duncan. Especially Duncan.'

'I don't understand.'

'Nigel Wade was merely to serve a purpose. I wanted to prove a point to my son.'

Ellen frowned. 'You mean you wanted to make him jealous?'

'No. I wanted to show him how easy it was to attract the wrong sort of admirer.' She gave Ellen a pointed look.

For a split second Ellen experienced a wave of sympathy towards Duncan. If she had grown up with this twisted, loathsome woman, who possessed all the love and warmth of Medea, she would have been driven to violence years ago. 'I think I should go now,' she said.

'I agree. I'll see you out.'

They stood at the front door in the hall, where it felt dark and dismal. Ellen couldn't get out of the house fast enough. She opened the door herself.

'Just one thing more,' Nadia said. 'You came here this evening full of self-righteousness, but you have to remember that I know exactly what I saw in your cottage that day back in April. You successfully fooled Duncan, but not me. I'd just like you to know that.'

PART THREE

September

The Song of the Hawthorn Fairy

These thorny branches bore the May
So many months ago,
That when the scattered petals lay
Like drifts of fallen snow,
'This is the story's end,' you said;
But O, not half was told!
For see, my haws are here instead,
And hungry birdies shall be fed
On these when days are cold.

Cicely Mary Barker

Chapter Thirty-Nine

Ellen locked the barn and wandered down to the stream. It was something she usually did at this time of day, finding it a relaxing way to finish work, and now that the summer was gradually drawing to a close she was determined to make the most of the remaining opportunities to sit outside.

It was nearly four weeks since the storm and all its associated drama, and during that time Ellen had neither heard from Duncan nor seen him. She had certainly made no effort to get in touch with him, other than to return his ring in a small Jiffy bag – there was no accompanying note.

The day after the storm she had taken the cottage and Spring Bank Dried Flowers off the market and thrown herself into her work, ensuring that there would be no time for her to reflect on her relationship with Duncan. For the first few days, she worked day and night, extending the number of hours the barn was open and even working into the early hours of the morning, assembling all manner of arrangements in the hope that by the time she collapsed into bed she would be too tired to interrogate herself. It worked. Physical and mental exhaustion kept the thought police at bay.

Until the day of Bernie's funeral, when in the quiet of the church she had found herself unable to avoid the list of questions waiting to be answered.

By the time of the funeral Jo-Jo had been discharged from hospital, had returned to Sheffield and soon after had parted with her daughter. They had spoken on the phone just hours after Jo-Jo had said goodbye to the grateful couple, and not surprisingly Ellen had detected a strained wistfulness to Jo-Jo's voice.

'They've called her Emily,' she said, 'and they're going to send me photographs on her birthday each year. They say they want her to grow up knowing who I am.'

'And how do you feel about that?' Ellen had asked.

'Confused, if I'm honest,' she'd said, 'but I'm still sure those people can offer her more than I can right now.'

How clearly Jo-Jo saw things.

Which was what Ellen had ended up doing while sitting next to Hermione in Crantsford's parish church. There were few empty pews. Bernie had been an immensely popular man and there were mourners from all over the country. All the residents of the Lodge, including the Management, had been there to show their respect and fondness for the old rascal.

But most of the words of the service had floated over Ellen's head while she had absent-mindedly flicked through her hymn book and thought of Duncan.

How could she have been so blind? had been the question uppermost in her mind. The answer was glaringly obvious. She had been fully determined to see Duncan in only one light – as her saviour. And that, together with her guilt for what she and Matthew had done, had made her incapable of ever questioning him. Through her own weakness and stupidity she had exalted and ennobled Duncan. Time and time again she had defended him, to Jo-Jo, to Hermione, to Simon and to Matthew, and all because she had so very badly wanted him to be her knight in shining armour. How pathetic she had been.

She was thoroughly ashamed of herself.

Matthew had asked her once why she thought she needed to escape. At the time she had refused to listen to him but, blast the man, he'd been right, she could see that so clearly now.

Now she swivelled her head and gazed proudly up at her little cottage and at the barn – her home and her business. She sighed. She had been so busy complaining and manipulating that she hadn't been aware of just what she really had.

During Bernie's funeral service one of his oldest friends had stood up to say a few words about the man he'd known since he was a small boy. He had quoted from Dante's *Divine Comedy* – 'No greater sorrow than to recall in our misery the time when we were happy.' It was the only part of the service that she could remember because it had echoed exactly what she had been doing ever since Roger had left her. All her energy had been focused on trying to achieve the lifestyle she'd led before. Her anger and resentment at what Roger had done had blinkered her to the point that, in her mind, a different life had meant a worse life.

She smiled. She was glad that she had resolved at least one piece of self-deception. Her life was certainly different from how she had once envisaged it but on the whole she had to admit that it was much more fulfilling, these days. She had plans too. She had given a lot of thought to Susie's idea about providing refreshments for customers. She would have to see about planning permission to extend the barn as well as approach the bank for a loan, and goodness knows what other obstacles she would have to overcome, but no matter, she was convinced it was something worth pursuing. As was taking on extra staff, and maybe even a few outworkers to help with making the arrangements.

Susie had turned out an absolute godsend, especially now that the girls were back at school, and Ellen didn't know how she'd managed without her.

Susie had also come to Hermione's rescue by taking care of Giotto and Botticelli.

She shivered and realised that the sun had long since slipped away. She got to her feet and walked over to the cottage. She gazed fondly at it. The honeysuckle around the door had now climbed past her bedroom window and was creeping along the guttering. It was beginning to lose its scent, but there was still just enough sweet fragrance left in the flowers to greet her as she unlocked the cottage door.

She made herself a cup of tea and prepared to sit down in her favourite seat by the window with a novel she'd picked up last week. Just as she'd opened the book and found her page the phone rang. It was Hermione.

'We're having lamb ragoût tonight. Care to join me?'

Ellen knew that the offer wasn't made out of loneliness – Hermione had made lots of friends since she'd moved into the Lodge.

'Try and stop me. What time?'

'Same as last time, about seven.'

It was out of sheer practicality, rather than giving themselves airs, that the gong was always sounded at the Lodge before meals. Ellen arrived just in time to catch the benefit of it. Hermione was there to greet her in the entrance hall and she took her through to the dining room. They had a table to themselves, though Hermione

390

usually shared a larger table with a few of the other residents.

'No need to ask how you are.' Hermione smiled, flapping open her napkin and settling it on her lap. 'You're looking well.'

'You too,' Ellen said. 'I only saw you a few days ago but I swear you've put on weight?'

'A few pounds,' Hermione admitted.

'It suits you.'

A waiter brought their soup to the table. 'Cream of chicken,' he announced cheerfully, then left them.

'I had a phone call from Jo-Jo this morning,' Hermione said, shaking an elegant silver pepper pot over her soup bowl.

'How is she?'

'Desperate to get off to university. She can't wait. And she's going to see Simon before term starts. I think she sees him as a bit of a guru.'

Ellen laughed. 'And how about her mother?'

'Getting better by the day.'

'And her step-father?'

'No mention of him, but she did refer to Duncan.'

'Oh?' Ellen looked up from her soup.

'She's decided not to press charges.'

Ellen frowned. 'But she should!'

Hermione shook her head. 'Look at it from her point of view. She wants to put the past year behind her. By going to the police everything about her would be dragged up. It can't have been easy for her, what with her mother and then getting pregnant. You have to admire her. At least she's not bitter. She's got the courage to pick up her skirts and make a dash for the next stage in her life.'

'And is there a little message in there for me?' Ellen asked, with a smile.

Hermione scraped up the last of her soup. 'Maybe,' she said.

'Maybe, my foot! And for your information I've already reached that conclusion myself.'

'What, all on your own? My word, Ellen, you're coming on nicely.'

'Sarky madam. But I still don't like the idea of Duncan getting away with it.'

'What is it that you dislike most about the episode? Jo-Jo getting hurt or your judgement of the man?'

'That's a terrible thing to ask.'

'I agree, but then it's never been my intention to have the merest hint of a saintly quality to my nature, though it's an admirable state of affairs to expect in others.'

'Ah, but it's our expectations that usually let us down.'

Hermione wiped her mouth with her napkin. 'Quite. But are we talking generally now, or specifically?'

Ellen drank some wine. 'I suppose my expectations of Duncan were way off the mark, weren't they?'

'He fooled us all to begin with.'

'When did he stop fooling you?'

'I can't say that it was any one moment. It was a combination of things. I can remember thinking that I didn't want you to marry him because if you did I knew I'd lose your friendship. I think that had a lot to do with colouring my view of him. But the real moment of concern was when he came to view the house.'

'What? When you made out you were away with the fairies?'

Hermione smiled. 'Yes. It was upstairs when he was insisting that I sell to him. There was such a look in his face. I could see that beneath all that poise and courteous behaviour there was a side to him none of us had seen.'

Ellen thought about this. 'I saw flashes of his temper but didn't want to acknowledge them. I tried desperately to ignore his faults, even though I found them worrying. I kept making excuses for him.' She shook her head. 'I made the same mistake with Roger. There were warning signs for years but I chose not to act on them. Why the hell do we do that?'

'Because we're frightened of the consequences, should we acknowledge that all is not well.'

'And another thing. Why do we refuse to listen to trusted friends who can see only too well what's going on?'

'You're not paying me a compliment, are you, Ellen?'

'Don't be ridiculous,' Ellen responded with a smile. 'But, seriously, when I think of Duncan now, I see him as a time bomb just waiting to go off . . . and poor Jo-Jo was unlucky enough to hit the detonator.'

'I would hazard a guess that his upbringing is mostly responsible.'

'Nadia, you mean?'

'In part.'

'You never told me how you knew La Carter. What was your connection?'

'It was more a connection with her dead husband, Donald. Have you ever wondered how the Carter family made their money?'

Ellen shook her head. 'Duncan never mentioned anything.'

'No, he probably wouldn't. Duncan would have preferred his father to have made his wealth out of something solid and respectable like slavery, but the bulk of the money was made through the silk industry. His father owned several small factories over in Macclesfield where they made dresses, handkerchiefs, scarves and underwear. Some said that Donald Carter was an astute businessman, but there were others who thought he was a hard-nosed scoundrel who later managed to make more money out of the war than was decent producing silk parachutes.'

Ellen considered this. 'Didn't you tell me that you and Arthur were once in the silk trade?'

'I'm impressed, Ellen. That means you actually listen to me from time to time. But you're right. When Arthur died I was left to run the family business but, like so many factories at the time, we weren't gaining orders and we were losing out to the foreign markets. I struggled on for a number of years and then Donald Carter made an offer to buy me out and I threw in the towel. I'd had enough.'

'Do you suppose Duncan ever made the connection between you and his father?'

'I shouldn't think so. Donald got out of the industry not long after I did and he became a man of considerable leisure. Duncan was only a boy at the time.'

'It must have been particularly galling for you when Carter Junior came along waving his wad of notes, determined to wrest Laburnum House from you.'

Hermione smiled. 'There was a touch of *déjà vu* to the situation, I'll admit.'

'Why did you never tell me about this when Duncan and I became engaged?'

'Would it have made a difference? Would it have made you any more able to dissuade Duncan from his chosen course?'

Ellen shrugged. 'Probably not.'

'It would have made me seem like a petty old woman

with a score to settle. And, besides, it was all in the past and there's really only so much of that that is worth hanging on to. That's why I'm here.'

'And it was the right decision, leaving Laburnum House?'

'I can't tell you how wonderful it is to wake up in the morning and know that the day is mine. I feel like I'm on holiday for the rest of my life.'

The waiter came and took away their empty soup bowls. A few minutes later he returned with the main course.

'Have the builders started work on Laburnum House yet?' asked Ellen, helping Hermione to the vegetables.

On the same day that Ellen had taken Spring Bank Cottage off the market Duncan had withdrawn his offer on Laburnum House, which had surprised no one. But what had come as a surprise was that the Management at the Lodge had approached Hermione, and within the week a figure was agreed upon and a contract drawn up.

'You wouldn't believe how quickly these people move when they get going,' Hermione said. 'The site manager gave me a guided tour yesterday. The place is barely recognisable, walls knocked down and great holes here, there and everywhere.'

'Bet it looks tidier,' grinned Ellen.

Hermione humphed. 'That's as may be. But now that you've insulted me I shan't mind asking you for a favour.'

'I always knew there was no such thing as a free meal. Go on, what do you want me to do?'

'Is there any chance you could get away from the barn for a few days?'

'I'd have to check with Susie. Why?'

Johnny Foreigner was making heavy weather of the hill. 'Come on,' Ellen urged the car, 'it's not as though this is Kilimanjaro.'

'Perhaps you ought to speak to it in French,' suggested Hermione.

'Any more from you and you'll be out and pushing,' Ellen replied, above the whining scream of the struggling engine.

'Is that any way to talk to a frail old lady?'

'Cut the lip, Grannybags, and keep your eyes on the directions and tell me where we are.'

Hermione tutted. 'Is this bolshiness anything to do with being nervous?'

Ellen kept her eyes on the road. 'Look,' she said, 'there's a signpost. What does it say?'

'It says A593 to Coniston to the left.'

'And is that what we want?'

Hermione flipped the piece of paper over in her hands. 'Yes,' she said, 'and then after a mile and a half there should be a narrow road off to the left.'

They found it and began a gradual climb upwards. Johnny Foreigner started protesting again.

'The car sounds as nervous as you,' Hermione fished again.

'If you're not careful I'll turn round and drive you straight back to Crantsford.'

'There's not room,' Hermione said, seeing the close proximity of the stone walls either side of the car. 'And, besides, you wouldn't deprive an old lady of a few days with her godson, would you?'

Ellen pushed the gear lever into first and wondered how she'd let herself be talked into this trip to Coniston.

'I haven't had a holiday in twelve years,' Hermione had said craftily over supper that evening at the Lodge. 'I could catch the train, I suppose, but there would be so many changes I would be sure to end up lost and possibly even mugged.'

Of course, she could have just refused to drive Hermione but then her sneaky friend would have sulked and, worse still, would have asked her why she didn't want to go and stay with Matthew.

Matthew had finished work on Susie and Bonkers's painting not long after Bernie's funeral and had returned home before the paint had even dried. In the end Bonkers had been so pleased with the results that he'd paid Matthew himself, which was what Ellen had suspected would happen anyway.

'There's his cottage,' exclaimed Hermione excitedly.

Ellen parked Johnny Foreigner alongside Matthew's old wreck and went round to Hermione's side to help her out. Behind her she heard a door open but she gave all her concentration to Hermione, wanting at all costs to avoid looking into Matthew's face and seeing, written large and pointedly, the words *I told you so*.

She didn't need to be told that she'd made a complete fool of herself, and if Matthew thought for one moment she was going to put up with any gloating nonsense from him she'd abandon Hermione and drive straight back home. If she had learned one thing from the past few months it was that she was going to take control of her life and stand on her own two feet, which included ignoring what anyone else had to say about what she should or should not do. It was she who called the shots now!

Oh, really, said a smug little voice inside her head. *Is that why you put your foot down with Hermione and refused to come?*

She watched Matthew kiss Hermione, went round to

the back of the car and busied herself with hauling out their luggage. And if there was going to be any romantic nonsense from him she would have to stamp on that as well.

Yeah, sure! I really believe you.

'Hi, Ellen,' he said, coming towards her. 'Here, let me help you with that.'

'I can manage.'

He smiled his wretchedly handsome lopsided smile and she felt her stomach lurch. Damn the man! Couldn't he at least have the decency not to look so ... so bloody desirable?

There! What did I tell you? Putty in his hands.

'I know you can manage,' he said. 'I'm just trying to be helpful.'

'Well, it'll take more than a few suitcases to convince me of that.' The sharpness of her voice surprised her, even the voice inside her head.

Not bad. Almost convincing.

He raised an eyebrow. 'Bad journey?'

'Yes. Look who my travelling companion was.'

Hermione laughed. 'Matthew, what dear Ellen needs is a big glass of wine and a good lunch inside her to sweeten her up. She's in the most terrible mood. I can't think why.'

I can.

Although it was mid-September it was still warm enough to sit outside for lunch. They sat at a big wooden table looking directly over the lake and an enormous hill that Matthew referred to as the Old Man of Coniston. Ellen noticed he was relaxed and jovial, in a way she'd never seen him before. He was handing round glasses of perfectly chilled wine and serving an assortment of cheeses and pâté with crusty rolls. Ellen didn't know whether it was the effect of the wine on an empty stomach or that she had been working so hard recently but with nothing to do but sit back and relax she found herself mentally unwinding. She listened to Hermione and Matthew chatting about the Lodge and stared out at the lake. It was heavenly.

After lunch they went for a short walk down to the water's edge. But Hermione said she was tired and fancied a nap so they went back to the cottage and while Matthew settled her into the spare room Ellen decided to take a look in his studio.

It was unbelievably tidy, with everything neatly pigeonholed. Shelves were clearly labelled with what was supposed to be stored there – jars of charcoal, boxes of palette knives, bottles of turpentine, hundreds of tubes of paint and just as many brushes. Several easels bore half-finished canvases, and beneath a window that overlooked the spot where they'd just eaten lunch was a massive bench. On this, and in isolation it seemed, was a large portfolio. Curiosity made her open it and when she'd had a chance to take in what it contained she found Matthew standing behind her.

'Fancy a row on the lake?' he asked, ignoring the startled expression on her face.

They took off their shoes, rolled up their trousers to their knees and dragged the boat across the shingle to where it was deep enough to launch it.

'You get in,' he said, 'and I'll give it a shove.'

The water was calm and the setting was tranquil.

'Is it always as beautiful as this?' she asked, trailing a hand in the water as Matthew pulled at the oars.

'You're seeing it at its best,' he answered. 'Most of the tourists have gone.'

Within a short while they were in the middle of the lake and Matthew's cottage was small and distant, partially hidden behind a clump of trees. They seemed very alone.

'That's Brantwood,' Matthew said, pausing with the oars and pointing to a large white house. 'It's where Ruskin lived, and over there is where Donald Campbell –'

'I'm not sure I want a guided tour,' Ellen said, thinking of the portfolio in Matthew's studio and all the sketches he had made of her. Did he really love her that much? And could she go on pretending that she didn't feel anything for him? While she had been engaged to Duncan she had tried hard to convince herself that he meant nothing to her, but now there was nothing to stop her from admitting what she really felt: that there had always been an attraction.

Except there was the small matter of the voice inside her head, whose name was Pride.

Her pride told her that just because Duncan was no longer in the picture it didn't mean she could automatically turn to Matthew. It was too obvious. He would think she was using him and he would sneer at her and accuse her of all sorts of unpleasant things. Oh, it was useless. She was a victim of her own making.

She looked up and found him staring at her.

'If you don't want a guided tour, Ellen, what do you want?'

She met his gaze and for a moment they were silent.

You dare! hissed Pride.

'A go at rowing,' she said, lowering her eyes.

The following afternoon after lunch Matthew took Ellen out in his boat again. It was even warmer than yesterday and Ellen could feel the comforting rays of the autumn sun lingering on her skin as she turned her face upwards. She breathed in contentedly.

'You like it here, don't you?' Matthew said.

'Yes,' she said. 'Why do you ask?'

He stopped rowing. 'No reason.'

She smiled. 'You never ask me anything without there being a reason. Go on, tell me.'

'Maybe later,' he said. 'How have you been, since . . . ?'

'Since what?'

'Since that . . . since that spineless jerk vanished from your life.'

She leaned over the side of the boat and dipped her hand in the cool water. 'Which one do you mean? Roger or Duncan?'

'Which do you think?'

She laughed. It was back to playing verbal ping-pong. 'Oh, Matthew, I'd forgotten how much I enjoyed our chats. But if this is the moment when you say *I told you so*, I shall be very angry.'

'I wouldn't waste my breath or insult your intelligence.'

'Good.' She flicked some water at him. 'And how have you been since you left Crantsford?'

He shrugged. 'You know how it is. Still waiting for that herd of wildebeest.' He watched her face closely, keeping his own perfectly composed.

'You wouldn't be much use to me if you went and got yourself flattened,' she said, with a smile.

This was too much for Pride. It began leaping up and

down inside her head. *See? See what I said? I was right all along. You're flirting with him. You've no shame!*

He swallowed. 'So what did you have in mind for me?'

I can't bear it. You're going to say something really stupid now, aren't you?

'Will you let me row again?'

Oh, a tease as well as a shameless hussy!

They changed places and when the boat had stopped rocking Ellen began to pull on the oars.

'You're very good,' he said, approvingly.

'Any reason why I shouldn't be?'

'None at all. You haven't answered my question, by the way.'

'Which one was that?'

'Dear God, Ellen! Have you been taking lessons from Hermione? I'm asking you what possible use you might have in mind for me?'

She ignored his question – and the voice of Pride. She squashed it flat with honesty and desire.

'Have you ever made love in this boat? Do you suppose it would capsize if we tried?'

He stared at her, unsure whether to trust his ears. But she gazed steadily back at him. He then shook his head and burst out laughing. 'It didn't cross my mind to bring either life-jackets or condoms!' Suddenly he leaned forward and kissed her.

She kissed him back, as she had on the first day they met.

When they finally stopped Matthew took the oars and rowed them to a sheltered spot further up the lake. They lay in the sun, wrapped in each other's arms. They talked. They kissed. And they talked some more. There was so much they needed to say to each other.

'I'm not on the rebound,' Ellen said, 'or, rather, I don't think I am.'

'I know you're not.'

'And I'm not using you as a replacement.'

'I know that as well.'

She raised herself up on her elbow and looked into his face. 'How can you be so sure?'

'Because I'm an arrogant swine. You told me that yourself.'

'Be serious.'

'As if I'm ever anything but serious.'

'Look, this is not the time to play one of our verbal games. Tell me how you can be so sure that what I feel for you is love? Maybe it's lust. Perhaps it's only your body I'm in need of.'

He raised an eyebrow. 'I'm hoping it's a bit of both.'

'Matthew, I need to be sure that you're sure, if you see what I mean.'

'Okay,' he said. 'It was because you cried that day we made love in your cottage. It was the one moment when you were incapable of covering up how you felt. There were other times, like the night of the croquet party, when I suspected you cared for me, but you were less vulnerable then and more able to disguise your feelings, but that day at the cottage I saw the real you.'

She thought about this, then lay back in his arms and laughed. 'It was a close thing that night in the summer-house, I can tell you. If you'd carried on kissing my hand I dread to think what might have happened.'

'Shall I have a go now?'

It was late afternoon when they reached the shore and tied the boat to its mooring post.

'Do you have any doubts, Ellen?'

She squeezed his hand. 'A few. But I don't care. I'm going to be reckless. I've no idea how we're going to make things work, not when you live here and I live in Cheshire.'

'You make it sound like we live in different countries. We're little more than two hours apart.' He drew her into his arms. 'I want you to know I don't ever want to force you into something you don't want to do. You've worked so hard building up your own business – nobody has the right to take that away from you.'

'You've read too many magazines,' she said, with a smile. 'You're too word perfect. And another thing –'

'Dear God! Do you never give up?'

'We barely know each other. We've spent little more than a few days together.'

He laughed and held her tightly. 'I know all I need to know. Now come on. Stop worrying. It won't be a conventional marriage, not with us living in two different homes, but it'll be wonderfully –'

She released herself from his hold. 'I haven't agreed to marry you.'

'I know,' he said. 'It's that tedious routine of one day at a time.' He kissed her tenderly. 'But I can live in hope.'

They walked back towards the cottage arm in arm.

'Do you think Hermione will be surprised when we tell her?' Ellen asked.

'Are you joking? If there's one thing you can rely on, it's Hermione always being one step ahead of everybody else.'

From the spare bedroom, Hermione peered through the window with her trusty old binoculars, which she'd thoughtfully brought with her. A satisfied smile spread over her face. Then she placed the glasses carefully in their leather case and went downstairs to offer her congratulations.

If you have enjoyed

Airs & Graces

don't miss Erica James's latest bestseller

Tell it to the Skies

Available in Orion paperback
Price: £6.99
ISBN: 978-0-7528-9336-5

Chapter One

It happened so quickly.

She had been hurrying from the market side of the Rialto Bridge, trying to avoid the crush of tourists in the packed middle section of shops, when a single face appeared in the crowd as if picked out by a bright spotlight entirely for her benefit. She turned on her heel to get a better look. And that was when she missed her footing and ended up sprawled on the wet ground, the contents of her handbag scattered.

Any other time Lydia might have been appalled at this loss of dignity, yet all she cared about, whilst a voluble group of Americans helped her to get back on her feet, was the man who had caused her to slip. She scanned the crowded steps for his retreating figure in the fine, drizzling rain. But he was long gone.

If he'd been there at all, Lydia thought as she relaxed into the chair and felt the downy softness of the cushions enfold her. The doctor had left ten minutes ago, promising the delivery of a pair of crutches in the morning. Her ankle was now expertly strapped and resting on a footstool. *Dottor* Pierili's parting words had been to tell her to keep the weight off her foot for as long as possible. He'd wanted her to go to the hospital for an X-ray, just to be on the safe side, but she'd waved his advice aside, politely yet firmly. Bandages, rest and painkillers would suffice.

'I still don't know how you managed to get home,' Chiara said, coming into the living room with a tray of tea things. She put the tray on a pedestal table between a pair of tall balconied windows that looked down onto the Rio di San

Vio. The weak, melancholy December light had all but faded and the spacious room glowed with a soft-hued luminosity. Strategically placed lamps created a beguilingly serene atmosphere, making it Lydia's favourite room in the apartment. She was a self-confessed lover of beautiful things; it was what brought her to Venice in the first place. Living here she was surrounded by beauty on a scale she had never encountered anywhere else. Venice's glorious but crumbling architecture together with its proud history combined to produce a profoundly sad and haunting sense of identity that appealed enormously to Lydia. It was the apparent isolation of the place that touched her; it was somewhere she felt she could be separate from the rest of the world.

She would always remember her first glimpse of Venice. It was early evening and as the *vaporetto* entered the basin, the city was suddenly there before her, floating like a priceless work of art in the distance, the low sun catching on the gilded domes and *campanili*. It was love at first sight. From then on she was a willing victim to Venice's trembling beauty and the spell it cast on her. Even with the myriad challenges that the city was forced to cope with – the growing threat of *acqua alta*, the ever-increasing crowds that were choking the narrow *calli*, and the graffiti (almost worst of all to Lydia) that was spreading endemically through Venice – it was still a place of dreams for her. Even the relentless chorus of 'Volare' and 'O Sole Mio!' coming from the gondoliers as they cruised the waterways with their cargo of nodding and smiling Japanese tourists could do nothing to diminish her love for her adopted home.

'You're either the bravest woman I know or the stupid-est,' Chiara said as she handed Lydia a cup of tea.

Lydia smiled, noting that Chiara had gone to the trouble of digging out her favourite bone china cup and saucer. 'Undoubtedly the latter,' she replied. 'That's certainly what your father would have said.'

'You probably did more damage walking on it than when you slipped.'

'He would have agreed with you on that point too. And said that for a forty-six-year-old woman I should have known better.'

Chiara crossed the room for her own cup then came and curled up in the high-backed chair next to Lydia. It was where Marcello always used to sit, his hand outstretched to Lydia as he quietly read the *Gazzettino*.

'I want you to know that this arrangement will only go on for a day or two,' Lydia said, keen to establish that she would soon be back at work, business as usual.

Chiara, all twenty-four years of her, gave Lydia a quelling stare, her eyes dark and shining in the muted light. 'Oh, no you don't. We can manage perfectly well without you.'

'That's what I'm worried about. I don't want you getting too used to my absence.'

'Now there's an idea. A boardroom coup.'

The shrill ring of the telephone in the hall had Chiara getting to her feet. Within seconds it was obvious the call wasn't for Lydia. Selfishly she hoped it wasn't one of Chiara's friends inviting her out for the evening; she could do with the company.

This neediness had nothing to do with her sprained ankle, and all to do with not wanting to be alone. If she was alone, she might dwell on that face in the crowd. And that was definitely something she didn't want to do. An evening with Chiara would be the perfect distraction.

It was a matter of pride to Lydia that she and Chiara didn't have the usual mother and daughter relationship. For a start Lydia wasn't actually Chiara's mother: she was her stepmother. It was a clumsy label Lydia had dispensed with at the earliest opportunity. Chiara had always called her by her Christian name, anyway.

Lydia had never told anyone this, but it had been Chiara who she had fallen for first – her love for Marcello, Chiara's father, had come later. They had met fifteen years ago, when Chiara was nine and Lydia had been employed to teach the little girl English. She received a phone call in response to one of her advertisements offering her services, and three days later a distinguished-looking Signor Marcello Tomasi and his only daughter arrived at her apartment in Santa Croce. She was a painfully shy, introverted child and it didn't take long to realize why: her mother, as her quietly spoken father explained, had died last winter. Nobody could have empathized more with the young girl. Lydia knew exactly how it felt to have your world turned upside down and inside out. Every ounce of her being made her want to take away Chiara's sadness, to make her face light up with a smile.

The lessons always started at four o'clock on a Saturday afternoon and took place in Lydia's tiny kitchen. She thought it would be a less intimidating environment for this fragile child than to sit at the formal desk in the sitting room. There would always be a pot of freshly made hot chocolate on the table, along with a box of delicious almond biscuits from her local *pasticceria*. Lydia's other students were never offered more than tea or coffee, or fruit juice if she happened to have any in the fridge. Gradually her young pupil began to grow in confidence, which meant she looked less likely to burst into tears if she got anything wrong.

Without fail Marcello Tomasi would return for his daughter as the bell from San Giacomo dell'Orio struck five. He would hand over the agreed amount of money, check that they were still on for the following Saturday and then wish Lydia a pleasant evening. However, one day, just as Lydia was opening the door for them to leave, Chiara did something that changed everything. She beckoned her father to bend down to her, cupped her hand around her mouth and whispered into his ear. Straightening up, he cleared his throat, rubbed his hand over his clean-shaven chin and said, 'Chiara would like to invite you to her birthday party next week.'

The thought of a roomful of over-excited, noisy Italian children held no appeal for Lydia. As if reading her mind, Marcello Tomasi said, 'It will be just a small party. I think Chiara would very much like you to be there. And so would I,' he added.

4

The party was bigger than Lydia had been led to believe, but it was very much a family affair with the only children present being a handful of Chiara's cousins, most of whom were younger than her and blessedly well behaved. After six months of teaching this man's only daughter and forming a strong, protective relationship with her, but exchanging no more than a few words with him, it was strange to be in his home; it felt oddly intimate. She was suddenly seized with the urge to snoop and pry, to find out more about this immaculately dressed, taciturn man. She knew that he worked on the mainland in Marghera, the nearby industrial zone that was generally considered to be the Beast to Venice's Beauty. She also knew, from Chiara, that he was *very*, *very* important and had *lots* of people working for him. Judging from the house – a two-storey, stylishly restored property a stone's throw from Ca'Doro – he had excellent taste and lived in a degree of comfort. But this scant amount of detail wasn't enough for Lydia; she wanted to know what he did for pleasure. Did he read? If so, what books did he read? What music did he listen to? What did he eat for his supper? More to the point, who cooked his supper? Did he cook it himself, or did he have help? Chiara had never mentioned anyone.

Even if she had had the nerve to carry out any actual unseemly rifling through Marcello's personal effects for answers to her questions, there was no opportunity to do so. Chiara took her excitedly by the hand and introduced her in overly rehearsed English to her many relatives, one by one. 'This is Miss Lydia, my very nice English teacher . . . This is Miss Lydia, my very nice English teacher.' The responses were all in Italian, which was fine by Lydia; she had been speaking Italian since she was eighteen. She might only have been in Venice for two years but she could manage a passable version of *la parlata*, the local dialect, which seemed to her to be entirely made up on a whim solely to vex outsiders.

Everyone at the party was very welcoming and took it in turns to press plates of tempting food onto her as well as top up her glass of Prosecco. But she took pains not to outstay her welcome; this was a family affair, she reminded herself. Shortly after the children had been called upon to sing for the adults, accompanied on the piano by Fabio, Marcello's brother – apparently a family tradition – she tried to make her exit as discreetly as possible, but Chiara was having none of it and announced to everyone that her *very nice English teacher* was leaving. Endless goodbyes then ensued until at last she was rescued by Marcello who, having instructed Chiara to offer her sweet-toothed great-grandmother another helping of *dolce*, steered Lydia away.

'I hope that wasn't too awful for you,' he said when they were standing outside in the courtyard garden, the cool night air making her realize how warm she'd been inside and how much Prosecco she'd drunk. She could feel the heat radiating from her cheeks.

'I had a lovely time,' she said truthfully, thinking how much she really had enjoyed herself.

'It wasn't too overwhelming?'

'Not at all. It was good to see Chiara so happy. She's a delightful child; you must be extremely proud of her.'

'She is and I am. I don't know if you're aware of it, but she's grown very close to you.'

'The feeling is mutual. She's charming company.'

'Are you busy tomorrow evening?'

'I don't think so. Why?'

'Will you have dinner with me?'

And that, six months after losing her heart to his daughter, was the start of her relationship with Marcello. A man who, ten years older than her, in no way fitted her idea of a typical Italian. He wasn't one of those rumbustious Italian men who constantly argue about politics and corruption in high places and claim they could change everything overnight if only given the chance. Nor did he have the infuriating habit of shouting '*Ascoltami!*' ('Listen to me!') every other sentence. And not once did he grab her arm to make sure he had her full attention during a conversation. Instead there was a quiet and intelligent

6

reserve about him. He was courteous to a fault and very astute. He realized and accepted that there was a part of her he would never know or understand. 'Your life is like a photograph album with occasional blank spaces where some of the pictures have been removed,' he said on the day he asked her to be his wife.

'Does it matter to you?' she replied.

'No,' he answered. 'I think it's those mysterious gaps I love most about you.'

Perhaps if he had pressed her, she might have shared more of herself with him.

The sound of Chiara's happy laughter, as she continued talking to whoever it was on the phone, broke through Lydia's thoughts and, not for the first time, she wondered how the painfully shy child she had met fifteen years ago had grown into this confident, carefree young woman, a young woman who had had to cope with the loss of both her parents before she'd turned twenty-one. Lydia liked to think that she'd played a part in Chiara's recovery from the death of her mother – Marcello always believed she had – but all she'd done was give the child what she had never experienced when she was that age: love and stability.

Having children had never been something Lydia had particularly craved. However, having Chiara in her life had felt exactly the right thing to do.

That night she slept badly, her sleep disturbed by a host of fragmented dreams. In one dream the siren sounded, signalling *acqua alta*. Venice was sinking. The water was lapping at her feet as she tried desperately to make it home to Chiara. But she was lost; every *calle* she ran into was a dead end. The siren continued to ring out. The ancient wooden supports creaked and groaned and finally they gave way and the buildings crumbled and slid slowly but surely into the lagoon.

She woke with a start and lay in the dark remembering a Bible story from her childhood, about the man who built his

7

house upon the sand. Pastor Digby had his long, bony finger raised accusingly to her; he was asking if she understood what the story was teaching her.

Once she'd allowed one memory to enter her thinking, others began flooding in too. Her next mistake was to attach too much meaning to the dream. Was her life disintegrating? Had she built her life on foundations that were about to give way?

She pulled the duvet up over her head, blaming that wretched face in the crowd. Who was he? A ghost?

Chapter Two

The following morning the promised pair of crutches arrived, as did a succession of visitors throughout the day, all of whom had been despatched by Chiara to entertain Lydia.

'Another one who's been sent to keep me company, I presume,' Lydia said tiredly after she'd buzzed up Marcello's brother, Fabio. His wet, bedraggled appearance was a clear indicator of the kind of day it was outside. The lower edges of his overcoat were drenched, his furled umbrella was dripping onto the marble floor, and his trousers were tucked into a pair of black, knee-high rubber boots.

'Would you rather I left you to rest?' he asked. From his coat pockets he retrieved a bag of *biscotti* and a bottle of Vin Santo. Smiling, he dangled them in front of her. 'I could always keep these for myself.'

'Well, seeing as you've gone to so much trouble, perhaps I'll let you stay.' She watched him take off his coat and boots, then set off awkwardly down the length of the hallway on the crutches, negotiating the rugs with care. Fabio followed behind in his stockinged feet. 'What dear, well-meaning Chiara forgot,' Lydia said, conscious that she was sounding less than gracious, 'in her attempt to keep me occupied for the day, was that I would have to be up and down like a yo-yo to let you all in.'

'In that case, I'd better stay until she returns so you won't be further inconvenienced.'

'Now you're just making me feel like an ungrateful bitch.'

He laughed. 'And with so little effort, *cara*.' He put his

gifts down on the coffee table and helped her to get comfortable on the sofa.

'So why aren't you hard at work?' she asked.

'I'm the boss; I can take time off whenever I want.'

'I'll tell Paolo you said that.'

He laughed again. 'It was Paolo who insisted I drop everything and come and see you after Chiara called.'

'Hah, so he's to blame.'

'I think you need a drink to sweeten that sour tongue of yours.' He fetched a pair of glasses from the kitchen and poured out two generous measures of Vin Santo. He opened the packet of *biscotti* and passed it to Lydia. Of all her visitors that day, Fabio was probably the most welcome. As Marcello's younger brother, there had only ever been a vague physical resemblance between the two men, but the bond between them had been a strong one, had marked them out as being cut from the same cloth.

'So how did you hurt yourself?' Fabio asked after he'd chinked his glass against Lydia's and sat down.

'Too silly to say.'

'Oh, come on, I could do with a good laugh.'

'I thought you were here to make *me* laugh?'

'I know a lost cause when I see one. What did you do, kick some poor tourist out of your way and lose your balance?'

She smiled, but didn't say anything. Instead she dunked a biscuit into her drink then sucked on it, aware that Fabio was watching her closely. She knew all too well that he could spot the slightest change in her a mile off.

'What is it, *cara*?' he said. 'You don't seem yourself. You look distracted.'

She wished that her brother-in-law wasn't so sensitive and perceptive. After Marcello's death from a heart attack four years ago it was his shoulder she had cried on, just as it was his hand, along with Chiara's, that she had held during the funeral service. He had always been there for her. She had joked once that it was as well he was gay or people would certainly have got the wrong idea about them. But right now she would give anything for him not to care so much for her.

'It's being stuck here,' she said, pointing at her ankle. 'I feel so useless.'

Looking far from convinced by her explanation, Fabio sat back and crossed one leg over the other. 'It's nothing to do with Chiara, is it?' he asked.

She took a sip of her drink, enjoying its dry, sweet warmth on her throat. 'Chiara's fine,' she said. 'And anyway, didn't I just say what's wrong with me?'

Fabio stared at her doubtfully. 'So if it's not Chiara,' he persisted, 'is it work? You've built up quite a business there; it's not becoming too much for you, is it?'

She shook her head. 'Work's fine.' Again, she was telling the truth. The business she and Marcello had started together had never looked in better shape. Shortly after he'd proposed to her, Marcello announced his intention to leave the chemical company where he was the research director. He had always felt that the nature of his work was at odds with his love for Venice – given the environmental effect the industrial zone was having on the lagoon – but he had eased his conscience by saying it was better that someone like him had a say in how things were done, than someone who didn't care. 'I want to do something new,' he told her. 'And it has to be something we can do together.' They soon came up with the idea of running a lettings agency, initially acting on behalf of private and individual owners, but eventually investing in property themselves. Before long, they had an impressive portfolio of apartments to offer clients, most of whom were British, American, French and German. After Marcello's death, and as a direct result of working the worst of her grief out of her system, the agency became even more successful. She now had a reliable team of girls working for her in the newly expanded office, including Chiara who joined the agency when she had finished her studies in Bologna two years previously. As architects, Fabio and his partner Paolo had played their part by helping with any restoration work that was required in the properties. They had also overseen the work carried out on this very apartment, which she and Marcello had moved into only eighteen months before his death.

The irony of her line of work was not lost on Lydia. Like so many Venetians who complained bitterly about the number of visitors to Venice, she actively encouraged tourists to pour in for the sake of her livelihood. There was also the more controversial matter of Venice's dwindling population. Hardly a day went by when there wasn't a piece written in the *Gazzettino* about the plight of young locals being forced to live on the mainland because they couldn't afford the sky-high prices here in Venice. Prices that had been inflated by outside investors. It was a problem that had everyone in agreement: something would have to be done. But meanwhile, life had to carry on and people made their living the best way they knew how, by welcoming tourists with open arms and giving them a thorough fleecing.

'If it's not Chiara or work that's bothering you,' said Fabio, 'is it loneliness?' He paused, and Lydia could see he was choosing his next words with care. 'Do you think it's time to move on?'

For a while now Fabio had been discreetly hinting that she ought to find someone to take Marcello's place. Lydia smiled. 'Oh, Fabio, I know how you worry about me, and I appreciate it, really I do. But it's not that. Not that at all.'

'*Sei sicura?*'

'Yes, I'm sure. To be honest, I'm usually too busy to give it a thought.'

'That's not healthy.'

'It's the way it is.'

'Then perhaps it's time you changed your ways. When was the last time you had a holiday?'

'Don't be ridiculous. What would I do with a holiday?'

He shook his head in what she hoped was defeat, but taking her by surprise, he said, 'Sometimes I think you go out of your way to punish yourself. For the life of me I can't think why.'

You don't know the half of it, she thought grimly.

12

All Orion/Phoenix titles are available at your local bookshop or from the following address:

Mail Order Department
Littlehampton Book Services
FREEPOST BR535
Worthing, West Sussex, BN13 3BR
telephone 01903 828503, *facsimile* 01903 828802
e-mail MailOrders@lbsltd.co.uk
(Please ensure that you include full postal address details)

Payment can be made either by credit/debit card (Visa, Mastercard, Access and Switch accepted) or by sending a £ Sterling cheque or postal order made payable to *Littlehampton Book Services*.
DO NOT SEND CASH OR CURRENCY

Please add the following to cover postage and packing

UK and BFPO:
£1.50 for the first book, and 50p for each additional book to a maximum of £3.50

Overseas and Eire:
£2.50 for the first book plus £1.00 for the second book and 50p for each additional book ordered

---

BLOCK CAPITALS PLEASE

name of cardholder ....

address of cardholder ....

delivery address
(if different from cardholder)
....
....
....

postcode ....

postcode ....

☐ I enclose my remittance for £........................

☐ please debit my Mastercard/Visa/Access/Switch (delete as appropriate)

card number ☐☐☐☐ ☐☐☐☐ ☐☐☐☐ ☐☐☐☐

expiry date ☐☐☐☐   Switch issue no. ☐☐

signature ....

prices and availability are subject to change without notice